Smoke Monkey International

By James Westhoff

To Elaine
Thanks!
Jim Westhoff

***

Elaterite Books

Smoke Monkey International

CHAPTER ONE

Oliver Easton wondered about the people chasing him. All young men, he figured, around his age. All close friends. Drunk and high, probably, and armed. And bloodthirsty. Drawing gunfire would be a new experience, if it came down to it. Yet another new experience. Like stealing the Jeep. Like screwing the girl in the red cowboy hat. Like shimmying down the rain gutter to avoid her boyfriend.

Or temporarily avoid. Still no sign of anyone behind him, but he knew they were coming. And with the busted needle in the gas gauge flopping side to side with each turn, there was no telling how much longer the Jeep would run. Which meant this chase might continue on foot, through the jungle, where so many more new and exciting experiences awaited him. Like death by constriction, he imagined. Or spider bite. Maybe something with a rusty machete. Or just lots of red ants.

Despite his concerns, he could still muster some positive thinking. For now, he was okay, alive, barreling around the tight, tree-lined curves, yanking the wheel, pushing the pedals. And the dark was coming on fast, which could work to his advantage. He hoped for a village, or a farmhouse, or a logging road of some kind, some place he might hide the Jeep, or at least hide himself.

This will all come down to focus, he thought, as the road twisted along, and a slurry of wet debris raked the Jeep's undercarriage. He processed through the adrenaline, cool as he could, with a detached interest in seeing just how well he could perform in a crisis. This had always been Oliver's way, to clinically observe himself. And so far, he *excelled* at this. Which was nice to know. He sought an explanation. Innate mechanical know-how? *Could be.* Panic-induced competence? *Hmm.* Something else altogether?

But what else? Luck?

It was hard to look at his current situation and call himself lucky. Certainly last night he *felt* lucky. She was partying with her girlfriends. He sat alone at the bar watching the Dodgers. She came up to get another round of beers. Americano? she asked, following his eyes to the English language telecast. Si, Nevada. She helped herself to the last of his peanuts and pushed the red cowboy hat back off her forehead. He turned to really look at her. She was drunk, smiling up at him. Dark skin, white teeth, white pearl earrings. Black jeans and a wispy red top, faded and stylishly threadbare. When the bartender came back with four sweating beers, Oliver paid for them. She carried three to her table and then came back and took the bar stool next to his. She sipped her beer. Whoos weening? she asked.

From that, to *this*. An almost perfect balance. The shitty and the sublime, all rolled into a neat package. He eyed the jungle, which now grew over the road in a linked canopy, bringing the darkness. Worth the chase, maybe. But not worth *that*. He shuttered. To be lost in there, and alone. On the run in the soupy wet blackness. The full botanical immersion. The accelerated cycles of life, death, and decay.

The Jeep had no side windows, so the constant breeze swirled through his sweat-soaked clothing. He hit a large rock or pothole and heard a loud clunking noise.

"Shit!"

Despite the humidity, his voice came out cracked and broken. He tightened his grip on the wheel and readjusted himself in his seat.

He expected, any second, to feel a loss of pressure in one of the tires. But the Jeep charged along with no sign of trouble. He exhaled, rolled his shoulder blades, and released the tension. *Thank God.* Thank God I can really *drive*. That I'm so damn *impressive*. He knew enough to temper the pride. But really, he allowed, who chasing me could ever catch up?

But still, Oliver, say you do make it to some village. What then? Word spreads quickly. Powerful and dangerous men are looking for an Americano. Who's stepping up to protect *you*? And what about your wallet and passport? If you do escape all *this,* are you then just going to go back and knock on her door?

He mashed a fist into his forehead. The cinematic cliché of it all. *Really*, Oliver, the high-speed chase through the exotic locale? The girl who forgets to mention her boyfriend is the half-crazed son of an underground crime boss? When the banging on the door started, and her brown face turned white as the bed sheet, he knew the whole story. He had watched that story a million times. He knew especially well the part where the girl does the throat-slitting gesture with two shaking hands, for decapitation.

He even found the Jeep keys in the sun visor.

Of course you did, Oliver. It's *Destiny*.

No, thanks.

Fate?

No! Stop that. It's not that kind of thing. It's not a *God* thing. It's a *jungle* thing. All of it. All *this*, just some complicated subconscious scheme to get me out here, desperate and alone. Because I fear it. I fear it so much. And fear is the ultimate catalyst. I play the firefighter arsonist, artificially generating the context for my own acts of bravery and heroism.

He refocused on the road. Before he reached the next corner, he glanced into the mirror. And there it was, a beam of light through the damp air. Then it straightened out. Two headlights. Then Oliver spun around the next corner, and all was black again behind him.

"Shit, shit, shit."

The pedal pinned to the floor. No more easing up around the corners. He had to start his turns even sooner, sliding closer to the edge of the road, closer to the jungle. Focus on driving.

Focus.

Again, lights filled the rear view mirror. The back window suddenly shattered.

Oh, Jesus. Okay, okay, okay. Keep driving. He ducked his head low. They do have guns. And they have a faster car than I do. I have to get off this road. I have to go in *there*. With the crocodiles, or caiman, whatever. With the death roll. The head-first submersion. Drown between those jaws, those crazy teeth. Then dismembered. Tossed into the air, chunk by chunk. Down the hatch.

Or boa constrictors and pythons, which did they have? Anacondas in Venezuela, just down the road. Sleeping on some bed of wet ferns, little twittering night birds. Condensation.

Drip, drip, drip.

Oh, *Oliver!*

Then the death swaddle, some meaty muscle *pulls* you into yourself. Little perverted eyes, red and beady. Engorged.

"How did he—"

"Engorged."

He came out of a tight turn and saw the road extend plumb line straight in front of him. Which was a mixed blessing. He could ease his white-knuckle grip on the wheel for a moment, but it also gave his pursuers a straight shot. The jungle began to recede from the roadside a bit too, and this change in his surroundings gave him some hope; a last little piece of sunlight.

And then it appeared. To his left. Parallel to the road, a chain-link fence. And just past it, a long flat clearing. A landing strip.

A paved landing strip!

Just then, the back end of the Jeep dropped, and he knew they had shot out one of his tires. But he still had steering. Ahead, he could see a small building. A control tower of some sort.

What if?

What if private planes park there? What if they keep keys in a locked box in the control tower? What if I smash the Jeep into the building, jump out, find the keys, hop into a plane, and fly away? What if I do *that?*

He checked the mirror again. Six lights now. Three cars. *Ridiculous.*

He would have to brake a bit to make the turn into the parking lot. Then he'd have just enough room to get the Jeep back up to ramming speed.

Ramming speed?

He shook his head and almost smiled. I guess I also have to jump out at the last second and barrel roll across the asphalt, because that's what you do.

He hit the brake, yanked the wheel to the left, set a line toward the windowed wall of the small building, and slammed the gas pedal one last time. Then he opened the door and looked down. The ground seemed to move much faster from that point-of-view.

He fell from his seat, protecting his head with his arms. He hit the ground and immediately started spinning.

He whirled in a silent, painless void. *Hold your head, hold your head, hold your head.* But then he heard gun shots and a loud crash. And then he stopped rolling.

First, for just a moment, no pain. And then, *pain!* Pain everywhere, which was good. No dullness, no dead spaces. Maybe nothing serious.

Somehow.

He sensed moisture from a wet lawn. He opened his eyes, tried to orient himself. He found the building, looked at the damage. The Jeep had crashed through the windowed front wall and continued clear through the back wall. He found that funny, despite everything, the cheap-ass Panamanian construction.

Then he hopped to his feet, looked back at the approaching cars, and limped as fast as he could into the building.

Pitch dark now, and no time to fiddle around for the light switch. His hands found a cluttered desk and a TV, and nothing else. He started tossing things around frantically, listening for the sound of keys. Two large ashtrays hit the ground simultaneously. A cloud of ash caked onto his wet skin. In a bottom drawer he discovered a small metal box. He shook it. Keys.

Thank you, Jesus.

The lights from the approaching cars closed in, almost to the parking lot. But at least he heard no gunfire. In the darkness, it would take them a few moments to figure out what he did and where he went.

He threw the box onto the concrete floor. Nothing. His hands shook. He picked it up and tried again. Nothing. One more time. Last chance. He raised it up as high as he could, and *slammed* it down. The box exploded open and keys scattered across the floor. He scooped up as many as he could find and ran out the back, through the second hole made by the Jeep. He felt more pain now, and couldn't help the limp. Something definitely wrong with his left knee. Blood from a mangled shin pooled in a sandal, causing his foot to slide around.

Keep going. Focus.

He turned around to see the cars slowing in the parking lot. Another gun shot, and he actually heard the bullet whiz by his head.

The planes sat parked in a neat row just outside the demolished building. All Pipers from what he could tell. Simple four-seaters, which he had flown before. Of course he had. He tried the door of the first one he came to and found it unlocked. Things had started to turn for him. It was obvious. He knew now that escape was possible. Probable even. The rapid succession of unfeasible successes built up a karmic momentum.

I deserve *this*. I do not deserve *that*.

His mind seized the uncanny, his imminent escape. *Thank you, God.*

He repeated aloud, "Thank you, God."

Soundless, in slow motion. Almost peaceful. A series of maneuvers to be completed. Their bullets would continue to miss. Everything that must happen will happen.

He climbed into the cockpit and started trying keys. The third one turned. The cabin lights came up. Fuel at maximum levels. He cranked the engine and watched the propeller turn. A bullet plinked off the metal body of the plane. He released the brake and started to roll slowly forward. The men, all six of them, emerged from the building, a hundred feet away. They ran in his direction, shouting. Then their guns started.

Oh, *shit*. They've got an arsenal.

The passenger-side window shattered and the glass crystals showered across his wrist. He taxied along, down the runway, hoping for enough room to take off. The plane picked up speed. He worked the gears and levers. Automatic. Faster. Almost there. Almost there. He turned his head and saw flashes from the gun barrels. Then he hit the green. He pulled back on the steering column and the plane jumped into the air a few feet before the end of the runway.

Liftoff.

Freedom. Flooding through the shot-out window.

A couple of seconds to let it all sink in. And then, "How the hell did I just do that?"

CHAPTER TWO

Ted sat at the huge desk station in the lobby of the fifteen-story SMI tower in La Jolla, California. He was so caught up in the newspaper story, that he didn't notice his coworker Twin standing right in front of him, glaring down in disapproval.

"I go up now," Twin said. Ted nodded without looking up. He knew that culturally Twin needed to be acknowledged, which made insulting him rather easy.

Twin cleared his throat and repeated himself: "I go up now. You watch station."

"Sure, dude."

"What you call me dude?"

"It's nothing. Don't worry. But you should see this first." Ted stabbed a finger at the newspaper. "There's a guy who claims he can—Twin, are you listening?"

"I go up now. I no interesting." He took off his glasses and rubbed his bloodshot eyes.

Ted stood up and did an exaggerated survey of the lobby. "The coast is clear, Twin. There's no one here. All quiet on the Western Front." Then he sat back down.

"I no understand what you talk about," Twin said. He put his glasses back on. Then he looked down at the ID badge clipped to his breast pocket and straightened it.

"Idiomatic expressions, buddy."

Twin shook his head, puzzled. "What you call me buddy?"

"Don't yell at me, Twin."

"I not yelling. This jus how I talk."

"In this country we treat people with respect."

Twin was bristling. "I respect! You no respect!"

"This story, Twin. Please, just listen. It's about a guy living in Honduras, some old scholar from Harvard, who claims significant archeological progress can be made through appeals to regional deities."

"I no understand what you talk about."

"Is that the craziest shit you've ever heard?"

Twin shook his head.

Does he not understand or not care?

"Apparently, this Dr. Lattistrom offers up nightly prayers to long-dead Maya godkings. A guy from Harvard."

Twin shook his head again.

"Think about the implications, Twin."

"You bad for work."

"Relax. You don't have to take this all so seriously, you know. You're allowed to just sit here and read the newspaper. Walk into any office building in America and you'll see guys like us just sitting there." Twin didn't respond. Ted wondered if any of this was getting through to him. "Are you listening, Twin? You don't actually *do* anything, you know. *I* don't do anything." Twin grunted. "We're just deterrents. Bodies. Like scarecrows, dude. We don't make anything. We don't buy anything or sell anything. There's nothing to learn or get better at."

Twin didn't say anything. He just turned and walked toward the elevators. Ted heard a ding, then the opening and closing of the doors.

Immediately, Ted pushed the newspaper to the side and focused on the computer. He logged them both in for the shift. Then he restarted the computer, holding down

14

the appropriate buttons as it rebooted. He knew the process by heart now. His roommate Jeff had explained it all to him, how to override the limits of his security clearance. He looked up from the screen to the bank of monitors on his left. He could see Twin exit the elevator on the twelfth floor.

He was talking to himself, Ted could see. Talking about me, he thought. About the bamboo he'd love to slide under my fingernails.

Once the computer rebooted, Ted found the lighting application and scrolled through the list of motion detectors until he located those for the twelfth floor. Then he set the video displays to follow Twin down the long corridor, and into specific offices.

He started all this, Ted reasoned. With his Eastern superiority. His moral high ground. I told him he couldn't have risked his life to come to this country just to work this crap job. But he told me I didn't understand anything.

Which maybe you don't, Ted.

As Twin moved down the corridor, he activated a series of motion detectors which brought up overhead fluorescent lights that went out after he passed. Permanent floor lights gave off just enough dim blue glow for Ted to see what was happening in otherwise unlit spaces. The whole building functioned like this at night, to save on electricity. Just before Twin reached the front office of Smoke Monkey International, the principle tenant of the building, Ted located the room on his sensor list and waited. When Twin opened the door and entered, Ted deactivated the sensor. The door closed behind Twin. The floor lights cast him in a gawky silhouette. He walked further into the room and stopped. Then he waved his arms at the sensor. Then he jumped up and down. Then he jumped and waved at the same time. Ted snickered. With his small camcorder, he filmed the monitor. He had been doing this sort of thing to Twin for the past two months.

15

I don't know why I do it.

You think you do it because it's funny.

I know I tell myself Twin deserves it, but that's not really true. I just can't believe he hasn't caught on yet.

Maybe he doesn't think it's possible.

What, the sensor-lock override?

No, the petty cruelty.

CHAPTER THREE

Marona Dilenta hired a woman she met in a department store to track her husband, approach him, and try to get him to sleep with her. She got the idea from a movie she watched one of those late nights, wondering where Coy was. The confluence of the film's subject matter and her own absent husband seemed so absurdly coincidental she wondered if it was a sign from above. Having already spent four years in a troubled marriage, Marona happened to be in the market for just such a sign.

The woman Marona hired worked in the shoe department, and she was young and busty and dopey, three things Marona was not. Marona was classy, she would tell you. She was forty-seven, and wore her long red hair in a tumble of graceful loops. She was fit and smart, with severe features that could range from mildly attractive to stunning, depending on the kind of day she was having. She met up with the woman in the department store's seventh floor coffee shop. She offered her a thousand dollars, which the woman accepted before Marona even explained the terms of the arrangement. The woman did want Marona to understand that she was no tramp, which was a tough comment to sell, with that extra-low neckline and earthquake fault of cleavage.

It took only two days for the woman to call Marona and tell her that she followed the husband around town a bit, and then down into the subway, where she sat next to him. They talked, exchanged numbers, and set up a date for tonight. Just like that.

When Coy called and told Marona he would be working late, she told him she understood and that she felt tired and would probably go to sleep early. He said that was fine and that he would see her in the morning.

She hung up the phone and sat there on the couch in the living room of the small but expensively decorated apartment, with the lights dimmed and some smooth jazz coming over the radio. She processed it all for a moment, and then did a giddy and delighted squirm across the couch. She let go a burst of unintelligible glee, which woke up their three year-old daughter.

"Go back to sleep!"

So full of shit, she thought. So absolutely filled to the brim with shit this man is. And I know it. She poured red sangria from a gallon jug and drank into the night until her eyes closed peacefully and she began to snore.

She dreamed of control. An exceptional dream. Not surrealistic babble, but a bona fide vision of some reality. Marona in a room, seated at a desk, staring at a bank of monitors. Twenty screens showing feeds from twenty different cameras. The lights are down. Smoke climbs from an ashtray into the still air. Each monitor represents a life. Follows a life. A man crossing a street. A woman watching TV. A child running under a pop fly. In the dream, Marona not only sees these people, but she manipulates the events as they happen. The man finds a twenty dollar bill and almost gets hit by a cab. The woman's TV goes out and she starts hitting the top of it. The boy slips, falls to the ground, makes the catch anyway.

She woke up, as people do from this sort of dream, with a shock to find it wasn't real.

"Poof," she said, spreading her fingers in the air, like she was signing *explosion*.

Then she remembered Coy and the girl. The dream was confirmation. This means something, she told herself. It's all connected. And there was more to it. An additional detail, which asserted itself slowly and then dominated the memory completely. Something on the desk where she sat. A carved figurine no more than nine inches tall. Ornate and polished, the work of a craftsmen. An idol of some sort, watching *her*.

Two weeks later at the hair salon, Marona met a different sort of woman, this one intelligent and physically slight, with tattoos, dyed black hair, and a pretty face. Marona offered her a thousand dollars to approach the husband seemingly at random and see if she could get him to ask her out. Again, Coy took the bait. This time he met the girl in a taco shop where Marona said he liked to go for lunch. The girl called Marona just a few days later and in a weepy, confessional tone admitted that she not only approached the husband and flirted with him a bit, but that she invited him back to her apartment that very afternoon and slept with him.

Marona comforted the girl and told her not to feel bad, saying it was not her fault she slept with a married man. She then deflected any concerns the girl had about whether this made her a prostitute, since technically Coy didn't know he paid for sex.

This time the satisfaction was even greater. Marona didn't really understand it herself. She had neutralized him apparently, by owning his every bad act. Perhaps, she wondered, this wouldn't work for other wives. Other women wouldn't be able to get past the infidelity. But Marona didn't mind that part at all. Her husband had always slept around. She wouldn't go around paying women to track and seduce him if she didn't already know him as a philanderer, and a good-for-nothing, and hadn't already made up her mind months ago to leave him, once they logged a few more years together and the alimony and child-support numbers climbed up to where she felt comfortable with them.

Through all of this, Marona continued to dwell on the profound and previously unfelt feelings of joy and excitement and giddiness that swelled through her body when the phone rang and she got to hear details from these girls about the encounters, the conversations, the moves, the lines, and the lies he told. So she kept at it, next hiring a real knock-out model type, tall and European, with a mysterious accent and fantastic clothes. They met while standing in line for a taxi and the woman would not even consider it for less than three thousand dollars, which Marona gave her because it was her husband's money anyway.

She heard back from the woman the next day, a story about how she followed the husband into a book store. She said she didn't even have to do anything, that he approached her with what the model referred to as an insane kind of confidence, which she had to admit was quite a turn-on, and how he offered to buy her lunch, which she accepted and enjoyed thank you very much. Then, as he paid the check, he rather bluntly proposed to the model that she join him in a hotel room that very afternoon for strawberries and champagne and who knows what else.

She admitted to Marona that the proposal delighted her. She found the whole crazy situation fascinating. She said she even considered sleeping with this charming man from this big foreign city. But she only made it as far as the hotel lobby before reason took hold and she turned around without explanation. The husband trailed out behind her, demanding with some amount of aggression, for which Marona apologized, to know what changed her mind. She improvised a story about virginity and Bulgaria and some other stuff, confessing her excitement to Marona over the phone, and thanking her, and offering her services in the future if Marona had any more sick schemes or weird games to play.

Coy's ability to conceal his encounters amazed Marona. She doubted she could ever keep such a straight face. He went about his routine, explaining away his stress and fatigue with stories about work. And this is where it got good. When he started on the fiction her face flushed and she reclined on the couch and just basked in the bullshit. This is what it's all about, she told herself. A story about Henry, how he messed up his best account after running late to a meeting, and then lied to the boss about the reasons the account was lost, and how Henry beat himself up over the lie he told, and constantly looked over his shoulder for the truth to come and find him, and how Coy had to work all these extra hours to cover Henry's ass by bringing in new clients and new accounts. Fascinating, Marona thought. He lies about lying. He makes himself the hero of the story. All for Henry. Good old Henry.

Always, there lurked the temptation to call him on it, to say you were not with Henry last night and you were not at the office, you were out giving it to some girl you met on the subway. But then it would be over. Nothing left but the big blow-up. Then the counter-attack. He'd call her a nutcase. Then divorce. Custody madness. And then...*nothing*. She depended on this mischief. It brought new joy and purpose to her life. She needed her husband. And not only that, she needed him to be every bit the dick he was being. The more he lied, the more he slept around, the more he invented tales of fraternal heroism, the better things got for her.

And what about her own culpability? This had gone pretty far by now. Three girls. Five thousand dollars. How might she look standing there in divorce court? Had she entrapped him? What if he just called her crazy? Did she

21

have a defense for that? What kind of mother runs around playing God?

With the fourth girl, things changed. She studied at NYU. Cute and brainy, but young. She accepted the money, but clearly had her doubts. She gave Marona an odd look, as if she could sense a new kind of desperation. Marona left the meeting feeling like a criminal who had let success go to her head. She was becoming careless. Not doing research. Not covering her tracks. Coy rejected the college student, who called Marona and spoke for only a few seconds. Didn't work, she said. I tried and he wasn't interested. I'm still keeping the money. Coy didn't fall for the girl because of her age, probably. He had standards. Limits.

Marona Dilenta, apparently, did not.

She noticed a change come over her husband, a distressing indifference. He seemed to get just as much satisfaction out of *rejecting* women. This will not do, Marona told herself. He even stopped with the lies about work, saying only that he had things to take care of. He read something in her. He saw a change. Maybe she sleeps around, he might have thought. That would explain the lack of questioning. The lack of protest when he made up reasons for not coming home. It would also explain her recent infusion of happiness. This rejuvenation. She must be getting some on the side too.

Marona kept returning to that dream from the night of her initial success. The image of the carved idol on the desk, so well-polished, gleaming in the light of the monitors, almost coming to life. The look it gave her overflowing with meaning. Her conscience? Someone watching her while she watched someone else. Sinister. Guilty. She remembered a line from a discussion in a theology class, maybe the only thing she learned in college that still stuck with her. What if God had the power to create the world, but not the power to control it?

This was all getting way out of hand.

So she just decided to start hiring prostitutes. Once she did it, she figured it was probably common. And probably not just wives who did it. Guys might do it too, to help out a hapless friend. Maybe they pay some girl to act interested and take him home and sleep with him. Because that's what she wanted her husband to do, sleep with these women. Go all the way. It made the manipulation more complete. It heightened her joy and her level of control.

Marona found the first girl's number in the sports page escort ads. She had always wondered if the girls in those pictures were really just prostitutes. She explained the situation over the phone, and they met at a fast food restaurant and talked about the plan, which the girl loved, just as the model had, making Marona wonder if everyone in the world secretly desired this kind of control over other people's lives. The prostitute looked a lot like the first girl from the shoe department, not necessarily pretty, but instead kind of slutty, with fake breasts, fake hair, and fake lips. Marona tried to imagine how her husband might react to this girl coming on to him, how her appearance, compared to, say, the European model's appearance, might influence the specific manifestation of his desire. Would it be different? Different how, specifically? And why? And if a spectrum existed for this sort of thing, where did Marona herself fall on it?

She told the prostitute to wait for her husband at the entrance to his office building and to follow him to lunch and just sort of wait for a good opportunity to catch his eye. Everything else would then take care of itself. Marona, having by now fully committed her life to this project, was anxious to experience as much of it as possible. She put on a wig and dark sunglasses, staked-out the prostitute while the prostitute staked-out her husband, and followed all the action from a safe distance.

Everything went according to plan. At first. The prostitute saw him on the street and smiled. He approached her and offered to buy her lunch. Marona observed this while pretending to stand in line at a falafel cart. Then, apparently, he offered to get them a hotel room. Not surprisingly, the prostitute went along with it. But when they got up to the room, according to what Coy told Marona later, he sat the prostitute down and said something like, what the fuck is going on? The prostitute played dumb. She launched into a story about how she never did this sort of thing, and that she actually came from a very conservative family in Missouri. Which he didn't buy for a second, since even in non-prostitute attire, the girl still looked rather slutty and experienced and for hire. So he kept at it. He told her they were going down to the lobby, where they could talk about this in public, where she wouldn't be able to make up any lies about him or throw the situation back in his face with rape charges. He was pissed-off by now, aggressive and mean, and utterly convinced that something was afoot.

And it turns out really all he had to do to get the truth was to offer her more money than Marona had offered. So he learned about the plan, and tied it back to all the other women. When he got home that night he told Marona they would be getting a divorce and that if she asked for a penny from him in the settlement, if she even mentioned the words *joint-custody*, he would go public with the story and tell anyone who would listen all about his sick psycho wife.

Marona discovered shame.

Shame!

Nothing could dilute it, and holy shit what soul shaker of an emotion. It beat her down and kicked at her head while she tried to sleep. It needled its way into every thought. Self-loathing seized upon every unconscious moment, blooming in her mind like some poisonous flower, toxifying everything. Coy was surprised by this over-reaction, which seemed grossly disproportionate to her actual crimes.

Grandmothers, she told him through chest-heaving sobs, who crash cars and kill their grandchildren, feel better than I do.

Well, it's not *quite* the same thing, he told Marona. But still, he took advantage of her personal disgust and piled on the insults, focusing mainly on questions of her sanity and fitness for motherhood. He called her delusional, said she lived in her own little world where it wasn't safe to raise children. He probably suspected he was being cruel, but convinced himself that her actions were the result of a deeper pathology which had contaminated their relationship from the start, and was the root cause of all *his* indiscretions.

Marona told Coy she didn't deserve custody or money or anything else from him. He agreed, though he must have known she would eventually gather her wits and come back fighting. She decided to leave town, apologizing to Coy for *dumping* their child on his shoulders. The last thing she did before she disappeared was to give Coy the phone number of the European model.

CHAPTER FOUR

Gob walked into the room with a beer in his hand. The rest of them sat on couches, watching TV. It was early Thursday morning. Ted's shift ended two hours earlier. He needed to get some sleep.

"It's gone again," Gob said.

"What is?"

"The newspaper, right? It's the fourth time this week."

Fetcher picked at an extinguished joint on a foil yogurt lid. "We should call someone," he muttered.

"Yeah," Gob said, "someone should call someone." He smacked the back of Fetcher's head. "How about *you* call someone?"

Fetcher coughed and ran his hands across his face, a gesture he did all the time. None of the roommates understood it. "I'm going to make coffee," he said, but he didn't move.

Gob stood there for a moment, waiting. "Well, fuck it, I guess." He sat down.

The newspaper thefts started three months earlier, around the time Ted began working the night shift. At first, it happened just once a week, if that. But the situation had escalated in recent weeks. And nobody at this point had mustered the energy to actively give a shit.

We are pathetic, Ted thought. College kids are pathetic.

He got up from the couch and staggered to his bag, which sat on the ground next to the front door and the ripe litter box. He yawned. He thought about his brutal schedule, working until two in the morning and going to class in the early afternoon.

He got the newspaper and the camcorder out of his bag and walked back to the living room. "Someone should change the litter box," he said. "It stinks like shit over there."

"Yeah," Gob said, exasperated. "Someone *should* change it."

Ted threw the newspaper onto the coffee table.

Jeff took his eyes off the TV and looked at it. "Where'd you get that?"

"At work," Ted said. "It's yesterday's." He sat back down on the couch. "You have to read this story."

Jeff reached over to an end table and picked up a different newspaper. "We got *yesterday's*."

"Did you see the story about the archeologist?"

"I didn't read it yesterday."

Of course you didn't.

Ted took the newspaper from Jeff and opened it to the middle of the front page section, scanning for the story about the archeologist. But he couldn't find it. He flipped backward and forward. "That's odd."

He picked up the newspaper he brought from work and located the story on page A6. Page A6 on Jeff's newspaper showed something different. No mention of Honduras or the Harvard scholar. "Look at that," Ted said, setting the two papers side by side. "They're different." They compared the two newspapers, checking the dates, looking for any other inconsistencies. But with the exception of the one story, replaced by an ad in Jeff's paper, they seemed identical.

"Sometimes they put out early and late editions," Jeff reasoned.

Ted shook his head. "Yeah, but this isn't that. I don't know why they'd cut such an interesting story."

Gob interrupted to remind everyone that the point of all of this was the fact that they did not have *today's* paper. "Yes, it's all very ironic that we have two copies of yesterday's paper, but I'm more interested in catching—"

"It's not ironic," Fetcher said, without taking his eyes off the TV.

"What?"

"It's a coincidence. It would be ironic if tomorrow instead of the paper being stolen we received two copies of it."

"This is ironic too," Gob insisted. "But it doesn't matter."

"No, it's not."

"I don't think you know what you're talking about, Fetcher."

The room fell silent. Everyone watched a commercial for dog biscuits. But Gob couldn't let it go. "The problem," he said, banging his fist on the table, "is that we paid for the newspaper to be delivered *here*. It's the principle."

"It's the principle, Mr. McMurphy," Fetcher said.

Gob threw his hands in the air. "That's not even the line. Go back and read the book."

Ted shook his head.

Four years of this.

It's enough.

"Check this out," Ted said, picking up the camcorder. He cued the footage of Twin on the view screen. He passed the camera around.

"Who's the guy?" Jeff asked.

"His name's Twin. He's from Vietnam or some shit. Really angry guy."

"What's he yelling at?"

28

"The motion detector."

"Does he have a twin?" Fetcher asked.

"I asked him the same question and he just got mad at me."

They all kept watching Twin jump up and down. "It's pretty funny," Fetcher said finally.

"Pretty funny?" Ted said, surprised. "Just *pretty* funny?"

"And kind of cruel," Gob said.

"Cruel?" Ted couldn't believe their reaction.

Am I way off on this?

Apparently.

When did everyone become so uptight?

"You'd be mad too," Gob said. "You escape from your homeland in the dead of night, risking everything to be here in this country, and then you finally get a job and have some stability in your life and you have to put up with some dipshit turning the lights on and off and picking on your name."

"Jesus, Gob," Jeff said. "You're acting more and more like a girl every day."

"Oh, fuck you."

"It's *To Kill a Mockingbird*."

"Thank you, Fetch," Jeff said. "And besides, it's a fair question to ask if a guy named Twin has a twin. How's that offensive?"

"But wouldn't it be ironic if he did have a twin?" Fetcher said, laughing.

Gob buried his face in his hands. Then he shouted, "No, you retard! It would *not* be ironic. You people are in college, aren't you? It would not be ironic. It would be a coincidence. It would be ironic if his name was Not-Twin and he had a twin."

There was a long silent pause.

"Wait, what?" Fetcher said. "Say that again."

Just then the toilet flushed in the small bathroom next to the living room. Ted and Fetcher looked at each other, puzzled. Then the door opened and Buttsweat staggered into the living room, looking very lost.

"Jesus," Ted gasped. "How long have you been in there?"

Buttsweat rubbed his face aggressively with both hands and then scratched his head. "I think I fell asleep," he said.

CHAPTER FIVE

The cracked stone path dividing the dirt lawn was littered with the armless corpses of He-Man figurines. Colorful paint splatters decorated the concrete stoop. Inside the house, the older kids took turns holding the younger kids inside the giant foil tube of the swamp cooler outlet. The cooler itself had been rigged by Cammie's father, Bruce Holder, a helicopter mechanic with the Idaho Army National Guard.

The engine buzzed monotonously, and was a non-noise to all who lived there. The output was a jet of cool air so forceful it made the window curtains flutter like laundry drying in a stiff wind.

Cammie, the oldest, sat alone at an enormous dining table in a quieter room, carefully reading a letter from her boyfriend Chuck, who lived in Chile, doing his two years missionary work. The contents of the letter were unremarkable. The same uninspired declarations of eternal commitment. The same tired metaphors to describe her beauty. The details of his work, which interested her not at all. "They keep slamming the door in my face," he wrote, "which only makes my faith stronger." She rolled her eyes. Never heard that one before.

Curious though, that he did dare to write her. Everyone knew the church forbid such communications. Missionaries were only allowed to contact home on Mother's Day. That Chuck took the risk, that he had the cunning to mail the letter to the restaurant where Cammie worked, suggested just the faintest little spark of something interesting. Livin' on the edge, Chuck-O.

A scream from the other room brought Cammie back to the situation at hand. Without getting up, she yelled, "If I hear another sound from your little sister we'll turn that thing off and all just stew in here like—"

"Sor-ry!" they sang in chorus.

The kids went mute. Cammie mistook the buzzing of the swamp cooler for a peaceful silence. Nothing came easier than babysitting money. She twirled the letter in circles on the table, looking at it. Chuck, she thought. Chuck Chuck Chuck.

She felt the wet nose of Taffy on her ankle and reached down to scratch the dog without looking at it. Dear Chuck, she thought, thanks so much for sending me the letter. Glad to hear things are going well for you. I, on the other hand, am not traveling the world, learning a new language, or spreading the word of Jesus Christ our Lord and savior. I'm babysitting. That's right, can you believe it? Mom and Dad are bowling. How awesome! At work, they're letting me peel potatoes and cook trays of bacon. They keep trying to get me to work in the front of the house, on account of how drop dead gorgeous I am.

Taffy scratched at the sliding glass door.

"You honestly don't remember how hot it is out there?"

She leaned over, and with some effort pulled the door open. A torrent of hot air flooded into the room like water through a hole in a submarine hull.

"Oh, God," she said, shutting the door the instant Taffy cleared the way.

She heard the rattle of dice in the other room. And then another perfectly synchronized yell. This time it said, "Yatzee!"

That night, an electric monsoon of purple lightning and sheet rain assaulted the high plains of western Idaho. Cammie sat at the dining table. She had hardly moved all day. She watched the flashes backlight the billowing curtains which hung in front of the cracked-open sliding glass door. Everyone else had gone to bed.

When the power finally went out, Cammie sat listening to the deceleration of the cooler fan. The house fell silent. There was no thunder. Columns of water slapped the door like the felt tentacles of a drive-thru car wash. Chuck Chuck.

Chuck-O.

As she stood up, she lifted the chair slightly so it wouldn't make noise moving across the hardwood floor. The house seemed strange without the cooler on. Everything came uncomfortably into focus. The still air began to warm. She tiptoed through the house feeling detached. She wandered into the front room and stood silently watching as the strobing lightning froze still images onto her retina. A piano. A couch. A table with books. A portrait of Jesus. Candlesticks on an end table. Her hand, held out away from her face. One finger. Three fingers. Thumbs up.

Down the hall, in the master bedroom, her father started snoring. She would wake him in the morning at three-thirty. His alarm had no power. She thought about how much fun he would have driving his Humvee to the base through the rainy darkness, plunging the vehicle into the flooded washes.

It would not occur to him until midday that Cammie stayed up all night to make sure he didn't oversleep. He would shake his head from side to side and smile. His colleagues would say, "What is it?"

He would say, "It's nothing."

And he would sit there eating a sandwich and think, not a boy or a man on earth deserves a woman as good as his oldest daughter. He would thank God for her.

But for now, Cammie's father slept on with his wife next to him. Six children asleep in three bedrooms. His oldest daughter standing troubled in a ghostly paralysis, knee-deep in the sticky muck of an unsanctioned religious experience.

A ground strike not far away soon brought the howl of fire engines. She went to the window and could make out a faint red glow on the horizon. She also noticed a car parked across the street that she didn't recognize. With the next flash of lightning, she could see the silhouette of a figure in the driver's seat, a woman with long hair.

Cammie almost expected this, the unexpected. She had waited all night for something, some physical manifestation of her mental condition. A tangible expression of the change which seized her that afternoon. It started with the letter. Then the disaffection she felt towards Chuck spilled over to her family, her church, her life. A full-scale detachment.

Dread.

Fear of the inevitable. That was it. She never thought much about the word before. But the second she identified the emotion, it began to throttle her. Panic, and a sense that the flow of blood through her body had reversed its course—her heartbeat now a tensing contraction.

She crouched on the couch and again peered out the window. An orange light flashed inside the car as the woman lit a cigarette. Cammie watched the driver-side window move down just a crack.

Yes, she thought. I need *exactly* this. The unexplained, the unforeseen. The unarranged. Who is this woman?

Cammie went to the closet, found an umbrella, and walked to the front door. With practiced skill, she quietly opened the door. She stepped out onto the porch and opened the umbrella. A gust of wet wind swept in and yanked it from her hands, sending it cartwheeling across the front yard. She watched it tumble in frozen images captured by the flashes of lightning. In the distance, the red glow of the burning sage plains intensified.

Undeterred, she set off across the yard, soaked to her skin in seconds. The water felt warm and heavy, and she slurped as it ran into the corners of her mouth. When she reached the street, the window in the car went all the way down. The interior car light came on. Through the rain, Cammie saw a striking mass of deep red hair and the kind smile of a middle-aged woman. She walked confidently towards the car.

When Cammie was close enough to hear, the woman said in a calm voice, "Hello, Cammie. Please get in. I want to speak with you."

Cammie nodded and walked around to the far side of the car. She must know me from somewhere, she thought, though I don't recognize her. Cammie opened the door, but then hesitated before getting in.

"Don't worry about your clothes," the woman said. "It's a rental."

Cammie climbed in, checking the back seat to make sure the woman was alone. Then she shut the door. The woman extinguished her cigarette, rolled up the window, and killed the interior light.

"Hi Cammie," she said.

Cammie wiped the water from her face and swept back her hair. "Well," she said, "this is really weird."

"Isn't it?" The woman said, nodding. "And you really *are* beautiful," she added.

Cammie looked at her, but could make out very little in the darkness. "What am I doing in your car?"

"My name is Susanna Copan. And this *is* exciting."

"Were you waiting for me?"

"I was."

"Specifically for me?"

"Specifically for you, that's right."

Cammie kept her eyes focused on the windshield. Rivulets of rain blurred the orange light of the emergency generator-powered street lamp. The sound of sirens grew louder. She made sure she could open the door quickly, if she needed to. The feeling of dread was entirely gone.

"So what's this about?" Cammie asked. "Please tell me it's not a kidnap ransom thing because my parents have way too many children to worry about losing me."

"Don't be nervous," the woman said.

"Why would I be nervous?"

"Seriously."

"Okay," Cammie said, with a bit of sarcasm, "then why don't you tell me why you're acting so crazy, staking out my house in a rainstorm in the middle of the night."

The woman looked at Cammie, forced her eyes to make contact. "We want to offer you a job."

"Offer me a job?" Cammie sputtered out a laugh. She didn't know what she expected when she crossed the street through the rain, but it certainly wasn't a job offer. "Is this," she gestured to the windshield, to the rain, to the darkness. "Is this, like, an interview?"

The woman smiled. "The interview phase is over. You got in the car."

"So what's the job?"

"It's more of an assignment."

"An assignment?" Cammie was beaming. This was suddenly great fun, this spontaneous weirdness. She was a sharp girl, and her instincts told her she had nothing to fear.

"That's right. We need you to take a trip to San Diego. We'll pay you five thousand dollars. It's all perfectly legal."

"What do I have to do when I get there?"

"We're not exactly sure yet."

Cammie nodded. This is crazy, she thought. Thank God something crazy is happening. Sensing a game in the woman's cryptic unspooling of information, she played along. "Who's 'we'?"

"My organization."

"What does this organization do?"

The woman laughed. She wiped a circle into the fogged-over windshield. "What do we do?" she repeated wistfully. "Well, that's a fair question."

Cammie waited for her to continue the thought. After a few silent moments passed, she looked at the woman, confused. "Well?"

"Well what?"

"What do you do, your organization? What are you asking me to do? This is kind of ridiculous, you have to admit."

"It's totally ridiculous," the woman said with a smile. Another pause.

"So that's it?"

"That's it."

"I don't even know what we're talking about," Cammie said. She felt the door handle and gave it a little tug, to make sure it caught. Good, she thought, still unlocked.

"You're deciding whether or not to take my offer."

"You want me to fly to San Diego?"

"That's right."

"But you don't know what you want me to do there?"

"Not exactly. We'll contact you at your hotel. We already have a room and plane tickets and all that. A *nice* room, Cammie."

"Five thousand dollars?"

"Five thousand now, and another five thousand in one year."

"*Ten* thousand dollars?"

"The second five thousand is yours only if after a year's time we are certain you have told not one single soul about this meeting, about me, about the organization, or about your assignment."

"I don't even know anything to tell anyone," Cammie said, somewhat exasperated by the whole conversation.

"There will be future assignments. If you're interested. All with the same policy. Your money is doubled if you can keep your mouth shut."

"It's all legal?"

"It's all legal. It's all safe. It's all, um, church-friendly."

"Well," Cammie said. She paused, sensing she needed to gather as much information as she could. "Can you tell me why you want me, specifically?"

The woman perked up. She smiled at Cammie, encouraged by a question she knew she could answer directly. "Why did we pick you? That's easy. You're the prettiest girl we've ever seen."

That one flustered her for a second. "The prettiest girl you've ever seen?"

"That's right."

She looked directly at the woman, whose arms were spread out before her, imploring. She thought about Chuck. Was she going to sit at that table for the next two years, waiting for the weary traveler's return?

"I'll do it."

"Dad," Cammie said in a whisper-shout. "Dad, wake up. It's three-thirty."

Her father rolled over, looked at the clock, and then propped himself up on his arm. "Is the power out?"

"It went out last night. You need to get up."

He thanked Cammie, and then dug around in a nightstand drawer until he found his emergency flashlight. He flicked it on and trained the beam on Cammie's face. "Your hair's all wet."

"Yeah."

Using her own flashlight, Cammie navigated the hallway and returned to the kitchen, where she started boiling a pot of water. She removed the plastic filter basket from the automatic coffee maker and set it on top of her father's enormous coffee mug. She added a filter and some decaf coffee grounds. When the water boiled, she slowly poured it over the filter, watching a foamy black sludge gurgle to the rim and then slowly drain. She added more water and repeated the process until she filled the mug.

Outside, the storm had let up. There were no more sirens in the distance. She hopped up onto the counter and sat there. Her hand moved to the side of her shorts, where she felt at a damp wad of bills. Five thousand dollars, all in twenties. She had to keep reminding herself that it couldn't have been a dream since she hadn't gone to bed yet. Now that her head had cleared a bit, her mind was full of questions.

How did they know about her? Who had staked her out? How did she feel about being watched, researched, discussed? She went over it again in her head. Plane ticket. Rental car. Hotel. Wait for the phone to ring. This message will self-destruct. Five thousand for this project, a test. More projects to follow, bigger projects. Always legal, always Jesus-friendly.

"I represent a clandestine organization," the woman had said. "You are now a covert operative."

Her excitement overrode any doubts. Her only reservation about the events was the timing. How had the antidote arrived so quickly? Not five hours after the dread had seized her, it had been cured. Her conscience told her to thank God. Her mind told her He had nothing to do with it.

Her father came into the kitchen, the dog following at his heels. Cammie handed him his mug of coffee and told him he would have to pick up breakfast on the road.

"Toaster's out." He thanked her and kissed her on the cheek. Then he picked the dog up off the floor and put it in Cammie's lap, where it squirmed uncomfortably.

As her father left the room, she thought about the folder on her bed, with the plane ticket and the car reservation. It was a little wet from the rain, plain green except for a small emblem on the front left corner. "SMI" it read.

CHAPTER SIX

"We have problem with light."

"What kind of problem?" Ted asked. He had the newspaper spread across the desk. He didn't look up.

"You go see. Twelve floor. Broken."

"Broken how?"

Twin looked confused. "Broken how?"

"Yes, how are they broken? That's what I'm asking. What's the problem?"

"Lights not come on."

"Well, I'll go check it out," Ted said. "You hold down the fort. We got electricians in at eleven-thirty."

"I know. I can read log. You go look. Twelve floor."

Ted stood up and groaned.

You sound like an old man, Ted.

I need to get more sleep.

He walked over to the elevator lobby and rode up to the twelfth floor. He strolled the halls and entered some offices, just to indulge Twin. The lights work perfectly. Big surprise, Ted thought. He wandered into the Smoke Monkey International wing and something caught his eye. On top of the desk in front of him stood a miniature idol, painted a dull gold color. He approached the desk and took a closer look. Maya or Aztec, he thought.

What do *you* know about Maya or Aztec?

He picked it up, to get a look at the detail. Its weight surprised him. Twin would no doubt be watching him on the monitor. He was going to have something to say about Ted touching things. But Ted couldn't help himself.

This is real gold. It has to be.

Isn't gold worth like seven-hundred dollars an ounce?

And this thing must weigh at least five pounds.

Then he looked around the office and noticed several more idols on other desks. And still more on file cabinets and supply shelves. One even stood next to the fax machine. Each one equally ornate and beautiful.

There must be twenty idols scattered around the office. A small fortune.

What's to stop someone from stealing all of this?

You are, dumbshit. The security guard.

He set the idol back on the desk after wiping it with his sleeve. He made his way back down to the front desk. Twin glared at him as he approached.

"Lights are fine, big guy," Ted said.

"What you call me big guy?"

"It's nothing."

"I see you," he said.

"What do you mean?"

"I see you in office. You no touch."

"That shit was solid gold, Twin."

"You no touch."

"You should go check them out."

"You bad man."

"Take it easy. I didn't steal anything." Ted patted the badge on the front of his shirt. "I good man!"

"You big trouble."

"Go take a look."

"I no look," Twin said with pride.

Ted noticed the employee handbook sitting open on the large desk. He laughed. "Can you even read that thing?"

Twin shook his head. Then he stood up. They had an understanding that generally Ted watched the front door and Twin did the patrolling. He gave Ted an angry look when they swapped positions.

"Why do you have to be in such a shitty mood all the time?" Ted called to him as he walked away.

The electrical crew was working on the sixth floor, installing wiring above the ceiling panels. They had piled most of their supplies on the floor of the elevator lobby, and moved constantly down the hallways and into various offices. All Ted had to do was keep his eye on Twin. He had the list of sixth-floor lighting sensors on his computer screen. The camcorder sat on the desk next to him.

Twin got into the elevator on the seventh floor and Ted watched him push the sixth-floor button. He also watched one of the electricians climb down his ladder, heading back to the lobby supply area. Ted killed that sensor just as Twin emerged from the elevator, into the near darkness. Twin stood there waving his hands at the sensor device in the corner, trying to get the light to come on. He put his flashlight on it, waving the beam around. Nothing.

Ted got it all on the camcorder. He watched as the electrician made his way towards Twin, the lights going on and off as he passed through sections of hallway. When he entered the lobby where Twin was standing, Ted reactivated the sensor, and the light came on. Ted put up the volume on the audio.

"Hey, it's Twin," the man said.

Twin looked confused. "You go out again, please."

"What do you mean?"

"You go out of lobby and come back. Light broken."

"The light seems to be working just fine."

"You go out, please. Then you come back."

"Hey, man, you don't have to yell."

"I not yelling. This jus how I talk. Please, you go out. Then you come back."

"Alright, guy, no problem." The worker turned around and walked out of the lobby. Ted killed the sensor and the light went out. Twin again stood in darkness. He spun violently around the lobby. He yelled something unintelligible. The man came back and Ted again reactivated the sensor. The lights came on.

"Everything alright?"

Twin didn't say anything. He sat down on the floor and held his hands out in front of his body.

Should I feel bad about doing this?

Because you don't.

No, I don't.

But you suspect maybe you should.

Yeah, I probably should.

But you don't.

No, not a bit.

"You okay?" the worker asked Twin.

Again, Twin ignored him. He stood up and walked quickly down the hall. Ted killed all the sensors except the one in an office where another man was clipping lengths of white wire. Twin marched along through the darkness, shaking his head, his lips pressed tightly together. When he got to the lighted room where the man was working, Twin ordered him out.

"You leave now."

"Is there a problem?"

"Light broken."

"They're working fine in here."

"You leave. You come back one minute."

"I'm working here, is this really—"

"You leave! One minute you come back!"

"Jesus, man. You sure you're alright?" He set the wire down and walked out of the room. Ted killed the light.

Twin made a terrible guttural noise, something Ted had never heard before. Then Twin ran back down the hallway. Ted could see both workers now stood in front of the elevator, talking. He killed all lights except the one in the lobby. Twin continued on through the darkness, still making the noise.

On his computer, Ted brought up the elevator call controls.

Maybe that's good for the night.

Ease off?

Yeah, maybe.

He does seem to be taking it kind of hard.

Maybe you don't know enough about him. He could be a refugee. Maybe psychologically he's sensitive to the concept of identity loss, of metaphoric invisibility.

Sensitive? Isn't that the point?

They had communists over there, didn't they? The whole death of the individual thing? Is this maybe hitting below the belt?

Twin entered the lit-up lobby where the men were standing.

"Can you just explain to us what the problem is?"

"Yeah, take it easy for a second."

Twin was silent. He hit the elevator call button.

Nothing happened.

He hit it again. Then again and again and again. Then he stopped pushing the button and stared blankly at the elevator doors, not knowing what to do.

"Easy, guy, let me get that." The worker reached passed Twin and pushed the button.

Ted reactivated the call controls and sent a car to Twin's floor. The button light turned green. Twin looked into the eyes of the worker, and then crumpled to the ground in silence.

"Shit," Ted said out loud.

He immediately turned off the computer and rebooted the system, hoping his tracks were covered. He put the camcorder in his bag and tried to compose himself.

The desk phone rang.

"Security."

"Yeah, I'm doing your wiring up here on the sixth floor. We got a problem with one of your security guards. I don't know. It might be a medical thing. He's like, slumped over and...well, I guess he's weeping."

CHAPTER SEVEN

Cammie flew from Boise to San Diego, connecting through Salt Lake. It was the first time she had ever been on a commercial airline. She had flown in small private planes with her father, who was a pilot in Vietnam. She had flown in helicopters with him as well. But the experience of airports and the cramped strangeness of the airplane was all new to her.

She had a first class ticket, and on the second leg of the trip she sat next to a man who drank at least eight glasses of champagne in less than two hours. He was a short, balding, dark-skinned man, who wore an olive green suit and seemed very uncomfortable. He adjusted himself almost constantly, mopped sweat from his bald spot with cocktail napkins, and aggressively leafed through magazines and catalogues, desperate to find an article he could get lost in.

Cammie waited nervously for the moment when both the booze and the lack of a suitable distraction got the better of him. Just around the time the co-pilot announced they were headed into their final descent, the man turned to Cammie and said, "Excuse me, do you go to college in San Diego?"

"What?" Cammie said, mildly irritated, as if the man had yanked her from a pleasant daydream.

"I'm sorry, I was asking if you go to college in San Diego. My daughter has been thinking about maybe the UC."

Cammie, raised to be a good girl, respectful and sincere, couldn't keep up her mock annoyance. "No," she said, turning to the man. "It's a, um, business trip." She liked the way it sounded.

The man didn't respond immediately, but instead remained in a kind of stasis for a couple of seconds, his eyes locked on Cammie's face. He broke out of it, shaking his head quickly from side to side, like a man who had just been sucker punched. "Excuse me for saying so, but you are quite an attractive young woman. I—please—I don't mean that to sound creepy. It's just—you caught me off guard."

Cammie turned away from the man. She did not blush.

He downed the last of his champagne. "Does flying make you nervous?" she asked.

"What—oh, the drinking? No, that's something else. It's been," he paused. He looked up at the ceiling of the airplane and smiled in a way that suggested he was not happy. "It's been a very strange past couple of weeks. I won't bore you with it. But to answer your question, no I don't mind flying, and no I don't usually drink this much."

"I see," Cammie said, nodding as if she knew exactly what he was going through. The conversation flatlined, and she began fidgeting with a peanut wrapper.

The man turned to look out the window. "Fire," he said, "look."

Cammie leaned over to see out the window. A dark cloud of smoke rose from an uninhabited valley far below. She nodded.

"What business are you in, if you don't mind me asking?"

She thought for a moment. "Gosh," she said. "I don't really know how to answer that. This is a onetime thing."

The man nodded. "I see."

"It's pretty weird, to be honest. I'm not supposed to talk about it. But they got me this first class ticket, and they're hooking me up with a car and a hotel in San Diego."

The expression on the man's face soured into a look of concern. He became serious. "It's none of my business," he said, "but you seem like a very sweet girl. Kind of innocent. Maybe a touch naïve. I don't mean that as an insult. I would just be careful."

"What do you mean?"

"It's not my place to say."

"I'm asking you to say."

"Are you confident that the people you work for have your best interest in mind? I mean, you're from Utah, right?"

"Idaho. What does that matter?"

"People in California do things a bit differently, if you know what I mean."

Cammie was now very interested in what the man was saying. His flustered and frantic body language suggested recent harrowing experiences may have left him in possession of some valuable knowledge. "Different how?"

"Look," the man said, throwing a glance out the window to see how long they had until the plane landed. "You're a pretty girl. My own daughter is a pretty girl too. And I worry about her. Every single day I worry about her. Because I know there are people out there who will try to take advantage of her. Let me ask you this, and you don't have to go into any details or anything. Just answer this one question."

"Okay."

"Were you asked to do what you are going to do because of the way you look?"

"Well," Cammie paused as she tried to think through exactly what it was she was being paid to do. And then it hit her. She blurted it out. "You think!" Then she quieted down and leaned closer to the man, whispering this time. "You think I'm a—a prostitute?"

"Oh, no no no," the man said, vigorously shaking his head. He looked out the window again. "Can I tell you a quick story? We're about to land, but I'll plow through it, if you don't mind."

Cammie was amused now. It was fun to imagine herself as some jet-setting prostitute, flying first class all around the world to meet with wealthy exclusive clients. "Let's have it," she said.

"Okay, so I used to be the manager of a restaurant in Pomona. It's basically a town outside of Los Angeles. I got into some family troubles that I won't...never mind that. Let's just say I'm recently divorced, and basically penniless. Someone bought me this plane ticket, which I would gladly have switched out for a coach ticket if I could have pocketed the difference." He looked out the window again. "Jeez, we're about to land. Quickly then. Okay, so I was pretty down and out, and my job wasn't all that great. And then one day, like around two o'clock when the restaurant was totally empty, this tall skinny man with funny thick glasses walks in carrying a briefcase. He's a crazy looking guy, and I immediately distrust him. He asks me if I'm the manager, and I tell him I am. He asks me if there are banquet facilities in the restaurant, and I show them to him. The banquet room is really quite nice. The building is on the top of a hill and the banquet room has floor to ceiling windows. The view is fantastic. This will do, he tells me. And then he asks if we can go back to the lounge and talk about some things. I've got nothing to do, so I say fine. We sit at a table and he puts the briefcase between us. It's a metallic briefcase, the kind you see in the movies that's either full of money or secret documents. It looks like a briefcase that might be handcuffed to somebody's wrist."

Cammie watched the man as he spoke. She encouraged him by nodding and smiling. He needed to tell this story, irrespective of its relevance, and Cammie's innate kindness told her to indulge this strange old man who would disappear from her life in just a few short minutes.

"So he opens the suitcase, and it's full of money. Just like in the movies. Stacks of twenties in bundles. Fifty thousand dollars, he tells me. I'm thinking, pardon my French, *oh shit*. I realize when I look at this money that I'm about to be made an offer that I will not be able to refuse. Seeing the money makes me painfully aware that I can be bought and sold. There is nothing I wouldn't do at that moment for that money. I'm terrified of what he will ask me to do."

"Which is what?"

"It's crazy. It's nuts. He tells me, get this, he tells me he wants to *live* in the banquet room for a month, no questions asked. He wants full run of the kitchen and the bar. That's it. I tell him, for the sake of argument, something he certainly must know. I tell him you can't live in the banquet room. This is a functioning restaurant. It's illegal, if nothing else. That's when he looks down at the money again. He smiles at me. This guy's a real nut. I'll lose my job I tell him. Again he looks at the money. And I start to think about it, and I just say yes. I figure there's a slight chance I won't lose my job over this, and it's fifty grand!"

"This is a true story?"

"True story. Just happened like two months ago. Notice," he said with a smile. "Notice I am not currently at work at this restaurant."

Cammie laughed as they told everyone on the plane to put seatbacks in an upright position and to fasten seatbelts.

"So I agree. He takes two stacks from the suitcase and hands them to me and says the rest of the money will be mine in two weeks. I tell him I want to get paid every day, as a percentage, and he agrees to it. And that's that. We shake hands and he takes the suitcase and leaves the restaurant.

"So I sit there and thumb through the stack of bills, really just in disbelief. And when the guy comes back, he's got this giant blue tumbling mat that's, I swear to God, as big as a queen-sized mattress. He's pulling and pushing it, and maneuvering it between tables and chairs. He gets it into the room and then leaves again. I'm watching this all in shock. I literally can't speak. He comes back with another mat, just as big. Then comes a long pole. Then a couple of metal supports. Then he comes with a dolly and takes a keg out of the bar and wheels it to the back room. I can't believe what I'm seeing. And then I don't see him for a couple of hours. I'm dying to know what he's doing in that room, and I'm stressed about what I have agreed to, and I'm worried that this could all be illegal or a sting or that in some way I'm going to end up without a job, without the money, sitting in jail.

"But for now I've got at least some of the money. About four thousand dollars. So dinner happens, and I tell the employees not to go into the room. And the guy doesn't come out. Not even to use the bathroom. So when I leave, I walk to my car and look up at the banquet room to see if I can tell what's going on in there. And what I see is absolutely crazy. The guy has all the curtains pulled away from the floor to ceiling windows, and he's in there, completely naked, practicing the high jump. He's set up a high jump rig and he's running and leaping and landing all in the nude. And he's quite good at it."

"That's ridiculous."

"You have no idea. Anyway. So the bottom line is that somebody sees him, calls the cops, he gets taken away, I lose my job and never see another dime of the money."

"But you've got this great story."

"Yeah...but who was that guy?"

"What do you mean?"

"Like, where did he come from? Where'd he get the money? High jumping naked in a banquette room?"

"Well, he was crazy, right?"

"That's what I figured, but I don't think so anymore. It was too calculated. Too strange. I don't know."

"I see," Cammie said. Tall buildings passed in the window. "We're landing," she said.

"I'm sorry," the man said. "I don't know why I told you all that. You're an easy person to talk to. You're really a good person, I can tell."

"And so are you," Cammie said. "I'm Cammie."

The man shook her hand. "I'm Sasha. The pleasure is all mine."

They smiled at each other and the plane touched ground.

"But wait," he suddenly broke in again. "The point. I must have had a point. Don't trust anyone whose motives aren't clear, okay? I know it sounds trite, but always know what you're getting yourself into when you take somebody's money."

Cammie thanked him for his advice and watched as he gathered up his things. She noticed a folder tucked into the side of his bag. It was a green folder, just like the one she had.

CHAPTER EIGHT

Gob sat on the couch watching the monitor. Everyone else in the house was still asleep.

"What are they?"

"They're figurines. Solid gold. They weigh like five pounds each," Ted said.

"Looks like there's a bunch of them."

"I counted twenty."

"You *counted* twenty? Jesus, listen to yourself. You should be careful."

"I'm not going to steal anything. But it's weird, right? To leave them just sitting out like that."

"What's the company?"

"They're called Smoke Monkey International. I don't know what they do. I looked it up though. Smoke Monkey is Maya. He was some lesser godking."

Ted had intended to show Gob the footage of Twin's breakdown, but changed his mind at the last second. "So I quit," he said. Gob nodded, still studying the video of the idols. "The hours are impossible. I keep falling asleep in class."

"I can tell it's tough on you."

"What do you mean?"

"You seem...I don't know...*removed*."

"Yeah, I'm just beat." Ted thought about it.

What else can I say?

Something about guilt and shame. That the feelings are pure and raw and awful. That they're real in a way that nothing else in this strange college bubble is real.

I can't tell him they took Twin away in an ambulance, that I followed the gurney as they wheeled him out of the building. That I tried to get him to look at me.

That he wouldn't look at you.

Gob handed Ted the camcorder.

"The newspaper?" Ted asked.

Gob shook his head. "Gone again."

Ted rolled his eyes. "We should do something about it."

"You're right," Gob said, "we should." They both laughed.

"No but really," Ted said. He thought about this person sneaking up to their porch. "It does make you angry."

"It really does," Gob agreed.

"They're going to steal *our* fucking newspaper?" Ted said, suddenly indignant. He stood up.

Gob laughed, surprised by Ted. "*Now* you're angry?"

"I'm angry, yes!"

And I like it. It's nice and distracting.

You're all over the place.

I'm refocusing. And my stomach hurts. And I have an idea.

You just sent a grown man to the psych ward.

I'm trying to move on. I'm inspired.

By anger?

Clearly!

"We're going to straighten this out," Ted said.

"By calling the newspaper? We should have done that weeks ago."

"No! We're not calling the newspaper. And we're not calling the cops either."

"You have a plan?" Gob asked.

"Damn right I have a plan. A goddamn brilliant plan."

The six roommates sat on the two couches. The TV was off. The music was off. This was serious business. Nobody had ever called a house meeting before.

Ted stood up and announced that it was time to deal with the newspaper thief. "Time," he said, rubbing his chin, "to engage the world with the well-spring of abstract thinking that bubbles up from the basement bedroom like gurgling bong water." They all nodded. "One of us gets up very early and shits in the newspaper." He paused. "And then we fold it back up and put it on the porch."

The roommates considered the suggestion.

Ted looked down at them all. He was beaming.

A few more seconds passed, and then they were all smiling. Then they were laughing. Their laughter became outrageous. Fetcher and Jeff fell out of their seats. Eventually, they carried Ted around on a chair, Bar Mitzvah-style.

Then they all got drunk.

They chose numbers. It could take a few days for the thief to show up. Gob picked the first spot. The next day, his alarm went off at four in the morning. He unplugged it semi-consciously by yanking the cord which ran along the floor by the head of his mattress, itself on the floor. But nobody came for the paper that day.

Fetcher was second in line. The following day, he got up on time, picked the just-delivered paper from the porch, made his way into the bathroom, and that was that.

"Mission aborted," he said.

"Details," they begged. They giggled. He was lactose intolerant. They all knew his was a suicide mission. Jeff, in his best Golem voice, wanted to know if it was "sssssoupy."

Gob had to pay a pre-arranged penalty for oversleeping—three nights on the dirty mattress in the garage, which sloped fifteen degrees. Fetcher they let off the hook.

Ted went third.

I always knew it would come down to me.

If you want something done right, you just have to do it yourself.

He had a hard time sleeping that night. When he finally heard the thump of the paper on the porch, he jumped right up to his feet. Twenty seconds later, he was squatting in the bathroom, training his ass on an image of First Lady Hillary Rodham Clinton. She would be giving a speech at the university that afternoon, to commemorate the naming of the library for Eleanor Roosevelt. Ted had tickets to see her speak.

He laid a number on her face that was fit for fluming.

Then, he quietly opened the front door. The morning was lightening. *Justice*, he said to himself.

He set the refolded paper gingerly on the porch, like he was handling nitroglycerin. Then he went back to bed and lay there for two hours, unable to sleep. The others were not kind when he finally appeared in the living room looking to get a cup of coffee.

"Can you pass me the sports section?"

"Uh, no, it's got shit on it."

"Has anyone seen the crossword?"

"Um, I think it might have shit on it."

"Hey, if anyone needs me, I'll be upstairs reading the toilet."

"Fuck you all," Ted said. "I have to get to class."

Round and round they went, and the reality of their plan began to punish. It was amazing, on the days the thief stole the paper, the task, for various reasons, had not been completed. Days the deed was successfully done, the thief stayed away. Nobody had read the paper in two weeks. Ted's ingenious scheme had become their ultimate humiliation. To buy something other than a toilet, and then go to the bathroom on it. Was there more absurd behavior?

But they pressed through the ritual daily, each with his own sense of dread. Lies were told about constipation or incontinence. Fears were voiced about upsetting some kind of universal balance through the mortal sin of vengeance. They were farther than ever from understanding the thief. Some blamed college, acknowledging how sated they had all become on exactly the wrong kind of knowledge. Shitting in newspapers? Really? It wasn't even that funny anymore. And what would it really accomplish?

But just as they were all ready to give up, on a day Ted half-heartedly did the deed, he woke to the sound of pounding fists on the front door.

He sat up in bed.

This is it.

As he walked down the hall, his heartbeat pulsed deep and pained. He had trouble getting his breath.

His roommates must have been awake, but nobody joined him. Which didn't bother Ted.

It doesn't matter. This is my idea. My shit. My problem.

The pounding on the door continued. He looked through the peephole.

The fire department.

The fire department?

This isn't good.

No.

Not what I expected.

It's not a shit-covered homeless guy. That would make sense.

Or even the cops. But firemen?

How does shit in a newspaper start a fire?

"It's the fucking fire department!" he hollered.

Another round of fist-pounding on the door. Ted opened it.

"Good morning, sir," said a middle-aged woman. She wore a yellow fire suit, complete with a small tank of oxygen strapped to her back. She had her red hat in her hand, and a look of great sadness and deep concern.

Two other firemen stood a few feet back. One was tall, middle-aged as well, and very skinny. The other was older and out of shape. They still wore their hats, and both glowed red with rage. Ted took a moment to search the porch for the paper, and it was gone.

"Sir," she said, "can we speak with you for a moment?"

Such beautiful red hair. Like she just came from the salon.

Jesus, man. *Focus!*

"Is something wrong?" Ted asked.

"Yes, yes something is very wrong."

"Is the building on fire?"

One of the men in the back suddenly stepped forward, with teeth clenched. "Sir," he demanded, "did you defecate in your newspaper this morning?"

It was the kind of question that the slightest hint of hesitation would answer on Ted's behalf. Surely, to ask this question of a man who had *not* shit in his newspaper would prompt any number of immediate and definitive responses.

"Is it...against the law?"

"You smarmy little bitch!" growled the other fireman, stepping forward. He was every bit as furious as the first guy.

He's going to punch me in the face.

Looks that way.

These are by far the two angriest people I've ever seen in my life.

Nice job.

What the hell happened?

"Guys," the woman said, still calm and professional, putting her arms out at her sides as restraints. She turned her attention back to Ted.

59

"Sir," she continued, "I don't know, can't honestly imagine, what your motivation might be for doing what you did, if it was some sick prank or what, but you should know how this morning has gone for two people who live just three houses down from here."

"Oh?"

"Do you know the Parsons? Addie Parson. She's ninety-seven years old."

"She's in the fucking hospital, you dick! I had to clean your shit off her face!"

"Dan, please."

Ted was shocked, "Oh my God, is she..."

"Is she what?"

"Is she going to...to make it?"

Dan stood right in Ted's face. His eyes were bloodshot and he spat when he spoke. "Make it where, you dirty asshole? She's ninety-seven. There's only one place left she's got to go, and you made sure she'll get there a little quicker."

"Yeah," said the woman, no longer holding back the dogs. "She's at this point non-responsive."

"Comatose, Dickweed!"

"Wait, wait, wait. How is this possible?" Ted asked. He ran his hands through his hair, trying to process it all.

"Addie Parson lives with her forty-four-year-old grandson, Craig, who's autistic."

I see.

Perfect.

I guess I should just kill myself now.

Guess so.

The woman went on. "Every day, Addie gives Craig fifty cents to go to the market at the end of the block to buy a newspaper from the machine. Apparently, sometimes Craig pockets the fifty cents and helps himself to a neighbor's newspaper."

Dan jumped back into the conversation: "I told them it wasn't no dogshit!"

The woman went on to say that on this particular day, Craig had taken *their* newspaper and given it, as he did every morning, to his ailing, bedridden grandmother.

"White fucking linen sheets!"

"Dan."

Ted tried to explain how things looked from his perspective. How they had tried everything to get the thief to stop.

"So you called the newspaper?" she asked.

"Well, no."

"The police?"

"No, but you have to understand we were being humiliated."

"And you wanted revenge."

"Well, in a way, yes. Within, of course, the limits of the law."

Dan, a little calmer now, broke in: "I wish to God what you did *was* illegal, and I'm not even sure it isn't. You should be locked up. Maybe when you get a look at this old lady with the shit all over her, you'll lock yourself up."

That doesn't make any sense.

Just let him have it.

Then Dan produced a photo, a Polaroid from the crime scene. The retarded grandson in hysterics, his hands clutching his head, sitting in the corner of the bedroom, presumably rocking back and forth. Then another shot of Granny, with a centerfielder's smear of brown across her cheek. And those vacant eyes. Then he saw a picture of the room without the two victims. It looked like a violent crime scene, with shit substituted for blood, splattered everywhere.

CHAPTER NINE

He estimated a northern direction as the plane pulled itself noisily through the darkness. The sky was overcast with no light from the moon or the stars. But at least he could finally relax. First, he assessed his injuries. He had cuts everywhere, all up and down his arms and legs, and a nasty tear across the top of his left ear, which bled actively. He took his shirt off and wrapped it around his head to put some pressure on the ear. He thought of all the dirt and grime on the shirt and wondered if in the end it would be a simple jungle infection that did him in. He snorted out a laugh.

Not crocodiles, silly, *bacterium.*

Then there was the issue with his knee. A hyperextension or a sprain or something. Most of the time it felt fine, but certain movements lit it up and he would make a high-pitched whiny noise and suck in air quickly. He didn't mind any of the pain however. He was alive. Certainly finding a place to land the plane, getting medical attention, and returning to the states would all be new headaches to deal with. But at least he was not staring down death anymore. At least he was not alone in a dark jungle attending his grim demise.

What he missed, however, was any sense of actual happiness. He felt relief. Tons of relief. But no happiness. Something big gnawed at his brain. Something he didn't really even know how to address. It was massive and terrifying, and it shut out any thoughts he might have had about sleeping with the girl, or how lucky it was that he knew how to fly planes, or any other issue that should have been dominating his thoughts.

He was thinking about the bullets. All of them missing. Just like in the movies. And the keys in the lock box. And the fully-fueled plane. All of it part of something he couldn't quite get his head around. When he was driving through the darkness, peeling around corners, eying that jungle with those headlights coming for him, escape seemed impossible. Truly impossible.

Yet it happened. Exactly as it had to.

The tiny prayers, how many had he made in the last two hours? Fifty? A hundred? The words fell out of his mouth automatically. *Did God just protect me?*

Did *God* just protect me?

Is that what happened?

A miracle? That's certainly what it felt like. Or...what if they missed on purpose?

Huh?

What if they missed on purpose? She was in on it. They were in on it. The chase. The keys.

No.

It's one or the other. God or man.

Enough of this. Let's go home.

When the sun came up behind him, he still had over half a tank of gas. He flew low over the jungle canopy, across Costa Rica, Nicaragua, and into Honduras. The sky had cleared. In the morning light, the jungle bloomed, bright, open, full of life. His nerves calmed enough for him to begin addressing his situation with some level of practicality. First things first, water. There had to be some water in—

He turned around and scanned the back of the plane. He saw two very large sealed cardboard boxes. And as far as what those boxes contained, nothing could be ruled out. He hoped it was bottles of water. He hoped it was not cocaine. Seized by a sudden compulsive curiosity, he contorted his body and fumbled around until he had one of the boxes on its side with the top facing him. The box felt very heavy. He worked a second key off the ring connected to the plane's ignition. Twisting through the pain, he sliced the tape away from the seam. He pulled the flaps open and looked inside.

What he saw set his mind at ease. It was not drugs, or body parts, or anything that might cause the plane owner to chase him to the corners of the earth.

Polaroid cameras.

About twenty of them. He laughed. Instamatics. He thanked God. Again. This time for providing him with just what he needed, a heavy dose of the mundane.

But he remembered that second box. His nerves tingled. It was slightly smaller than the first box, which told him it probably had different contents. Again he contorted himself. He manipulated the second box's opening so he could reach it. This box was much lighter. In fact, it felt empty. But he could sense the shifting of contents. With one eye on the windshield, his knees bracing the steering column, he cut at the seam with the key, pulled out the flaps, and looked inside.

Confusion.

"What the hell?"

Colorful nylon swatches folded into pie shaped wedges. Nylon cords. Miniature carabineers.

Cute little tiny parachutes.

He smiled. He looked at the first box. The Instamatics.

Hmm. The Instamatics. The adorable parachutes. The single engine plane.

What's this guy up to?

Perplexed, he considered any explanation he could think of. You own a small plane in Panama. You are...*what*? Parachuting Polaroids to indigenous tribes? Is that it? What kind of man—

React *now*!

To *lightning*!

To a brilliant bolt of purple suddenly blocking his flight path. He hit it square on and the left wing was severed from the plane. He began to dive before he could even grasp what had happened. Then the plane started to roll. He could do nothing to stop the spinning. He hit the upper jungle canopy while still moving somewhat horizontally. He heard scraping, saw birds take flight, and then he felt the impact.

He never actually lost consciousness, but there was a period of shock in which he was unable to move or focus his mind. Crash, he thought. Crash. You are crashed.

You are alive.

You are in a tree.

You are upside down.

He managed to get the door open and undo the lap belt. These first few movements brought him no pain. He felt fine.

A miracle.

Another miracle?

He poured his body out the side of the craft, onto a thick tree branch. He could smell fuel and something like lawn clippings from all the destroyed greenery. Hugging the trunk, he shimmied down to the floor of the jungle. It was the second time in twenty-four hours he had shimmied down something. Thirty years, he thought, and I maybe never shimmied once.

Branches broke above him. He dashed from under the tree as the plane fell from its perch and slammed into the ground. He climbed back into the cockpit and looked again for something useful. He found nothing.

He studied the dense jungle around him. *Perfect.* Had he crashed the *Jeep* into the jungle, he might have only been *sort of* isolated in the wilderness. But *this.* He looked around at the blankets of greenery. This is the real deal, Oliver. "The whole enchilada," he said out loud.

Strangely though, he felt none of the earlier fear. He was charmed now, impervious. Improbable escapes, crash landings, all so some jaguar can rip my head off? Unlikely.

He studied his surroundings more intently. The only non-vegetative feature he could see was a tall mound of earth about a hundred yards away. He started walking toward it, with a mind to climb up and get some perspective.

But before he could move, a searing headache seized him—an *eyeball* headache. A glaring whiteness filled his vision. He stumbled, barely able to keep himself from falling over. He clutched his head, and the pain subsided as quickly as it had come. He blinked his eyes. Vision began to resolve itself.

He remembered the lightning bolt.

What the hell was that?

He would have to think about it later, because now, as his focus returned, he noticed something very strange about that mound in front of him. It was too symmetrical. He walked to the base, crossing a trickling stream, where he stopped to wash his wounds and drink. Then he labored to the top of the mound, about a hundred feet above the jungle floor, remarking the odd consistency of the slope and the stunted growth of the groundcover.

The view from the top didn't help at all. He was still far below the canopy. He told himself he would need to walk west. Follow the sun. There will be settlements. Think practically, act logically. Stay hydrated.

But something's weird here, he thought. With this mound. He felt reluctant to move on. He felt...

Something.

Something what, Oliver?

He stood still and listened. Where did that lightning bolt come from, Oliver?

He sniffed the air. He looked at his dirty hands. The dizziness returned. He sat down. He lay down. He slept.

When he woke, the sun seemed not to have moved. Yet he felt thoroughly rested. He descended the mound by the far side, aware of a dull cramping soreness in his lower back, as if he'd slept too long in the same position. Halfway down, he stopped to stretch on an outcropping of white limestone.

When he continued on, he quickly came across another outcropping, identical to the first. He stood on it, thinking. Something occurred to him. Something improbable. He studied the hillside, the dirt and shrubbery. He pulled on a large fern and it tore easily out of the ground. He clawed at the dirt. Beneath it, more limestone. He continued the process obsessively for several hours, until he uncovered a series of perfectly square blocks.

This is no mound of earth, Oliver.

He climbed down to the base and walked around it, back towards the side he initially ascended. He located a place where a narrow section sloped up at a much steeper angle. He fell to his knees and started digging at the base, compelled. He pulled away the soft mud and uncovered a sheer white wall. By placing his hands flat against the cold stone, and raising them up and under the accumulated biomass, he was able to dislodge most of the sheathing debris with little effort. He exposed six feet of wall and studied it closely for any deliberate marks or inscriptions.

He didn't find any. He sat back on the damp ground and considered the facts. Beneath this superficial layer of organics, a large man-made structure was waiting. Had *been* waiting a long time. Was as yet, undiscovered. Was probably, *what*, Maya? Aztec?

What country am I in again?

What movie am I watching again?

He thought about booby traps, curses, poison darts, and gold.

He studied the spot where the white wall disappeared into the ground. He crab-walked over, got to his knees, and began to dig *downward*. Three-feet of subterranean wall, and then nothing. So then he started tunneling *inward*, the ground cold, clumpy, and easy to move. By evening he had excavated a passage four feet long beneath the exposed wall. He continued to work frantically through the night in total darkness.

By morning, this passageway was ten feet long, sloping at a slight downward angle. And it was bordered on all sides by smooth stone. He had somehow connected his crude tunnel with a preexisting one. Nothing about that surprised him.

He labored on, inching closer to his inevitable discovery. He dug and dug and dug.

And then his hands hit hard cold stone. He wormed back out of the hole and reentered feet first. When he reached the stone he kicked at it. It moved, sliding back slightly. He kicked again. More movement. He kicked and kicked and kicked. Finally, the stone dropped away and the tunnel instantly flooded with a cold dank wind.

Back at the plane, he swirled his t-shirt around in the gas tank. He built a torch. Then into the tunnel head first. He lit the bundle with matches from the bar. He crawled along, and then paused at the brink of the emptiness and looked ahead. He saw a large open chamber. He climbed in and stood up. He brushed himself off. In the center of the room stood a large rectangular stone. And on top of that stone Oliver saw a small carved idol.

His heart swelled. Waves of joy pulsed through his body. He approached the idol and studied it in the torchlight. He set the fire on the stone floor. Then, he carefully picked up the idol and cradled it expectantly. The face that glared back at him was almost cartoonish, with oversized eyes and pointed ears.

Oliver looked at the large stone. Then back at the idol. He pressed it to his heart. Then he set it on the ground. He placed both hands on the stone and felt around. Intuiting this, as he somehow intuited everything else, he discovered a seam one inch from the top.

The lid.

He put his fingers on the portion of the stone above the seam. He pushed. It moved. Of course it moved, Oliver. He slid the lid far enough over to expose the contents of the box. He reached down for the torch, brought it to the edge and looked inside.

He smiled. "Mother of God," he said aloud.

CHAPTER TEN

Ted put the Polaroids on the coffee table and walked out of the house. Then he drove to the university.

What now?

Don't look at me.

I have no idea how to handle this. First Twin, and now Addie Parson. I can't just go to class.

You could drop-out. Sell your books.

Is that where this is headed?

Well, apparently you're a sociopath.

For real. Two people in the hospital.

You did that.

Me.

He shook his head.

My shit. On *her* face.

He couldn't believe how that sounded.

The mother of veterans, probably.

The proud survivor of two world wars and the Great Depression.

Her own mother probably came to California in a covered fucking wagon.

He pounded his fist on the steering wheel. He squinted until his mind cleared.

That's it then. Call it.

May 6, 1997. Ten thirty-five AM.

Even though it was still early, the campus was already crowded with students. He had to park in one of the shuttle-accessed satellite lots. On top of everything else, it had begun to rain.

Noah's flood.

It *never* rains in San Diego.

I have brought down the wrath of God.

He waited in his parked car until he saw the shuttle approaching. He grabbed his bag full of books and made a dash for the stop, where several other people hunkered down under umbrellas. He would have made fun of them yesterday, carrying their umbrellas around San Diego in May, necessary or not. It seemed too calculating, required too much analysis and foresight. Trying to control everything. Just let life happen, man. Roll with it. Get wet if you have to. So what?

But now these people just confirmed his place, unfit for selection. See the clouds, dumbass? Maybe instead of shitting on old ladies, you should take a minute to watch the news.

Or read the newspaper.

Because of the rain, the shuttle was packed. He had to cram into the aisle and balance himself by holding onto an overhead plastic strap. His bag of books was on the wet floor, braced between his feet. He hung his head low, like a bad dog, as the musty shuttle rocked its way towards the center of campus. More stops, more wet students. He didn't the mind the crowd, the misery on every face, the wet air, and the closeness of strangers. The collective suffering actually helped.

He felt the breaks come on. The tires squealed a little, and the shuttle made a hard stop. He heard the doors hiss open. He heard a timid *thank you* to the driver. The doors hissed shut and the shuttle continued. He looked up, to check their progress.

The bodies in the aisle in front of him swayed back and forth. They separated just perfectly for a moment to give him a clear view to the front of the shuttle, the road ahead, and the new passenger.

She was soaking wet, like she just crawled out of the ocean. Her face glistened in the yellow light. A sea nymph, Ted thought.

She's *flawless*

That damp sweater, all heavy with rain water.

The way it sticks to her body in a haphazard perfection. Such spontaneous beauty.

And you in such a fit of self-loathing.

Strange timing.

The others in the aisle re-swayed to obscure her once more from view.

I'll talk to her, he decided. Just approach her and ask her out.

Such brazen acts didn't come easy for Ted, but things didn't matter so much anymore. He certainly wasn't afraid of failure. How much worse could things get?

You shudder a bit when you ask that question, don't you?

I don't know. I don't know anything except *that*. The way the wet wool clings to her breasts. Clearly, life can be renewed.

Focus, Ted. You're dropping out of college, remember?

She was gone by the time he got off the shuttle, as if she had teleported away. He could see everyone else jogging across the lawn. But not her. It was strange. Impossible.

He stood pivoting, scanning for the girl, his bag of books drenching in the rain.

What the hell?

A disappearing act.

He jogged to the Student Union. Once under the overhang, he walked to the textbook store and headed to the back counter. He unloaded the books from his bag.

"These books are all wet," the man at the register said.

"Yeah, it's raining out," Ted said. He felt like being an asshole, especially here. He always hated these book return guys. They dressed in fine suits, like they worked on Wall Street. Just how much money did they make off this racket, sitting on their asses, fleecing college kids?

"I can't buy any of these," the man said. "They're no good to me. Once the covers dry, they'll warp. People are very particular about book covers."

"You can't give me anything?" Ted asked. He went on to explain that he was dropping out of college, and that being here in the textbook store was a highly symbolic moment. He told the man he simply couldn't leave the building with these books.

He left with thirty-five dollars. He had paid almost five hundred dollars for those books. He stood under the overhang and watched the rain.

Okay.

So what now, Ted? Now that you are officially a college drop-out.

Did I really just sell all my books?

You did.

Am I over-reacting?

He ran his hands across his face.

You did this because you feel awful. You're ashamed of yourself and your bad behavior. You've gone over all this.

I have to leave.

You have to leave.

Yes. I have to get away from here. I have to go to work. I need a shitty job. A punitive job. I need long hours and shitty bosses. I need psychotic colleagues. I need—

To be punished.

Yes.

He made his way back through the rain towards the shuttle stop, not at all concerned about getting wet. He stood waiting. Everyone stared at him. All those nice, focused, shame-free students.

Don't start acting crazy, Ted.

Start?

The shuttle arrived and he filed into the back. He took a seat. It loaded slowly, as people who had been hiding under the eaves of close buildings made the dash across the lawn to the shelter of the shuttle. He watched for the girl, but figured it was hopeless. Nobody would be on his weird schedule, taking the shuttle to the center of the campus and then leaving so quickly.

The doors hissed shut and they were off. He wiped the fog from his window and studied the campus. They passed the venue for Hillary Clinton's speech. It was hard for him to believe that he so recently thought it would be interesting to watch the First Lady speak. Just days ago.

That's college.

See what it did to you? The First Lady? Really? Commemorating Eleanor Roosevelt? You cared about *that*? About getting stoned and sitting on a folding chair and listening to a speech?

Ridiculous.

College *is* ridiculous.

This little bubble, like this shuttle, cramped and muggy. All fogged over. No wonder I'm running around like a maniac, sending people to the hospital. I'm done.

Good for you.

Then he felt the slowing again. The squeaking breaks. The force of an unplanned stop. The doors hissed open. He heard a soft *thank you*, just like before. The shuttle continued on its way. He stood up to get a view of the front. The aisles were packed just as they had been on his first trip. But there she was, somehow even wetter this time. The white sweater still stuck perfectly to her body. Strands of

74

hair were plastered to her cheeks. The students swayed in the aisle, obscuring her, revealing her, in and out of view like the sun behind a patchwork of moving clouds.

Her arm gripped the overhead strap. As the shuttle jostled along, she swayed in a seductive dance.

For me! For Ted!

Oh, boy.

I'll try again. I'll ask her why she rides the shuttle with such an irregular schedule. I'll confess my crimes to her. She'll absolve me. I'll go get my books back. It's fine, it's fine. Everything will be fine.

You just said you were done.

Look at her!

The shuttle slowed as it approached the first stop. His car was still a mile further along. The rain had intensified to the general grumbling of people who now had to get off the shuttle and deal with it. Through the window he saw her step outside.

"Excuse me!" he howled at the people ahead of him, those still standing in the aisle. "This is my stop!"

With no place else to go, the people in the aisle were forced to exit the shuttle and wait in the rain. Outside the door was a scene of chaos. People getting off. People getting back on. Umbrellas going up. The rain plopped in big tropical drops. He looked for her, but she was gone again.

How does she do that?

He turned in circles, searching the mass of coats and hoods. No white sweater. Already, the aisle standers were filing back onto the shuttle.

Then he saw something.

Over there!

A whitish sweater moving between two cars in the lot. But he wasn't sure. It was hard to focus through the rain.

That's a dude, Ted.

Suddenly, behind him, the doors hissed shut. He wheeled around. Through a rubbed-clear section of the fogged front window, he saw her, back on the bus somehow. She gripped the overhead plastic strap and swayed as the shuttle pulled away. She looked at him. She shrugged her shoulders.

Did she shrug her shoulders? I don't know.

Maybe.

What does it matter? What does anything matter?

He started shivering. The rain was cold and his car was still a mile away.

He planned on leaving town early the next morning. He would go to Valvert, Idaho, a resort town in the mountains he knew from childhood vacations. He put a call in as soon as he got back from campus. They were indeed hiring, and they had plenty of dorm space available.

Then what am I doing here? he wondered. He was sitting in his car in front of Mel's house. She was having a big party that night.

I don't really care about saying goodbye. In fact, the more people I see tonight, the more likely I'll chicken out and stay. So what is it?

It's the girl, Ted.

Of course.

Not that she'll be here.

But you never know. Maybe she's a friend of a friend. And at least it stopped raining.

He walked up to the house. He knew some of the people there, but his roommates were running late. They might not show up at all, which was why he took his own car. After four years he had learned the group could not be relied upon to make quick decisions.

He wandered through the house, looking for the bathroom. There was a line. Instead of waiting, he went out back to the side yard of the house and peed in the ivy. Just as he zipped up, a window on the second floor opened.

Can they see me down here?

76

He recognized the face in the open window, Stephanie or Susan. She had dated Jeff a while back. She looked upset. Ted could hear banging on the door behind her.

She's the reason for the line.

Then he saw her throw something. She throws like a girl, he thought. It hit him on the shoulder and fell to the ground.

No. Not possible.

Oh, Ted.

He looked at his shoulder and could make out a dark stain on his white shirt. He pulled the spot to his nose and sniffed. It was shit. He looked at the ground where the rest of the turd propped up against his shoe. Then he looked up, horrified, in time to see the girl slam the window shut.

"Gross!" he called out in the darkness of the side yard. He took off his shirt and threw it on the ground. "Curses!" he hissed, looking up at the sky, his wild shaking fingers gripping the air like striking claws. He hopped the fence and walked to his car.

If not the wrath of God, then what? What other reason would an attractive woman have to throw feces out a window at a college party?

You think it was *aimed* at you?

I don't know, maybe she's vegan. I've heard they have airy unflushable turds that bob on the surface like rubber duckies. Maybe in a panic, with a desperate mob banging at the door, she fished it out and tossed it into the yard. Maybe God is punishing her too.

Maybe for her the wrath of God is an unflushable turd at a house party.

That makes me the co-victim of a divine two-for-one.

So he left the house party, left college, left San Diego. Just *left*.

77

CHAPTER ELEVEN

"Climb down from the bed of the rusted-out pickup truck. The one that brought you here to us, these thirty-five miles from the Guatemalan border. You've never seen coffee growing before. The dreary tangle of thin branches and yellowing leaves saddens you. Document this and all we have spoken of. Tell Him the story. About the chicken bus. Run the peeping chorus through your mind. Forget nothing. The flung pebbles and the trailing cloud of dust. The Maya couple, fellow passengers, short and simple. Married so young, she is tossed into you as the truck whips through the tight mountain curves. She apologizes, though the words are strange and mumbled. She is ashamed in your presence. What can you do? The hut where they are dropped off is made of mud. The truck barely stops. You'd never seen the bloodied tree stump where chickens are killed, and now you have. The rusty machete embedded in the wood rings terrifies you. Remark these two, their isolation, their struggle to grow corn.

"Your life, sweet Marona, is the subject of today's prayer. Smoke in the moonlight. Stand at my side. Lean against the pocked stone. The iconic imagery endures. Burn it all into my mind. You and I, here in the moonlight, atop this Hieroglyphic Staircase. This living document. Pre-

Hispanic. Like you Marona, generating orbits and satellite suitors. *He* is my family now. And so what of yours? That husband. Picture him. See yourself leaving. Again, you are climbing down from the pickup and standing in the mud waiting. You do not know where to go. You do not know what to do. You are waiting. It is the present. You hardly recognize it. Breathe deeply. You stand there as rain begins to fall. By the time it reaches you, its source has dissipated. Just like starlight. They call them sunclouds, moisture out of the clear blue sky. His miracle. One of many.

"You are lost to us. The jungle devours Your contribution. They sing of the others, lock them in books, rid their legacies of the roots and vines. Their creations again bleaching in the sunlight. Possibly forever. Connect Yourself to the new apostles. Squirm beneath the ire of Your detractors. Through You we come to understand faith. The penitent shall have a hand in creation, in rebirth, in retroaction. We pray for justice, for knowledge. We pray for the mandate. Our numbers grow. While You sleep, they double. Your dreams of the future are here realized. Now a chance for retribution. Usurp the usurpers, whose flames are now but sputtering mudpots. Recall. Reanimate. Gods create men to create gods. Awake and seize the new light. The future is on hold, attending You."

She sat down at his side, just far enough away to avoid the shit smell. The jungle night moved in an eerie state of flux. Mists cooled the radiant rocks. The moon flared in and out of the clouds. Winds jostled the heavy air and slowly rocked the jungle canopy, which surrounded them at eye-level. Invisible creatures filled the scene with strange calls. Two stationary travelers in a shifting world. Strange how he caught the smoke in the moonlight, she thought. It did look remarkable. *Iconic*, did he call it? Iconic of what? A place? A person?

An idea?

The professor's absurdity was tempered only slightly by a sense that if supernatural weirdness did indeed exist, it would exist in places like this.

But she hadn't gone there to pray to dormant godkings, or rub elbows with obsolete academics. She traveled to Copan because she saw a pamphlet stapled to a corkboard next to the customer service counter at a produce market in Berkeley. Are you looking for something different? it asked her. She read on, interpreting. Have you made a wreck of your life? Looking for that very deepest corner of obscurity? Do you long for the company of people far crazier than you are?

Well, she found it. Professor Eugene Lattistrom, and all his silliness. And the knowledge that her own silliness, her awfulness, was permitted. Hideous flatulent men dressed in tree bark, who spend their days and nights talking to jungle ghosts, are not in the business of passing judgment. But even you, Lattistrom, seem grounded and sane in my monstrous presence. This will take time, and great energy, to diffuse.

Marona had joined the professor as a show of support, to thank him for taking her on as his assistant. One more day with the shovel and the buckets, and that might have been it. Back to New York City. Full surrender. Public allocution. Lawsuits, humiliation. Possible jail time. But she did wish he would leave the personal stuff out of it. This unusual old man sitting in prayer, talking about her husband. It was almost too weird to be believed.

The professor passed gas and resumed. She looked over at him and shook her head slowly. I've found something, she thought. I don't know what it is, but it's something.

"Join me in the mess tent. Devour the gazes one by one. These men are lonely. They have taken Maya wives, some of them, because they have forgotten about women like you. Eat Salisbury Steak. You don't even have to chew.

Push it against the roof of your mouth and suck out the seasonings and juices. Wash it all down with red wine. It is your party, Marona. This is your party. But you remain calm and quiet. Build within them a curiosity. Let it sustain them. Laugh loudly, then return to silence. That is your way. It is devastating. Let them marvel, as I marvel, how your boots stay so clean, so shiny and black. Let them assume that you too have fallen for Him. Let their heads spin round like drunken monkeys. In half-time. In quarter-time. The way the stars spin over our heads, their lost light like you, Marona, moving through the universe, bracing for impact."

She studied the professor's conical hat, which he made by coiling a long flat strip of tree bark. It may as well have read "Dunce." But she admired the professor, in a way, for his obliviousness, feigned or otherwise. He had become reviled in the camp and seemed not to even notice. Many of the graduate students resented his current project. He had been their idol. She learned that many of them grew up reading his books, watching his documentaries on PBS. He looked different then. He made an effort. The students came here looking to study under the greatest Mesoamerican archeologist of all time, and found this lunatic instead. They saw it as criminal, the way he continued to siphon off funding for his project. He had not produced a single grain of useful scholarship in three years. He was a Kurtz now, they said, trampling on his own progress, disparaging academia. A delusional fool with a mad obsession. The mind, the work, the legacy, all reduced to the banality of religious obstinance. They might have accused him of having gone native, but Childers said they asked the natives, "and they were all like, what the fuck is with this guy?"

"Peace, Marona, listen to the nightbirds. We all pray together. This is Your world. It is clear to us. Remember yourself, again, in this pickup truck. See the small child in the multi-colored woven dress selling blue liquid in a bag. Focus on the yellow straw. Do not ask, who would ever buy that? Do not fret for the future of her business. She will grow into a woman as you have. Corn will sustain her, not your fears. Light another smoke. Let the mists consume it. Feed the airy waters. Consider the words you will use when time aligns with your purpose. When prayer is compelling, when the phone is ringing in the tent camp and they say, 'Miss Dilenta, there is a little girl on the phone who wishes to speak with you.'"

Marona coughed out her smoke. "Can you just leave her out of this?"

"Mommy, Mommy is that you?"

She stood up and tried to get him to look at her. But his eyes were locked ahead, staring into the jungle. There will be no mingling of insane jungle prayers and the awful reality of my situation, she thought. Her tone became severe. "Professor Lattistrom, in all seriousness, I'm not comfortable with you talking about my daughter, okay?"

He continued on, entranced. "Mommy!"

She smacked the conical hat from his head. "Dicknose," she said, "I told you to knock it off!"

"I miss you."

She stood up and crushed the cigarette into the spike of her boot heel. "I'm trying here, Professor. I'm making a really fucking huge effort here with you, okay? Is it your plan to burn *every* bridge?"

"I am not the girl with the blue liquid for sale, Mommy."

She gave the professor a shove, causing him to topple over onto his side. He shook his head cartoonishly, and his eyes popped open wide, like a drowning victim responding to CPR.

Then he struggled to his feet and looked at Marona, who was fuming. "Shall we?" he asked, gesturing to the stairs. He offered her his arm.

"You're an asshole," she said. But as his fat, wobbly body moved penguin-like down the uneven limestone steps, she found herself softening. Her rage turned to pity. Here is a poor man who is losing his mind.

He clapped his hands together loudly and smiled over at Marona. "Time for wine," he announced.

Life at the Copan excavation site had little in common with what Professor Eugene Lattistrom experienced when he first went there to study the ruins twenty years earlier. A younger generation had now seized control, and they brought with them all their modern influences. They were not pioneers, as Lattistrom once was. They wielded machetes only to be photographed. They embraced the bad food as "part of the experience." They wanted the sour milk. They compared the severity of their prickly heat bumps, like veterans comparing war wounds. They publicly scratched at their mosquito bites and then dismissed concerns with bravado. It's nothing. It's cool. I can take it. They craved hardiness, embraced it as an essential component of field work. But Lattistrom, back in the day, would have much preferred if Copan had been discovered in the lobby of the Ritz Carleton. Because the Maya were the story. All this heat and jungle nastiness was an unfortunate side-effect to be endured, and never embraced.

Nothing happened for its own sake with these new guys. No experience was allowed to simply float down the river of time. Cameras and videos and journals and souvenirs and tattoos. This is *me* doing *that*. Vials of dirt from a first dig. Building muscle. Getting a tan. Pride in shirt stains that won't come clean. Mud on my boots *this* thick! Building petty temples to honor themselves. Auto-anthropology, Lattistrom called it. Which requires no specialized degree.

"It's all horseshit," the professor announced when they got back to camp, once he changed into some real clothes, drank a glass of wine, and started acting like a reasonable human being. "They want it to be like the good old days, which were actually terrible. People got diseases and *died* out here. The locals didn't help us or work for us, they hated us for exploiting their heritage. But we did it anyway, and didn't always feel great about it. But I guess these new kids are typical. They're so proud of themselves because they can make it out here. But so much has changed. It's a piece of cake now. They act like it's the end of the world if the power goes out. We didn't have power. Just vats of toxic bug juice and neckerchiefs to keep the vampire bats away."

"That's why people wore neckerchiefs?" Marona said, amazed.

"Got you," he said, smiling.

She punched his arm. That was the surprising thing about Lattistrom, not how ridiculous and delusional he was, but rather how downright normal he could be.

"There's an old saying about people in this line of work, that there should be another group of scholars studying us." He went on, telling Marona how much joy he used to get out of watching the new folks suffer. "They write papers about how specific environmental factors effected the trajectory of the civilization, as if those factors were abstract concepts, like numbers or letters. But then they get here in the field, and those factors are still there; the rain, the heat, the mud and bugs and disease. The brutal nasty shovel work in the punishing humidity. And they somehow act surprised by how bad it is. And you think, didn't you just spend two years learning about how this shit took down an entire civilization? Made people act crazy, throwing virgins into volcanoes and all that. They think these godkings wore jaguar skulls on their heads because it looked cool. But that's not it, Marona. They did it because jaguars were scary as hell, and they killed and ate babies and destroyed families. I say if you want to study the Maya, just go stand alone in the jungle for three hours and feel that fear. That's as close as you're ever going to get to them."

"Is that what you're doing now?" she asked.

"Exactly, Marona. I'm so glad you're here. That you understand. It's not that complicated is it?"

"You're attempting to understand the Maya by praying to their gods."

He nodded. "So what's the big deal, right?"

She laughed. "It does sound crazy."

"It's ingenious is what it is. And by the way, you don't have crazy people in Manhattan, all high and mighty?"

Before she linked up with the professor, Marona had been out there with the rest of them, with her shovel and bucket, serving her penance. Every single structure in Copan had been reclaimed by the jungle this past nine hundred years, and to even get a clear look at anything, the dense tropical biomass had to be stripped away. There was local labor available for that sort of thing, but any archeologist worth his salt, even amid this new wave, had to have dirty hands. The work was tedious and gross. The muds and mosses were infested with all manner of creepy and slimy invertebrate. The pungent odors of decay and renewal stuck to bodies and clothing. The landscape rebelled against its own removal with stickers and thorns and toxic oils.

And then there were the howlers, monkeys cursed by the gods, or so the natives said. They moved through the jungle canopy in huge groups, their collective noisemaking psychologically devastating to the workers below. They sang in the tones and frequencies of the underworld. Ceaseless and deafening. You dared not look up and lock eyes with one of them. You prayed for their passing like you would for tornado funnels or enemy bombers.

"They see it all as a context for their own heroics," the professor continued, "which is fine for volunteers like you, Marona. Your only compensation *is* the experience. But

85

these grad students and site managers, these newly anointed professors, really have no business romanticizing anything. They have it all backwards, and that's why they'll never understand. It's not about the experience. It's about the Maya. They reinvent the camp a million ways, while the subject stays fixed in time. It's all about grooming now, and fitness, and allergies, and proper footwear, and sleep cycles. People go jogging! They bring kids to this place, like it's a vacation resort. Can you imagine?

"So now I'm considered washed-up. There are trends and fads within each sub-field and I've apparently fallen outside newly accepted methodologies. I've lost my influence. These snarky up-and-comers trample on my back while at the same time they stand tall on my shoulders. They make fun of my clothes. They even make fun of my pencils. Like it's not cool anymore to write with a pencil. It's crazy.

"But thank God for the vegetarian dining options, the chemical toilets, the Larium and anti-venom, right? Because how could we possibly do anything without it? Now it's all about covering debris heaps with blue tarps, about staying dry and using anti-fungals preventatively. If I hear another archeologist say the words 'stream integrity' or 'invasive species' my head will come off.

"Where are the wood fires, the poker games, the girlie magazines? Where are the care package doughnuts? The rooster alarm clocks?"

He slammed his empty glass down on the table.

"At least there's still wine," Marona said.

"Yes!" he cheered emphatically. He refilled their glasses.

Marona smiled at him. She didn't understand exactly how, but it was working. She felt a little better every day. Thanks to Lattistrom.

He went on. "Professor, they tell me, sunscreen *and* a hat. I'm an artifact to them by now. Someone told me I reminded them of Colonialism. An *era*. I think they're dense, these kids. An era? Every time I see you Marona, I just think Industrial Revolution. I mean, *Colonialism*? Come on! I'm from fucking *Reno*! What's with the accent, they ask. What *accent*? There's food in your moustache. Your fly's undone. Well you know what else, asshole? In 1979 I deciphered the Ascension Stele which identified Head on Earth as the founding godking in Copan. Remember that? Remember reading about that back when you were stewing in your own shit-filled diapers? But no, it's all about my halitosis, and my secret crazy jungle prayers. They treat me like I'm a retarded schoolboy. I get more high fives than handshakes.

"I'm a joke," he said finally, pausing to wince at the sound of these words. "A liability. Me. Eugene Lattistrom. I used to be the Carl Sagan of archeology. Billions and billions of tiny gold earrings."

"You're right. I remember you from TV. God. Now that you mention it," she said. *He's changed so much.*

"They act like what I'm doing now is somehow contaminating everyone's work. They say I'm divisive, misanthropic, and overly naturalistic."

"I heard cartoonish and annoying."

"Or just totally lame, dude. I try to explain it and they don't hear me. It's called Theological Archeology. Don't look for it in the journals, I just made it up. I tell them my current method is, in fact, the oldest form of archeology, and really the only one that was available for countless centuries. They try to get me drunk. Only for you, sweet Marona."

"Sante."

"Kids with six months in the field haranguing me with evidence of my own supposed contradictions and academic hypocrisies. They ask how such an influential mind could so easily reject the very foundations I myself established. They take it personally that I refuse to stand behind my vast body of academic writing, the stuff that got them all fired up to be archeologists in the first place. I try to explain that I don't reject the work I've done in the past; I'm proud of it. I've just moved on. It's weird with these kids. It used to be you gave older people the benefit of the doubt. You figured that even if you didn't understand them, their actions were based on a larger life experience than the one you had. So you deferred. But now, with these wiseguys, my age makes my actions seem like the output of a broken mind, one that is creaky and old and outdated. And my reaction, which is more like a defense, is to simply play the part they've cast for me, the smug old fart.

"'You used to be a linguist,' one guy yelled at me. 'Now you act like a fucking Mormon!' They curse at me, Marona, can you imagine? 'There is stuff only you can do, yet you refuse to mentor anyone!' It's all in my books, I tell them. 'You used to be all about interpretation. Now all you care about is discovery!' But there's no difference, Marona. 'We have showers now, you know. Like with hot water!' I try to explain, insects are attracted to the smell of detergents. 'So, what's with the fucking outfits, Shitting Bull?'"

"They don't call you Shitting Bull," Marona interrupted. "Do they really?"

"Shitting Bull, Bronto, Fatso, whatever. If they had any *idea* what I've been through. I'm the key to this whole operation. No Lattistrom, no funding. *Poof.* No passion, no public interest. Without me, the Ascension Stele is a rectangular jumble of weeds, mosses, and lichens. The Hieroglyphic Staircase is just a graven picture-book covered in monkey shit.

"They think I'm up to something. That's how the young mind works these days. Nothing for its own sake. Everything is a conduit to something else. I feel sorry for them. The big picture's never right there where they can see it. There's always an angle, a subtext, some nefarious motivation. 'What are you really doing?' they ask. Well, I tell them. Prayer and sacrifice. They don't believe me though. 'Self-denial is Buddhist,' they say. 'The Maya were not Buddhists,' as if I didn't know. They say I don't brush my teeth. They say my bark hat makes me look like a Klan member. And so I tell them, I *remind* them of something they should have learned on Day One, that basic assembly methods yield similar artifacts cross-culturally whose symbolic meaning is entirely dependent on specific contextual social constructs. 'You're an asshole,' they tell me."

"Well I don't think you're an asshole," Marona said. She stood up and kissed the professor on the cheek. Then she walked back to her tent and lay down on her cot.

CHAPTER TWELVE

"On the drive," Ted said, "there were moles." He was practically crying when he said it.

"Moles?"

"Carpeting the road. Corpses end to end. Shoulder to shoulder."

"And?"

"And I screwed the waitress in Wells. In the parking lot."

I thought you weren't going to tell anyone.

This guy isn't anyone.

"You paid her?"

"What?"

"You paid her."

"Well, yeah I paid her. What do you think?"

"I think you should change your bags. We should both change our bags."

Ted pinched his cooking coat and pulled it out from his chest. "I'm almost dry. I'm fine. But listen. What do you know about suffering?"

Salton Steve stood up to fetch two more warm beers from the closet. With his back to Ted he said, "Suffering? Like work-suffering? Dishwashing?"

"No, *suffering* suffering. For real suffering."

"I know it's all relative is about all I know."

"That's not exactly helpful."

"You asked me what I know, and that's what I know. Some people kill their grandkids in traffic accidents. I don't know anything about that. What about you?"

"I know the moles helped."

"Helped what?"

"Helped mitigate my own...concerns. Which is crazy, right? The *dunk, dunk, dunk*, rolling them under my tires. And I was only doing twenty-five, because I was so horrified. And the big rigs would pass me doing sixty-five, seventy, and it was *dunkdunkdunkdunkdunk*. It was disgusting."

"But you felt better?"

"Yeah."

"Watching the little guys suffer?"

"Oh, I don't think they suffered at all. But it was the first real distraction I've had in a while. Maybe it put things into perspective, or something like that."

"Like we're all just moles blindly crossing the highway of life?"

"No. No, fuck you. You're making fun of me."

"I'm not making fun of you at all. And how do you know they were moles? I mean who even knows what a mole looks like?"

"I do. And they *were* moles. They have these little pointy faces."

"What were they doing outside in the middle of the day? I thought they lived underground. That's why they don't need eyes."

"They have eyes."

"I thought they were blind."

"You can have eyes and still be blind."

"Yeah, if something happens to you. But not in nature. Things that don't need eyes don't have eyes. Like those cave trout."

"Cave trout?"

"Yeah."

"Bats have eyes."

"Bats aren't really blind. It's just a saying."

"Okay, maybe they were voles."

"*Voles*?"

"Yes. Maybe."

"What the fuck is a vole?"

"What the fuck do you care? There were creatures. It doesn't matter. Little creatures, and they were dying like crazy. And it made no sense."

"They were probably prairie dogs, Ted."

"They weren't fucking prairie dogs, Jesus. They were *tiny*."

"Mice then."

"Mice don't migrate en masse in the middle of the day."

"But voles do?"

"Apparently!"

Salton Steve started giggling. "You're a funny guy, Ted."

"Why are you provoking me? You don't even know me."

"Because I'm an asshole."

"Apparently!"

Ted stood up and walked to the closet. He took out another warm beer and opened it, staring at Salton Steve in mock-defiance. He chugged the entire beer and tossed the can on the floor.

Salton Steve laughed even harder. "Sit down, my friend. Have another beer and sit down. This is fun. Tell me what the problem was."

"What problem?"

"The problem. The suffering, you know. What the hell happened to you?"

Ted took out two more beers and sat on the floor next to Salton Steve. "No, no, no," he said. "I don't think so. You don't seem like the kind of person one ought to confide in."

"Oh, stop."

"I'm serious."

"Is it a long story, Ted?"

"It is, yes."

"Please tell it to me, Ted."

"Not tonight."

"Can I try to guess it?"

"Guess my story?"

"Yeah, if I can."

"Fire away."

Salton Steve stood up and walked in a short plaintive loop while he spoke. "Okay, well, let me see. You're far too chipper and enthusiastic about kitchen work to be a real blue collar type, which would suggest you came here more for the experience than out of desperation. Which means this isn't your real life. You left your real life behind. You're trying to close the door on something. Probably something that happened in college. Maybe you dropped out. Maybe you did something disgraceful in college and you freaked out and came up here to hide and punish yourself with shitty labor."

Um.

It's still pretty vague. And you're not so atypical.

"Go on."

"I was going to say date rape, or even some kind of substance abuse, but I don't think so. Not you. I think it's something weirder. You did something really weird, didn't you? And maybe there were unintended consequences. You probably weren't sure who to blame, but taking all the blame yourself didn't sit right either. You felt victimized, but you couldn't figure out how or why or even by whom. How am I doing?"

"Keep going."

93

"Well there's probably a girl in there somewhere. A real beauty. Some screwed up relationship or unrequited obsession. Actually, I bet it was someone you didn't even know. Like someone you would just see in passing, and you'd probably tell yourself you were going to do something about it, like ask her out. But you never did. That part's easy. So this whole enterprise in Idaho is your version of burying your head in the sand, which doesn't feel quite right to you, probably because you thought you were tougher. You probably thought college had prepared you for something. That's what the prostitute was all about, proving to yourself that there were new directions for you to go, different types of experiences to put some distance between yourself and all that weirdness you can't wrap you head around. But ultimately you know deep down you're too sensitive, and you'll never root that out, and you'll never be able to actually change anything meaningful about yourself, so really why drop out of college at all? So there's the regret, and the pride that won't let you fully acknowledge it. The only thing saving you from these realizations is this trumped-up melancholy, which is really just some effort to shame-away bad deeds and help yourself believe there's a significance and gravity to the events in your life when really you know it's all small time, small man, small town shit, right. What did you do, Ted? Something really really terrible and horrible and awful, right? Just the devil in human form sitting on my floor, right Ted? What was it? What'd ya do? Did you really fuck a prostitute?"

"Yes."

"Sure."

"I did!"

"Did you cut her head off and bury her in the desert?"

"What? No. Jesus, no. What the fuck?"

"Just slapped her around?"

Ted stood up. "What the hell's wrong with you?"

94

"Did you do it in the car? Did she have nice tits? Did she press them in your face like this?" Salton Steve placed his open palms on his face, and then began to cackle loudly. Ted left the room and slammed the door. But he could still hear Salton Steve's absurd laughter as he walked down the corridor to his own room.

His roommate Luc was asleep when Ted got back. He stripped down to his underpants and climbed onto the top bunk. He was about half-drunk. He lay there organizing the odors of the room. Luc wouldn't let him open the window because of the mosquitoes. There were general kitchen smells, coming off both their clothes. Plus Luc's fat man smells, body odor, and the ghosts of a hundred dead farts. And something French he couldn't place. Eventually, he fell asleep wondering, do I smell *American*?

In the morning Jackie had him polishing silver up in The Idaho Room kitchen. They only did a dinner service, so none of the cooks were around. He sat on a king-sized white sheet making his way through an assortment of brunch hardware, chaffing dishes and champagne chillers, service spoons and forks. Napkin rings. The polish was bad for his skin, so he wore the pink gloves Jackie gave him. He did like being there in that huge spacious kitchen all alone though, with the only light coming from a row of rectangular windows running along one of the walls. He tried to keep his thoughts focused and immediate. This was labor done for kings. He ought to have a title. Who, past to present, has done this work? Stand them in a row, in authentic period clothing. His own name seemed class-appropriate. He imagined they were mostly British, history's silver polishers. In France they called them Argentiers.

Maybe.

Maybe I get high from all these fumes.

Across the room the service elevator door opened. Backlit, and coming through the half-light, Ted could see the outline of a body, dressed as he was in the standard-issue kitchen bags, holding the handle of a large blue plastic ice bucket. Unlike Ted, however, this body wore a tall cylindrical cardboard hat. As she walked toward him, her face caught the window light. He saw her youth first, the smooth glow. Closer now, she was smiling. That perfect face he knew. Which was impossible. Seven or eight days since the shuttle ride, and the girl, and the rain. Turning up in Valvert?

Impossible.

"You're all alone here?" she asked, stopping next to Ted.

"All alone, sort of."

"They don't have lights?"

It's her.

Impossible.

But still.

"I prefer them off when it's just me in here."

"It's like an old church compared to downstairs," she said.

Ted quickly took off his pink gloves and set them on the floor. "I know. I hear it can get crazy down there. You're new here?"

She looked slowly around the room, nodding. "Yeah," she said.

She's stunning.

That's what you said on the shuttle.

It can't be the same person. It's not possible. I'm hallucinating from the polish fumes.

"And you're a cook?" he asked.

"Prep cook. So not really."

"Trust me, from where I sit, with the silver and the polish, you're a cook. A chef even."

"They're not going to let you cook?"

96

"I don't think so. You know Jackie?" Ted looked around. "I'm kind of stuck with her."

I'm kind of her bitch.

Say that.

I'm not going to say that.

Please.

"I'm Ted, by the way."

"Cammie," she said. They both nodded.

"Can I tell you that you look familiar?"

"Oh?"

"You're not from San Diego, are you? Go to college there?"

She hesitated for a second. A change came over her, just for an instant, and then she was back. "No, why?"

"Was that a tough question?"

"No, I just..."

"You look like someone I saw there just a few days ago."

"Wasn't me." She adjusted her hat unnecessarily.

She's nervous.

Like all beautiful women in your dudely presence.

She's lying.

"Never been there?"

"I've never even been on a plane. I'm from Boise."

Just then, the fluorescent lights came on and Jackie walked into the room. She was holding a squirt bottle of glass cleaner and a roll of paper towels. "You know where they keep the ladder?" she asked.

"Yes."

"Well, go get it."

Ted smiled at Cammie.

"I guess that's your cue," she said, and walked over to the ice machine.

Salton Steve took two beers from the closet and sat on the floor next to Ted. Their wet dishwashing coats hung from the ski racks next to the door.

"She's awful," Ted said.

"A terrible human being from what I can tell."

"She has me cleaning all the jewels on the chandeliers in the dining room. Do you have any idea what a pain in the ass job that is? Each chandelier—and there's at least fifty of them—has like a hundred of these little jewels, that have never been cleaned. Ever. I'm up there on this rickety ladder, craning my neck, and shooting this glass cleaner up in the air, which most of it just drips right down onto my face, and into my mouth. Between drinking glass cleaner and inhaling silver polish, I'm going to be dead before the end of the month. But since they've never been cleaned, there's this huge contrast between what I've sprayed and wiped, and what's still dirty, and the contrast looks way worse than when they were all equally dirty. Nobody would have ever noticed. But now, if I miss just a tiny spot."

"You could talk to Kevin."

"I think Kevin's terrified of her. Who wouldn't be? Thank God she spends most of her time on the loading dock smoking. She always comes back to the kitchen with some new supply or something, so it looks like she left for a reason. Today it was a bundle of rags. She spent twenty minutes with me sniffing rags, trying to find the less greasy ones for me to buff the silver. She kept holding them to my face and telling me to sniff. It was humiliating. Then she gave me some lecture about how everyone in Laundry is an idiot and how they wash all the housekeeping linen with the kitchen linen, which she's sure is a violation of health codes, and if the Michelin people find out, there goes The Idaho Room's five-star rating."

"You prefer washing dishes?"

"Obviously. I actually like washing dishes, when I get to do it."

"You're good at it."

"Thanks."

"Is that pride in your voice?"

"Maybe. Because it's weird that I'm good at it. I'm great at it. I get tons of compliments from the kitchen staff."

"But not the restaurant staff."

"No."

"They don't give a shit."

"No, they don't. And by the way, what was the deal with your pant leg the other day?"

"What was the deal with yours?"

"Well, I got mine wet chasing some kid's sweatshirt into the creek. I slipped. I was on my way to my first shift. But I don't know about yours. I'm suspicious."

"Suspicious?"

"You had the identical issue I did. You showed up with your pant let all twisted up. Just like mine. You didn't even know me and you were fucking with me."

"It was my first day too."

"I know. So I had to go into the bathroom and ring all the water out, before I met Kevin. But the pant leg was all twisted and weird looking. He kept looking at me funny, so I explained what happened. He asked me if I was wearing Valvert issue non-slip shoes when I slipped. I told him I was. We laughed about that. But then you show up ten minutes later and your pant leg is all wet and twisted too. What was that?"

"I watered my pant leg down before the shift and then twisted it dry. Like you did."

"Why?"

"Why?"

"Yes, why?"

"You think it had something to do with you?"

"It clearly did."

"Not everything is this world is about you, Ted."

"But this is. Which is creepy. Explain the pant leg."

"I can't. It's just something I did."

"You saw me slip into the creek?"

"I don't remember."

"That's ridiculous. You're ridiculous, coming down that ramp on the first day, with your wet shoe making fart noises. You had this goofy-ass grin, and you made that crack about which one of us was the boss."

"So?"

Ted rolled his eyes and stood up. He bent down and touched his toes. Then he walked over to his coat and felt the sleeve for dampness.

"I'm out."

"What are you getting so angry about."

"I'm not...I'm just. It doesn't make any sense. You don't make any sense. The girl—you've met her—she doesn't make any sense either. And Jackie's nuts. This wasn't all supposed to get crazier."

"What wasn't?"

"Life. I don't know."

"I saw the girl too. It's kind of unreal."

"That's my point. Girls that look like that don't work in greasy kitchens. They don't peel potatoes for eight bucks an hour."

"Just sit down, Ted. Get two more beers and sit down. And calm down."

Ted shook his head. Then he obeyed.

"What do you think her story is then?" Salton Steve asked.

"Well, it's got to be some kind of power trip. She's threatening, because she's so hot, and maybe her boss down there is some married troll who can never have her. And he's bitter, so he's punishing her. He's trying to deactivate her charms by sticking her in kitchen bags and making her wear that hat."

"Which only makes her hotter."

100

"I know! We used to have this *beautiful* woman who worked for the gas company come over and light the pilot on our water heater, which *for some reason* was always going out. She had this absurd brown and yellow jumpsuit, with her name on a patch, and Gas Company written on the back. It was devastating."

"So if she's being manipulated, this girl, why would she put up with it?"

"I guess she needs the job, right? Same reason we all put up with it."

"And what are your chances, do you think?"

"With her? Zero."

"Where's your confidence, Ted? She's just some potato peeler, you said."

"What are *your* chances?"

"No, no, no. She's not for me."

"Not your type?"

"No, literally. She's not *for* me."

CHAPTER THIRTEEN

Weeks passed, and Lattistrom continued to spend most of his time with Marona. But one night she didn't show up for dinner and he became worried. He went to her tent and found her face down on her cot. He took a seat on the floor without saying anything. He listened to her troubled breathing and noticed the picture in her hand. She sniffled occasionally, and he knew that she had been crying.

This marked the first moment of real doubt. He had been at it for well over twenty years, lost in a dream. Which was fine. Ideal, even. But now, with Marona, reality set in, as he knew it eventually would. She lay there, his weeping catalyst. A woman he cared about, who he needed very badly, who was suffering.

And now I twist the knife in the wound.

All for You.

"Are you hungry?" he asked.

"No, thank you."

A joke then? "They've refried the beans."

"I'm fine, thank you. I think there's a chair, if you're staying."

"Do you want me to leave?"

"I don't really care what you do."

"There's no chair though. Remember I broke it last week?" He hoped this would lighten her up, because it was funny when it happened. She had howled. They were both drunk that night. He crashed to the floor and sat there dumbly for a second before he realized what had happened.

"Maybe you should requisition another," she said. "Aren't you, like, the boss?" She hadn't moved. The professor tried not to leer, but the black skirt she insisted on wearing had slid high up her legs.

She is a beautiful woman, he thought. But that is irrelevant. It will help down the road, but for now I must stay focused.

"Why don't you write her a letter?" he suggested.

"She can't read. She's three and a half."

He had guessed correctly. This was all about her daughter. "Draw some pictures for her, of the temples."

Marona rolled over and wiggled her skirt back into place. "What the hell am I doing here?" she asked.

"You could put some wildflowers in with the drawing."

"It's just going to make my husband think I'm even crazier, when he finds out where I am."

"You told me you weren't going to worry about him anymore."

"I'm not worried about him. I'm worried what he might say about me to a judge. It's best if everyone just thinks I'm in San Francisco. That at least makes some sense." She sat up and scanned the room. "Is there any water around?"

"Let me get you some."

"It's fine."

"Really, I don't mind."

"Are you going out tonight?"

"I go out every night, you know that."

"I see. I'm sorry. I feel like I haven't been sincere with you, with all the praying and carrying on. My heart's not in it, you know?"

"Marona, you don't need to apologize for anything. You are trying to improve your life. That's admirable."

"My *life*," she snorted. "Right."

"Things will get better," he said.

Marona looked at the professor, believing she saw only kindness and caring. She smiled at him. "Can you leave me out of it though, you know. All that stuff about my daughter. It can't be necessary."

He shrugged his shoulders. "I can't promise you that. Your presence brings an energy."

"Can I have some wine beforehand?"

"Before we go out? Well, the ritual does require sobriety."

Marona took her duffle from under the cot and opened it on her mattress. "Who says it requires sobriety? I thought you were making this shit up as you went along."

"I'm not making anything up. And it's not shit. Come on, you know that. You alone should know that. I base my rituals on interpretations of their written documents."

"You've found mention of the need for sobriety?"

"In a sense. There is something."

"I'm not going to get shitfaced," she reasoned. Then she took a dark red turtleneck from the bag and held it up. "Eyes closed."

The professor shut his eyes while she changed her shirt.

"Okay."

He opened his eyes. "Is that a different shirt?"

"Are you going to get me a glass of wine or not?"

"I'll be right back."

The tent flaps shut behind the professor and Marona stood all alone, looking at the small photo still cupped in her palm.

You are in fucking Honduras, Marona. You have lost your mind.

She set the photo on the mattress. The image haunted her. The bright smile of her daughter. Cuter, really, than all the other little girls. The smile compelling her to confront her shame. The professor's advice: don't avoid the pain. Incredibly profound, or just incredibly obvious? An idiot savant, or just an idiot? A complex, spirited, vibrant woman, or just a shitty mother?

"Hon-*fucking*-duras? Really? Honduras?"

She bent over unconsciously to stretch out her sore calf muscles. Her fingers touched her dirty bare feet, her unpainted toes. She counted to ten, instinctively. Ten distracting seconds.

"El Salvador. Guatemala. Costa Rica." She spoke in a loud, exaggerated Spanish accent. She smiled at the absurdity of it all. Ten toe rises, for her shin splints. "Nicaragua. Panama."

Then she crouched down in a track-start, her left foot on top of her right calf. Ten seconds. Switch. She scanned the floor for insects, spiders, cocoons.

Nests. Pods. Chrysalises. *Chrysalisi?*

"Columbia!"

Snakes.

"Marona, you in there?"

"Go away. I'm busy."

"Have you seen the professor?"

"Venezuela!"

"Huh?"

"Go away!"

She did a butterfly stretch on her cot. She swiped away dirt brought up by her feet.

"Hey!" she called out. "You still out there?"

A pause. "Did you say something?"

"Yeah, come here."

The flaps parted and Paul Matters entered the tent. His eyes immediately focused on Marona's legs, which were tanned and gleaming, taught in the stretch. He was a graduate student in charge of a quadrant of residential structures. His suit of Marona consisted of making up stupid questions to ask her during mealtime.

"Did you find the professor?" she asked him.

"No. Do you know where he is?"

"What do you need him for?"

"Oh, there's a question about cemeteries."

"I see."

Several awkward seconds passed in silence. Then Paul gave in. "So what do you think these tents are made of?" he asked. "It's like canvass, but waterproof. It's weird."

"Don't know."

"Yeah, it's strange. Good surface though." He felt the wall some more.

"Excellent surface," she repeated, torturing him with his own ridiculousness.

Amazing, Marona thought to herself, that all I would have to do right now is take my skirt off and it would probably be one of the top five most significant moments in this young man's life. I wouldn't even have to do anything. Just take my skirt off like I've done a million times. She shook her head at the thought of it. That I could be so low down. So beat up. So racked with negativity. Shame. Self-doubt. You name it. That I could be this close to tears. And still have that much power.

Just a kiss on the ear. One little kiss on the ear would literally change his life. His priorities. I could make the Maya absolutely meaningless to this guy. I could destroy an entire civilization with one stupid kiss. Men have nothing like this. Nothing close to this. Yet they rule the world. It makes no sense.

"What's east of Venezuela?" she asked him.

"Oh, gee, I'm terrible with geography."

"Is it French Guiana?"

"Or just Guiana?"

They both laughed. "What the difference?" Marona asked.

"In French Guiana they—"

"What?" she asked, her legs now straight out in front of her. She reached for her toes. She could feel his eyes scan the exposed small of her back.

"There should have been a joke there," he said. "Like they eat a lot of croissants."

"That's not funny."

"No, I agree. It's not funny."

"In French Guiana they...don't use soap," she said.

"That's not funny either."

"It's funnier than yours."

"But it's still not funny." He looked around the room. "Do you mind if I sit down?"

"What about the professor? The cemeteries?"

"Huh? Oh."

"Nine hundred years, so what's another minute or two?"

"You've heard that one?"

"It's a wonder anything gets done at all around here," she said.

He gestured to the floor. "May I?"

"Knock yourself out." She bent her left knee in a thigh stretch. The best way to do it was to lie flat on her back. But she figured that would be too suggestive. Already, they're probably wondering what this guy's been doing in my tent for the last fifteen minutes, she thought. Maybe he'll make something up. Or at least a lie of omission. What were we doing in there? Wouldn't you like to know.

"What about Paraguay?" he asked.

"What about it?"

"It's over there somewhere."

"Paraguay," she said, smiling. "You don't hear a lot about Paraguay, do you?"

"Almost nothing."

"I don't think I like it."

He laughed a bit too loud, not quite sincere. "You don't like it? Just like that?"

"Just like that."

"What about Uruguay?"

She switched knees, shaking her head. "I think I hate Uruguay even more than I hate Paraguay." He's never going to tell me I'm being stupid, she thought. He's never going to say this is lame, you're lame, I'll see you around. We could go through every country on the globe.

She stood up, which made Paul visibly uncomfortable. He's afraid of me, she thought. He's infatuated with me, but he's *afraid* of me. How does that work?

"You didn't work today?" he asked her.

"I don't, you know, really *work*."

"Oh, right. You're with the professor. His assistant."

"That's correct."

"So what exactly do you do, if I may ask?"

"You may not," she said playfully. "Eyes closed."

"Huh?"

"Close your eyes. I'm changing."

He shut his eyes, squinting to prove he wasn't peeking.

Maybe this is evil of me, she thought. Am I leading him on? Giving him false hope that we'll somehow end up in bed together? But can I really be expected to take responsibility for *his* fantasy world? The tension was invigorating, though. The flutter of his eyelids. What must he be thinking? Would it be too flirty sounding to just ask? An invitation for him to say something embarrassing or crude? Because then I'd have to ask him to leave. That's how that works.

She quickly slipped out of her skirt and pulled on a pair of expensive designer jeans. In the distance the dinner bell rang. "You can open your eyes now," she said, marking the slightest hint of disappointment in his eyes when he looked at her and realized she was not naked.

"We must persevere despite the howlers. They test our devotion, our commitment to this solemn purpose. She writes a letter in her mind. Tell her they mean her no harm. See this mad world we belong to. A world that craves Your influence. We ask for You to awaken. To show us Your great temples. Show us Your value. Know there is need for strong influence, for knowledge. Prove to the world these buildings we uncover are not the empty shells of a dead world. Fill them with Your energy. See how easily we are distracted. Families struggle through fogs and are separated. Pettiness rules our lives. Provide the proof of a deeper world. Focus. Clear Your mind. Silence the monkeys. Will them back to peace. Rescue them from their torments. See the moon emerge. See its reflective fires across the backlit canopy. We are in the air."

"I can't do this."

"Peace."

"I'm going down."

"Stay, stay."

"I have to go home."

"You can't."

"She needs me."

"Pray with me."

"Oh, shut up."

"Faith."

"She's going to grow up and want to know what the fuck I was doing down here. She's only three."

"There is another way back."

"No, no there isn't."

"Faith."

"Good luck with all this. I can't do it. Not now."

"What if you could bring her here?"

"Why would I do that?"

"To continue our work."

"I'm not interested in the work. You know that. This is limbo for me. I'm in a holding pattern. I don't know what I'm supposed to do. If I go home they will put me in jail."

"You don't know that."

"My husband filed charges."

"Judges can be sympathetic."

"I fled the country."

"Well, yeah, you *did* flee the country."

"Thanks. Good night. Good luck."

"Wait."

"What?"

"Do you feel that?"

"Oh, Jesus."

"No, seriously. Like a cold wind."

"Yeah, it's called a cold wind."

"Give me ten more minutes. Please. You can't leave tonight anyway."

"How am I such a disaster?"

"Pray with me."

"Oh, Lord."

"Ten minutes. Come over here. Put out the cigarette. Sit in the circle. I told you drinking was a bad idea. It's distracting you. And you're distracting me."

"Okay."

"We are two now and our numbers will grow. We are here. Where are You? What's that? The howlers have fallen silent. Peace now. Hear it. We call to You."

"We...call to You. This is so stupid."

"Two voices. Clear. Know our struggle to find faith. Understand how our lives get complicated. See through it all. We are here."

"We are here."

"And we believe."

"We believe."

"Mark the time, I...I...I..."

"Professor?"

110

"...it's..."

"Are you okay?"

"...it's..."

Then he fell over.

"Oh, give me a break." She shook him. "Hello? Wake up...This isn't funny...You better damn wake up...I can see you're still breathing...I'm going to leave you up here, I swear to God I am."

CHAPTER FOURTEEN

Cammie sat on the floor of her dorm room, stretching. Rooms in the women's dorm were not only bigger than those in the men's dorm, they were also all singles. The *Book of Mormon* lay open next to her, with a hairbrush stuck in the middle to keep her place. She studied the color of her left arm, which was becoming quite tan. She stood up and walked over to the closet. A plastic bag of fabric dangled from the hanger pole. She untied it and brought it over to the floor. She took up a handful of the fabric and set it against her arm. The color almost matched. Two more weeks in the sun and it would be perfect.

But that was becoming an issue, the sunbathing. She *loved* sunbathing. Growing up in a big family, with all the chaos and noise. Just put on a swimsuit, lie down on a towel in the backyard, or wherever, with the lotion, the glasses, and the Walkman. It was essential, the secret to her good nature and her patient, positive outlook. Her brothers and sisters all knew better than to bother her. They had all learned that painful lesson at least once. The dreaded typewriter. The letter of apology finger-stabbed into your chest while she sat on your stomach and pinned your arms with her legs. And then the silent treatment, the nasty looks. It could ruin your whole day.

But finding a place to sunbathe in Valvert wasn't easy. She didn't have access to a nice private backyard, and employees weren't allowed to use the resort pool facilities. She could plop down on the lawn between the two dorm buildings if she wanted, but other employees would mistake her intentions. Which was a shame because it was right there, with good sun and trees and flowers. She considered more remote options. She could hike up to some nice alpine lake and lie out on the granite. But should she really do that? By herself? Those places were not so isolated. Hikers were everywhere, and creepy mountain men, and sketchy hippies. It might not be safe for a girl.

Unless she brought a gun. Her dad would tell her to do that. It comforted her to think about her father. He would say bring a *big* gun. She laughed. A bikini, a leather holster, and a .44. Maybe a sash of bullets. No telling how a guy might react to seeing that.

What she needed was a companion, a guy, a girl, either way. A friend in this place. Easier said than done, she knew. Why did everything have to be so complicated? Guys had no interested in friendship, not with her. Not if it involved bikinis and sunbathing. And it was just as tough with the girls, who were always so predictable, resenting her, or misreading her. Plus, most of them worked in housekeeping, a weird clique of its own. She needed a guy like Chuck around. A Mormon guy. Someone who set limits on himself, who wasn't allowed to see her in *that* way. At least overtly. But Chuck was boring. The church was boring. She sighed. She shook her head. She put her hands in the air and gestured in supplication.

Then she resumed her stretching. Head on knees, fingers on toes. Count to ten.

She could understand what happened to some Mormon girls, especially the pretty ones. How they hopped on the back of a guy's Harley, and rode off into the sunset. Which is kind of what Mom did, she realized. Dad must

113

have been a real bad-ass in his time. The tattoos, that mysterious silence about Vietnam, and what went on over there. He was scary sometimes, and forceful. A family man now, sure, but before the kids and the house, what had really drawn her mother to him?

Not his piety, that was for damn sure.

Unfortunately though, the pickings in Valvert seemed awfully thin, awfully *tame*. Just a lot of guys like that guy Ted. Guys. Just *guys*. Maybe something going on, maybe not. You have to do a little digging, she knew. And then you end up *involved*, and you're in there before you really know what's going on. Maybe there's some attraction. Maybe he makes you laugh sometimes and wouldn't be an embarrassment if you brought him home to your parents. But maybe a creep deep down, or something like that. Something you find out years later. No way to know. Maybe he turns out to be gay, or a gambling addict. At least the bad dudes weren't hiding anything.

She switched to a butterfly stretch, pressing the soles of her feet together. She also did torso twists while rotating her shoulder blades.

I must be lonely, she realized, always thinking about this stuff. About boys and men. She remembered what a friend told her back in high school, about a group of guys at a party who all admitted they had thought about Cammie Holder when they masturbated. A *lot* of guys, the girl emphasized. A *lot*. Cammie wasn't even sure what that meant. It sounded awful though. And true or untrue, it certainly wasn't flattering. It freaked her out. It made men seem scary and primitive and compulsive. Why her? What had she done? She didn't wear fancy clothes, didn't do anything special with her hair or makeup. Not like some of the other girls. In fact, she consciously downplayed her looks all the time.

But why? Was it her fault men reacted this way around her? Why not embrace the situation? Let them fawn over her. Break their poor hearts. Why not that? Get aggressive. Take the reins.

She smiled. Not me.

She stood up and shook her whole body out.

Enough of this. Life is good.

I'm *rich*.

She liked to say that. It felt a bit dirty, and sinful. It was wrapped in secrets, and lies, and covert meetings. And best of all, it was *true*. Ten thousand dollars for San Diego. And another twenty thousand for *this*, for Valvert. Susanna Copan had appeared again, two nights after that whole weird shuttle bus in the rain gig, after the flight home. She still acted cryptic and odd, but complimented Cammie's debut performance. She set out the conditions for the next assignment. Ten thousand now and ten thousand more in a year, according to the usual terms. Just get a job in Valvert, Susanna told her. Live in the employee dorms. Three months, maybe less. And that's it. Twenty grand, just to get out of town, which was something Cammie *needed* to do anyway.

Thirty thousand dollars! Plus what she made working. How good would it feel to tithe all *that*?

And beyond the money, her association with Susanna Copan kept her life unique and interesting. It provided an extra element she knew other people were missing. People like Ted. He needed a Susanna Copan in his life, to add that extra level, that secret life, with secret *missions*. Fancy hotel rooms and bundles of cash. She glanced up at the ceiling, trying to determine if it was high enough to skip rope.

She strolled the familiar path through the tourist village. The town was steadily getting busier. The restaurants all seemed to be on a wait for lunch, at least for the outdoor seats. Families sat on the grassy banks of the little creeks, their tiny kids fussing with the mallards. She

115

understood the appeal. Valvert *was* a nice place, glorious even, on a warm summer day. The kind of destination families returned to, year after year, for generations.

But the world was not perfect. Not even in Valvert. A rich girl with a secret life could still lose the positivity game if properly beguiled.

It always came back to this stuff. The looks from men. From *dads*. Thirty grand didn't change a thing. With son on his shoulders, wife's hand in his own, gawking at Cammie. Then looking away. Then looking back again. Then the arresting glare of the wife/mother. The blatant rudeness, anger unshielded even by dark designer glasses. Resentment. Despite wealth, family, sunshine, and vacation. Focus on Cammie.

How strange. How unfair. I'm wearing a cardboard Tower-of-Pisa hat. I'm wearing an oversized cooking coat and baggy kitchen pants. I am Staff. I should be invisible to you. You are not here for me. Go play tennis. Stop acting creepy.

At least there didn't seem to be any problem at work. People acted surprisingly normal in The Spot kitchen. They told her what to do. They yelled at her, criticized her, jostled her when she stood in the way, and threatened her with demotion to dishwork. It was nice to be treated like everyone else, joked with, picked on, ignored. A system of value and worth that made no concessions. The laws of seniority and merit. Logic. Fairness. Justice. Potatoes.

"How long are you putting them in the steamer?"

"I set the dial, like you told me."

"Twenty minutes, right?"

"Yes."

"Twenty minutes or twenty years?"

"Twenty minutes."

"They're mush." Alfonso squeezed a potato through his fingers. "Look at this. I've had diarrhea that was better organized."

116

She loved it when they said things you shouldn't say around a girl. Any girl. Offensive and gross. As long as it wasn't creepy towards her. She didn't mind when they talked about kitchen work affecting their balls. Their crassness and vulgarity was all fine, the cursing and farting and frank sexual chatter.

Even the waitresses treated her well. They overlooked her, or asked basic questions about supplies. She felt none of the contempt she sensed from other women. They worked too hard to care. Busy with their lives. She loved it, the whole chaotic mess. The men behind the line, the waitresses impatient at the expo counter, or filling drinks, loading trays, *heaving* trays. The sarcastic banter, the palpable stress. The whole operation on the brink of total failure, a delirious mess, yet somehow functional, successful, highly regarded by repeat visitors.

Watching it all, Cammie reveled in her seasonal status, thankful for what she had, a non-dishwashing job, a non-hostessing job. *That*, she didn't think could handle. And they'd asked her a dozen times already. A new dress for every shift. Hair, make-up, and a nice fake smile. A nice slow walk to the table. Giving Granny a hand. Pulling out chairs. Handing menus to leering men and ticked-off women. Unhappy people who had no business being unhappy. Embittered by the indignity of a slow round of golf. Enjoy your meal. You can find me in the kitchen with my head in the deep-fryer.

But peeling potatoes? No problem. Prepping avocados and straining eggs. Fine. Three months. Less than three months. Eleven weeks. Eleven weeks of bacon trays and spice grinding. Head down. Some stretching, some hiking maybe, some phone calls home. Simple. The time would fly.

"Do you know where cold storage is?"

She looked up.

"Anybody in there?"

"Sorry."

"I said, do you know where cold storage is? You been down there yet?"

It was Alfonso. He stood over her, wiping his hands on his apron. The sweat mark on his conical hat had reached a good seven inches.

"No, I haven't been down there yet."

"Okay," he handed her a ring of keys, holding one key in his fingers. "This key. You go out the back, around to the loading dock, down the main corridor, like you're headed to the IR. Third door on your left. It has a small window. There's a walk-in in the back full of berries. Bring like a dozen baskets of each kind. And six bags of potatoes. There's a cart in there. Load it up. Then take the service elevator at the end of the hallway back up here. You can lift the sacks, right?"

"Yes." She repeated the instructions. He nodded. Key in hand she walked out the back of the kitchen.

CHAPTER FIFTEEN

Ted woke up from a long nap. It was about midnight and he was done sleeping. He could hear Luc below him, snoring.

I've got to fix this sleep schedule.

You're too anxious.

It's not anxiety.

You see them in your dreams.

Twin and Addie?

Yes.

Okay, so?

Move on.

I could go out, but I'm not supposed to hang around the Valvert bars. Not that I'd want to.

You could go to Oresite.

And sit in a bar, alone.

You'll meet people.

And then what? Get drunk, drive home and get a DUI?

Fine, why not go down to the rec room? Watch some TV. Read a book.

The rec room smells like urine.

Then take a walk. Look at the horses. Or, they're always saying bears invade the campground up the road.

I could go look for bears.

Might see a bear.

Could be cool.

Might see some white lightning.

How come white lightning is always only in the distance? How can some things exist only in the distance?

Like what?

Like death.

You sound like maybe you should call your parents.

But he didn't think his parents wanted to talk to him. They were still upset. His father insisted Ted pay back his wasted tuition if he didn't finish his degree. Ted tried to convince them that this was a good thing, his going to Valvert. He told them that college had become a toxic place for him psychologically, and that even though the decision seemed idiotic—since he only had five weeks to go until graduation—it was one he had to make.

They probably thought he was talking about drug use, not shitting in newspapers.

In the end, he drove to Oresite, a slightly larger town about a mile outside the Valvert village. He saw a few people milling around outside the bars, guys mostly. Guys and their friends.

No thanks.

So what, then?

Cigarettes.

Great idea. It always seemed like a huge mistake when you quit.

He drove to the Circle K and bought a pack of Camel Lights. He sat in his car smoking, watching a few local teenagers loiter. One tall blonde guy with no shirt on stood over his BMX, working the front break so the back tire rose up under him, and then bounced to the ground. His friend, also shirtless, wrote something on the sidewalk in blue Icee, which he spit out through a long red straw. There was also a girl, who may or may not have been with them, who had dyed black hair and a black Misfits t-shirt. She cursed for attention, too loud into the payphone.

"You got any weed, dude?" Ted looked to his left and saw a blue-haired guy about his own age sitting on the curb, his mountain bike thrown down in the dirt just behind him.

Where'd he come from?

He looks shifty. And he's filthy. But that's a nice bike he's got.

Full suspension.

He's probably a ski season left-over. Harmless. Maybe homeless, but not *homeless*.

Ted apologized for not having any weed. Then the guy asked if he wanted some. He said he knew a guy who sold it. "You give me a ride over there, we can split a bag," the guy said.

Ted looked at him more intently. "Sounds fine," he said.

He introduced himself as Travis, from Sandy, Utah. A self-described Mormon shithead. He piled his bike into Ted's hatchback. Travis also had a small backpack which he kept at his feet. They drove along the dark streets paralleling the Bigpine River. Ted played an obscure tape, some old Jethro Tull, stuff his roommates never let him listen to. And Travis knew all the words.

"It's so ironic that you happened to be playing my favorite album of all time!" he yelled over the music.

"It's a *coincidence*!"

"It sure is! I fucking love Tull!" He banged his head to the guitar riff.

They sang along, testing each other on deeper verses. Twenty minutes into the ride, and Ted felt like he was back in San Diego with one of his long-time college buddies. More than anything else, it felt comforting.

Then Travis said, "Dude, do you want to see my sword?"

"Your *sword*?"

Travis leaned over and rummaged through his bag. Like a magician pulling a three-foot wand out of a one-foot top hat, Travis produced a Samurai sword. A genuine, full-sized Samurai sword. He handed Ted the scabbard and took the wheel. Ted unsheathed it half way. He pulled to the side of the road. He got out of the car. He fully unsheathed the sword. He seemed to know how to hold it. He understood its balance, the logic of its weight and design.

I love this sword.

Yes!

I love swords! And weapons!

"I need to hit something with this!" he stammered.

"I know you do!"

Ted walked to the front of the car, leaving Travis still sitting in the passenger seat. He posed in the headlights. He made slashing motions, and ridiculous guttural Kung Fu noises.

Swords and weapons!

Yes!

I had no idea.

He slashed and grunted some more. He felt a natural competency. Travis stepped out of the car and held up a grapefruit. He nodded. "I'm going to lob this to you."

"Yes you are."

"Think you can cut it in half?"

"Just throw it," Ted said.

The entire motion was silent. Lethal. The fruit-corpse bled-out on the asphalt. He demanded Travis throw another.

"I'm out, dude."

"Here," Ted said, throwing the dirty halves back to him.

Now they were quarters. They forgot all about the pot dealer. Thirty minutes later they walked out of their third gas station mini-mart, having purchased every available piece of fruit in Oresite. It was two in the morning. They had six limes, four apples, a bushel of bananas, and a box of cereal. They drove to the ski area parking lot and sliced fruit. Then they sat on the hood of the car, music coming softly from the open windows.

Ted asked Travis why he carried the sword around. Travis dragged on a cigarette and said, "To hunt."

"Bullshit."

"I live off the land."

"Bull*shit*."

"No, I do. I live in the forest. I hunt for my meals."

"You hunt for your meals with this sword?"

"I also eat at TacoTime. It's very postmodern."

"What do you kill?"

"Whatever," he shrugged. "Badgers."

Badgers? "Bull. Shit."

"Swear to God," he said. He explained that he hid in trees above their holes and pounced on them when they came out. He said badgers hardly ever looked up.

"Isn't it bad karma to eat carnivores?" Ted asked.

"I've never heard that."

"I just made it up."

"Interesting."

"Do they ever fight back?"

Travis laughed and nodded vigorously. He handed Ted the sword and gingerly undid the buttons of his shirt. His entire torso was covered in scabs and scars. He looked like a boat propeller chopped him up. He looked like he needed to go to the hospital.

"Jesus!"

"It's the life of a warrior."

"You're messing with me."

"No."

"Are you crazy?"

Travis looked up at the sky, dead serious all of a sudden. "I get by," he said, with a touch of sadness in his voice. "I used to drink a lot. Now I hunt badgers. And deer. I fish a lot too."

"How about wolverines?"

He shook his head. "I don't fuck around with wolverines."

"I see," Ted said. He nodded like he understood. "I don't fuck around with wolverines either."

Later, they pulled up to a house on a street of small seasonal ski cabins. There were no lights on anywhere. Travis got out of the car and came over to Ted's window. He said he needed some money.

I should have seen this coming.

It's kind of disappointing.

But then Travis told Ted not to worry, that his mountain bike in the back of the car was worth twelve hundred dollars. Ted gave him forty bucks and watched Travis go around the back of the house. He sat there in the darkness waiting.

Travis came back quickly and showed Ted the sack of weed. Ted knew immediately that Travis had had it all along.

Why didn't he just sell it to me outright?

Maybe he was lonely.

He did say he lived alone in the forest.

As they pulled away from the house, Travis immediately rolled a joint. He suggested they drive out to some hot springs he knew of. He told Ted where to go. Ted remembered the road from past vacations. It led to one of the base lodges at the ski mountain.

They smoked.

Ted asked about badgers. Travis confessed they weren't really all that good to eat.

"Like most carnivores."

"Is *that* true?"

"I don't know," Ted confessed.

"You got all kinds of theories, don't you?"

124

"Well," Ted said, somewhat defensively, "you don't see a lot of carnivores on menus, do you? Lions or bears or tigers?"

They both thought about it.

"Shark," Travis said, beating Ted to the punch. The pot was strong.

"Yeah, shark. Good one."

"Ever had it?"

"No."

"No. Me either."

A protracted stoned pause, then Ted said, "Aren't all fish carnivores in a way?"

"I guess."

"Kind of ruins the theory."

"Kind of does. Kind of ruins everything, in a way."

"Everything."

"Every last single thing."

"Ever on earth..."

"Yeah."

Ted drove on. White lightning in the distance. He told Travis his theory about it always being in the distance.

That made Travis laugh. "Not always," he said. "I got struck by lightning when I was eleven, in Alta."

"How's that?"

"Exhilarating."

"Did you get hurt?"

"It curled my hair."

"What?"

Travis swept his hair over his shoulders and held a lock for Ted to see.

"I can't see shit."

"Well it's curly."

"And blue, if I recall."

In the headlights, Ted saw the outline of two people walking on the side of the road. They had their arms awkwardly slung over each other's shoulders, for stability.

As the car got closer, Ted saw two girls in tank tops and short skirts. He watched in disbelief as the one walking on the outside turned into their approaching lights and raised her thumb. Ted and Travis exchanged glances, then high fives. He pulled over so Travis could talk to them. The girls turned to look.

Too young.

Way too young.

Bummer.

And not very attractive.

High schoolers on vacation. Snuck out of the condo. Got drunk.

They asked for a ride, in flirty slurs.

Then Travis did a funny thing, he rolled up the window so he could discuss it with Ted. The girls appeared to take offense. "We should give them rides home," Travis said. "Deliver them safely to their parents. No funny business. Good karma."

"I like the idea."

Travis rolled his window back down and told the girls they could have a ride. He got out of the car and put the back seats up so the girls could fit. He moved his bike to the very small space behind the back seats. It stuck half-way out the open hatchback. As they drove, Travis did most of the talking. He found out that the girls were indeed in high school. Travis gave them a couple of hits off the joint, and then he showed off his sword. They giggled stupidly.

They should be afraid for their lives.

You planning a homicide?

No, but they're seventeen-year-old hitchhiking girls and the guy who picked them up has a Samurai sword.

They dropped them at a well-lit condo, right on the way to the hot springs. The girls thanked them and everyone exchanged awkward hugs from the front to the back of the car. They watched the girls slink up to the front door and slowly open it.

"That was an interesting non-adventure," Travis said.

"Completely uneventful and mundane," Ted agreed.

"Really thought our night was going to take a turn there."

"So did I. So did I."

"What if they'd been really good-looking?"

"That's an interesting question."

"A very interesting question."

Somehow Travis found the parking lot for the hot springs along the dark road. They must have been ten miles outside Oresite by then. Ted heard no cars and saw no lights other than the stars. But a very faint glow on the horizon suggested an impending moonrise. They stumbled across the gravel lot, both now bleary-eyed from smoking. Ted followed Travis up a soft mud path through the darkness. He could hear the river ahead of them. He could smell it throwing moisture into the dry air. In fact, everything smelled amazing—the hot sage blowing down off the hills, the wet greenery from the valley, and the muddy earth of the riverbank.

"Here is a world!" Ted called out, inhaling melodramatically. "When comes such another?"

"Huh?"

"It's Julius Caesar."

"Julius Caesar can suck my balls."

They walked to a rocky clearing where the river swept through a half-moon bend. Right in the center of the arc, just along the bank, steam rose from a dark pool. To Ted's surprise, Travis took off his clothes and shuffled across the rocks. Then he slipped down into hot water.

We're getting naked, I guess.

Oh no! Better hide your wiener!

Shut up.

He took off his clothes and eased himself into the water. The pool was just a couple of feet deep, and scorching hot.

"This is the best part," Travis said. He moved to the side of the pool closest to the river. By moving around a few rocks, he directed a thin channel of cold river water into the pool. This way, they perfectly regulated the water temperature. Their frantic conversing, which seemed earlier to have exploded out of them, now subsided. They both fell into silence. The moon crested above a stand of fir trees and lit up the small gurgling rapids. Every few minutes Travis slunk out of the pool and sat in the river.

When they finally left, Ted felt stone sober again. At the car, Travis pulled his bike from the back and thanked Ted for the ride. They were both too zonked from the hot water to make a big deal of their fast friendship. Travis told Ted his lean-to was just up the road.

They shook hands, agreeing to meet up again the following night at the Circle K. Ted watched him pedal down the road, into the moonlight.

When he got back to his dorm room he still had about four hours until his shift started. He climbed into bed, set his alarm, and shut his eyes. Beneath him, Luc tossed and farted. Then he started to snore.

CHAPTER SIXTEEN

On top of the table, one layer of clear plastic resin encased a second layer of jet black crude oil. The salt and pepper shakers were miniaturized sections of tubular pipeline. Earl Bish, founder and CEO of BC Petrol, opened his mouth to speak, but stopped himself. He grinned across the table at his wife. His fingers played in a bowl of almonds.

"It's the boy, isn't it?" she asked.

Bish nodded.

"Oh goody," his wife said. Salton Steve was her favorite work topic.

Bish exhaled. Then he put his head in his hands. "There's something wrong with that kid," he said.

"Well, you've always—"

"And it's not just him, I'm thinking. It's all of them. All these kids. I mean..."

"Oh, honey," she said, her still-youthful voice measured and consoling, as ever.

"You should see him. Maybe I'll invite him over sometime. Maybe you can help him. It's been a few years since the boys were teenagers, and maybe I've blocked a lot of it out, what all that was like. I just can't image that they were *ever* like him. Such a miserable..."

His wife stood up and left the room. Earl sat in a daze, thinking about his conversation with Salton Steve. She came back into the room with a bottle of red wine, an opener, and two glasses. She opened the bottle, smiling at the pop of the cork. She poured the wine.

"Manhandled," Bish continued. "Just *destroyed* by adolescence." He took a deep drink of wine. "His feet, my *god*, I couldn't stop looking at his feet, like he should be in the circus."

"Earl."

"I'm serious. And this greasy hair. If it was a fashion thing maybe I could get that, but it's not. It's, I think, neglect, or worse, just ignorance."

"Ignorance?"

"I think, yes, of hygiene. It's serious."

"Dear."

He shook his head and then laughed. "I have a hard time even looking at him," he confessed.

"It's okay. Have some more wine." She smiled. "I won't tell."

He looked at her and returned the smile. He took her hand and squeezed it. Then he took up the glass of wine and drained it in a big gulp.

"Gently!"

"Fill 'er up!"

She refilled his glass.

"So where does this come from?" he continued. "This attitude. This awkwardness. I don't know how some of these kids survive their teens."

"Yet most of them do. It's a phase."

"A *phase*? This is different."

"I'm just trying to—"

"It's this whole sense that life is a burden. Which I know in some cases it is. But this kid doesn't live in Ethiopia. He has prospects. Abilities. *Unique* abilities. He could very well take me over one day, if he ever got his shit together."

"Language!" she gasped, with mock outrage.

"It's the devil juice."

They both laughed. "Careful with that stuff."

"But he can't even finish a sentence, Carol. Can you imagine? He gets going and then the waves of self-doubt kick in and he just mumbles his way through the rest of the thought. It's a tragedy really, when you consider how much this kid could actually tell us. He makes me angry."

"I can tell."

He finished his glass. She refilled it before he could even set it down. "I want to throttle him. To shake him." He made feigned slapping motions, hitting Salton Steve with his palm, then the back of his hand, then the palm again. "Come on! Get your head straight! Get your act together! Stand up for yourself! Look me in the eye! Shake my hand like you mean it!"

"Yes, Earl!"

He rose from his seat and stood with his hands on the back of his chair. He took a deep breath. "Ooh, headrush," he said. "A good one."

She looked at Earl lovingly. He was so funny sometimes. She knew this was all sort of an act, his outrage. He never let himself take work too seriously, something they both knew was the secret to his success. Employees were a constant source of entertainment, not frustration. His attitude kept him young. She waited for him to continue.

"There's something a person learns when he gets older, that you can't just sit there and let life have its way with you, that at some point you have to stand up for yourself and take control. You have to take an *active* role. Stop getting kicked around. It's a beautiful thing when it happens. But it's a tough road. And I guess once you make the journey you don't have heaps of sympathy for people who haven't put in the effort yet, who are still struggling."

"Like Salton Steve."

"Yes! And I know it's awful to pick apart people like this, especially someone who is young and having trouble, but he'll get through it. Hopefully. He's just got to push through this."

"And he will. They all do."

"Except the ones who kill themselves."

"Except for them, yes."

"They don't push through anything, those ones."

"No they don't. You're right."

"Weaklings," he said. He smiled down at her. He was driving her crazy, he could tell. She kept urging him on, to get to the point, and he kept letting the wine distract him.

"Sinners," she added.

"*Sinners*, yes. Good one, dear."

"So what happened?" she asked finally.

He savored her eagerness. He climbed back into his chair and leaned in close. "So, anyway, he came into my office, this Salton Steve, and by the way what kind of a name—"

"Earl," she interrupted, her voice placid. "Just tell me the fucking story."

Grinning, he continued: "He walked in like he regretted his entire existence. Like it was all just some big terrible mistake. He was slumped over, staring at the floor. Just so damn depressing. You hear about people sucking the life out of a room, well, I'd never actually witnessed that happen. No smile. Nothing. Just this pulsating anti-charisma. He's well over two meters, and he probably weighs less than you do." He nodded, seeing it all so clearly. "Wife, when I say he was gangly...my God. And barely three dimensions. Which got me thinking about biology and human development and why it seems so essential that young people endure this part of life, why they emerge from their younger, carefree years into this dark world of pulverizing discomfort. Why does it happen?"

"I don't know."

"I looked at this kid and really could not imagine him ever having a normal life, you know, pulling it together enough to start a career, charm a young woman and get married, raise children. You know, the basics. This is a kid who you can't even picture going into 7-Eleven and figuring out how to purchase a soda. I imagine him walking in there and then twenty seconds later just running out in tears. I mean, *nothing*. There was *nothing* there. Just a bad haircut, bad acne, asymmetrical and blotchy facial hair, an Adam's apple like a peach stone. This brutal Canadian paleness."

"I understand Earl, but what did you say to him?"

"Tell me Carol," he went on, "does this exist elsewhere in the animal kingdom? Does it happen to badgers? Are there awkward miserable badgers? Or snakes. Do snakes have a stage where the other snakes have to slap them around and tell them how to be snakes? It almost proves our uniqueness on earth, as God's chosen people, because we really are so different. We have...this *affliction*."

"Maybe that's the point of it, Earl, to give us a chance to practice sympathy. Because that's exactly what you're struggling with right now. You need to practice. *This* is how you feel sorry for someone. So you know how to do it. So you recognize it in others, when *you* need it."

He thought about what she said. He nodded. "I think you should listen to the man talk, dear, okay?"

"I apologize, Your Grace."

"That's alright." There was an awkward pause. She dipped three fingers into her glass and flicked wine into his face. He pretended not to notice. "Would you believe his shirt was half tucked, half untucked, with the tucked part going into his underwear, which was black? What kind of a mother lets her son wear black underwear?"

"One who doesn't like to do laundry."

"That's disgusting. You're a disgusting woman."

"I apologize, Your Grace." Again she flicked wine at him.

"You've had what, half a glass, and you're already toasted."

"Continue."

"His collar was wrinkled."

"Damnation!"

"I've had wrinkled shirts. I get that. But the collar you almost have to *try* to mess up. And this shirt he was wearing, just a plain white shirt, looked honestly like it was being used as bedding for cats, like it was all balled up against the side of one of those carpeted cat beds. Like he picked it up, shook it out, wiped some of the hair away and that was that."

"Because when it comes to fashion, there's Earl Bish and then there's everyone—"

"Silence!" He held his palm to her face. He looked at his empty wine glass and cleared his throat. She refilled the glass. "The problem, and this is where I feel a little justified in my criticism, is that it all makes him look stupid. Like intellectually deficient. Which he isn't. Not by any stretch. He's certainly smarter than you. Which is just another reason for him to try and work it out. Because people are going to go around making assumptions about him. If you look dumb and act dumb, well."

She smiled widely.

"I'll not have your insolence!"

"You were saying, about looking and acting dumb?"

"There's a voice I use in my head when I think about him, his inner monologue, this kind of deep oafish complaining drone, like *I can't believe I have to do all this math homework. I can't believe I have to clean my room. I can't believe you're only supposed to use one hand when you masturbate.*"

"Earl Bish!"

"That's right! Masturbate masturbate masturbate!"

She pretended to swoon and then dabbed wine on her temples.

"I'm being cruel, I know. But on the other hand, I'm probably also going to make him rich, so I guess I'm entitled. But that shirt. I can't get it out of my mind. Misbuttoned. Honest. He actually failed to get the buttons lined up. At one point I thought it all had to be intentional, like some big goof on me. Like a set-up, or a con of some sort. Like he's really some mad genius taking me for a ride. Some scheme beyond my ability to comprehend."

She coughed.

"Would you like me to describe his tie? It was yellow and green striped, extra thick, with the back hanging down further than the front. It was the kind of tie a woman would wear if she dressed as a man for Halloween. I think it was corduroy. Where does one even shop..." He broke off, shaking his head.

"Be strong."

"It doesn't even seem necessary to mention that the pants were wrinkled and too short and that he wore white running socks with black shoes. I also think he was wearing his Junior Mountie belt."

"Well, that's cute."

"No. Not cute. Braces. And of course braces. It goes on. You think I'm wrapping this up. I haven't even told you about his glasses. You'll think I'm exaggerating. Those big thick glasses that make your eyeballs seem oversized. Can a person be both cross-eyed and wall-eyed at the same time?"

"I'll fix you a bath. Would you like that? And cookies?"

"Help me, Carol." It was hard to tell where his sarcasm ended and the real pain began.

She took up his hand and looked him in the eye. "Well for one thing, Earl, your own children all wore braces. They all wore Junior Mountie belts—"

"With their Junior Mountie uniforms! When they were eleven! Not to work!"

"Maybe his family—"

"Not an excuse. I pay him a salary."

"He's a miner, Earl."

"No, he's not. He *works* with miners. But he hasn't driven a Bobcat in four months."

"I'm just trying—"

"Try harder!"

They locked eyes. She still held his hand. "*You* try harder," she said, her voice calming. He leaned over the table as if to kiss her, but seized her wine glass instead, and began to chug. She just kept staring at him.

Bish set the glass down and picked up the empty wine bottle. He turned it over in his hands, as if he didn't understand its purpose. He squinted at it. Sniffed it. Tried to put it in his mouth.

"I'll be right back," she said.

Once she refilled their glasses, he continued. "If he could have done just one thing right, you know. A perfect tie knot. Business appropriate footwear. Anything. But no. Of course no. Nothing. Sorry kid. If the goal of it all is to practice sympathy, then I failed miserably. Because all I feel towards this kid is anger. I mean, I *get* it that teens have acne. I had acne. That's not his fault. But he made it his fault with his attitude and the way he carried himself. There's a lot for this kid to overcome, but a good attitude, good posture, a firm handshake, that can do it. There are ways to move beyond one's limitations. But he has none of that."

"What's the story with his parents?"

"No idea."

"They're LDS?"

"Hell no!"

"How do you know?"

136

"Kids who can dress for church can dress for a meeting with their boss."

"Well I don't know what to tell you then."

"You should try sometime, Carol, to have a conversation with this one. You'll want to throw yourself out the window."

"Like James Castle?"

"Who?"

"Never mind."

"Please don't interrupt me, woman. There's another weird thing; he said *sir* and *please* and *thank you* and all that, which just means that there *is* someone helping him with all this, and I want to meet that person, that parent, and ask them how they allowed things to go so terribly wrong for their son. I want to get a look at Mom and Dad just from a biological standpoint. They're probably perfect specimens. That's how it works with these things."

"Helen of Troy begets the Elephant Man."

"The problem, *my* problem, and this is probably where you're going to want to start paying attention, is that I need to get information out of him. It's not like I was having dinner at a friend's house and had to chat with his kid for a minute or two. This was, basically, an investigation. A rather serious one, in fact. So I asked him finally, once the shock of him wore off, I asked him if he knew who I was."

"Yer, uh, Mr. Bish."

"What do I do?"

"Yer like the boss of the comp—um—the, like, the company, I guess."

"That's correct. Do you know why I've asked to speak with you today?"

"Um, well, sir, not really. I mean, I guess, uh, no, not really."

"I think you do know. Just relax, son. You're not in any trouble."

"Well, I, uh, what was the question again?"

"I asked you if you knew why you were here today."

"Um, I guess, well it's about the mine, or, I don't know."

"That's correct. I want to ask you about the mine."

The boy nodded.

"Has anyone talked to you about the mine?"

"I've, um, well..."

"Yes?"

"Well, I guess I heard some stuff."

"Okay, let's try it this way. You're just going to talk, okay. Just tell me everything you know about the history of the Collins Lode. Do you understand?"

"Uh huh." He took off his glasses and rubbed the sides of his nose. Bish noticed he looked even stranger with the glasses off. *What a mess.* Salton Steve told Bish he noticed the Collins Lode while looking out the window of the transport helicopter that took him out to the P4 derricks where he worked all summer.

"What do you mean you *noticed* it?"

"I just saw it, like, from where I was sitting."

"Just saw it?"

"Uh huh." When the kid nodded his mouth hung open.

"Can you explain that to me?"

"Hmm, let's see, I'll try to remember. There was, like, this mound that I saw—"

"Yes...and..."

"And it was, like, I don't know, like I guess out of place or something."

"You noticed something was different. Out of place. From way up in the sky?"

"Yes, sir."

"What did you think that meant?"

"Um, hmm." He squeezed his nostrils between his fingers. "Can I please have something to drink?"

138

"Of course." Bish made a call over the intercom and Sherry brought in a soda. She also topped off his coffee. *Good old Sherry.* Bish repeated the question.

"Uh, just that, well, like...hmm."

"Son, now listen. You're going to have to do better. I need...well...let me put it to you this way. Are you listening?"

"I'm listening, yes."

"I want to offer you a raise. How much are you making right now?"

"I make six twenty-five an hour."

"Okay, son. I'm willing to double what you make."

"I, uh, would like that." His eyes were glued to the floor.

"Good, that's good. But you need to tell me what I want to know. Okay?"

"Okay, uh, sure. I'll try."

"Thank you."

Bish suggested they take a walk. Maybe the office was too stifling. They just did a couple loops around the block. Though Bish was able to get him talking a bit more coherently, he still didn't really learn anything. Salton Steve said he noticed from the helicopter that there was a large moraine rising out of what looked like an old river bed. But when Bish pressed him on how he knew there would be gold in the river bed, he couldn't explain it any better than to say he just knew it. Bish asked him if he had had other experiences in his life where he just knew something, without understanding why he knew it. Naturally, the boy didn't understand the question. Bish put it another way.

"Do you know what it means to be psychic?"

Salton Steve stopped walking, and for the first time all day he looked Bish right in the eye. Just for a second. "Uh, I think so," he said. He sounded scared. Bish wondered if it was not in fact his terrible experience with adolescence that had turned him into an incoherent wreck, but rather this strange affliction which he felt separated him from the rest of the world.

"Have you ever thought that you might have psychic abilities?"

"Sir?"

"Are you psychic?"

"Well, I can't, like, read people's minds or anything."

"No. Of course you can't. But you sometimes know stuff?"

"Yeah, I guess, sometimes."

They sat down on a park bench. "You realize that's impossible, right?"

The boy looked at the ground. "Um, uh, what do you mean?"

"I mean that it's not possible for you to just know stuff. That doesn't exist."

"Um, I don't know."

"What don't you know?"

"I...it's just...I don't know."

Bish stood up. "Look up. Look at me, okay. Okay. Look at me."

"Okay, I'm looking."

"You need to explain this to me. In English. I need an answer."

"I told you, I can't explain it." There was the smallest hint of anger in Salton Steve's voice now.

Bish decided to push him. "You have to explain it."

"I don't have to do anything."

"It's a con isn't it?"

"A what? A con? Mister—"

"That's right. You're scamming me. You knew about the Collins Lode. You discovered it with your dad when you guys were hunting or something."

"Excuse me, my father's dead."

"Well, whatever."

140

"Whatever? Geez. You asked me to come see you and I tried to, you know, answer all your questions and all. But you don't like what I'm telling you and I can't help that."

"You're telling me you're psychic."

"You're the one who said that!"

"I said that wasn't possible. So how about some answers kid? About the mine. About the mine that's brought in over twenty million dollars to this company. Tell me how you knew what was down there."

The poor kid looked like he was going to cry. "I don't know how I knew and that's the truth. I got lucky I guess. Whatever you want to call it."

"Have you ever told anyone about this?"

"About what?"

"This ability you claim—"

"No. Nothing. Nobody."

"How do you feel about it?"

"I don't like it."

All the stammering was gone. The self-doubt. Even the sniffling.

"Why don't you like it?"

"It...I guess it scares me."

"Why does it scare you?"

He looked at the ground again, and started fiddling with the tab of his soda can.

"Psychic? Earl? What in God's name has gotten into you?"

"You explain it then."

"Luck."

"This kid has no luck."

"Everyone has *some* luck."

"But I'm the one who's benefiting, not him."

"Well, dear, that's how bad it is for him, I guess. His good luck only helps others."

"Poor bastard."

"It's very ironic."

"Well, his luck is about to change. I told him he would be working directly with me, if that was okay with him. I told him Sherry would be taking him shopping that afternoon. Maybe you should take him."

"I would like that."

"I told him I was going to make him a very wealthy man. He just nodded a lot. We stood up. He shook my hand. Limp and damp. Is there anything worse?" He dipped his fingers in the wine glass and moistened his right palm. "Here, try it."

She shook his hand. "Eww," she said. She jerked her hand back and did an exaggerated full-body twitch.

"Gross, right?"

"Icky."

"I told him I believed him after all, that I was sorry to have pressed him, or angered him, but that I needed to know for sure. And the truth is, Carol, I think there *is* something going on with him. The fact remains that he picked the thing out of the clear blue sky. The biggest gold deposit in our whole outfit. Like he was picking horses. This kid. What explanations are there really? You mentioned luck. So, out of the vastness of British Columbia he just pointed?"

"I don't know, Earl. I'm tired."

"It's not possible to be that lucky. So he knew about it. Like I said. From his father or something."

"But then why not develop it himself? Why not buy up the land. It doesn't cost much way out there. Buy it and sell it, right? That's what you'd do. What you *do* do."

Earl nodded. "You're right."

"What if his abilities are not supernatural, just super-informed? Could the world's greatest petroleum geologist identify a gold mine from a helicopter?"

"Who knows? Petroleum's different."

"But that's his training. Could this Salton Steve be the world's greatest petroleum geologist? Is that logical?"

"This kid who can't tie his own shoes?"

"I'm just saying."

There was a long pause. They both stood up. They embraced. They swayed in a slow dance. Then he pushed her back gently and set his hands on her shoulders. "Psychic ability," he said. "I won't consider it."

"But he seems to think that's how he did it. And that's important."

"I'll have to see if I can get him to do it again."

"Would that convince you that he has...*powers*?"

"Would it convince you?"

"It might."

CHAPTER SEVENTEEN

It was about noon. The brightness outside nearly blinded her. She blinked her eyes for a moment, standing on a freshly mowed lawn. The sounds of children filled the air. It took her a moment to realize where she was. She saw the large skating rink in the distance, and to her left, the outdoor seating of her restaurant, The Spot. She had never taken a break by going out this back door.

Such an absurdly nice day, she thought, wishing she too was on vacation. She watched kids twirling around on the ice. A tall figure was picking them up and throwing them into the air, and then setting them down carefully. A bunch of kids, actually. And a row of parents lined-up along the railing, snapping pictures. Some diners on the patio stood, also caught up in the scene.

The man was huge. Abnormally huge.

Is that...Arnold Schwarzenegger?

Can't be.

That's Arnold Schwarzenegger.

There he is.

On skates.

Holy Cow.

Her face lit up. She watched him play with the kids. What a nice fellow, she thought. So gracious. So giving.

How do you like that?

Arnold Schwarzenegger.

Man, where's *my* camera?

CHAPTER EIGHTEEN

I dropped out of college to do this, Ted thought. I still can't believe it's an actual job people do.

His Royal Silver Polisher.

What?

I don't know. Took a dump in the electric kettle? Am I losing my mind?

It's the fumes.

Right. The fumes and Jackie. She's such an awful old woman. You're not allowed to be both senile *and* stubborn. She tells me to do something one way, so I do, and then she criticizes my technique minutes later.

Insanity.

Everything has to be done properly, but properly is an amorphous concept. Don't use so much polish. Do you know how much it costs? Gads! you're not using enough polish. If we run out we can always buy more.

They're *all* maniacs.

Salton Steve is a maniac. Why does he keep bringing me the newspaper in the morning? I'm not comfortable with that.

Given your history.

Right! He claims he's just being neighborly, that it's important to stay caught up. Don't want to get lost up here in Idaho, he told me, and forget we live on a little thing called Planet Earth.

And what about Cammie?

Well she turns *me* into a maniac. I'm always a bit shocked when I see her, so she's always apologizing for startling me. Such a turn-on I'm sure. I can hear her on the phone to her girlfriends—not only is he handsome and rich, but he's *skittish* too.

She caught him most recently stuffing his face with fresh berries down in the walk-in. It was cold and smelled like spilt Italian dressing.

We could have had a moment down there, he thought, making out against the produce boxes, maybe getting locked in accidentally. I'd have to break her out with the fireman's axe. All bad ass. Saving her life. Or we could have done it next door, in dry storage, on the rice sacks.

She told him she saw Arnold Schwarzenegger at the skating rink.

"Cool," he said.

One word. Not a single fully realized Schwarzenegger-thought. Only, oh my God, we're down here all alone. Say something funny. Say something interesting. Grab her and kiss her. Run for the hills.

Would it kill me to be charming? Oh Schwarzenegger, right, hear he's got a house in Valvert, plays golf with Bruce Willis, shot a hole in one on a par five, that's how strong he is, orders like six plates of steak tartar and drinks raw egg mimosas, no shit, yeah, I know, I am kind of funny, and cute, right, not as cute as you are, do you like blueberries, do you want me to feed them to you, do you want me to feed you blueberries with your shirt off, how about that. Let's take the hat off, shake out your hair, yeah, well hello it must be colder in here than I thought...

Knock it off, Ted

And Travis was gone. Ted never saw him again. He went back to the hot springs six nights in a row. But there was no sign of him. He even yelled his name in the darkness near where he thought Travis kept his lean-to.

Maybe the badgers got him.

Maybe the Bushido got him.

Definitely *something* got him.

Ted did buy a sword though. He drove to a shop in Boise on his day off. He took it into the forest and started chopping at stuff. Dead twigs still on trees. Nothing fleshy to be found though. No flying grapefruits. Nothing to hunt. He realized a Samurai sword in a pine forest was not all that exciting. What he really wanted was a machete in the jungle.

Too bad about Travis.

He was cool.

That was a good night.

Friends are good.

And you don't have any.

It was true, he really didn't have any friends. He had talked to his old college roommates about their upcoming graduation, but he sensed a huge distance. He told them he washed dishes, and didn't mention the silver polishing. Even with them, it was hard to be honest about what he really did in Valvert. He could sense they all still worried about him.

Afraid I'm cracking up.

Which you are.

Literally.

He looked down at his hands. They were eroding from the silver polish. That morning he poured lotion into the deep lines and it disappeared like water down a drain. His hands could absorb a whole bottle, somehow, and still look like scale replicas of the Grand Canyon, with their own little hoodoos, buttresses, archways, amphitheaters, and free standing buttes.

Ever since he met Cammie, he wouldn't allow himself to be seen in those pink gloves. So he went in bareback and his hands paid the price, a fact he kept hidden from Jackie, who wouldn't understand his aversion to pink gloves.

God, I *hate* her.

She's not that bad. You're overreacting.

No, I do hate her. Maybe it's irrational. I don't care.

It's her cigarette breath.

Yes!

Well, you're stuck, so see if you can learn something.

Why is she so miserable?

Why indeed?

He studied her, the expressions, the body language, the interactions with others. He was more aware of emotional states now that he had experienced a few new ones. Shame had crept up on him after Twin and Addie. It was more painful than he would have expected. He wasn't going to get caught off guard again. He would try to learn from Jackie, about bitterness, so when it overtook him in life he would at least recognize it.

And not overreact.

That word again. I did overreact, didn't I?

Of course you did.

I dropped out of college and left the state. Some people, most people, when they do something shameful, don't even notice. Or at least they don't dwell on it. Maybe I *am* too sensitive.

Like Salton Steve said?

Yeah.

Not easy to give that guy any credit.

It's not.

But he did get a lot of things right.

Too many.

What's that supposed to mean?

It means I don't like to be so...

Predictable. Normal. Obvious.

But I'm not. I mean how many people would have dropped out in my situation?

149

How many people would even be in your situation? Shitting in newspapers.

It's funny again, isn't it. I mean when you look at where it landed me. It was funny at first, then it wasn't. And now it is again.

Maybe you wanted to leave college and used that as an excuse.

Is that what I did?

It's possible.

Maybe I should ask Jackie.

Bad idea.

I left too early. She's stayed too long. Maybe we could have a conversation about that. I mean, she must have some kind of pension retirement thing set up, right? She has grown kids, her own house and car, money to gamble with. She doesn't parade around the IR because she has to, financially. So why does she do it? I've never seen her share a smile with anyone in the kitchen, never seen her even have a real conversation with anyone unless she was down on the loading dock smoking. Maybe some of the higher-ups respect her, but they hardly ever deal with her. Maybe she stays for the physical activity. Walking up and down the corridors to smoke has to be better than sitting on a stool in a casino.

They call her The Gargoyle.

She must know that. It's cruel. But she's just as cruel. And so miserable. Or sad. I just don't know. But she's clearly unraveling. Cursing mop buckets. Kicking the vacuum. Sniffing rags. Nothing in her world ever comes clean. I work for Sisyphus.

You're *Sisyphus'* Bitch.

Perfect.

First she swept the floor. She did it slowly and deliberately, not wanting to send dust up into the air.

Sound technique.

She wore a green knitted apron.

"You've had that apron a while?"

"It's not an apron, dummy. It's a *smock*."

"How do you spell it?"

"What the hell kind of a question are you asking me?"

Her mouth moved when she worked, like she was reading. *Pair of Jacks pushes in Jackpot, loses in Vegas.* Then she stopped, leaned on the pole for support, farted inadvertently, and continued. *Door to the loading dock swings out from the inside, in from the outside. It's bassackward.* She eyed Ted's fortress of chafers. Dirt in there she couldn't get to. *It's my loading dock. They get water in my ashtray one more time I'll kick their asses back to May-hee-ko. With the hoses all the time. Just love to spray things down.*

"Kevin, Kevin, Kevin!" she called. He scurried over to her, impatient and annoyed. "These carts can't go here," she said.

"You have to talk to the servers. Talk to Simon."

"Simon's an idiot."

"I don't understand your point." He walked away.

"Kevin, you've got to—"

"Jackie, I'm too busy to deal with this. Just move them. Write a note. I don't care."

She kept sweeping, not seeming the least bit bothered by the conversation.

That's the insanity. Right there. Kevin's dismissal should have enraged her. But it didn't.

Subject exhibits a lack of consistency.

A lid slipped off one of the pots and banged around on the floor, comically loud, protracted in the library calm of the kitchen. A pox-on-your-house glare from Jackie. Smoke break.

A revelation!

Smoke breaks can be induced.

It's possible to make her leave through carefully crafted displays of stupidity. Get her blood up and she goes away.

Ted blew air into his palms. His hands *ached*. One crack in his thumb webbing actually started to bleed, which meant the silver polish was going to get into his blood stream.

It's already in your blood stream, from the fumes.

Maybe I can find some of those clear latex medical gloves.

Have you seen any?

Not one pair, and this is a kitchen. Maybe it's an aesthetic issue with chefs in high quality restaurants, that they need direct contact with the food.

Like a form of unprotected sex.

Jackie reappeared and tossed Ted a bundle of rags. "These are special," she said. "They come from housekeeping. No grease."

Bet I can get her to take another smoke break.

This is entertainment?

We'll see.

"I've been meaning to ask you about that, Jackie. What is grease exactly?"

"Grease?"

"Yes."

"Grease is grease. What kind of question are you asking me?"

"It's a serious question."

"What's grease?"

"Yes, like what *is* it?"

"Holy Hanna," she muttered, not angry so much as disappointed.

"Is it fat, or oil, or juice? What is it?"

"*Juice?*"

"Yeah, juice. Like drippings."

"Jesus, *drippings*?"

"Like from turkeys."

"My God, son, is there something wrong with you?"

"Why's it such a stupid question? Nobody ever explained grease to me. That's all. What's the big deal?" She leaned on the broom stick, shaking her head. He poured it on. "Because you hear about grease on heavy machinery, like for lubrication."

"*Lubrication?*"

"Is it the same stuff?"

"I have no idea what you're talking about."

"You said these new rags are from housekeeping so they don't have grease on them."

"Yes..."

"So how do the kitchen rags get grease on them?"

"They get grease on them because they all get washed together."

"I don't understand."

Suddenly, a look of horror overcame her. "My God! What's wrong with your hands?"

Ted rubbed them self-consciously together. "It's from the polish."

"Holy Christmas. I didn't know what I was dealing with here. You haven't been wearing gloves this whole time? Do you know what's in that stuff?" She went to the closet to get Ted his new pink gloves.

"I'm not wearing those."

"What do you mean?" She tore the bag open.

"It's emasculating."

"In English."

"They're pink."

"So?"

"I don't need them."

It's working.

Tread lightly.

"You have a job to do here and it's not up to you to make these decisions."

153

"I am doing my job!"

"Put these on."

"I don't want to."

She grabbed his wrists. Her lips were pushed so tightly together they turned white. "You will put these on!"

"No!" He moved his arms around slowly so she couldn't get a grip. He was careful not to knock her in the head. "I don't want to!" He turned to the others, to see if anyone else in the kitchen was watching.

They all were.

Chef Kevin, Luc, Bruce at the sauté station, two waiters folding napkins. Massive grins on every face.

"I don't want to!"

"Hold still!"

He stopped moving. He hung his head. He felt the powdered rubber move over his fingers. Soothing. Blissful.

He took them off the second she left for her smoke break.

Victory!

He marched over to Kevin. "She's awful," he said.

"That was great."

"I'm glad you enjoyed it. Are there any latex gloves, you know, the clear ones?"

"Dry storage, downstairs. Let me see your hands." Ted held them out. "Yeesh!"

When Ted came back, Jackie would not look at him. Her silent muttering intensified. He watched her disappear into a closet. Then she came out pushing a mop in a mop bucket. She wheeled the bucket into the middle of the room and returned to the closet, still in a silent rage. When she returned, she had three containers of cleaning products. She set all three containers on the floor next to the mop bucket. She took a minute to rest and clean her glasses. Ted watched her pick up the first container and study the label. She moved her mouth as she read and seemed completely oblivious to anything else that was happening. She looked like she needed a long nap.

She can hardly see.

Even with her glasses on, she had to hold it right up to her face to read the label.

She dumped a substantial quantity of the liquid into the mop bucket, leaned over, and set the container down next to the other two, her face just inches from the bucket. She picked up the next container and repeated the process, pulling it right up to her face, reading the label while moving her lips. She unscrewed the lid and dumped a good amount into the bucket. She put the lid back on and leaned over to set the container on the ground.

Ted watched her do this. He watched her jerk her head instantly away from the bucket. He watched her body go limp and crumple to the floor, boneless. Her head knocked against the side of the mop bucket, causing it to overturn. The chemicals pooled around her motionless body. Then the mop pole smacked the tiled floor, announcing the end.

CHAPTER NINETEEN

Exactly two months after Marona Dilenta arrived in Copan, the same rusted-out pickup truck deposited another volunteer excavator at the muddy entrance to the tent camp. He stood on an uneven wet board laid out across a large puddle, with a single small duffle in hand. His eyes scanned the camp, the rows of dirt-splattered canvass tents, the familiar rickety sign attached to a splintering pole, which read "Harvard University." He looked up at the trees, the clouds, a large black bird in flight, taking it all in with a cold analytical scowl.

"This fucking place..." he muttered. "You make your move this time, *Eugene.*"

But then he ran a hand across his face and transformed himself. He was now Heinrich Airhorne, free-spirited wanderer, in his travel-worn leather sandals, cutoff camouflage pants and deeply stained white undershirt. Big toothy grin. Enormous thick-lensed glasses. A nasty head of tightly curled hair which he kept long and greasy, and which swung back and forth when he walked, and looked like a wet mop cleaning his shoulders. An absurd man. He rolled his shoulders a couple of times, like a swimmer on the blocks. He exhaled and smacked himself hard across the cheek.

He followed the worn path of dark compacted soil. He compared notes with his previous visits. A tall pile of boards and disassembled scaffolding suggested that the tedious restoration of the southern ballcourt was probably complete. From one of the tents he passed he could hear two Italians arguing. Still apparently a bad idea to bring your girlfriend on a volunteer jungle excavation vacation.

The tail of a black snake disappeared into the undergrowth in front of him. He stepped over a line of red ants.

He noticed something new about the camp. Someone had painted the words "Dig It" on the side of the mess tent in cutesy bubbled letters. Doesn't change anything, he thought. Still a place to eat and drink. An empty gesture. *Dig It*. Lame. The professor's losing his influence. It may be time. After twenty years. What about *Copancakes*? And didn't this place used to be lousy with squirrel monkeys?

My name is Heinrich Airhorne.

He tossed aside the flap and entered the large musty dining room. He set his bag down, and while framed in the doorway, backlit in a towering silhouette, he bellowed deep and melodramatic, "Jackson, I have returned!"

Various heads turned in his direction. A general cheer of enthusiasm rang out. He danced a goofy jig, tipped an invisible hat, and bowed graciously to the room of about twenty diners. Applause. A Maya woman in the back, who tended the warming trays, rolled her eyes and turned to her friend, who crossed herself.

Marona Dilenta, sitting alone at the corner table was equally unimpressed, mostly on account of his hairstyle, which was offensively bad, absolutely the worst she had ever seen. A dead cat from a gutter stapled to the back of his head. A tarred roofing swab.

He circled the room, vigorously shaking hands with everyone. Sometimes smiling, sometimes severe. Sympathetic to upsetting news. Affable with introductions.

He stopped at each table, taking care to crouch like a catcher so the people sitting didn't break their necks looking up at him.

Marona watched it all from behind her book. Something about this guy...just so weird looking...almost intentionally so.

His long arms swung around pale and skeletal as he animated the conversation. He kept losing his balance and had to steady himself in his crouch by bracing his bony fingers on the dirty cement floor. But those he spoke to seemed genuinely uplifted by his presence—when he asked after their families or inquired knowingly about their research. He patted backs, gave full bear hugs. And he laughed. He hardly ever stopped laughing. His eyes squinted tightly behind those thick lenses. Marona's suspicious reaction to the guy made her instantly self-conscious.

Just how jaded am I? she wondered. Root him out. Find him out. What's the tell, the tick, the inconsistency? What deception and why? The guarded skeptic. That's the new Marona.

Everyone seemed grateful to have this new energy around. She noticed the same enthusiasm that had boiled up around her. They had nearly thrown a party when she arrived. And it was happening again, with this guy, only more organic. No questions asked. Trusting. Themselves therefore trustworthy. Her own suspicion branding her suspicious. An outsider. The only one alone at a table. These days *she* was the one they eyed from behind *their* books. But at least she had great hair. Dark red and flowing in nice curls, not those creepy wet zigzags. Buzz them off, she thought. To have him in a chair in front of her (he'd probably still be taller) with the high-powered clippers, the industrial ones you have to plug in all the time. She would start at the back. Then up and under, to his forehead. Again and again and again. She would need gloves that went all the way up her forearms, and an Asian airport mask. Fishing waders. She imagined a group of scientists in lab coats picking up the shorn locks with long metal tweezers, one by one, and dropping them in an orange haz-mat receptacle. The looks on the scientists faces the same mix of fear and disgust Marona gets when she roots around in the garbage disposal to fish something out.

But thanks to this new arrival, the dining room was transformed from a dreary hospital cafeteria to a rollicking beer hall. The local ladies in the back frantically popped beer caps. "No cold," they repeated, shaking their heads, pressing the backs of their hands to the sides of the bottles. Someone slid one absently across Marona's table and she caught it before it crashed to the ground. They were including her, but just barely.

The guy spun in frenetic circles, knocking bottles with anyone who stood in his way. A smile like beams of light through a dark cave. This was charisma on a massive scale. A dangerous scale. Marona could light up a room as well, but she usually needed black leather boots and a tight-fitting sweater to do it. Attention to her was given instinctively, biologically. But his was charisma in spite of himself. A hardier brand, tougher to come by. Nobody was pre-set to appreciate *this* guy. Just the opposite. And it irked her, she had to admit. It threatened her own emotional stranglehold on the camp. She kept her head buried in her book, slugged the warm bottle in large gulps, and pretended not to notice a thing.

He continued his rounds as things settled down a bit. When he finally arrived at Marona's table, she affected distraction, sopping up runny beans on a plate with a corn tortilla. He made an exaggerated stop, and stood there in a state of theatrical paralysis. His smile faded. His features softened. He primped himself with exaggerated flourish, brushing his hair from shoulders and then checking his breath in a cupped hand. Somebody on the other side of the room chuckled. All eyes were on the two of them.

"And who might you be?" he asked, dipping towards her. She looked up, feigning exasperation. The whole thing seemed choreographed. He knelt down to her level. "Sorry to interrupt."

"It's fine," she said, with a calculated softening. She set the book on the table. "I'm Marona Dilenta."

"Heinrich Airhorne," he said. They shook hands. "The pleasure is all mine."

She nodded. *Airhorne*? Really? A bullshit name if ever there was one.

"Can I ask how it's possible a woman like you would be sitting here all alone?"

"It's not a big deal," she said, tapping the novel which lay open at her side.

He asked if he could have a seat and she told him to knock himself out.

He sat. He picked up the book and looked at the cover. "*E.T.*?" he said, snorting out a quick laugh. "Like the movie?"

She nodded.

"The book of the movie?"

"The novelization."

He shook his head back and forth and pushed his glasses back up onto his nose. "Is it any good?"

"It's fine."

"You got it here?"

"There aren't a lot of choices."

With a mouthful of beer he nodded vigorously, then swallowed, "No, no, no there aren't. Don't I know it. Last summer I read *Little Men*."

"Little *Men*?"

"Yeah. Here. In Co-Pan of all places. Awful stuff."

"I see."

160

"Couldn't put it down, though, right? Isn't that the way it sometimes goes?" Then into song. "Isn't that the way they say it goes..."

Oh God, make him stop.

As their conversation progressed, little quirks in his behavior became more pronounced. She had barely noticed them at first. His smile expanded and contracted as he spoke, and the volume of his voice rose and fell with random emphasis, like some unseen sound tech toyed with his modulation knobs, his peaks and valleys coming apropos of nothing.

Maybe he's retarded, she thought. She hoped. She downed the rest of her beer and wiped her hands on a napkin. They both nodded in the awkward silence while he conducted a brazen examination of her body.

"But really," he said, "that's a pretty stylish get-up for digging around in the mud, isn't it?"

"Well I'm just very careful out there I guess."

He nodded. "That's impressive, impressive...but you like it here?"

"I do."

"You sound about as convincing as my ex-wife did at our wedding." Instant, maniacal laughter. Then instantly ceasing. He wiped his brow. "That's a joke," he said.

"I see."

One of the site managers, Head on Earth specialist Dr. Furizuki-Webber, entered the tent and immediately made his way over to Airhorne. He slapped him hard on the back, "Didn't think I'd see you here again!"

"Evan!"

"What's up, man?" He looked down at Marona, "And how are you this evening?" She shrugged. "You met Airhorne, I see."

"Unfortunately for her, right!" Airhorne banged the table.

"He's an old hat here," the doctor said to Marona. Then turning to Airhorne, "This is your, what, third time in Copan?"

"Forth!" he said.

"You're a glutton."

"We're all gluttons."

"Great to see you." Furizuki-Webber patted his belly and gestured to the buffet table. Airhorne turned his attention back to Marona, who had taken up her novel again. He apologized for interrupting her.

"No, no," she said, putting the book back down. "It's fine."

"Are you a student or a volunteer?"

"I'm a professor," she said.

Heinrich fumbled, embarrassed, "I'm, I'm sorry," he said. Then after a pause, "I thought you looked too young to be a professor."

Marona smiled at him. "Nice, but I'm a volunteer, actually."

"And a liar."

"Yes, and sometimes a liar, Mr...*Airhorne* is it?" she said, smirking. "Is that German?"

He fumbled for a half-second. "Alsatian," he said.

"Four times to Copan. You must really love it here."

He began speaking as if a jackhammer had just started up at the side of her table, even cupping his hands around his mouth, "Don't ask me why," he yelled, "but I just can't seem to stay away."

She played along, yelling right back at him, "What, you said you can't find a good toupee?"

"I can't..." he laughed, shook his head, and truly at the top of his voice bellowed, "I can't seem to stay away!" The rest of the room watched, transfixed. Airhorne then leaned in close to Marona. She wouldn't look at him.

"Is there something wrong with you I should know about?" she asked, staring down at the tabletop. He

162

brushed his hair from his shoulders again. Marona recoiled. "Can you not?"

"Marona Dilenta," he said. His voice soft and creepy.

She brushed her fingers at him. "Can you just...move along please?"

He slammed his fist down on the table, threw his head back, and burst into crazed laughter. Then he pushed off from the table—she saw him do it—and fell straight back in his chair and landed on the floor. He lay there for a second, eyes closed. Then he instantly popped up to his feet and took another bow. More applause. Then he sprinted out of the room, like an unathletic kid running to first base for the first time in his life. The applause continued long after the tent's doorflaps swayed to a standstill. Marona picked up her book and pretended not to be impressed.

Full of shit, she thought, this Airhorne character. I've seen it before. How absolutely full of shit you are, and I know it.

That night she joined the professor at the top of the Hieroglyphic Staircase. The evening was particularly foggy. No sign of the howlers. The jungle itself, mostly hidden, had a quiet giddy energy, full of actors waiting backstage. The nightbirds cleared their throats, tested a few calls. She had been going with him most nights, telling herself it was not safe for him to go alone. Whether he was putting her on or not, the other day when he passed-out and fell over, didn't really matter. He was either sick or crazy, and someone ought to keep an eye on him.

On this night he wore his most absurd outfit to date, normal slacks and a basic t-shirt. He hand-dyed them all blue using local ingredients purchased from a woman in the village. He did it in one of the shower stalls and the results were comically bad. The coloring came out blotchy and multi-toned. The natural dyes had not set yet because of the brutal humidity, so his skin was also tinted blue in places. He had a particularly large smear of color across his forehead, where a similarly dyed baseball cap had rested. The hat was gone, and now his wiry long hair was tangled in a big chaotic mess.

"Your day approaches," he began, sitting cross-legged atop a flat stone alter. Marona lit a cigarette. "Let us not mark the ascension of a lesser man. Let us celebrate Your divinity through the denial of the imposters. Show us the way as our numbers grow. The people, they crave miracles, inhabit worlds of fantasy in Your absence. Reveal this larger world. Deny the need for speculation. Help us understand faith's true intention. Reward the ages. Compliment our histories. Make this the world, our world, Your world. The *New* World.

"See how we tumble through expectations, impulsive, riddled with mistaken intention. Crammed into our seat of power, we fly, we drive at, we engage full steam a void. A tower of nothingness. We hurl ourselves at walls. We leap into great darkened caverns. Swing our arms as one deflecting bats. There is no direction for us to travel, so we travel inward, across the shipping lanes of entitlement. We fight for our lives, for what we deserve, and for what You deny us. But tempt us just a little with the fruits of revelation, and watch faith drench Your alters. Watch us wear a path in stone just to be by Your side.

"Let us welcome today the new arrivals, who have come to labor under Your great shadow. There are so many of us, more alive now than have ever died. I am here, with Marona. We will generate the fold, through our labor, for You. All for You. Out there, through these mists, these swirling cold fires, hard roots grip Your temple. You are buried beneath the ashes. The detritus of our spent fires. We see the others, frozen in time. Faces etched in stone. Where are...*You*?

The professor sniffled, a noise Marona had never heard him make. She was pulled from her own reverie. About

164

pretzels. She studied the professor in the darkness. She stood up and walked to him, shifting her cigarette from one hand to the other. "Is everything alright?" He turned to her and she could see just well enough to tell he was a blubbering mess. Blue streaks ran down his cheeks and into the folds of his neck. Her heart broke for him. Such a sad old man, maybe now, at this moment, accepting his failure. She put a hand on his shoulder.

"I knock and I knock and I knock," he said through the snorting and sniffling. He wiped at the tears, spreading more dye from his sleeve. A melting blue gumball. "It's insanity."

"Faith isn't easy."

"It's a trap is what it is. It's a trap for the human mind. It's sick. A sick game to play on a person." Marona rubbed his back, still standing at his side. "You run and you run and suddenly you wake up and you are in the middle of some great open expanse and there's nobody else there, and you have to call out louder, you have to press harder, and you're so completely invested you can't give up, because you think it's all a test. If you just go a little further, you'll get there. And so you go a little further and a little further, and the world starts to fade. Marona," he said, now turning to see her face. "Is it you?"

She laughed, "Is *what* me?"

"Is it through you...is it...God...this sounds mental. Have I gone mental?"

"It's okay."

"You're the only thing...that's come out of this. The only miracle."

"No," she said, "I'm no miracle."

"But you are. You are standing right here in front of me. Why are you here? What other explanation?"

"Professor, I think you need a break."

He stood up and tried to compose himself. He faced Marona and put his hands straight forward, onto her shoulders. "This is madness, I know. I can see that. But there's something out there." He turned from Marona and shouted in a voice that seemed to come from a man thirty years younger. "Behold! Behold the glory! Doubtless we strive!"

She tried to restrain him. She pulled him close to her body, not worried that the blue dye of his outfit would stain her black skirt. "Don't," she said quietly.

"Are these the trials?"

"I don't know."

"What if these are just the trials?"

"I don't know."

"This shit can drive you nuts."

"I know it can."

"It's insidious. I think my faith is stronger now than ever before."

"Why don't we call it a night?"

He was heaving, his head buried in her shoulder. "It's such a dark lonely road."

"It's okay."

The professor sat back on the alter and refolded his legs, as if he was going to continue with his prayers. Marona stood next to him, wanting very badly to return to camp. But she could also feel herself being pulled into this vortex. The trap. The curiosity overwhelmed her. Something *was* happening. There was a force of some sort driving all this, going all the way back to her dream. The one of control. The professor had created something out of nothing. There was passion in it, desire and longing. There was pity and rage. The building blocks...not of life, biologically...but of lives, and faith. Inertia conjured from the abyss. The professor, Marona realized, has been working miracles of his own. She sat at his side and took up the prayer.

"Hello," she began, "I am new here to this place. What I have seen tells me You have done great works. The devotion You inspire in the professor tells me You will once again do great works. We offer ourselves to You here as humble travelers who have stumbled upon Your generous legacy. We know, buried deep in this jungle, is hidden an alter appropriate for Your worship. It is lost, as the faith which sustained You years ago was lost. Now the faith has returned, and so it is the time to reveal to us the tools we need to give You the love You deserve." She looked over at the professor, whose head was bowed low. She couldn't see his face.

She couldn't see the broad mischievous grin.

She couldn't sense the depth of his satisfaction.

She continued on as the words, occasional nonsense, poured out of her. A purging of broken thoughts, deeply cleansing. "Pretzels," she announced, "like mammoth tubes of glacial displacement folded as the post-penitent arms of a stubborn child, in denial of righteousness, as seen here, in the cracked intentions of swindlers and con-artists, chipped salty men who feast on the desperate crumbs locked down in vertical corners, pinching out sustenance, robbing the blind, the mind, the unkind."

"Faith obliterates oblivion."

Not a peep from the monkeys. Marona and the professor traded off until the mists were backlit by the light of the rising sun.

They returned to camp. Hand in hand, they entered the mess tent. The weary eyes of the morning shifters all turned to meet them. The professor's appearance was an instant shock to everyone. His blue outfit, his blue-stained skin, couldn't mask the fact that he appeared many years younger. He seemed alive, optimistic. Relevant. Marona too was smiling. Her beauty now in full display. They seemed happy, these two, as neither had been in a long time. At this hour, such a display was hard to stomach.

Breakfast, for some reason, was roasted chicken. A drunken Heinrich Airhorne joined them at their table.

Thick hardened mud still caked his body, left over from the previous day's field labor. He needs a good hosing down, Marona thought. He and the blue professor both.

They tried to ignore Airhorne by diving head-down into their meals. Both were famished. Marona felt like she'd just run a marathon. Which was weird, this exhaustion. Physically she'd done little more than go up and down a staircase. But really, so much more had happened, all this channeling of energies, the focusing and evaluating. It was big, apparently.

She shook her head as she pushed her fork flat against the plate, snaring rice grains in the fork tines.

"Hell of a day, no?" Airhorne asked, holding a sweating beer bottle against his cheek. "So fucking hot."

"It's five in the morning," Marona said.

"Five in the...*what?*"

"Have you been drinking since the sun went down?"

"And then some!"

At a table in the corner, Marona noticed three heads piled on folded arms. A fortress of spent beer bottles filled every inch of unused space. The slightest twitch from one of the guys would cause a domino effect of broken glass. It was such a perfect passed-out spectacle Marona had trouble believing it wasn't all staged.

"Hello there mister professor. Chu remember me?"

Chicken leg in hand, the professor looked at Airhorne. "Yes, I remember you Heinrich. You still owe me thirteen dollars."

"You were counting cards!"

"We've been through this."

Marona liked the professor's dismissive tone, his display of mental clarity. Airhorne didn't deserve his full attention. To think, just five hours ago she considered the professor maybe too feeble and confounded to be left alone. He seemed so much stronger now, so much *better*, despite the fatigue. She found herself wondering about his true age.

"Didya hear about the residence quadrant dig today... err...yesterday?" Airhorne stammered.

"Yeah, we heard they found stone floors."

"Oh, shit," he laughed. "We found fucking stone floors alright. We looked *under* those motherfuckers."

"I see. *And*?"

"Bodies, dude. A whole fucking family. All bones. Some creepy ass shit. Shouldn't the bones all be gone by now?" Airhorne pulled a granola bar from his shirt pocket and started eating it.

The professor picked up his napkin, wiped his face, and looked hard at Airhorne. "You looked under the stone floors?"

"That's right, my brother."

"And you found remains?"

Airhorne suddenly changed, his focus now completely on Marona. "Hello. My dear. You need *me* in your life."

"Is that so?" she laughed, thinking Airhorne shouldn't drink. His power is gone. Just a little flea now. Impotent. At least the hair is tucked up under his fishing hat.

"Heinrich, focus." The professor snapped fingers in his face.

"I am focused...on her..."

"Hey! Over here. Hello!"

"How's the book, sweetheart?"

"Heinrich!"

"Yes mister professor, jeez. We found lotsa stuff. It was Professor Chin or Chong, I don't know. It was his idea."

"Because there aren't any graveyards," the professor suggested. He turned to Marona. "No graveyards in Copan. No stupas, either. Big mystery."

"That's...what *he* said. Chong. Nice fellow."

"Anything buried with the bodies?"

"Jack and shit, my man."

"How many bodies?"

169

"Six skulls." He turned to Marona. "Freaky shit. *Skulls*, dude. Just buried in the ground. You ever just think about *skulls*?"

She laughed. She decided she actually liked Airhorne when he was drunk. "Not really."

He knocked himself on the head. "Got my own right here."

This was clearly a major discovery, and the professor suddenly looked less like a freak in a blue costume, and more like a pranked Harvard professor. She rarely heard him talk straight-up archeology. She often forgot he once dominated his field.

"Chang says we're going to pull up every floor in the quadrant." Airhorne turned to Marona and whispered, "We're like safe crackers."

"Heinrich, were any of the remains adolescent?"

"Little skulls, yeah dude. Little skulls, big skulls...just fucking *skulls*. Everywhere. Hard core shit. I'm all freaked out that I got some curse or something from moving them all around, like disturbing their peaceful slumber or some shit, right Marona?"

"I doubt you have anything to worry about."

"I don't know. What do you think, professor?"

"Nothing to worry about."

"No," Airhorne said, his voice changing slightly, a strange sinister look in his eye. "Nothing to worry about, hey? Tell me...I shouldn't do this when I've been drinking...stop me, Marona, before I say something I might regret."

"Why would I do that?"

"Ha ha. Professor Lattistrom?"

"Yes."

"Professor Lattistrom from B.C."

"Excuse me?"

"The Smoke Monkey, right?"

"What about him?"

"You tell me."

"Maybe later."

"A great secret, Marona."

"Why don't you get some sleep, Heinrich."

Turning to Marona, in a fake, beer stinking whisper, he said, "He's not from Canada, that one. But he likes to go there. Don't tell anyone, okay?"

"Heinrich, I think you're drunk."

"I'm certain I am. Volunteer's prerogative. Look at all those bottles. They make a killing off of us. We fund the whole fucking project, probably that's what I think. But I'm tired suddenly."

"You want to go rouse your buddies, maybe?"

Airhorne stood up, then bent over and touched his toes. "Mister not from Canada, you lady from Olympus, I say good night!"

He brushed aside the tentflaps just as one of the guys asleep on the other table twitched violently and sent a cascade of beer bottles crashing to the floor.

CHAPTER TWENTY

Oliver Easton was anxious when he entered the lobby of BC Petrol headquarters in Vancouver. Passing the distracted security guard with a salutary nod, he took the elevator to the tenth floor and headed in the direction of CEO Earl Bish's office. He carried his briefcase in such a way as to not betray the fact that it was extremely heavy. He was nervous, emotionally taxed. A successful meeting was essential. Bish *must* come on board. Without Bish, he would have to make his offer to some smaller firm. Or make no offer at all. He had not allowed himself to consider a rejection seriously. He believed in the momentum of it all, and had from the beginning.

He had faith.

And faith's bonus B-side, the absence of doubt. All those lost hours put to better use. His life unrolling before him, like a carpet. But he felt nervous none the less. Nothing was fated. He would not allow himself to take it *that* far. Not yet, at least. Bish was his own man, with his own carpet. And when it came to asking a devout Mormon, father of three, CEO of the very highest public profile, to break domestic and international law, it seemed prudent not to assume Bish was going to jump at the chance to lose everything.

But there *was* money in it for Bish. Heaps of money. And a story. It was on his rollicking tale that Easton hung his hopes. What made BC Petrol special, ideal for his purposes, was the well documented fact that it was run by a living, breathing man. Earl Bish was a public figure, a social moralizer, frequently seen and heard throughout Canada and the United States. A CEO with a human touch, a sense of humor, and an unapologetic devotion to his faith. He was unconventional and philanthropic, trolling for entry-level employees in blood banks and homeless shelters. He was also whimsical and spontaneous, well known for embarrassing himself with karaoke at the Petrol Picnics, for which his company was notorious.

And he would take a meeting with just about anyone who asked.

In the spacious waiting room, the kindly secretary gave Easton a caffeine-free diet soda with a green straw. Then she sat at her desk and resumed applying Liquid Paper to a document.

Unaware, he thought, watching her, of all I have experienced, of the great work I have planned. As your own story is hidden from me. I am an international fugitive, would you have guessed that? I have an alias, and falsified documents. I speak Spanish fluently. I once punched a guy in the face on a boat dock and he flew into the water. *Flew* through the air, do you hear me, lady? When he resurfaced, he shook his head and wiped his face in disbelief. You'd have thought you were watching a movie.

It could really be anything, right? You and me both, lady. It's amazing. Providence. Here's something for you. A gift I could give. In Cambodia, you're not supposed to eat dog. But if you do, it's best with vodka and bananas. There you go. Give me twenty-four hours and a slide projector, and I'll give you a Maya schooling that will stop your heart. This man in your waiting room, this future attendee of the Harvard University Graduate School of Archeology.

Just ask me about God. Please. (But not when I've been drinking.)

I am Oliver Easton, lady.

Yes, *that* Oliver Easton.

Scheming for the good of all mankind.

Oliver Easton of Smoke Monkey.

OE, The Martian.

There were angry voices coming from behind the door. This won't do, he thought. I can't have him in a foul mood. But have faith.

There.

Amazing.

It *does* make it all easier.

Before everything happened, he thought nonbelief was the easy road. It was the religious kooks who really had it rough, managing their hypocrisies. But once you set your wheels on the rails, he discovered, it just became an issue of stamina. No doubt. Not like the atheists had. The *what ifs* could keep a guy up at night. But not Oliver Easton. Not now. He had a plan. A stranger one he could not imagine. And he had the assurance that he would either succeed, or fail in the service of an ideal, which was in fact no failure at all. It was the same nutty logic that drove him crazy when he saw it in others, years ago, before he ever went down to Panama. But people change. Hallelujah.

His fingers danced nervously on his thighs. He imagined this was always the most dangerous part of any screwball scheme, the securing of accomplices. How do you bring up embezzlement with a coworker? How does one sibling talk to another about killing their parents? Once Bish heard the proposal, he might just call the cops. It was possible.

I'm going to have to take the chance, stand there naked.

No. Not naked. Shrouded in faith.

Armored.

God, it was there every single time he needed it.

But he wouldn't need it for this. Easton relaxed. Bish would accept the offer. He had to, as a resource man, a gold and oil man. Sure Bish prayed on Sundays, piety and all that, but he did still have those dollar signs for eyeballs. Once Easton opened that briefcase, every option would be on the table.

He wiped his palms on the sides of his slacks. He sipped the soda waiting for the door to open. What a metaphor, he thought. The door. Was there a stronger one on earth? Right now it's closed. But it will open soon. I will pass through it. I can shut it, slam it, break it down, build it up, turn it to glass, to iron, lock it, unlock—

"Mr. Bish will see you now."

He stood up and walked towards the office, passing a young man on his way out. A very tall young man, in fact, flustered and red-faced. Exceptionally awkward and overdressed...or...I don't know...maybe those aren't even his clothes.

The office was enormous. Fittingly tasteful. A decorative vile of black liquid sat on the otherwise empty oak desk. A small fire burned in a corner furnace. A panorama of windows. This was the building's top floor. Bish stood waiting, hand extended, "Pleased to meet you...mister?"

"Treadwell. Andy Treadwell. Thank you for seeing me."

"So what's this all about?"

"I'll just get right to the point, if that's okay with you," he said, without sitting down.

"I like you already."

"May I?" He gestured with his briefcase to the desktop.

"By all means." Bish was excited. He met men like this all the time. Speculators, swindlers, and con artists. It was one of the highlights of his job. His favorite were the ones who tried to sell him maps with big X's on them. But he had never seen one of them do what Andy Treadwell just did, which was open a briefcase on his desk and dramatically spill solid gold chunks out all over the place and then silently sit back with a big fat grin and light up a cigar.

"Call my wife!" Bish yelled. Then he lowered his voice to an affected maniacal whisper. "Tell her I'll be home late tonight." He giggled. He took up a small nugget, which appeared to have been chipped off some larger piece. In fact, it all looked like it came from something larger. He knew instantly that it was gold of the finest quality and purity. "Where did you..."

The man took in a long drag, and pulled a second cigar from his chest pocket. He twisted it sideways as an offering, then exhaled. Bish accepted it, and the light. He sat back in his chair, puffing the cigar to life. The two men watched each other. Good show, man, Bish thought. Really terrific work.

"Your name's not Treadwell, is it?"

Easton laughed. "No, it's not."

Bish nodded, and then walked over to the door to make sure it was locked. "Let me guess," he said, "you want me to melt it down. Throw it in the smelter like I just pulled it out of the Rocky Mountains." He sat back down. He blew smoke at the ceiling. "And pay you out a cut. A...*healthy* cut."

Easton nodded.

"You can imagine, I'm sure, that a man in my position puts himself at considerable risk by even having this conversation."

Easton nodded again.

Bish continued. "I'm going to need you to take off your clothes, first of all, which I will then put in the furnace you see in the corner. I have some clean sweatpants over there, in that cabinet, and I'll have Sherry bring you in one of the delightful t-shirts left over from last month's Petrol Picnic."

"I understand."

"I will then need to shoot a quick video of you, in which you swear an oath upon the Bible that you are not a member of any law enforcement agency in this country or any other.

"Of course."

"And at that point we can *begin* to have a discussion about the *possibility* of working together."

Really, for Bish, this was the equivalent of somebody just walking up and handing him hundreds of thousands of dollars. Once he eliminated the possibility of this being a sting of some sort, the process of converting this gold into cash was simple. Just throw it in the smelter. Prime work on the Collins Lode. Up in smoke. Indisputable.

He considered this man, who sat silently smoking on the other side of the desk. It was ingenious, in fact, the proposal. Exactly the right thing to do, if you are a man looking to quietly turn a bunch of gold into cash. Sure, he stands to lose half of its value, *my* cut, but at least the process will be neat and tidy. A greedier man would do this differently, on the open market, and probably end up in big trouble. He knew that the heart of the negotiation would be about information, which was far more valuable to Bish than the actual gold.

After all, Bish *had* money. Plenty of money. The fresh currency was this briefcase man, his alias, his life and his story. Worth the risk. Bish would take a relatively small cut in exchange for a full accounting. Starting with the man's real name. Then the history of the gold. Where's it from? How'd you find it? Is anyone else looking for it?

How much of it is there?

A seventeen-year-old Salton Steve, three blocks away, in an elaborately furnished penthouse apartment, adjusted the receiver signal to pick up the full bass in Bish's voice. He raised the volume, unplugged the headphones, rerouted the audio input, and sat on his couch with a cold beer, pleased as punch, as the super top secret conversation taking place in that office played out in optimized sound, all thanks to a state-of-the-art listening device transmitting from the light fixture above Earl Bish's desk.

CHAPTER TWENTY-ONE

"No, sorry, not your fault."

"You don't understand. There's a trend. I keep doing this."

"Sorry, Ted, you're just not that powerful."

"I made her angry, intentionally. She was flustered. She mixed up the chemicals and died."

"Look, the bitch mustard gassed *herself*. You didn't do a thing."

Ted winced at the comment. "That's another part of it. I *didn't* do a thing. I just stood there, like what was happening wasn't real. It's getting crazy, this feeling. Like I'm watching a movie. I'm disassociating."

"Stop it."

"I am, really."

"You're *disassociating*?"

"Yes."

"Do you even know what that means?"

"It means I am disconnected emotionally from the events that are happening in my life."

"*Disconnected emotionally*? And what does *that* mean?"

"It means things feel wrong. My emotional response is inconsistent with the events I'm reacting to."

"*Emotional response*? Jesus. What goes on in college these days? You're overcomplicating everything. You say these things and they don't make any sense. She died and you feel bad. That's it. If it helps for you to feel something strange is happening in your life, fine. That's fine. Something actually is. But you're doing a shit job of explaining it. So either stop trying, or get a deeply emotional and disassociative wet fart on the side of your head."

"You think I'm so naïve."

"You are, trust me."

"You—"

"And ignorant."

Ted stood up and turned to the door. Then he turned back and looked down at Salton Steve. "You're wrong," he said. "Wrong about everything. You think you know who I am."

"I do."

"You think you know what I've been through."

"I do"

"Jesus, listen to yourself. Who would put up with this shit?" He went to the closet and took out two more beers. He handed one down to Salton Steve. "And how can you call her a bitch like that?"

"You saying she wasn't a bitch?"

"That's not the point. She's dead."

"And you're going to grant her some kind of critical asylum because her heart stopped beating? You're sanctifying her. It's disingenuous."

"Big word."

"Yeah, and used in its proper fucking context, Poindexter."

"I'm just trying to be a little sympathetic."

"Bullshit. She was a bitch in life so she gets to be a bitch in death. So there."

"Cold."

"It's a cold world."

"What happened to you, I wonder? Because you're way off on this one. It *is* wrong to talk shit about dead people. I can feel how wrong it is. And I'm allowed to feel guilt about the small roll I played. So you don't need to waste any more time trying to convince me that I'm wrong."

"You *are* wrong."

"You don't have many friends, do you?"

"I'd ask you the same question."

"I have lots of friends."

"In another state. Why don't you call them up right now? Is it that you don't have much to say. Your self-described absurd existence doesn't even warrant a phone call, does it? Do your buddies even know where you are?"

"Yes."

"But that doesn't matter, does it? It's actually shocking how little it matters, isn't it? But what does matter is that you are here with me. That makes me your friend. You have one friend. Same number I do. And unlike you, I actually like my friend."

"There's Travis."

"Who the hell is Travis?"

Ted shrugged.

"Exactly. Now sit down and drink your beer and talk to your friend and accept that this is your life. And if you don't like what your life has become you can get back in your car and keep driving. Because that *always* works, right?"

There was a pond in the center of the valet reception area where a black swan sat on a nest amidst a stand of reeds. She watched Ted as he cut along the water's edge on his way to the back loading dock. He was muttering to himself, opening and closing his eyes, gesticulating and shadowboxing. She fluttered her wings to make sure he saw her.

Ted stopped, looked at the swan, and then looked around to see if anyone else was watching him. He couldn't recall anything about the walk from his dorm room to where he stood at that moment. No tourist faces or landscaping odors or bird noises or shuttle exhaust. He couldn't even remember scouting for Cammie, which he always did when he walked around Valvert, hoping to catch her in non-work clothes, in black spandex jogging pants and a sky blue sweaty sports bra, as the fantasy went.

He did remember Jackie though. And Twin. And Addie Parson. And Salton Steve. He said he knew what Ted had been through, said it with such certainty Ted was scared to push him for specifics.

In college, they called it a Hard Zone. Sitting at a stop light at the bottom of a freeway off-ramp, not remembering even getting on the freeway, merging, reading signs, reacting to other drivers. Now he crouched in front of the swan and fed it grass.

I killed her.

You didn't kill her.

I can't go in there.

Stop it. I'll tell Salton Steve on you.

Fuck him.

He speaks the truth.

Fuck you. I'm just going to feed this bird.

You have like two minutes to get to work.

Fuck work.

You're regressing.

And what does *that* mean?

It means people who feed birds are nuts.

Maybe I'm nuts.

Maybe you're a melodramatic narcissist. You didn't kill Jackie. Like he said, you don't get to put that on your plate.

He tried to pet the swan, but it recoiled its long neck and lifted its wings. "Do you eat flowers?" he asked it.

He looked up and saw two tuxedoed doormen staring at him across the reception lot. They were laughing. He stood up and gave them both the finger.

Okay, I'm good.

Tantrum over?

Yes.

Good. Now get to work.

Right away he noticed all his unpolished silver still sitting on the floor, exactly where he left it. He walked to the back of the kitchen and found Kevin in his office, on the phone. His moustache draped across the mouthpiece like roots over a boulder. Kevin held up his finger. *Give me a second.* He looked troubled, like maybe he'd been there all night. Rather than wait around for him to get off the phone, Ted went back to his little workspace next to the primary dishwashing station.

He studied the site of Jackie's sudden demise. All that remained was an anti-bloodstain on the tiling, a Jackie-shaped gleaming outline of exceptional cleanliness, caused by the powerful corrosives which had pooled around her corpse when the mop bucket overturned.

He really had no memory of the aftermath. Who took control? Who did the CPR? Where did he stand the whole time?

The sleeping kitchen was now a calming vigil of appliances and cookware, many of them saddened by the loss of a dear friend. A copper pot hanging above the expo-line bowed slightly with reverence. Plastic cocktail swords on the service bar aligned at attention. And the dear mop, upside down, a shambles of shock and outrage, backed into the corner like a mental patient.

He returned to the array of silver items scattered across a sheeted square of kitchen floor. He slipped into his pink gloves and set upon the implements with some vague notion of trying to honor Jackie.

Kevin came over to Ted and asked him if he wanted to go down to The Spot and get some breakfast.

They rode down in silence, everything so somber and cold and dead feeling.

This sucks.

Period.

That's it, huh? It just sucks.

And leave it at that.

Damn him.

The elevator door opened. And there she sat, right there, peeling potatoes with comical intensity, her tower-of-Pisa hat down low across her brow.

Alternating currents.

Bingo.

Ted moved instinctively toward her, but a firm hand on his elbow directed him to the far side of the kitchen, to dry storage. He sat on an overturned pickle bucket, waiting. Salton Steve showed up seconds later, with his massive stupid grin, pointing in Cammie's direction and nodding lecherously.

"They're fucked right now," he said, taking a seat on his own pickle bucket.

"What?"

"They just lost both dishwashers down here. Plus the thing with Jackie. Hope you're ready to work. A lot."

"Fine with me," Ted said.

"That's what I say. Bring it on." He laughed. "What else are we going to do around here, right? Hike in one of the four surrounding mountain ranges?"

"No thanks."

"Fly fish in some of the most picturesque locations in all of America?"

"Yeah, count me out."

"Mountain bike through aspen forests, kayak the Bigpine, play golf, tennis, shoot rifles, ride horses?" Kevin was on his way back. Salton Steve continued along, whispering, "float around in hot air balloons, hunt mushrooms, ride the concrete toboggan course, dig for gems, lounge in the hot springs?"

"No, no, and no." Ted said, playing along.

Kevin had three breakfasts and a large mug of coffee. He sat on a pickle bucket and passed the plates. "So here's the deal," he said. "Things are really tight right now. We've lost four employees in the last twenty-four hours, and there aren't a lot of spare bodies around to fill in."

Ted looked at Salton Steve. "Four?"

"Yes, four," Kevin said. He spoke like an officer giving orders. "You guys are going to have to step up. Ted, I'm going to need you to stay down here and wash dishes until we can get some help."

Ted seemed to remember *two* guys usually working The Spot's dishmachine, to handle the volume. "It'll be just me?"

Kevin sucked coffee out of his mustache. "Just you. That's right. Then you take a couple of hours off and come back and work the night shift in the IR kitchen. We'll get you a second uniform, so you don't get too nasty. Salton Steve—" Kevin paused at saying the name aloud, "you're going to help prep upstairs with me in the morning, and then you'll do pots and pans in the IR at night."

"How's overtime work here?" Salton Steve asked.

Good question.

He's smart.

Don't seem too eager.

"Time and a half."

That sounded like decent money. Ted had never worked more than thirty-five hours in a week. Now he would be working eighty or more. Plus, he had free room and board.

I'm about to be stinking rich.

Literally.

"And no more silver polishing?" Ted asked.

185

"We'll have to get someone else."

Ted just nodded. Kevin finished up by telling them that Jackie's death was a very big deal in Valvert, particularly in the minds of the management, owners, and veteran staff. There would be a couple of events in her honor. Kevin also told them that Jackie's main function in the food and beverage department was to make sure everything looked *appropriate* to a resort and restaurant of the highest quality, and that they would all be expected to collectively pick up the slack and mind the details. He praised Ted's earlier initiative in finishing up the silver from the day before without having to be asked to do it. He told them they would basically be doing the work of four people for the next few days and that he was glad that those available to him in this difficult staffing period were at least intelligent, self-motivated, and professional.

They both thanked Kevin for his kind words, though Ted suspected none of them were meant for Salton Steve, who crammed folded bread into his mouth and nodded aggressively.

Once he finished breakfast, Ted took his position behind the cramped quarters of The Spot's dishwashing station. They had not had a dishwasher there all morning. The line cooks did their best to keep things reasonably controlled through the rush, but even still, the scene that confronted Ted was absurd. He gawked at the plates piled cartoonishly high, the sinks clogged with bits of breakfast scraps and pinkish water, the floating toast crusts and plastic jelly lids, the full glass-racks stacked five-high on the ground with juice remains dribbled all over the floor, which was slick as ice in some places and sticky as hot gum in others. Nobody came over to show him the ropes. Nobody welcomed him to his new place of employment. He barely had time to consider the fact that Cammie worked just a few feet away, his new immediate colleague.

He rolled up his sleeves and set his thoughts to the task at hand. He pushed the big green button on the machine, and it groaned to life.

He started by picking up the glass racks and feeding them through one by one. Then he dumped the bucket of soiled silverware onto a flat plastic rack and sent that through once. Alfonso saw him pulling the silverware from the machine and yelled to him, called him Cody, and told him to always run silver through twice. As the machine fumbled through its cycles, Ted heard Alfonso's voice trailing off, "Idaho state law."

In a matter of forty-five minutes Ted had completely resolved the situation. He was even ahead of the game. New trays of debris were devoured and processed lightning quick. The servers and bussers couldn't see who he was, this mysterious whiz-kid, hidden behind the wall of glass racks. They knew him only as two darting hands, grabbing and dumping, spraying and disposing. He even had time to fill a mop bucket, adding nothing stronger than standard dish soap, and clean the floor.

With the lunch rush officially done, Alfonso came over and quietly praised his work, telling Ted there was nothing more important than stepping up when the bosses were down. Then he did something strange. He told Ted to be careful not to appear too good or too enthusiastic.

"What do you mean?" Ted asked.

"You're not looking to get promoted are you? Like to management and all that?"

"No. Not at all." He hadn't even considered that.

"Because they'll promote your ass if they think you're a good worker. They'll make you a manager. Some kind of bullshit manager. Then your life is pretty much over."

"Yeah, but working hard got me this gig, right? This promotion. At least I'm not upstairs polishing silver anymore." Alfonso burst out laughing. Ted got defensive. "What?"

"Did you just call this a *promotion*?"

"I did, yes."

"Are you retarded?"

Why would he ask me that?

"Why?"

"Dishwashing in The Spot might be the worst job in Valvert. You know you're the go-to guy for vomit right?"

"Vomit?"

"That's right. Or a Code Brown. Children eat here. Little children."

"Code Brown?"

"Think about it. You get to do anything the bussers won't do."

"Such as?"

"Anything bathroom related. Think of the worst thing that can happen in a restaurant bathroom."

That's an easy one.

"Turd in a urinal," Ted said with confidence.

"What?"

"I saw that once, in Anchorage. At a diner."

"And who do you supposed fished it out?"

"I don't know."

"You did, buddy. *You* did."

Ted nodded, but Alfonso's attempt to quash his enthusiasm wasn't working. "I still say anything's better than polishing silver." He presented his hands as evidence. Alfonso sucked in a quick breath and jerked his neck to an awkward angle. "They pulsate when I sleep."

"That's wonderful. And by the way, a turd in the urinal doesn't even crack the top ten."

"Give me the top ten."

"I'm not going to...just think vomit, okay. It's *way* worse."

"I disagree."

"We're not having a debate. Just trust me."

"One time at a party someone hit me in the shoulder with a fresh turd."

"What did you do about it?"

"I think I dropped out of college."

Alfonso laughed. "Well at any rate, enjoy your *promotion*." There were finger quotes and snickers. "And think about what I said. Good, but not *too* good. You want to stay in restaurants. You want to meet good people, work in an agreeable atmosphere...not get drug tested, that sort of thing. Stay put. Work hard enough to stay valuable, pick up shifts. But don't go crazy. Not to mention, you working like this makes the rest of us, particularly kitchen managers like myself, look like lazy sacks. My advice is to hit the bong in the AM, and to hit it hard. Take it easy. You're washing dishes, not saving children in burning buildings. Learn to love the chaos, the funk. Look at the bags under the eyes of some of the servers here. The old breakfast ladies. Live in those bags. *Be* those bags, you hear me son?"

"I hear you."

"Now for lunch. Whatever your sick heart desires."

He took his plate of blackened trout to the usual spot in the back of the kitchen. Cammie was there, all alone, eating a bowl of cereal.

Shit. Not now.

It's your big chance.

I'm not prepared. I'm going to make an ass out of myself.

But look at her!

Milk ran down her chin and she smiled up at him, dabbing it with her coat sleeve.

Devastating.

She's embarrassed.

Ted apologized for interrupting her. "No, no," she said. "I'm just back here alone pouring milk all over my face." She used her feet to slide a pickle bucket in Ted's direction. "Please, grab a seat,"

"Ted," he said.

"I knew that, jeez. Bet you don't—"

"Cammie." he said.

Was she kidding?

"It's all so sad around here today isn't it?" she said, speaking in a low, serious voice.

"Because of the thing with Jackie?"

"Were you there?"

"Happened right in front of my face."

"Oh, my lord. What did you do?"

I did nothing. Nothing at all. I just stood there and looked at her and waited for somebody else to act.

Well don't tell her *that*.

"I can't even remember," he said.

"Really? Just kind of a big blur I bet. Same thing happened to me when Nana fell down the porch steps. It was like one minute I was eating a hotdog, and the next minute I was in the ER."

Nana?

"I'm sorry, was she..."

"She died. It was awful."

"I'm sorry."

"It's fine. It was like years ago. So what happened, though, with Jackie? I heard she was yelling and then just grabbed at her heart and fell over."

"Who told you that?"

"I don't know, one of the girls in the dorm. Sherry...or Shelly."

"That's not what happened at all. She wasn't yelling or anything. She just mixed the wrong chemicals in the mop bucket and the fumes stopped her heart."

Cammie suddenly looked like she was going to cry. "That's terrible."

Ted could barely keep himself focused on the conversation.

I want to marry her.

You mean have sex with her.

It's not even that. She's just so *good*. And pure.

And hot.

And straight-forward. Simple and sincere.

And she smells fantastic.

Eating cereal! A whole kitchen of delights, and she has Honey Smacks. And a funny-looking hat.

And long legs.

And a black sock bunched into her shoe.

And tanned ankles.

And stray shoelaces caked in potato gunk. How many instances of unconscious beauty could she cram into twenty four hours? A whole lifetime?

It's *depressing*.

I can't eat my fish.

"You're not hungry?"

"It's...I'm waiting for it to cool down."

"No you're not."

"Huh?"

"You are *not* waiting for it to cool down. That's the most ridiculous thing I've ever heard." She grabbed his plate and held her hand over the fish. "It's cold Ted."

"I'm...waiting for it to...heat back up?"

"You're a weirdo."

"Alfonso thinks I'm retarded."

"I like Alfonso." She gave Ted his plate back.

"Because he said that about me?"

"No, he's just nice. Treats me...well he treats me just like he treats everyone else."

"Is that so unusual?"

"Well, you know, I'm a girl in the kitchen. The only one other than the waitresses, but they're kind of their own thing. He just doesn't make exceptions."

"And you like that?"

"I do. It makes it easier to do my job. I'm going to eat that if you don't."

"Why didn't you get something good? Cereal seems kind of..."

She wasn't kidding. She pounded the last of her cereal milk like it was a shot of whiskey before a bar fight. Then she set her bowl on the floor, grabbed the fish off Ted's plate and savagely tore it in half. "We can't have trout," she said. She stuffed her face.

Wow.

Jesus.

I'm in love.

Suddenly, Cammie moved to wipe her oily fish hands on his pants. Ted jerked away instinctively and tipped over his bucket. He fell onto the damp floor, holding his plate as level as he could. The whole incident made a tremendous commotion, the pickle bucket vibrating like a conga drum, his heavy knife and fork clanging around on his plate.

Cammie looked horrified. "Oh, my gosh, I'm so sorry. I was just pretending. I wasn't going to really..."

"It's fine." He climbed back onto his bucket.

Such an asshole.

Way to make it look like there's nothing more horrifying on earth than the idea of this girl putting her hands on you.

"The bucket just tipped, that's all."

She laughed. "It sure did."

He checked the wet spot on the side of his leg. "Impressed?"

Cammie pretended to fan away the vapors.

Then Ted stuffed the remaining half of the fish into his mouth and held up his own oily fish hands.

"You better not," she said, smiling.

Then Alfonso poked his head around the corner. "None of that, folks. Party's over."

"We were just..." Ted stammered.

"Cammie, I need you to run to cold storage. Berries."

She stood up, smoothed her pants gracefully with the clean backs of her hands, and left without saying goodbye.

"They're going to need you at four upstairs, Ted. You might want to get yourself home, relax, you know, change out of your clothes. Don't blow your big promotion now!" He held his thumb and index finger up to his lips, encouraging Ted to get high before he came back to work. "Oh, and did you get the pots and pans in the back yet?"

"Pots and pans?"

"By the back sink."

"No idea what you're talking about, to be honest."

Alfonso seemed disappointed with himself. "Right, first day down here. In the back there's a second station." He shook his head. "Sorry, I should have said something. You're going to have to get that sorted-out too, before you go."

Ted walked to the very back of the kitchen and immediately understood why they usually kept two dishwashers on in The Spot's kitchen. Every conceivable cooking implement, from a small single egg fryer, to a massive eighty-quart cauldron, lay scattered across the small dump counter and the surrounding floor. The two sinks were overflowing with bacon trays and steamer vessels.

Two hours.

Maybe three.

I'll be lucky to finish before my next shift.

Just think about the money. And Cammie.

There's an iron pot overturned on my head that they keep whanging with a heavy spoon as they turn my body in circles.

Fatigue set in. *Work* fatigue, something he never knew before. Cleaning the pots and pans was almost as bad as polishing silver. The work was awkward and frustrating. He kept splashing nasty water in his mouth, or pinching his fingers between the large pots and metal sink. Plus, he was the only one left in the kitchen. The restaurant shut down from three to five. Someone even turned the lights out and he had to yell, *Hey, I'm still back here!* Some pots had been there for hours and needed to be soaked, then scrubbed, then soaked, then scrubbed. At first the hot water had soothed his hands, but now they felt like wet strips of tenderized flesh. He only had two large cauldrons to go. He was saving them. He wasn't sure why. His shift upstairs started in twenty minutes.

I'm a soggy mess.

What's the plan?

He looked down at the two cauldrons, oatmeal on the left, grits on the right. He got down on his knees.

We thank thee father for this hot cereal.

Then he dramatically thrust his hands deep down into the mixtures.

A hot gasp of erotic pleasure.

Oh, *wow*.

Warmth.

Creaminess.

Soothing satisfaction.

Vaginas.

Elbow-deep.

He closed his eyes. Naked women on clouds, flying, soaring with seabirds over rocky headlands. Peace. Silence. Calming succor.

He pulled his arms out and opened his eyes. The world again. Grounded. Cold and vivid. He ran to dry storage and got a black plastic trash bag. He held it open as he poured in the remainder of the mixtures. He picked up the bag to test the weight. Ten pounds or more. He set the bag down and tied it off. Then he frantically began scrubbing the pots clean. A burn ring half-way up each pot simply wouldn't come off. He set them to soaking and looked at the clock. Ten minutes. He slung the bag over his shoulder, ran through the kitchen, hit the lights, and slunk out the back door like a cat-burglar escaping with the goods.

He tore-ass through the village, practically knocking kids off the narrow paths. Nesting black birds, sensing a threat, dive-bombed at his head as he ran the gauntlet. Five minutes. In his dorm room. Luc gone. Perfect. He slung the bag into his side of the closet and threw a shirt on top of it. Then he ran back out of the dorm, back through the village, and back into the lodge, all the while trailing a chorus of wet shoe farts.

He walked down the ramp with one minute to spare, panting and smiling. Kevin took one look at him and called in his emergency requisition. Ted was sent over to Uniforms for a second fitting and told to be back in an hour.

CHAPTER TWENTY-TWO

They met two more times that week, circling each other like boxers at the start of a fight, each trying to glean what he could about the other's deeper motives. On the surface there was the gold, and good old-fashioned human greed. And if that was the whole story, then the transaction could be quick and simple. But Bish was more interested in the mystery of the man than the money. And Easton needed Bish to do more for him than just write a check. For both men, it came down to trust, something tough to establish between two strangers conspiring to break the law.

Or *laws*. Bish guessed there had been some theft, and smuggling, and various customs and border violations. And Easton, little as he knew about mining regulations, assumed governing bodies required detailed documentation of all mineral extractions, and their subsequent transformations and output value.

Not to mention tax evasion, times two.

Clearly, there was more at stake for Bish, who was a public figure at the head of an enormous corporation. But Easton was gambling as well. Bish could simply take the gold and melt it down. What claim did Easton actually have? What recourse to the law, in a country he entered illegally with contraband?

But that wasn't going to happen, Easton was certain.

And Bish's initial read on Easton told him it was safe to move forward, even though the guy had lied about his name right out of the gate. But that was understandable. It was preferable, in fact. It deepened the mystery, expanded the level of intrigue. Such people were risky to deal with, but they were also a lot more interesting.

What worried Easton most about Bish was his professional eye, and his well-honed ability to judge character. How else does a person achieve that level of success? Which meant he would be probing, and suspicious, and difficult to deceive.

Their second meeting took place two days after Easton first walked into Bish's office. Bish took him for a hike on a popular trail just outside town. The unexpressed purpose of the outing was to give each man a chance to poke and prod a little, to try and round-out the picture. So they talked about family. Easton said he was orphaned at a young age, and had no children or siblings. Bish, a dutiful Mormon, was the father of three, and grandfather to eleven. Easton already knew this from his research.

"It's a sad thing for a man to be without family," Bish said. "My family gives meaning to my life far beyond anything."

"Beyond the church?" Easton asked.

"They're the same thing. It's all connected."

"And where does this massive company you've created come into the picture?"

"Well, it provides wealth for sure. And that provides comfort and security. And I love the human side of what I do. I like this." He gestured to Easton, the surrounding aspen forest, and the view of the blue Pacific in the distance. "You know, *this* is business. Meeting people. Hearing stories. Collaborating."

"I was surprised how easy it was to get a meeting with you."

"I've always had an open door. And look at the opportunity it brought me."

"Well, I'm grateful," Easton said. "I mean, on a personal level, you can help me become a very wealthy man."

"But no one to share that wealth with."

"It's okay. I'm young still. I've benefited from a certain amount of freedom in my life. I've done the kinds of things a family man just can't do."

"I can't imagine."

"I was a pilot on the Panama Canal, you know. I used to take giant tankers through the locks. I've been everywhere."

They sat on a bench. Bish expressed a wistful desire to travel as well. He said his company kept him too busy to really get away. "A week in Hawaii here and there, but nothing crazy. No open-ended adventures."

They sat quiet for a moment, both happy, relaxed and pensive. Easton had not counted on liking Bish so much. He had considered him just a pawn in the overall picture. But as they sat there getting to know one another, Easton began to reconsider some aspects of his plan.

What if I had help? he wondered. A collaborator, or at least a confidant? He thought about how that might change things. There were not many people on earth with Bish's knowledge and experience. And there were complex logistical issues on the road ahead, unforeseen hurdles and pitfalls. I could really use a man like Bish.

He decided to test the waters. "Can I call you Earl?"

"Of course."

"I want to be honest with you, Earl. My name is Oliver Easton. It's my real name." Bish nodded. "There's a much larger story to this gold. Nobody else knows this story. And I want to tell it to you, but I'm afraid to."

Clearly, Bish was greedy for the information, and Easton detected a touch of madness in the man's wide grin.

198

"I want to hear your story." Bish said. He wiped his palms on his thighs. "I'm dying to hear your story, to be honest. And I understand your apprehension. I understand just how important the issue of trust is."

"There are secrets you would have to keep for the rest of your life. I don't know if anyone is capable of doing that. I mean, no offense, but you have a wife."

"None taken."

They laughed. "Men tell their wives everything."

"You've obviously never been married."

They laughed again. "I'll tell you what," Bish said. "I'm willing to bet that gold you brought into my office was not legally obtained. I'm not saying you're a criminal. I'm just saying that once we start working together, your secrets become my secrets. Your crimes become my crimes, see?"

"I guess I don't understand why you'd take that risk."

"Because I'm pretty good at covering my ass. It's nice when what you do for a living is essentially throw stuff into an eleven-hundred degree smelter. The story, the secret, the origins of the gold, that all dies the second it hits the heat. And consider this, do you know how many private Canadian citizens contribute more income tax dollars to the general coffers than I do?"

Easton threw up his hands and guessed. "None?"

"That's right. None. Plus there are political contributions. Philanthropy. Nobody's looking at me, you know?" Easton nodded. "Just remember," Bish continued, "whatever secrecy you need from me, I also need from you."

"I understand," Easton said. He thought hard about it. He pushed dirt into little piles with his feet. It would feel so good to just tell somebody. The whole story. And he would be doing Bish a favor. The guy seemed ravenous for information. He smiled at Bish.

"You're killing me, Oliver."

"Okay." He took a deep breath.

199

Salton Steve, in dark sunglasses and an old cowboy hat waited on the trail just beyond the two men. He pretended to study the city below through a pair of binoculars. He couldn't hear a word the two men were saying to one another. He took off his hat and glasses and strolled down the path.

"Hey," Bish called to him.

Salton Steve stopped and looked at his boss. "Mr. Bish. Hey. What brings you...uh?"

"Business meeting." He looked over at Easton. "This is Mr...Underhill. Terry, this is Salton Steve, a remarkable kid. He's been with us for three years now. Remarkable abilities."

"Nice to meet you," Easton said, shaking the boy's hand.

"I can see my house from here," Salton Steve said.

"That's good."

There was an awkward pause. "Well you all, um, have a nice day." They all said their goodbyes. Then Salton Steve skipped off down the trail.

Bish immediately turned to Easton. "That kid's psychic."

"What do you mean?"

"He's like a human divining rod. It's unbelievable. You send him up in a helicopter and he can see subterranean resource deposits. Oil and gold. Whatever. It's actually a bit creepy. I can't tell you how much money he's made me. And he's a pretty rich little shit himself. When I first met him he was the most socially awkward human being on the planet. He's made some strides though. But it's guys like him. Guys like you, with your suitcases full of gold, that make this all worthwhile to me. Now are you going to tell me this story or am I going to have to beat it out of you?"

CHAPTER TWENTY-THREE

At first, a slow trickle of dishes in the IR kitchen. Everything pleasant and calm. Everyone focused and competent. Ted was happy to be back on his home turf, away from the chaos one-floor below. Here at dinner, they would be preparing and serving expensive meals to leisurely diners, no time crunch or turn-over to deal with. Easier work, and less of it. And Ted was pulling in time and a half.

Plus, his new uniform gleamed spotless and dry. Almost like not being at work at all. He studied the deliberate professionalism all around him. Luc drizzled golden raisins on a salad of Boston lettuce, his whole fat body bent over the plate, his face attentive to the final resting place of each individual ingredient. Kevin, at the grill, pushed his thumb into a lightly seasoned ribeye. Just next to him, Bruce stood at the sauté station, adding a flair of sherry to a floating pan of veggies, the whole scene awash in flames. Nick the fryer massaged cut calamari circles in a bath of buttermilk. On Ted's side of the line, the expediter passed plates to tuxedoed food runners, and the service bartender shook castanets of gin and ice. Ted watched a server stab a cocktail onion with a plastic sword, his tongue tip poking from the side of his mouth.

And Salton Steve over there at the pots and pans station, a ridiculous man, right? Six and a half feet tall, though he couldn't have weighed more than a hundred and fifty pounds. His hair a tangle of tight receding curls. Big thick glasses. Total absurdity. His hammed-up work personality was so different than what Ted saw of him in more private situations, his transparent enthusiasm for his boss and co-workers, with his golly-gee handshake at the beginning and end of every shift, moving his arm way up and down, the way salesmen in cartoons shake on deals.

And he was a terrible dishwasher. He worked slowly and methodically, with an expression of intense concentration. His industrial steel sink overflowed with bubbles. Sleeves rolled up as he bit down softly on his lower lip. Then from the towering white foam, he pulled out the object of his focus, some sauté pan. He gazed upon it with true pride. He dunked it in the rinse sink, to free it of bubbles, then gazed at it some more. Ted watched this from across the room. Disbelief in Salton Steve's eyes, that something could be so perfect. Pure delight, as he held the pan up to the overhead lights.

Clean, the very definition of the word!

But not even close.

Ted could see it from where he was standing, the caked-on sauce residue, the egg still clinging to the rim, the oil smudges on the handle. He watched Salton Steve set the pan on the drying counter and turn his focus to the next item. He watched Bruce catch the first gust of a coming storm. Deeply weeded by a sudden onslaught of appetizer tickets, he unconsciously grabbed the sauté pan from the drying counter, his true focus miles away. He gave it a quick glance, and ran a rag around the inside to clean out all the stuff Salton Steve had missed.

The kitchen swelled to life. They had a full-house that night, the first real test of the season. The energy level rose, metered and controlled. Waiters, bussers, chefs, expediters, service bartenders, dishwashers, everyone going hard. Everywhere, people actually enjoying themselves, fully engaged in their life's work, in the act of creation.

Downstairs, Ted had noticed, The Spot's workers behaved like a company of conscripts reluctantly called to battle. Here, in the IR kitchen, the crew acted more like idle Marines finally given the order to charge. Yelling, laughing, joking. Pans crashing to the ground. Broken plates. Broken bottles.

"Fire twenty-five!"

"Refire twelve ounce! Need it rare!"

"Baked potato yesterday!"

"Mop! We need someone with a mop by the hostess stand!"

"Can someone *please* clear this shit out!"

I love this. I love the powerful whoosh of water that kicks in every time I feed a tray of dishes or a rack of glasses into the machine. I love the savage gurgle of the industrial-grade disposal and the warm comfort of the overhead sprayhose slung over my shoulders like a python. I love my technique, my process, my success.

And when there was a lull, that five or ten seconds when he could breathe, Ted would look over at Salton Steve, and catch the expression of a boy in a field of clover, watching butterflies flutter under a blue summer sky. Smiling, giggling to himself. Bubbles everywhere. Slow motion. Bubbles on the tip of his nose. Soaking wet. Just scrubbing and scrubbing and cleaning nothing.

But Salton Steve was tolerated in the kitchen, despite his ineptitude, for the simple fact that he gave the servers hell. The kitchen staff hated the serving staff, who held a lot more power in the organization than any of the chefs did, based on the fact that many had worked in the IR for ten to twenty years. The servers were mostly local boys, while the kitchen staff, except for Kevin, were all imports from the corners of the world, few lasting more than a handful of seasons.

The source of the animosity, not surprisingly, was money. Ted had heard all about it. Chefs considered themselves artists. Many in the IR kitchen had formal training at renowned institutes overseas, and were still making payments on hefty student loans. But they made on average one-third what the servers pulled down on a typical night shift. Servers had no formal training, no specific talent as the kitchen staff saw it, other than knowing how to smile, kiss ass, and carry trays, which really food runners did most of the time anyway. It was brutally unfair. They never tipped-out the kitchen staff either. A steak with a sixty-dollar price tag, which Kevin ordered from the distributor, received at the loading dock, stored in the walk-in, seasoned on the line, cooked on the grill, and plated to perfection, would put twelve dollars in the pocket of the server who simply wrote down the order and put up the ticket. That twelve dollars amounting roughly to Kevin's entire hourly wage. And Kevin made a lot more than the other cooks. Luc told Ted he only made eight-fifty an hour, slightly more than dishwashers made, and he held a degree from the Cordon Bleu, had learned pastry prep from Jacques Pépin himself!

It should have been the other way around, the cooks argued. The people *making* the food should get the tip, right? Not the people who wrote down the order. Which was more important? Why did people really go to restaurants? For the food or the service? Certainly service was important, and there was an art to doing it well. But still. How about at least fifty-fifty on the tips? It made no sense. Not to mention, servers had no prep-work, and very little side-work. Maybe fold some napkins, refill the salt and pepper shakers. Kitchen staff came early and left late, had to worry about food temperatures, cleanliness, and health codes. A million little things that really mattered.

And the worst insult of all, worse than anything, was the way any mistake the servers made could easily be blamed on the kitchen. Put down medium instead of medium-rare. The steak comes out over-cooked. Well, I'm sorry, the kitchen is very busy. Sometimes *they* make mistakes. *They*! Let me go have them fix that for you. You wanted to punch them right in the face, Bruce had told Ted. Half the time the kitchen had to remake the order, which affected Kevin's bottom line, which in turn affected everything from staffing funds to Christmas bonuses. And again, the servers were not impacted at all. Sometimes customers even praised them for deftly rectifying their own mistakes!

And what could a kitchen worker do about it? Slow down food preparation? Make an intentional mistake? Of course not. That would all come back on Kevin's shoulders. It was a situation of such maddening paralysis that most people Ted talked to just shook their heads and told him they didn't want to talk about it.

Also unwise, Ted discovered, was asking the cooks how they felt about preparing the servers their post-shift meal, dealing with that sense of entitlement in their voices when they made special requests. The Chicken Caesar, but blacken the chicken and give me some of those tortilla straws instead of croutons. And put it on a plate, not in a bowl, and stick the lettuce in the freezer while the chicken's cooking, would you? And can I get a side of asparagus heads? Blanched if you don't mind. With some of that fresh béarnaise. And you got a banana you can flambé back there? No whipped cream, thanks. Wads of twenties bulging in their pockets.

And what, Ted asked, did the servers do with all that money, over a hundred grand a year? Bruce told him they skied and fucked and snorted cocaine.

There were about six of them, nearly identical. Each in his mid-forties, hair dyed a blondish red, fairly long and parted to a big sweep of bang that magically stayed put just above the eyes. They were all handsome men, well-built and tanned, exceptionally vain and cocky. They were loud, crude, and condescending. If they needed something from the kitchen staff, they ask for it parenthetically, while they carried on a conversation about whose wife they'd had sex with the night before. Ted took offense to the way they slid trays of dishes and glasses onto the dump counter at his station, without even a glance to see who was back there on the receiving end. And he knew that the servers were supposed to break down their trays, rack their glasses, and separate the silverware and linen, which they never did. None of this was right. None of it was fair. And there was apparently nothing anyone could do about it.

Until Salton Steve showed up.

He was their only defense. A true secret weapon. The kitchen staff would never make as much money as the servers, but now they had a way to get their revenge without compromising the quality of food or the good name of the restaurant. Nobody asked him to do it. How could they? He had simply assessed the situation and figured out a way to make himself valuable without having to break a sweat. Ted thought the whole scheme was ingenious. The minute things got moving for the dinner shift, Salton Steve transformed himself into a clumsy half-wit. With his slapstick lunacy and his feigned obliviousness, he burst into the lives of these servers like a crazed visitor from another dimension. Ted watched it all from the primary dishwashing station.

It started with introductions. The instant a server entered the kitchen for the first time that shift, Salton Steve made a point to shut off his water, set down his pot or pan, partially dry his hands on a dirty wet rag, and walk over to the guy with his arm extended. The server would generally wave or possibly bump knuckles, immediately becoming awkward and defensive. Then Salton Steve would fumble with the guy's name, like it was his personal quest to remember everyone.

"Craig!"

"It's Carl."

"Carl, right. Carl. Tall Carl. Tall Carl."

"Sure."

"I'm gonna remember this!"

"Okay."

"So you ready to make some money tonight?"

"Uh, yeah, I guess...look I have to..."

"Gonna be busy? Do you think?"

Doug came in.

"Danny boy!"

"It's Doug."

"Right Doug. Doug on a rug. Doug on a rug."

"What the—"

"Work work work, we never get a break do we?"

"Look out, I need—"

Salton Steve moved his hand up and down like a man at an old-fashioned cash register. "Cha-ching, cha-ching, right buddy?"

Always slightly in the way, tall and imposing, but friendly, sort of harmless, not the kind of guy you could just yell at for no reason.

"Carl!"

"That's right, you just—"

"But I got it right!"

"Yes, you—"

"High-five, buddy, knock 'em dead out there. Make some mo-nay!"

When Carl turned to Kevin for an explanation, Kevin just shrugged. What do you expect for seven dollars an hour?

As the shift wore on, Salton Steve found ways of needling himself into each server, just enough to make things weird and unpleasant, to establish a presence every time they set foot in the kitchen, a presence they could not control, a presence unburdened by any real responsibility. He was like a sadistic grocery-store bagger who asks fifteen times how your day is going.

Anytime a server hesitated for even a second, with a heavy tray, or a confusing order, Salton Steve was there to offer unwanted assistance, his whole uniform sopping wet from dish duty. He would stand a little too close, talk a little too loud. And he usually had a nasty chewed up straw sticking out of his mouth.

Carl counted orders of shrimp cocktail on a tray, comparing them to what he wrote on a small pad of paper.

"Do you need some—"

"No! I'm fine. I just need—"

"Anything at all Collin, really, don't hesit—"

"Please! Just...can you just—"

"There are six shrimp cocktails."

"I know...I'm fine...I'm trying to think!" The twisted, bitten straw made a sneaking foray into Carl's personal space as Salton Steve denied the man the ten seconds peace required to just gather himself together and prioritize the needs of his tables.

A small sink was set up near Ted's dishwashing station where servers could wash and dry their hands. Ted watched Salton Steve come over to the sink, take the soap and drying-rag over to his dishwashing station. He pumped a couple of squirts of the soap into his soak sink, and put the rag across his shoulder. He didn't look Ted's way when he did this, didn't wink or anything. He had a vast array of potent cleaners on the rack just by his side. What could he possibly need the hand soap for?

Ted had a front row seat. Seth, a particularly nasty server, set two plates on the counter (without putting the silverware in the appropriate container) and looked at the side of his hand, which had a streak of brown sauce on it.

No problem, I'll just head over to the sink and...where's the fucking soap. Does that asshole...

Ted watched him glare over at Salton Steve, who had calculated the moment to appear lost in the joys of his labor. It was hysterical, the look of private rage on Seth's face, the indignity of this escaped mental patient getting his goat. Salton Steve's little gift. Just to brighten up the day. It was amazing. Such disproportionate anger. *I'm going to fucking kill that stupid motherfucker who keeps taking the damn soap!* Ted could read it all in his eyes.

So at that point Seth had two choices. Either let his hands stay dirty, which was unacceptable, or march over to Salton Steve's station and take back the soap, which would mean addressing the freak and subjecting himself to some kind of inane conversation. It was brilliant. Ingenious! Just take the soap. Business was not affected. Neither was quality, performance, or any other tangible marker. But psychologically, it devastated Seth, who treated people like shit and deserved everything he got. Salton Steve might very well have the power to ruin this guy's *entire* day! When he got to Salton Steve he had completely lost his composure. Salton Steve, bubbles on his face, saw him coming. "Hey, Sean, how's it—"

"You can't keep fucking taking the soap!"

"Whoa, buddy. How about you step back and count to three?"

"I'm fucking serious! And I'm not your buddy!"

"Here," Salton Steve held up the dispenser and offered to pump a few squirts into Seth's palm, like you might do for a three year-old.

"Give me that!" He grabbed the soap dispenser and marched back to the sink, yelling over his shoulder, "You can't keep taking the fucking soap! It stays over here! You have your own soap. This one stays *here!*" He slammed it down on the side of the sink. "Got it?"

It was almost embarrassing to watch. He knew he'd made a fool of himself and that every member of the kitchen staff delighted in his degradation. Ted had never witnessed such skillful manipulation.

I'm glad he's on my side.

You're sure he is?

At least in here, yeah.

Salton Steve held up his hands like he was being robbed. "Just doing my job, Sean."

"It's fucking Seth! My name is *Seth*!"

CHAPTER TWENTY-FOUR

When the professor became sick in the mess tent, and violently vomited his empanadas onto the floor next to his dining table, just about everyone looked to Marona to do something about it, to help him to his feet and get a napkin to sop up the gunk from his beard. She was still in line when it happened, waiting to add a glass of tamarind juice to her tray. She rushed to the professor, who sat staring straight ahead, a worried look on his face, anticipating a second wave of nausea. She took a seat next to him, on the clean side of the table, and spoke quietly, reassuring him, asking if he needed anything. Water? Fresh air? More empanadas?

She seemed genuinely concerned about him, which disappointed the others in the room, who hoped the situation might expose Marona's true character. They wanted to see her abandon this dear friend in his hour of need, and thus reveal what they all assumed, that Marona was using the professor. Not that anyone could fathom why she would use him. But the alternative, that she just liked him, and enjoyed his company, was absurd. Nobody liked him or enjoyed his company.

It was possible, the others supposed, that Marona had bound herself to the professor simply to limit the amount of actual labor she had to do. But then again, volunteer excavation was nothing *but* labor, and if she had no interest in that type of work, why come all the way down to Copan in the first place?

She certainly didn't deserve it, this lack of trust. She had been nothing but friendly to everyone. Even still, some felt The Marona Enigma had run its course. At first, they had thanked God for her, a bone fide object of beauty, whose inappropriate attention to high fashion, in the muddy wet reality of the excavation site, fueled endless daydreams amidst the monotony of scraping limestone and hauling wet dirt. Who among them had not taken a private moment to marvel at her sleek skirts, her short shorts, her black boots, or her tight fitting tank tops rimmed with perspiration?

But by now, they all realized that the infatuations would never lead anywhere. Which just made her a tease. And that was obnoxious, to go down to some remote jungle camp and prance around in front of a bunch of sex-starved history nerds. Was she that desperate for attention?

It was more fun to imagine that she had made some sort of deal with the devil, and now the devil was throwing up on the floor. But instead of turning tail, as they all expected she would, the bitch acted like a saint, smoothing Lattistrom's greasy hair, bringing cups of water to his lips, and consoling him.

She got him to his feet, struggling to support his weight. She looked around for assistance. Nobody offered any. She rolled her eyes at the room and nodded. As the couple made their way to the door of the tent, it could not be missed, the orange vomit stain on the side of her black skirt, which was otherwise immaculate, and clung to her hips, damp in the soft humidity.

They were left with their pettiness, their cold dinners, a puddle of puke chunks, and the reinforced notion that they would always be baffled by the behavior of beautiful women.

CHAPTER TWENTY-FIVE

At the end of the night they were the last two left in the kitchen. Ted swept the floor and Salton Steve followed him with a wet mop.

"Beer?" he asked Ted, "and carrots?" The goofball character had departed, and Salton Steve was back to his abnormal old self.

"Yeah," Ted said. "I'm all jacked-up for some reason."

And rich. He made good money that day, maybe the most he had ever made in a single day.

Couple of beers.

Then zonk out.

Then do it all over again tomorrow.

And the next day.

And the next day.

Cha-ching!

"You bring the carrots."

"I don't have any carrots," Ted said.

"Then fuck the carrots!" Salton Steve yelled at the empty kitchen, throwing his mop violently against the ice maker. It clattered to the ground, which started him into a deep belly laugh that eventually turned into violent hacking.

I'm glad he's on our side.

They split up at the liquor store. Ted went up to his room quickly and changed into clean clothes. Luc was gone. He saw the bag of grits and oatmeal in the corner of his closet. More than anything, it reminded him of just how long a day it had been.

When he got to Salton Steve's room, he found him sitting on the floor with a twelve pack at his feet, still wearing his wet uniform and trying to get a station to come in clear on a little radio. Ted immediately regretted coming over. Exhaustion had caught up with him.

My bed is calling me.

It's not your bed that's calling. It's those oatmeal and grits.

"So what the hell went on in there tonight, messing with all the servers?" Ted asked, taking a seat on the ground and cracking a beer.

"We can talk about work," Salton Steve said, "if you want." He took a big slug from his beer.

Yeah, why would we talk about work?

To prevent him from psychoanalyzing you.

"It's like the golden rule, right?" Ted asked.

"What is?"

"Don't talk about work after work."

"It's a good rule, but it's not the golden rule."

"What's the golden rule?"

"Don't get into sexual relationships with co-workers."

Ted scooted a few inches away, but Salton Steve missed the joke. He continued to fiddle with the antennae, and Ted could sense irrational frustrations building.

He's exhausted too.

You should really just leave.

"Do not," Salton Steve said firmly, without looking at Ted, "*ever* drink beer and eat carbohydrates and fats at the same time."

"Okay."

I'm not sure I can handle him tonight.

Finish your beer and let's—

Suddenly, Salton Steve slammed his fist down hard on the radio, but the fuzzy signal didn't improve. "You metabolize the beer *first*! And then everything else just rots in your gut."

"What are you—"

"Do you know this, Ted?"

"What are we talking about?"

"Nutrition, Ted."

"Nutrition?"

Oh Lord.

Salton Steve finished his beer in one long drink and had another one ready. He tossed his empty can into the corner of the room and opened the next one. "Do you know this, Ted?" he asked again.

"I'm tired, man, to be honest."

"You must learn this now, while you are young, so you do not become *fat*." He spoke with a slight accent, overly enunciating each syllable.

"Okay."

It's not charming.

It's not funny.

Salton Steve picked up the radio and threw it at the wall on the far side of the room. "Nutrition!" he hollered.

Ted finished his own beer and stood up. "I have to go. I just...I can't. Not right now."

"Please sit down. I just don't want you to forget, Ted, about the—"

"Yes, the carbohydrates and the fats. I won't forget."

"Good."

"But it's weird, right? What you're doing. Yelling about nutrition. Can I just get you to admit that?"

"It's important, Ted."

"So, no? This is the bottom line for you? No real answers to questions?"

"Ask me a question."

"Why are you lecturing me about nutrition?"

"Ask me a real question."

"Okay, what are you doing in Valvert?"

"Why am I here?"

"Yes."

"Well, I came to get some time alone, to write."

"You're an author?"

"I write children's books," he said.

Ted nose-gasped and shot snot down onto his clean shirt. "Bullshit."

"No, I do. But it's tough going. This kitchen work is just a side gig to make some extra dough."

"What have you written?"

Salton Steve stood up and walked to the closet. He came back with a short stack of paper held together with a thick black binder clip. He threw it onto Ted's lap.

Ted read the cover page. "Even Airplanes Have Assholes."

"It's true."

"You're insane."

"You could read it and give me notes."

Ted set the papers aside and looked up at Salton Steve, who towered high above him. "Bullshit," he said.

Salton Steve smiled and sat down. "Unsatisfied with my response?"

"Unsatisfied, yes. But not unamused."

"Okay, well how about I'm here washing dishes because Valvert is one of the few places that hire ex-cons," he said.

"You were in jail?"

"Just got out."

"For what?"

He took a deep breath and grabbed another beer. Then he gave Ted a nasty look.

Is this some taboo, asking ex-cons about their crimes? It's like asking a war vet how many kills he has.

"Marijuana possession," Salton Steve said finally.

"Oh," Ted said. "You went to jail for that?"

"It was eighteen pounds. And it was Texas."

"I see."

"I did three years."

"Jesus. Were you coming up from Mexico?"

"Kansas."

"How'd you end up with eighteen pounds of marijuana in Kansas?"

"I picked it along the Freedom River. It's everywhere in Kansas. Which is a big, badly kept secret. You just have to know where to look for it."

"I had no idea. Three years still sounds like a lot of time, even in Texas."

Salton Steve smiled. "Well, the Feds got involved."

"The *Feds*? Like the Federales?"

"Come on, Ted, the *Feds*, like the Federal Government, the FBI. You heard of them?"

"Yes I've heard of them. Why you?"

"I'm on a watch list. I have a special designation."

"And what's that?"

"I can find or make drugs out of anything, anywhere."

"That's your designation?"

"Yeah, there's nobody else like me. I'm...well known."

"Bullshit."

He became serious. "Bullshit?"

"Sounds like bullshit."

"Do you know there are three agents in Valvert right now watching me? I was dosed my first night in town. LSD in my beer."

Well that's disappointing.

He's just a garden variety kook.

"Why would the Feds dose you with acid? That doesn't make any sense. They carry around acid?"

"You don't believe me?"

"Not really."

218

"I've also had notebooks stolen from me by men in black suits. I was doing research at the University of Texas in Austin."

"Men in black?"

"They also poison pages of certain texts."

"I'm not following. What texts?"

"It was years ago. I was trying to learn how to synthesize heroin. It's all in chemistry textbooks. But they put this invisible substance on certain pages. You get it on your fingers and it makes you violently ill."

"Sounds like more bullshit. Sorry."

He looked at Ted intently. "You love that word, *bullshit*, don't you? And I love a skeptic," he said.

Ted shook his head and smiled. "But listen to yourself. Can you blame me? Do you even realize that you're that guy? Salton Steve is that guy, that crazy guy who thinks everyone is out to get him. But really you're just a dishwasher in Idaho and, no offense, nobody gives two shits what you're up to."

"You don't know what you're talking about, little man."

"You're delusional." Ted said. "You're trying to compensate for your own insignificance."

"There's that college kid. I love it. You're right at that age, aren't you? It's a perfect age. You're so naïve, yet you believe so strongly in your powers of observation. You're about six months away from climbing back into that hole where you belong."

Ted took a long drink from his beer. "You say with a straight face that federal agents put LSD into a beer you were drinking. That doesn't happen."

"How do you know?"

"I just know."

"It's beautiful, and revolting. And kind of *cute*. You actually think you know something."

"I *do* know something. Not much. But I know you're full of shit."

"I didn't want to have to do this, but someone needs to set you straight."

"Give me a break. You should hear yourself."

"You're a little child, and it's time for you to go to school."

They both cracked new beers. It had become a sort of stand-off.

At least this is interesting, right?

Just be careful.

"So I'll give you a choice," Salton Steve said, very proud of himself all of a sudden. "Which part of my story would you like me to prove?"

"I'm not driving to Texas."

Salton Steve laughed. "Are you even old enough to have a license?"

"Fuck you."

"Am I contributing to the delinquency of a minor? Because you seem a little tipsy all of a sudden."

"Yeah, someone should call in the *Feds*."

Salton Steve snickered. "Ok, we'll do it this way then. Analgesic, amphetamine, opiate, or hallucinogen?"

"What?"

"Just pick one."

"I don't care."

Salton Steve stood up. "Wait here." He started for the door and then froze. He put his hand to his forehead. "Hang on." He walked over to his closet. "I have something for you. Because I like you. Because I'm invested in you."

Invested in me?

Run for the hills.

When Salton Steve turned around he held a small golden idol in his hand.

What the fuck?

Sprint for the hills.

"Where did you get that?"

"Don't worry about it."

"No, I've seen something like it before. What the hell's going on?"

"I doubt that very much. This is an authentic artifact."

He handed it to Ted. It was heavy, as he expected it would be. "You need this. You need the wisdom it will provide. Put it in your room. But don't leave it lying around in the open. It's very valuable. It will help you."

Smoke Monkey.

From San Diego.

Smoke Monkey International.

And?

And what? I don't know. I don't know what to think.

Who is this guy?

Salton Steve disappeared out the door. Ted sat there transfixed, staring at the golden idol. And the golden idol stared back at him.

Twin.

You no good for work.

Twenty minutes later, Ted was looking at the flattened radio box, which was now an improvised laboratory table. A small purple caterpillar was trapped under a glass. Next to that was a bouquet of flowers, some with thick stalks and small purple petals, others with narrow stalks topped with closed yellow pods. Next to the flowers, not surprisingly, were two small mushrooms, their stems caked in brown dirt. Salton Steve smiled down at the display.

"Put that aside for now," he said, pointing at the idol.

"Where did you get this?"

"I don't want to talk about that anymore. Just do like I said. We can talk about it later. Now focus. You're supposed to be telling me all about how full of shit I am."

"I'm having second thoughts," Ted said.

"Focus here, little man." He pointed at each item. "Pain killer. Upper. Downer. Hallucinogen. Still don't believe me?"

"Where did you get that idol?" he stammered.

"Forget the idol. Jesus. Pay attention."

"I'm not eating any mushrooms," Ted said. "I have to work tomorrow."

"The fireweed's probably a bad idea too," he said. "The Vikings used to eat it during battle, because it got them all blitzed-up. They ate their own testicles too."

"*What*?"

"Before battle. As a sign that they would fight to the death."

That was unnecessary.

Even if it's true.

"Why would you tell me that?"

"How about the pain killer?"

"It's okay. I believe you. I think I'm getting tired."

"Where's all that bravado now? Gonna let the crazy guy win this round?"

"I apologize."

"Just try a little," Salton Steve said, lifting the glass off the caterpillar and holding the bug in his palm. He was still in his work clothes. "This is *Alasterias Nolcum*." He rubbed it with his finger and the caterpillar rolled itself into a tight defensive ball. Then, gingerly, with his thumb and forefinger, he began to pry it back out of its ball. As the caterpillar resisted, it secreted a small amount of translucent blue liquid which pooled in a groove of Salton Steve's palm. He set the caterpillar back on the table and replaced the glass.

He held his palm up to Ted's face. "Now," he said, "try this."

Ted objected, "I'm not—"

"It isn't piss, I promise."

"You go first."

Salton Steve hesitated. "You want me to go first?"

"Yes!"

"You don't trust me?"

"No!"

222

"Fine, I'll go, but you have to go right after me."

"What's it going to do?"

"It's a pain killer. Ready?"

"I wish you hadn't told me that about the Vikings."

He dipped his pinky into the liquid. Ted did the same. Salton Steve counted to three and touched the liquid to his tongue. Then Ted did it.

His mouth went instantly numb, like he was shot up with fast-acting Novocain. His tongue started to swell.

"Thith theels thunny," he said.

"Thrink thum theer."

They both lifted their cans. Ted tried to swish the beer around his mouth, but ended up just spitting it all over the carpet. Liquid drained from the corners of Salton Steve's mouth. They both started laughing. Salton Steve pulled at his lips. "Thlap by theek," he said. He picked up Ted's hand and brought it to his cheek. Ted nodded. He slapped him. Salton Steve fell back on the floor laughing.

Ted kept drinking beer, managing to keep about half of it in his mouth.

"Do do deleve be?"

"Deth!"

"Did dit thill dulthit?"

"Doe!"

CHAPTER TWENTY-SIX

Their next meeting was back in Bish's office. Salton Steve sat ready in his apartment with his headphones, his notepad, and a twelve pack of beer in a cooler next to the couch.

Easton dangled the story in front of Bish until they both agreed on terms for the sale of the gold. Bish conceded seventy percent to his own thirty, in exchange for the full story, starting with the gold's discovery and leading all the way through this mysterious plan Easton kept alluding to. Bish estimated the value of the gold in Easton's suitcase at about seven hundred thousand dollars. Easton told him that was roughly a third of what he'd brought up to Canada. So Bish would get six hundred thousand dollars. Easton, a million and a half, in cash.

They shook hands. Bish poured out the Blue Label. He leaned back in his chair. "To Oliver Easton."

"To Earl Bish...and the Smoke Monkey."

"The what?"

"Don't you want me start at the beginning?"

Bish nodded. "I'm all ears, Oliver."

"I'm all ears, Oliver," Salton Steve repeated to the vaulted ceiling of his penthouse.

Easton wiped his damp palms across his thighs. He honestly didn't know where to start.

"How about a question?" Bish asked.

"Let the man talk!" Salton Steve called out.

Easton nodded. Bish, calm and cool, leaned in close to Easton and simply asked, "So where'd you get it?"

"Honduras. You tell nobody."

"Not a soul. On the *Bible*, you saw me do it."

"I still can't believe you brought the *Bible* hiking."

"Holy Christ, will you two shut up and start talking!"

"So," Easton began, "seven years ago I got into some trouble with a lady down in Panama." Simultaneously, Salton Steve and Earl Bish relaxed a little in their respective seats, took a sip of their drinks, and let Oliver Easton's tale wash over them. "There were some seriously thuggish-type people hunting me. I snuck out of her apartment, stole a Jeep, and drove out some crazy dirt road while they followed me. They had guns, and managed to take out one of my tires just as I arrived at a small regional airport. I jumped out of the moving car, found some plane keys in an office, and took off in a small four-seater. They were shooting at me and the plane the whole time. I was, miraculously, unharmed. I want to stress that part to you, as a religious man. The word *miraculous*. This story I'm telling is a story of faith, okay, it's not about greed or graft, or anything like that. I'm telling you, they must have fired a hundred rounds.

"But I got away. Somehow I escaped, everything happening exactly as it had to. So I'm flying away to freedom, like I've got this charm on me or something. And then, on my mother's grave—and I've run this through my head a thousand times—just as the sun came up over the Central American jungle, a bolt of purple lightning shot up from the canopy and severed one of the plane's wings clean off. Surgically precise."

Bish winced. *Lies. Damnit.* He was disappointed. As Easton told his story, Bish's calculating business side took over. This man is not being honest, he realized. He's hiding something. How did I not see it before? He began to regret their agreement and was angry with himself for not doing a better job on this guy.

"I crashed into the jungle. Still unhurt."

"Miraculously."

"Yes, *miraculously.* That's right. Almost immediately after I got to my feet, I was drawn to a hill rising out of the jungle. Something seemed strange about it. I started climbing around and eventually discovered some large limestone blocks. I realized I had found some kind of hidden building, a temple or something."

"Just like King Solomon."

"You don't believe me."

"No, I don't."

"No, I don't," Salton Steve echoed.

"That's part of my central problem, which I'll get to in a second. But nobody is going to believe what I say, even though it's the truth."

"You're lying about something, Oliver."

"Nice work, Earl," Salton Steve said.

In a deadpan voice Easton said he was not lying. He looked worried.

But Bish continued to look on skeptically. "No lies, *please.*"

Easton took in a deep breath. "Look, I found a temple in the middle of the jungle. The gold...you think there's some easy explanation?"

"Maybe you stole it, Oliver."

"I did steal it."

"You did!" Bish pounded the table.

"Yes! From the temple! From Smoke Monkey, okay. But I didn't really steal it. It's on loan."

"Oh, wow," Salton Steve said. "This is *beautiful.*"

226

"Go on," Bish said. He leaned over and refilled the small glasses.

"So at this mound, a compulsion drove me to start digging around the base. I found a doorway clogged with mud. I spent hours and hours pulling out dirt until I reached a stone door, which I was able to kick open. I built a torch and entered a room. A tomb, in fact. Inside, I found an enormous stone coffin. I worked the lid off and looked inside."

"Gold?"

"And a blue light."

"What blue light?" Salton Steve asked.

"And gold figurines, about nine inches tall. Little idols. And underneath the pile, skeletal human remains resting on a bed of golden orbs, like potatoes. Oblong, varying in size. About three hundred pounds worth.

"Three hundred pounds of golden potatoes?"

"That's right."

"Unbelievable."

"Unbelievable," Salton Steve repeated.

"So then what?" Bish asked, now back onboard. He decided the story, with all its improbability, was at least *potentially* truthful. Based on the potato detail. And with his skepticism now tempered slightly, he was able to enjoy the story all the more.

"What was the blue light?" Salton Steve demanded. "Ask him about the blue light again!"

"So naturally, I was in shock. In shock about the gold and the temple and the remains, but also in shock over the way they were all discovered. The way I found the plane keys, the way their bullets kept missing, the purple lightning, and the survivable plane crash. Then the sort of magnetic attraction to the tomb, this sense that I was being pulled towards my discovery. It was a deeply unsettling feeling, and in no way a natural human experience. I felt as though I had been *brought* there. Called."

"Summoned."

"That's even better. I felt like I had been summoned. So what to do, right?" Easton asked. "What options?" Bish was nodding, as he started to understand the special predicament. "The knee-jerk desire to just grab as much as I could carry and run, barely even registered in my head. It wasn't even an option. I was still stuck on the idea that I was brought there. *Summoned*. I was standing, mind you, in the middle of a dark tomb. A man's decayed corpse below me flickering in the torchlight. There were strange blue lights. Do I believe in this kind of thing, I asked myself. What do I believe in? Or, rather, what *don't* I believe in?"

"I understand," Bish said.

"This skeleton. This temple. The absence of autonomy. I said, who are you? To the bones. I started talking to them. Can this all be coincidence? Is there such infinite random potential in life? Are there limits? Can things this weird really just *happen*?" He shook his head. "I don't think they can."

"Come on, with the religious bullshit." Salton Steve muttered. "Can't a guy just find gold in a hidden temple and be done with it?"

"No," Bish said. "Things like this do not just happen for no reason. Of course they don't."

"I agree. I committed in my mind, in my core."

"You took the leap."

"Exactly. I took the leap, thank you. What a perfect cliché. I took the leap of faith, and had to therefore tune all my future decisions to that frequency. This entombed body had brought me to his resting place. He was in possession of an *ability*. He could create in this world things I did not think possible. The universe buckled. Total—"

"Liberation."

"Yes!"

"Through faith."

"Yes! Thank you!"

"So then what?"

"Yeah," Salton Steve seconded, "then what?"

"I spent three days in the tomb. I had to keep returning to the crash site for torch fuel. There were cameras too, in the plane."

"What cameras?"

"I don't know, just boxes of cameras."

"You have pictures?"

Easton shook his head, sensing his credibility waning once again. "No, no pictures."

"Why not?"

"I was afraid to. I don't know. It didn't seem right."

"How so?"

"It's hard to explain. But I sensed this was all about faith. There's no need for pictures. I have to make you believe me. Like this."

"Oh, please. Are you buying this Earl?" Salton Steve began bouncing a tennis ball against the wall.

"I prayed at the side of the coffin. I'd never prayed in my life. Not like that. I asked who he was. I asked why I had been brought there. And while there wasn't exactly a direct response to my questions—"

"There never is."

"Shut up and let the man talk!"

"I heard answers. I say *heard*. That's not quite the right word. I became aware of answers, and the name, Smoke Monkey, whispered in my ear."

"What you describe is common for people coming into their faith, this awareness. Like a sixth sense, right. A certain transmitting of knowledge."

"Horseshit!"

"Exactly."

"Go on."

"I came to understand his purpose, and therefore, my own purpose. This man, this godking, who I now know as

K'ak' Joplaj Chan K'awiil, is a dormant power, fueled, as are all pagan gods, by the faith of their followers—of which he had but one. I've learned that human beings build their own world, gods and all, through the power of imagination, and that this world grows smaller and smaller, as we set up limits and deny the impossible. Through my prayers he grew stronger."

Salton Steve spit beer across the room.

Bish was nodding.

"So my purpose, as I sit here in your office, is not simply to sell this gold. I must take this opportunity, this discovery, to further the cause of faith, which is the destruction of earthly limitations and the throwing off of veils."

"I think I understand," Bish said. "But let's connect the dots, okay. I thought you were here for money. Is that not the case?"

"Basically there were two options. Report my discovery, or don't. If I reported it, I would instantly fall under suspicion. They'd assume I'd taken some of the gold. Or they'd take the gold themselves and blame it all on me. We're talking about a very unstable country here."

Salton Steve stood up and got his world atlas down from a bookshelf.

"The tomb would eventually be excavated, catalogued, and added to a long list of significant Maya archeological sites, important only to scholars and the occasional tourist. The tomb, and Smoke Monkey himself, would experience a brief moment of scholarly attention, and then fade into the background like all but a select few high profile mummies and monuments."

"Or…"

"Right, or…" Easton cleared his throat. "Or instead of bringing him to the world, I could bring the world to him."

"What do you mean?"

230

"To discover him." His fingers were in quotes around the word *discover*.

"Smoke Monkey?"

"Yes. It's the only way."

"I don't understand."

"For you, in your faith, there is comfort I imagine. Multitudes of like-minded...Saints, you call them. Mormons."

"Right."

"Plus the larger Christian world. Billions of people. Thousands of years. World-wide. Massive structures. The weight of history. A collective experience. But you are still just one man with a relationship to God, right?"

"I guess so. There's my family—"

"No. Just you."

"Okay."

"Well, I'm the same. Absent all that other stuff, the history, the legions. Just me and my god. He seized me in the stride of my life and set me on a quest. It is no different than the quest of your own faith. It is fundamental to my being. My life's goal, to do the greatest service. To what end, I don't know. But I find I am wired for faith. It is my new life."

Bish looked at Easton sympathetically. He decided the man was indeed truthful. But he was also very naïve. "Oliver," he said. "I certainly can appreciate the particulars of your spiritual awakening, and I understand the desire to commit oneself to the cause of faith..."

Easton looked confused. He cocked his head to the side.

"Get to the point, sir." Bish said.

"Oh, right. Well, I cannot simply announce to the world that I have discovered a god and expect anyone to think me anything but crazy. But if I can generate the circumstances in which this god's existence is allowed to organically reveal itself to a mass of people, there is at least a chance he may take root in the modern world."

Bish was shaking his head. "You can't do that."

"Can't do what?"

"You can't manufacture divinity."

"Why not?"

"Yeah, why not?" Salton Steve asked. He thought about that question for a long time, barely hearing the rest of the conversation.

"You just can't," Bish said. "There is only one god. *God*. That's it. Everything comes from him."

"Well, God is a relationship, right? A two-way street. And I think religion has shown you can at least engineer the human side of it, the faith part."

"To what end?"

"Well, the preservation of the principle. Why do you send out missionaries? To propagate a belief system. Right? Why does God need you?"

"This is getting—"

"Knowledge of Smoke Monkey's existence, his *continued* existence, may help people liberate themselves from the cold restraints of this calculated world. Once I have established myself as a respected scholar, I will begin public prayers. Theological Archeology. I will create a situation in which it appears to a great many people that I have received a communication from...elsewhere. That I have, through the abstractions of faith and piety, produced tangible worldly results, a buried treasure, a fantastic temple, a God, with a capital 'G'."

"A scam."

"A necessary deception. Do we really have to look too closely at your own Mormon faith to find instances of willful disillusionment. Don't try and tell me your own church hasn't pulled some shenanigans."

"It's an interesting idea, really. I like it. I like you, Oliver, and I'm glad we're doing business together. But as for this miraculous discovery you hope to stage, it'll never come off."

"Why do you say that? Please. There's no precedent for this sort of thing that I'm aware of. I'm sure it's got holes throughout. But you don't think the overall concept can work?"

"No. And I'll tell you why. Nobody's going to believe you. Once you claim your epiphany and show the world your temple, they're all going to say you're full of crap, that you knew it was there. How can you convince anyone that you didn't have prior knowledge?"

"Because most of the gold is still in there."

"Excuse me?" Salton Steve said, snapping back into the conversation. Having found Honduras in the Atlas, he now began looking more intently at the "Maya Structure" icons. They were all over the place.

"I intend to take the long road. It's been seven years already, most of it spent slowly smuggling out the gold I did take, which I will only use in the service of Smoke Monkey. I've been accepted to Harvard. I'm attending in the fall. I intend to make a very public display of basic scholarship. I'm going to take years to do it. Maybe twenty years of hardcore traditional archeology. Group field work miles from the tomb. Never a moment on my own, away from colleagues. Then wham! One day, like a bloodhound in a trance, through the forest, to the tomb. Some will doubt me. But some will see a miracle. A manifestation of the impossible."

"What about the plane?"

"I've scattered the plane, piece by piece, far and wide. Remember, I'm seven years into this thing. You have no idea how much work I've put into it. Most people will not be able to conceive of a person spending twenty-seven years hatching a plan this absurd. That's the key, sitting on all that gold. If I really had discovered it in secret, wouldn't I take it? Wouldn't anybody?"

"You *did* take the gold."

"Not all of it. Just a little...and don't forget, Smoke Monkey is real. The purpose of the deception is only to expand belief."

"Okay," Bish was nodding now, coming around to Easton's logic. "I understand why you're so fixated on secrecy. I'm the only man on earth who can call your bluff."

"Exactly. But you wouldn't do that now would you, Earl? Because you swore."

"My lips are sealed."

"Mine aren't!" Salton Steve had his finger on Chiquimula.

"Still though, Oliver. I have to tell you you're way off. What you're saying is of course polytheistic nonsense. You have to understand, from my point of view. To perpetuate such things is in violation of my contract with the one true God."

"See, you're nuts too, Earl. You just don't see it. If our places were reversed and you were telling me the story of your own faith, you alone, who wouldn't call you nuts? Magic glasses, magic undies, the red sun, the golden tablets, the Garden of Eden...in Missouri. The mud people? Really? The *mud* people? Come on. What must they have said about Joseph Smith?"

"Are you comparing—"

"Absolutely."

Salton Steve removed his headphones and unplugged the jack so he could hear the rest of the conversation through the speaker system. Then he took off all his clothes. He stood flush against the room's back wall. "To manufacture divinity," he said to himself. "Now that's something to shoot for. I'll be sure to keep my eye on you Mr. Easton. And Mr. Bish, I hope you know how to spell the word *extortion*." Then he took off running, full speed across the room and leapt high into the air, his momentum carrying him well over the fiberglass bar supported by two metal stands, and then down, onto his back, onto the double-stacked thick blue tumbling mats.

CHAPTER TWENTY-SEVEN

Kevin asked him to come in half an hour early that day, to help with a project before the night shift. As Ted walked down the ramp he noticed a large rectangular box on a metallic table in the center of the kitchen. All the chefs stood at their stations prepping for dinner. Bruce thrashed at veal cutlets with a cooking mallet. It was savage, brutal, and extremely loud, but nobody made any indication they even knew it was happening. Luc was at the dessert station sampling some dark sauce with his pinky. Kevin, coming Ted's way, said something to Luc, who apologized and agreed to use a spoon in the future. The Michelin people were strict in their attention to detail, especially when health issues were concerned.

Kevin met Ted in the middle of the room by the prep table. He took a look at Ted's enthusiasm for this *special project* and smiled.

"What's in the box, boss?"

"What's in the box?" Kevin repeated. They both looked down at it. He handed Ted a pair of kitchen shears. "You cut the straps. I'll be right back." Ted took the shears and moved around the table, snipping at the thick yellow ribbons which held the lid in place.

"Tomorrow's Luau Day out on the rink lawn," Kevin called out over the sound of Bruce's thrashing. He was rummaging through a supply closet. Then he headed back Ted's way carrying a large metal pole. Ted cut the last of the straps. The pole was at least six feet long, three inches in diameter. Kevin set it on the table next to the box.

Bruce stopped pounding at his cutlets. Ted looked around the kitchen. Everyone had stopped working.

Why is everyone looking at us?

Luau Day.

Oh, shit.

"Tell me Ted, you ever spit roast a hog?" As Kevin spoke, he slid the lid off the box, revealing an enormous fleshy pig, all pink and wrinkled and grotesque.

I eat that?

You love to eat that.

Ted had no idea pigs could get that big. He focused on the snout, which looked like a pink tube sock collected at the bottom of an ankle. "That's pork," Ted said.

"That's pork, son. One hundred and thirty-seven massive pounds," Kevin said, slapping its hide emphatically. "Now, about this pole."

Ted looked at it in horror. "Wouldn't it be more authentic to bake the pig in a hole in the ground?"

"It probably would be more authentic, Ted, yes. Thank you. We'll have to consider that for *next* summer. So," he said, rolling up his sleeves, "one of us gets the mouth and one of us gets the asshole."

Ted heard a mumbled *that's what she said* from someone on the line behind him.

"I'll take the *mouth*," Ted said hopefully.

"Good," Kevin said, "a sense of humor. You're going to need it."

They flipped the box over and the unhappy pig rolled out onto the gleaming steel of the table. Kevin took up the pole and backed away. Ted stood by the head of the pig and fed the pole into its surprisingly tiny mouth.

"Now go back by its rump," Kevin directed. More snickering. "When I push, you push back." Ted put his hands on the pig's butt, and waited for Kevin to start pushing.

The curly tail!

What do you remember about porcine anatomy?

Enough to know it'll be a gruesome barbarous coring. We're going to tear through the center of this pig, and more than just a shiny metal pole is going to be coming out of his backend.

His?

Ted looked more closely. *Hers.*

Then it's the first one right under the tail.

Thanks.

Ted braced himself. Kevin pushed. He could hear the tearing of internal tissue, as twelve inches of metal disappeared down the pig's throat. Ted pushed back with his hands and shoulders until progress ceased, one cold buttcheek on his neck.

"I'm going to pull it out and ram it in with some force."

The snickering turned to belly laughs. Someone slapped their prep counter and sent up a vibrating chorus of metal implements. Kevin was sweating.

This is getting creepy.

I don't like the look of Kevin's mustache one bit.

Kevin thrust the pole in and let out a grunt. They were two feet in. Then he pulled the pole all the way back out. It was covered with bits of flesh and a thick translucent slime.

Then he brought the pole over to Ted's side of the table and handed it off to him with a smile. "We do this like they built the railroads," he said. "Start at both ends and meet in St. Louis."

Ted moved the little tail to the side and fit the pole into the pig's tiny asshole.

238

"Push eet een there. You are zee *boss*!" Encouragement from Luc. Ted clutched the pole, straining for the best way to get a grip. It was slippery and wet and awkward to master. He put one hand against the flat back-end, to get some purchase, and used his other hand to guide it. He wiped his brow on his shoulder and tried to focus.

"Maybe you should get a running start!" Bruce yelled.

"Maybe you should go fuck yourself!" Ted called back without turning around.

But a running start.

That's interesting.

He couldn't shake the image. He had to set the pole down, to compose himself. The delay caused everyone to consider the same image. Within seconds the room erupted. It was collective laughter like he'd never heard in his life. Bruce actually fell over coughing. One of the front desk managers poked her head in the kitchen entrance to see about the noise. She saw the pig and the pole and left horrified. More explosive laughter.

Kevin, as the boss, tried to stay composed. He braced himself on the pig's head and wiped his eyes continuously with the back of his hand.

Ted moved away from the table unafraid, took up the pole, and held it like a vaulter, at a forty-five degree angle. Bruce lay on his back now, writhing like an overturned cockroach. Ted could hear strange deep huffing noises coming from Luc.

Is he laughing *in French*?

Kevin stopped him before he could make a serious attempt. Ted nodded and approached the pig. He fit the pole back into the opening and circled it around with some force, like he was trying to put an umbrella in the sand. Then he rammed it home. The pole hardly went in at all.

"I'm no good at this sort of thing," he confessed to his audience. Recovery giggles. Bruce held his hand in the air. He couldn't take anymore.

"You're next, Bruce," Ted yelled. People coughing and sucking for air.

"Focus," Kevin said, mopping his brow on his sleeve. "We got to get this done."

Ted pushed again. Some progress. The vibrations of tearing intestines resonated along the pole. He pulled out and rammed it back in. Three times, four times, lost in the intensity. Locked in. Stoic. Suddenly dead serious. *In*. Out. *In*. Out. Complete detachment.

Eventually he got there.

Relief.

Satisfaction?

Shouldn't we have gutted this thing first?

When he hit Kevin's hole, the pole shot through, triumphantly emerging from the pig's mouth, which surprisingly had not changed its expression throughout the whole ordeal.

There was applause.

Salton Steve came bounding down the ramp. He took a bow and thanked the room. Then he caught sight of the impaled pig and the blood drained from his face. "Oh, God," he said, with all the weight of tragedy. One last great burst of laughter. A snot rocket down the front of Kevin's white cooking coat.

"You're next," Ted said to Salton Steve, but this time the joke fell flat.

He ran into Cammie again in cold storage. He had his spit pig in tow on a cart. Conversation would come easily. He proudly slapped the fleshy hide with a big smile on his face.

"Amazing," she said.

"Total barbarism."

"Which end were you on?"

That's exactly the right question.

"The asshole," he confessed.

240

"How did you—"

"Running start," he said with a straight face. The pig, somehow, had given him a bit of confidence.

She nodded, considering his answer. Then she smiled brightly. "Wait, no you didn't!"

God you are beautiful.

"It wasn't easy."

"Cause back at home," she said, with an affected country twang, "we just drop them ass first from the roof and let gravity do the work."

Ted laughed. "Who holds the pole?"

"We rotate."

"How do you get the pig on the roof?"

"We raise them up there, with the sheeps and chickens."

"Smart. Do you kill them before you drop them?"

She thought about that. Then she nodded and pursed her lips.

Every new expression.

"We wait till they die of old age."

Ted wasn't sure if they were having a serious conversation or not. He just stared at her face as she talked. When she stopped talking, he kept on staring.

I should stop staring.

You should *say* something.

He looked at the bag in her hand. "Whatcha got there? Corn?"

She held up a bag of corn. "Yes, this is corn."

Help me.

Stay on the pig! The pig!

"Wait a minute," she said suddenly, excitement in her voice. "Luau Day?"

"That's right." Ted fished the T-shirt from his back pocket. He held it up. She reached into her own pocket and pulled out the same shirt. "We can be twins!" he said. He sounded like a twelve-year-old girl. Cammie just nodded.

241

CHAPTER TWENTY-EIGHT

The humidity of the jungle made Marona Dilenta's hair frizzy, which was driving her crazy. The real culprit was dandruff, a condition she couldn't abide. She wore her tight-fitting black tops every day, almost as a uniform, along with her skirts and calf-high boots. Under no circumstance was she going to allow herself to be seen with white specks on her shoulders. The problem, one she had battled on and off throughout her life, was caused by a yeast that loved perspiration and ambient moisture.

The whole thing was a complex nightmare. She used anti-dandruff shampoo to kill the yeast, but that made her hair dry and brittle. She wasn't able to use conditioner since that would create new oil deposits on her scalp for the yeast to feed on when they regenerated. And even if she did want to use conditioner, her own bottle ran out weeks ago, and there was not another bottle of a suitable brand within 200 miles of the camp.

She started picking at her scalp at night while she sat with the professor on top of the Hieroglyphic Staircase. She would zone-out completely, lost in the slow cadence of the professor's spoken prayer. With her head bowed, she would create a part in her hair, run her finger along the line until she found a patch of raised skin and scratch it out. Then she would create a new part just to the side of the previous one, and repeat the process. It could take an hour to survey her whole head, a hour without thought, or sensory awareness of any sort.

And then they would go back to camp, she would go to sleep, and wake up a frizzy mess. Which was unacceptable. Survival at the camp had always been contingent on her outward togetherness. The clothes, the boots, the hair. She took pride in her unflappability, of working against expectations. She wanted to show them all that a pretty woman from the city could handle herself in the jungle just as well as anyone else. At the core of all this was her innate snarky desire to expose vanity in others, particularly in those who outwardly condescended to the very notion of vanity. It was the same thing in her nature that led her to set traps for her husband five months earlier, an obsessive need to make men look foolish and simple.

At the camp, she targeted the pride men took in their own griminess. The dirt colored sweat stains on their work clothes, their unkempt hair, their disregard for muddiness as a variable condition. Some of the men, she knew, did not brush their teeth or even soap-up after eliminating. These men relished this lifestyle. This myth of hardiness, a blue-collar approach to scholarship. At least women wore their vanity on their sleeves. Men liked to pretend they did not craft their identities the way women did, that it was beneath them.

But there was simply no reason why a person could not go through life at the Copan excavation site maintaining the same standards of cleanliness and hygiene that were expected everywhere else. It drove her crazy. Just look at the natives who worked around the camp. The women in their immaculate colorful dresses. The men in their clean pressed tees, their well-tailored denim, their nicely-trimmed moustaches and carefully parted hair. Guys like

Heinrich Airhorne would come to dinner with dirt on their faces. Why not spend five minutes washing-up? What possible joy was to be had in making sure the boys knew you had been hard at work? Of course they knew! They worked at your side all day!

Just because you live in a tent in the jungle means you are unable to wash your hands or brush your teeth or change your socks or scrape the mud off your shoes? Ridiculous! If it were laziness, she could handle it. And they all wanted it to seem like it was laziness, that it came from a point of view of not caring. It made her crazy. They did care! They cared tremendously.

And they calculated this disguise to impress each other. Or, even more pathetically, to impress her. Like they were all husky firemen or something, all covered in soot and rescued babies. Pathetic. Maybe if these men came into the house after a long day of laboring on the farm, smelling of sincerity and hard work, she might find it attractive. But then the first place *that guy* would go would be to the shower. Because his sense of self-worth did not come from showing off his dirty ankles, it came from putting food on the table for his family.

And it was all so transparent in this particular batch of guys. For many, it was their first go at a wilderness-type experience. They were academics mostly, who spent more time in the library than in the woods. Picking grime out of their ears at dinner and wiping it on their forearms demonstrated some degree of masculinity? Really? Excessive body odor, a condition that could be fixed in three minutes with a simple bar of soap, was supposed to be a symbol of something? It was supposed to say something to the room?

All it said to Marona was, not only am I full of retarded male vanity, I also smell like shit, and will dirty up your bed if we sleep together.

So if she could saunter into that mess tent looking like she just stepped off of 5th Avenue—beautiful, sophisticated, *together*—well then it might just make them all seem a little bit trite and silly. Of course she chose to ignore the fact that she did not work as an excavator, like the others did, that her job as the professor's assistant kept her away from the muck in the field. She could be as hypocritical as anybody. She knew that. She had flaws. They were well documented in her own psyche. But this preposterous male fronting needed to be dealt with.

And of course, the others completely misunderstood her efforts. Men like Airhorne saw her togetherness as its own perverse stab at vanity. Not that he or anyone else *minded* if Marona had some pathological need to look her best at all times. But they certainly didn't see the subtext.

All of this made it extremely inconvenient to Marona that she looked like the jungle might be getting the best of her. Her hair was a disaster. Even in a ponytail it frizzed-out. Which caused a chain-reaction of neuroses. She started wiping at invisible flakes on her shoulders. Not only that, she developed a kind of social tick where she would try to smooth her hair when she talked, by pressing her palms flat against her skull and then sliding them down repeatedly. It looked like she was petting herself when she did it.

And now, a nail fungus of some sort had taken root in the cuticle of her left pinky. The nail grew out all soft and misshapen. It was depressing. Things were feeding off of her. It was enough. It was time to go.

Strange that the only real benefit she got out of the Copan experience was her friendship with Lattistrom, some deluded and disgusting old kook. At least nobody could accuse Lattistrom of posturing. It was just the opposite with him. A little vanity might actually help his cause.

She worried how he would do without her. She worried that their friendship, and her willingness to embrace and humor his absurd notions and behavior had pushed him a little further out to sea. And now she was just going to leave him there.

So *damn* depressing. All of it. Her hair. These stupid men. The professor. This whole dead civilization. All these people spending thousands of dollars on their educations so they could dig around in somebody else's jungle searching for relics from the past. Taken as a piece of the world, as a piece of the human experience, the scene at Copan was just a mass of pathetic humanity firing off blanks. It all seemed so pointless. Where could she go in the world where lives had meaning and people did not act like petty little children?

At least she had some perspective on New York, and her husband, and all that had happened. That was something. Her daughter was something. Something neglected. How did she have the gall to make a project out of exposing male ridiculousness, while simultaneously letting months in her daughter's life pass without a word from her mother? It was just one big cycle of awfulness. All this misplaced energy, following the professor around, sitting on ancient structures in the middle of the night watching him pray. He had become her surrogate charge, in the absence of her daughter. It was wrong. Even her own prayers left her nothing. They were turning into private ruminations on the subject of her life and how things had gone so wrong for her so quickly. So that was it.

But where would she live? What would she do? How could she get her daughter back after all *this*?

What would she say to her husband? *Ex*-husband? She wasn't even sure if she was still married.

The passing time had certainly erased the sting of her mistakes, but not his. Everything he had done, cheating since the beginning. *That* had set her on this path, *his* dishonesty. When she held their two cards side by side, he was clearly the more hateful person. He was a dick, right?

Yet she was the one to shuffle off humiliated. She was the one to give up custody.

Why had she caved so readily? Why had she felt so ashamed for exposing *his* flaws? She tried to think back over the months. It seemed like an overreaction now. All the way to Honduras? Like some escaped Nazi war criminal. All she had done was pay a few women to sleep with her husband. How had she let it all get so twisted in her mind?

Compared to Coy, these men in Copan were actually quite tolerable. If she was going to expend any more energy on the subject of male weakness, it would all be for him. She walked around muttering to herself, cursing Coy and her former weak self. She would land in New York City like an invading armada, kick his ass to the ground, rescue her daughter, and set up a life for herself that built on her intellect and her charms.

Thank you.

She caught herself. Thank *you*? Thank *who*?

You're welcome.

Stop that! She was not going to let that happen. But she already heard the professor's voice in her head. Faith will set you straight. You are never going to be able to stop people from acting like assholes. You are never going to be able to prevent your own hypocrisies. You need to come to some sort of an understanding with the world. Find how to live within it. Think of the nights in the jungle, the moonlit mists, the scurrying feet of the little night creatures we keep at bay by our circle of light. You must not walk out of here, Marona, without tipping your cap to our bold purpose. You have been assisted, do you not see that? And not by me. But by your reluctant faith.

It *was* possible. Not the existence of some dormant deity. That would be crazy. But certainly the ability of faith to heal. The hours atop the Hieroglyphic Staircase, focused outward. It built something within her, an emotional toughness. And that toughness had become essential. It was her new source of energy. It would be at the heart of each new decision she made. This weird something born out of jungle mists.

She sat on her cot and picked at her fungused nail. She decided to give it one more day. She would stroll the excavation site, as she often did, to make a basic record of what type of work was being done. She did this to help the professor fill out some paperwork the university requested in order to keep the requirements of the site's main grant satisfied.

The dinner bell rang. She could hear Airhorne in the next tent, "If you move any of my fucking men, you're dead. I have twenty-six armies in Siam. We eat and we're back here in fifteen minutes." She heard the sound of the flaps slapping shut and the trailing off of voices.

She was just going to go to dinner. That was her plan. But she did not like Heinrich Airhorne at all. He made her uncomfortable. Everything about him was inconsistent. Sometimes he was passably handsome, other times grotesque. Sometimes playful and fun-loving, other times cold and aggressive.

She came out of her tent and looked around. Nobody there, which was not surprising. Beer was free during the dinner hour. She walked casually to Airhorne's tent and said, "Hello?"

No answer. She pulled the flap aside and poked her head into the tent. Empty. She scurried inside and went over to the table. She looked at the game board.

Where on earth is Siam?

She found it in Asia, covered in red plastic pieces. Airhorne's red. She started picking up random red pieces from all over the board, but not so many that he would notice. Then she put them in the clear plastic rectangle that held the unused pieces.

CHAPTER TWENTY-NINE

Kevin had one of the most stressful jobs on earth. He was under huge pressure to maintain the Idaho Room's five-star rating, which meant micromanaging costs and quality and staffing. Plus, he ran the grill station most nights. And while he always seemed to be calm and composed, the perfect man for the job, Ted suspected there might be a veiled maniac lurking behind that moustache.

When Kevin showed up at the loading dock the morning of Luau Day, looking nervous, Ted too became nervous. He had never seen that side of Kevin. They both wore their Luau Day T-shirts.

"We've never done it like this before," Kevin confessed, as they wheeled the brand-new spit roasting barbeque to the rink lawn, and parked it next to The Spot's outdoor patio. "I hate an open kitchen, and this is going to be about as open as they get. We'll just have to keep the fire low and steady. That's the key."

"What am I going to be doing?"

"Just sort of watching and managing. Going for anything we need upstairs. Talking to people. It'll be you and the girl from The Spot."

"Cammie?"

"Yes, Cammie." He looked at Ted. Ted looked at the ground. "Just don't get distracted. She'll be our insurance policy. If this thing starts to go south, she'll be the face of the operation. Who's going to yell at her?"

"I wouldn't know how."

Once the barbeque was in place, Ted walked back to the loading dock to get the coals, which came in two huge fifty-pound bags. He took up the first bag and heaved it over his shoulder.

There's no way we're going to need all this.

He clutched in at the second bag, with a mind to impress Cammie. It hardly moved.

What we should have done was put the bags on the barbeque before we wheeled it out to the rink lawn.

But we didn't.

So two trips then.

Looks that way.

But then he heard a voice behind him, a thick accent, "Do you need a haand wit daat?"

No way.

He turned around, and there he stood, Arnold Schwarzenegger, like a locomotive engine, his giant white teeth grinning down at Ted. He looked strange in shorts and a T-shirt. "Hey," Ted said. "Uh, sure."

"No problum." Schwarzenegger took up the second bag with greater strain than Ted expected. "Vear aar vee gooing?"

"The skating rink," Ted said. His helper nodded as they started walking. "You look familiar," Ted told him.

"I get zat a lot."

Ted marched proudly out onto the lawn, Schwarzenegger in tow. Proud that Arnold's burden was no bigger than his own. Kevin had wheeled the pig out and it sat on the cart with a foot of metal coming out of each end.

"Ouch," Arnold said, eyeing the pig, as they walked up to Kevin and set the coals against the barbeque. "Hello,

Chef. Thees leetle von here thinks he can carry two beeg bags and I told heem he's crasy." Ted took no offense.

"Well thank you sir, for helping us out," Kevin said.

"No problum." He shook hands with Kevin. "I came here looking for you, Chef, becaas vee are hafing a paaty toomaow night and I vant you to breeng ova yoo vife so I can proof to Bruce Villis that not all chefs are omosexvuals."

Kevin laughed. Ted was giggling to himself.

He really does sound kind of stupid.

I could listen to him all day long.

"I'll be there," Kevin said. He was as star-struck as Ted was.

Then Arnold turned to Ted and said, "Vy doon vee breeng zis leetle von visth you if he is strong enough to make it up zee stairs. You know vee can see my house zrom here." He pointed to a stone mansion on a distant hillside. "And you should breeng a friend visth you, and please leef zees metal poles here. Vee vant no funny beeznis, okay."

"Sounds great," Ted said. "Thanks so much."

"Okay, and Chef, jus make somesing simple. Not five courses or anysing like zat," Kevin's face went sour. "I'm keeding, my God you should see youself. Veee have a caterer, jeez."

When Schwarzenegger turned to leave, there were already five or six kids gawking at him from a safe distance. He threw his hands high in the air and roared. He lumbered towards them like Frankenstein's monster and they all scattered with delighted screams.

Kevin spread the charcoal inside the barbeque, coated it in lighter fluid, and set it all on fire. Even with Schwarzenegger gone, they still had a bit of an audience. Mostly, it was families on bikes who had come to watch people ice skate. Some asked questions about the upcoming event, while others kept their distance, sensing Ted and Kevin might be in for a wild ride with a hot fire and a hundred-plus pounds of pig. Most of the kids focused on the impaled beast draped across the top of a stainless steel kitchen cart. Ted caught a few skeptical glances from younger girls, who shook their heads disapprovingly and straddled their bikes.

Kevin tried his best to engage anyone who wanted to talk. Many of the Valvert guests spent several weeks a year at the resort and Kevin was well-known to them, well-respected as a chef. Ted tried to do his part, but nobody seemed interested in talking to him.

One young girl, six or seven years old, couldn't stop staring at the impaled pig. Ted could see the little gears in her head spinning, the way her face ran through a wide range of puzzled contortions. He admired her curiosity and thought he could help her out by answering a few questions. Her father stood ten feet away, talking to Kevin.

"You staying for lunch?" he asked the girl.

"I wouldn't eat that," she said.

"Do you like bacon?"

"Yes."

"Do you like ham?"

"How'd they get the pole in there?"

Ted looked over at her father. "We put it in there."

"How come?"

"To cook the pig."

She looked at the flames coming off the charcoal.

"Did it hurt?"

"It didn't hurt the pig, no."

"I think it would hurt."

Again, he looked at her father.

"What's your name?" he asked her.

"Cara."

"Cara, the pig was already dead when we put the pole in there."

"Did you kill it?"

"No."

"Who killed it?"

"I don't know, Cara."

"How did he die?"

"I don't know that either."

"Can I touch it?"

"No. That's not a good idea."

"Why not?" She continued to stare. Then something changed in her, instantly. Her face tightened into a ball as she tried to squint-away an emotional onslaught. She shrieked, threw her bike down on the grass, and ran over to her father, wrapping her arms around his leg.

"What's the matter?" a voice asked. Ted turned and saw Cammie standing right next to him, wearing her Luau Day T-shirt.

"I don't know." They both stood watching the girl, who continued crying. Her father put his hand on her head, but went right on talking to Kevin.

"What did you say to her?" Cammie asked.

"I didn't say anything."

"Maybe we should cover the pig up until we start cooking it. It's kind of grotesque," she said. Ted hardly heard her. She was stunning, as usual, bright-eyed, smiling in the sun.

He pointed to the mansion on the hill. "See that big house over there?"

I got this.

Do it now, before you lose your nerve.

"Yes."

"Know who lives there?"

"Who?"

"Your boy Arnold."

"Really?"

Before he could go any further, Cara's father walked over, holding Cara's hand. "Ted, is it?"

"Yes, sir. This is Cammie."

He looked angry. "What did you say to my daughter?"

"Nothing, really. She asked me about the pig."

"She's terrified."

"I saw her looking at the pole, you know, thinking about it. Maybe she's a little weirded-out."

"By the thick pole coming out of its ass?"

"That's probably what did it."

"I'm a little weirded-out, too," the guy said, focusing on the pig.

"It is kind of hard to look at," Ted said.

"I agree," Cammie said.

The man looked at Cammie, really seeing her full face for the first time. Ted studied his reaction, out of curiosity. The man's eyes got wider, his posture a little more rigid. He smiled. "You work here?" the man asked.

"Yes I do."

"Cara," he said. "Cara, dear, look at the pretty lady." The little girl unburied her face from her father's leg and looked up at Cammie. She smiled.

"Hi, Cara," Cammie said in a nurturing voice.

"I'm Tony Reznack," the man said, offering his hand to Cammie. "Cara and I have been coming to Valvert every year, just the two of us, since her mother passed away."

Cammie looked at the little girl. "I'm so sorry."

"We love it here though," Tony said. "It was her mother's home away from home."

"Ted!"

Jesus, what?

Kevin called him to the barbeque. Ted walked over, while still looking at Cammie. Tony had moved in a little closer. He was talking and she was smiling.

"Time to cook a pig," Kevin said.

At the barbeque, Ted held his hand over the white coals, and pulled it back instantly. "Hot!" he said.

Kevin looked at him like he was an idiot. Ted turned to watch Cammie again. She was laughing. She looked amazing.

Shit!

Kevin told him to run the spit motor's extension cord to an outlet on the outside of the building. When he got back, he saw Kevin had wheeled the pig over to the barbeque. Tony and Cammie chatted away like old friends.

"Shouldn't she help us?" Ted asked.

Kevin looked at Ted. Then he looked over at Cammie. "She's with Tony Reznack."

"Who's that?"

"His grandfather sold this land to Earl Bish Sr."

"Who's that?"

"Jesus, Ted."

"I'm sorry. I'm from California."

"Earl Bish built Valvert in the 1930s. The first ski area in America. His son, Earl Jr. owns this place. He's your boss. He lives in Canada. These guys are all ridiculously wealthy."

Cammie stood by the ice rink now, next to Cara. Tony sat on the ground, fixing something on her bike.

"They're all Mormon. Like a big family."

"Isn't Cammie supposed to be helping us?" Ted asked again.

"She's doing her job. If Tony's happy, we're all happy."

Ted was angry. "You're pimping her out!"

"She's a hostess, Ted. It's called hospitality."

"She's a prep cook."

"Not today. What are you so worried about, anyway? I'm sure Tony Reznack doesn't have what you have." He gestured to Arnold's house on the hill. "A certain invitation."

"From what you tell me about him he's probably going too."

Kevin laughed. "Actually, you may be right. I bet he *is* going."

"And he's single?"

"Notoriously."

255

Notoriously?

Ted panicked. "What does *that* mean?"

"Don't worry about it. He's twice her age. Let's do this."

Kevin took up his side of the pole and heaved it into the device. Then Ted did his side. Kevin flicked a switch and the pig began to rotate slowly over the hot coals. It certainly looked like they knew what they were doing. A few guests standing around applauded. They took a bow.

Then Ted heard Cammie make a loud squeaking noise. He was expecting it. He watched her shake hands with Tony, and give Cara a dainty hug.

She skipped over to Ted and Kevin.

"He invited you?" Ted asked.

"What do you mean?" She looked at Kevin. "What's he talking about?"

"To that party."

"The Schwarzenegger party? How did you know? Tony just asked."

Tony.

Christ.

"That noise you made."

"Are you going too?" she asked.

"Yes I'm going. He invited me this morning. I...I was going to ask you to go with me."

She looked mortified. "Oh, Ted, I'm so sorry. I had no idea."

"Brutal," Kevin muttered.

Then Ted heard a loud sizzle. They all heard it. They all spun around and looked at the pig. A big drop of rendered fat plopped onto the coals, igniting a temporary column of blue flame.

Another drop. Another column.

"We're going to have to keep our eye on that," Kevin said.

CHAPTER THIRTY

Marona entered the mess tent and saw Heinrich Airhorne sitting with the professor, blathering away. Lattistrom was trying to ignore him.

"Marona!" he called out. "Save me from this lunatic."

She walked over to the table. There were no empty seats. "Uh, Heinrich?" the professor said.

Marona could see Airhorne didn't want to give up his seat. He looked around. Grimaced. Then caved. "Only," he said, "only because it's you, Miss Marona."

"Thank you," she said, smoothing her frizzy hair with both palms.

"What kind of name is that, by the way?"

"Spanish."

"Spain Spanish or Americas Spanish?"

"I don't know, Heinrich."

"Oh, and watch out. My kale had a snail." He pointed at his service tray which sat in the center of the table.

"I'll keep that in mind."

Airhorne vanished. Marona sat down next to the professor, who slid his meal over to her. "You want these taquitos? I think it's goat."

"Just wine," she said. She picked up the professor's glass and took a large sip. She studied him. He looked awful. Dark stains covered the front of his shirt. His hair was extra matted and greasy.

"I'm leaving Copan," she said.

The professor nodded without looking at her. "I'm not surprised."

"I've got a daughter."

"I know. I understand."

"You'll be okay."

"I will be okay." His reaction puzzled Marona. She had expected him to put up a fight, tell her how much he needed her. He leaned in close and his face lit up with a huge grin. He was trying to hide it from the others. "Something's happened," he whispered. "I couldn't wait to tell you."

"You *did* wait," she said. "What happened?"

"I was taking a nap. I had a vision."

"Oh, Jesus, Professor."

"I saw a man sitting in near darkness. There was a blue glow in his hand. I could only really see his silhouette. He was dressed as a Maya godking." Lattistrom stopped himself to make sure nobody was listening. Then he continued. "It was in a cave of some sort. Or a crypt."

"What did this man look like?"

"I couldn't see clearly."

"I don't know, Professor."

"You don't seem happy for me, Marona."

She put her hand on his shoulder. "I'm sorry. I am happy. If you're happy."

"You have to come with me tonight."

"I will, of course. Did he say anything to you?"

"Nothing. But I got a feeling, you know. A sense of warmth. Of love."

In a way Marona was glad she wouldn't be there to witness the professor's ultimate breakdown, his final acceptance of failure. It was coming soon. Tonight would probably move him one step closer to the edge. It was going to be sad and ugly, and that was that. What could she do to stop him? Not a thing. She knew that by now.

"What do you think the blue light was?" she asked, humoring him.

"It's his life-force. It's growing. We brought him back to life, Marona. You and I."

Airhorne returned to the table with a chair. The professor slumped and became miserable again.

"Why don't you leave him alone, Heinrich?"

"You're worried about the professor? He's going to be fine."

Marona studied him. "Are you ever not drunk?"

"You ever played Strip Risk?"

"You're such a cliché Heinrich. Heinrich Airhorne. What's your real name, anyway?"

He hesitated a second. "Why don't you ask Lattistrom here the same question?"

The professor picked his eyes up off the table and looked at Heinrich with an intense, predatory glare. "You should watch yourself, Heinrich." The professor's voice came out strong and forceful. It was not the first time Marona had seen glimpses of youthfulness in Lattistrom. This time it made her suspicious.

"What's he talking about, Eugene?"

Lattistrom's eyes were locked on Airhorne's. "It's nothing. It's just...they doubt me. They come and go." His voice trailed off. He continued to glare at Airhorne, something building up inside of him. Then he stood up suddenly and grabbed Airhorne by the collar, his face red with rage. "I've been here for twenty years, asshole!" He slapped Airhorne across the face. "You can go to hell!" Then Lattistrom released him and stormed out of the mess tent.

Airhorne sat down and smiled at Marona. He rubbed his cheek. "Priceless," he said.

That night they walked to the top of a small temple built just to the side of the great staircase. Broad steps led to a flat platform once used for public address by the godkings of Copan. From this point they could look down at the grounds of the city center. The night was cool with patches of fog and a gibbous moon. In the jungle, the howlers screamed intermittently. It was not difficult to imagine how similar the scene might have been nine hundred years earlier. The professor sat dressed in his rags and a new conical tree bark hat. Marona wore a college sweatshirt and black leggings. They faced one another. The professor began his prayer. Marona, who had prayed with the professor in the past, could not manage it anymore, her thoughts too focused on the future, getting home and sorting out her real life. She came with the professor for the same reason she always came with him, as a gesture of friendship, and to make sure nothing happened to him.

She brought her hand to her head instinctively, and started scratching her scalp. God, it would feel good to take a proper shower. Maybe she would spend a night in Guatemala City before flying home. A nice hotel. Did they have nice hotels? A good meal. Get cleaned up. Get her head screwed on tight. She didn't want to show up in New York looking like she just wandered out of the jungle. Though that wouldn't be bad as an excuse for her absence. She came down to Central America for a couple of days to think things over and had wandered off a trail and ended up lost. She could even play it off as kind of heroic, a tale of survival. Only the thought of my daughter kept me going.

The professor yelped suddenly and started pawing at the sides of his head like he just walked through a spider web. Then he went silent and fell over to his side, motionless. He had done this sort of thing before, and Marona had no patience for it this time. She shook him. "Get up, Professor."

But he didn't move. She put her ear to his mouth to make sure he was breathing, which he was. She let out an exasperated sigh. "What am I going to do with you?"

Then his eyes opened. He took a moment to get his bearings. He turned away from Marona and vomited. He looked back at her, clearly disoriented. Then his eyes studied the structure they sat on, like a man coming out of a coma, trying to make sense of an unfamiliar environment. It was all very convincing.

"What's wrong with you?" Marona asked.

He looked at her and opened his mouth, but he couldn't speak.

"Are you hurt? Are you sick? What do you need?"

As his senses returned, the professor's wide-eyes softened and his mouth expanded into a broad grin. "Marona?" he muttered.

"Right here. What is it?"

All pretense was gone. The crotchety old professor was gone. He stood up. He tore off his robe with a swipe of his hand and stood naked in the jungle air. There was a brief and terrible odor. Then he raised his hands to the sky and called out, "I hear you!"

"Hear who?"

"The priest."

"I didn't hear anything. Eugene?"

"This way," he said, and took off down the steps with the agility of a man twenty years younger than he was.

Confused, and not wanting to be left alone, she started after him.

But she couldn't keep up.

The camp was quiet when she got back. First she went to the professor's tent, but it was empty. She did not know what to do. Had he wandered off into the jungle alone? Was he still naked? Please just be in the bathroom, or the mess tent.

261

She checked both places. No sign of him.

She started to panic. She would have to raise an alarm, which she really didn't want to do. The professor was already an annoyance in the camp. If Marona had to wake everyone up on his account, it would only make things worse for him. People would file petitions with the university. *The professor has become a liability and we fear for his personal safety.* He would be removed, possibly by force. It would be ugly. That was if she could even find him. She *had* to find him. She couldn't let him lose all this. He had put over twenty years of his life into Copan. It was all he had.

Airhorne, she thought suddenly. He would help her. He was just a volunteer, like her. He couldn't petition anyone for anything. But would he help her? Would he help the professor? Is he even sober?

He'll do it for me, she thought. Maybe. But at what cost? *That* didn't matter. She was leaving anyway. They would all be out of her life soon enough.

She was already walking towards Airhorne's tent.

"Heinrich," she whispered. She listened. "Heinrich!" she shout-whispered. Nothing. She pulled at the tent flap. It was unlatched. She flicked the switch and the bald bulb above his cot glowed with soft yellow light. No sign of him. Where the hell is he? she wondered. In someone else's tent? She smiled at that thought, despite herself.

She checked the professor's tent once more. Nothing. She was out of ideas. She was going to have to ring the dinner bell, loud and long, until everyone knew the professor had finally lost his mind.

But wait.

There was still one place she hadn't looked. She jogged to her own tent. Of course he would be there. It was the only explanation. She felt better, even a little silly for panicking like she did. She would have a talk with him, a real talk. You really need to rein-in this Smoke Monkey business.

I just hope he has some clothes on.

She pulled the tent flaps aside, walked in, and flick the light switch.

A man was sitting on her bed.

It was Coy.

Her husband. Or *ex*-husband.

Here. Right here in Honduras. Where nobody on earth knew she was.

She stood motionless, staring at him with wide, disbelieving eyes.

"No," she said.

She turned the light off. Then turned it back on.

He was still there, smiling.

CHAPTER THIRTY-ONE

The pig was on fire. A dense plume of black smoke coiled into the air and drifted over the ice rink, where it hung captured under the giant awning. People stopped skating and sat with their shirt collars pulled up over their mouths and noses. Kevin had covered the coals with several baking pans, but the fire squirted out the sides and continued to attack the pig. Blue drops of molten flesh bounced off the pans and splashed down on the ground and continued burning like napalm, scorching black holes on the green lawn.

Kevin looked horrified. He had very few options. The whole spit-roast mechanism glowed white hot and leaked liquefied lubricant from the rotation motor. They couldn't get close enough to the flaming pig to take it down. It pulsed an angry red through the heat-distorted air and looked like some malevolent demon. Ted imagined it suddenly animating, jumping down off the barbeque and chasing tourists around the lawn area. He saw it charge across the ice rink, leaving a trail of melted hoof prints. He wanted it to come for him, to corner him while spewing white smoke from its charred snout, the pole still sticking out of both ends. He imagined the pig reaching up to its mouth and drawing the pole from its body like a knight unsheathing a great sword. Before he bashed Ted's skull to bits he might stare at the cowering human and say something like, "What's the matter, am I *bacon* you nervous?" And then Ted himself would be up there roasting over the coals, cored and spinning, his arms and legs bound, while other pigs in pantless tuxedos passed a pleasant afternoon on the lawn, mingling in small groups and sipping slop martinis.

Kevin tossed rags on the fire, but they were greasy and just ignited and made everything worse. Ted stood around with Cammie, useless, waiting for Kevin to tell him what to do. He felt a pulling on his pant leg. Cara was standing next to him. She looked at the burning pig and then looked into his eyes. "You are a very bad man," she said, with all the authority of a hanging judge.

"Back up, Cara," he said. She began crying.

"Where's your father?" Cammie asked.

Wouldn't she like to know.

You're pathetic.

"Guys!" Kevin called to them. "Get that kid out of here!"

The pig started making high-pitched squeaking noises, as tiny jets of air were forced out from the inside. "Is it going to blow up?" Ted asked, a certain fascination in his voice.

"I don't know!" Kevin barked. He was beside himself, reacting as if it wasn't just the pig going up in flames, but his entire reputation as well.

The gathering had swelled to a crowd. Some people on the lawn still wore ice skates. They were curious, jovial, and full of dumb comments about how they wanted their pork cooked. The whole scene had become the afternoon's entertainment, a comedy of errors. For many, this would be the highlight of their vacation. They took pictures and filmed videos of Kevin's frantic search for a solution. Kids scrambled around, yelling and screaming, delirious from the excitement. Certainly, nobody except Kevin minded that this was happening.

Some edible meat might even be salvaged if they could just put the fire out. In fact, the flaming pig might even be a great boon for Luau Day. What better conclusion could these onlookers hope for than to ultimately sit down and enjoy a plateful of the main attraction? If Kevin had been able to keep some composure, he might have even convinced the crowd that this was all an intentional part of the cooking process. *You see folks, don't be alarmed, what you do is you torch the outside and that locks in the juices and keeps the meat moist and tender.*

Can I get mine with the extra poisonous machine-grade lube on the side?

Kevin came to Ted's side, and in a low dejected voice told him to get the extinguisher.

Poor Kevin. This is a grand, expensive, public failure. And it's going to be shameful.

Not for you.

I know, but I don't even like to be around it. The extinguisher foam is going to toxify the flesh. We're going to have to throw the whole damn thing in the trash.

Poor Kevin.

Poor pig.

Ted came back with the extinguisher and stood as close to the pig as he could get.

Cammie's watching, isn't she?

Don't fuck this up, Ted.

Kevin dropped his hand like a general giving the order to a firing squad. Ted let the pig have it. The whole process only took a couple of exhilarating seconds. A bright white cloud and that was that. The heat and smoke dissipated. The party ended. Kids stopped running and a group of teens actually booed them from the ice rink bleachers. The crowd dispersed. Ted looked at Kevin, who was fixated on the pig.

"What a damn waste," he lamented. And Ted knew Kevin was talking about the life of the pig and not the money he'd spent on it. Ted and Cammie stood next to him, shaking their heads at the tragedy. Kevin told them he had a reverence for the animals he served in his restaurant, that as barbaric a thing as it was to butcher and cook animals, it served a justifiable purpose. "But this was murder," he said, "plain and simple." He told them it was all his fault and that he was going to have a very hard time sleeping that night.

Then they heard fire engines in the distance. Kevin threw his hands in the air and groaned. Cammie disappeared and soon returned with a large sheet, which Ted helped her throw over the pig, to downplay the spectacle. But the heated extinguisher foam had altered its state and was now a wet soupy sludge. It quickly soaked through the sheet revealing the blackened pig flesh underneath, like a wet T-shirt. She told Kevin they'd need several more sheets. "Don't worry about it," he said, sounding tortured and miserable. "I'll be in my office if anyone needs me."

"What should we do?" Ted called after him.

"I don't care. Clock out. Go home."

"What about the pig?"

"Luau Day's been canceled."

Ted and Cammie looked at each other and shrugged. They studied the barbeque mess, the burnt pig, the soaked sheet, the blackened lawn underfoot. "At least it didn't explode," Ted said. Cammie nodded.

"You weren't really going to invite me to that party, were you?" she asked.

"I was," he said. "But it's okay that you already have a date because I know of a certain eight foot tall psychotic dishwasher I've been dying to ask out."

Two firemen walked up to them and asked what was going on. Cammie told them about the pig, and said everything was under control. One of the firemen, tanned and very manly, nodded and gawked at her.

I know that look.

You've *mastered* that look.

I bet he can't hear a word she's saying right now.

The firemen eventually poked around the barbeque, determined the crisis was over, tipped their hats and left. But seconds later, one of the firemen returned, running with his hat in his hand. He stopped in front of Cammie, smiled, and handed her a piece of paper. Then he turned and ran back to where the other guy stood waiting for him. They high-fived. Cammie unfolded the paper, read it, and closed it back up. Ted asked her what it said, and she told him the man wanted to know if Ted was single.

Ted smiled.

And she's *funny*.

Now how is that fair to anyone?

"No really, what did it say?"

She shrugged. "It's cute. Just a little thing."

"He likes you, doesn't he?" Ted taunted.

Cammie turned her face in mock embarrassment.

"Does it ever get old?" he asked her, "all the attention?"

"What attention?"

"Oh stop it."

"Are you flirting with me?"

"I'm just asking a question. But if I *was* flirting, at least I would have the guts to do it to your face instead of writing it down on a piece of paper like some seventh grader."

"You're *jealous*?"

"Of Prince Valiant? Listen, lady, a dishwasher has no time for jealousy."

"I thought you were a silver polisher."

Ouch.

She did not sound impressed.

"So are you going to call this fireman? Or are you too busy with Tony?"

"You *are* jealous."

"Maybe a little."

She looked around uncomfortably. "What do we do with the pig?" she said.

The barbeque was still very hot and there were already several magpies dancing around on the lawn, waiting to move in. Ted looked around the ice rink and noticed several large potted trees being used to block access to a set of bleachers that were off limits. One by one, Ted carried them over to the scene of the crime, and built a circular blockade around the barbeque and sheet-covered pig. Cammie seemed impressed by his ingenuity, and they both agreed they'd done all they could do.

They walked back to the employee dorms and Ted asked her if she wanted to go down to the river that afternoon and eat some sandwiches or something.

"By myself?"

"No, with—"

My God.

Where did she come from?

"I'd love to, Ted," she said, smiling as ever.

Oh boy.

Oh boy, oh boy!

"Super," he said.

Ugh. I know. I know.

Super?

I know!

She's going to ruin you.

Of course she is. I don't have any choice with this.

You were kind of back on your feet, you realize.

I don't realize anything.

Plus it's hot out. When she comes down to the river she's going to be in shorts and a tank top.

And a pony tail.

And she's going to be surrounded by the beauty of Valvert and the tranquility of the river. There will be fucking *songbirds*, Ted.

I know!

Plus, you cornered her by asking her out, knowing she had expected to be at work and couldn't possibly have other plans. She has no excuse not to go with you, which means she might not even want to go.

She might hate me for even asking.

Right?

They split up at her dorm and agreed to meet back there in an hour. Once she was out of sight, Ted sprinted across the lawn to his own dorm building. He bounded up the steps four at a time. He could barely control the urge. In his room, he took up his sack of toiletries and the large garbage bag from the closet and went into the bathroom. He entered the last shower stall, set down his bags, and took off his clothes in the changing area. He started the shower. The water came out hot almost instantly. He stood under it for a few minutes. Then he got the garbage bag and brought it into the stall. He opened the bag, letting in some of the shower water. The oatmeal and grits had congealed. He used his hands to stir up the mixture. The hot water returned it to its previous state of creaminess. Then he moved the shower nozzle to spray against the wall. He picked up the bag and poured its contents over his head and stood there in meditative paralysis for a solid ten minutes.

When he left the dorm building to go pick up the food, Cammie was already out front, sitting against an aspen tree wearing exactly what he'd hoped and feared she'd be wearing, which was not much, cut off shorts and a simple green tank top. She had a magazine about horses. He asked if she came early because she couldn't wait to meet up with him. She told him straight-faced that, no it wasn't that, it was the fact that she worried about the sandwiches. "I'm kind of a bread freak," she said. "I didn't think I could trust you."

"Anything else I should know about you?"

"I'm Mormon."

Is that supposed to be funny?

It's not.

No, it's not funny at all.

It's code for keep your grimy heathen mitts off me.

She's setting up boundaries.

Like a pro.

They went to the Village Deli together and stood in line feeling like tourists on vacation. Ted recognized the guy behind the counter from the dorms, and studied his face when he took their order. No doubt he knew Cammie, or at least recognized her.

And she's with me.

Don't, Ted.

He paid for their sandwiches and they took the picnic to a riverside park where large boulders lined the bank so you could sit and dangle your toes in the water. They ate and talked about work. Ted felt more relaxed since his shower. The sun was warm on his back and he was in the company of a beautiful girl.

Just manage my expectations and it'll be a fine day.

You can see her nipples, Ted.

He looked down at the water.

She asked him to tell her something about himself so he said he dropped out of college with only half a semester to go. He told her he came to Valvert because his family had always come there on vacation, that his mother had a cousin who used to own a local business in town.

Cammie told him she was from Boise and had come to Valvert just to get away from it all. She said she was trying to put some space between herself, her church, her family, and a mass of "obsessive dudes." Ted looked at the water again when she said that. She told him she had no interest in college, that Mormon girls only went there to find husbands. She'd been bumming around Boise, living at home, babysitting and working in a restaurant, and it all made her seem like a woman desperate to be snatched up and married. Around town, she said, they called her The Prize. She wanted no part of it.

"So it does get old, all the attention?"

"It does. I mean, what did I do?"

Wore cut-off shorts.

Smiled a lot.

Didn't act like working in a kitchen was beneath you.

"At church," she said, "grandmothers try to set me up with their grandsons. It's gross. The phone is always ringing. Let's play mini-golf. Let's see a movie. It's all my parents can talk about at dinner."

"Why do you think you get so much attention?" Ted asked. He wanted to know how she saw herself.

"I don't know. Because I'm single. I'm marrying age. People tell me I'm pretty."

He just nodded. She looked at the river. He could tell she didn't like talking about this stuff. Or there was an apprehension, or *something*. Which was fine. She said she just got in her car and drove to Valvert without telling anyone she was going to do it, that she chose Valvert since nobody from Boise would be caught dead there. She'd just knocked on the door of the personnel office and asked if they had any openings.

They switched back and forth, filling in the pieces, what had happened in their lives to bring them each to that spot by the river. Ted confessed to her that in many ways this whole diversion to Idaho, the griminess of washing dishes, was a kind of penance. He told her he did something terrible at school, and that he was ashamed of himself. He was moving closer and closer to just letting the whole thing out, about the newspaper and Addie Parson. And Twin. He wanted to tell her about himself because he genuinely needed to talk to someone about his life—someone other than Salton Steve—and she was the best person he knew.

So he looked at her. Sitting on a boulder. Her shorts riding up her legs, her tan skin, her slender arms, her youthful silhouette. Her profile perfectly backlit by the sinking sun. Beads of sweat on the back of her neck.

It would be so much easier if she was just a conceited bitch.

No it wouldn't. You need to thank God she's not a conceited bitch, because you'd be just as drawn to her, if not more so.

He asked her if she had ever done anything she was ashamed of.

She thought about it. "Not really. I've done some things that have made me feel weird. But nothing shameful. Not in the way I think you're talking about."

"It's awful," he said. "I'd never thought much about it. But it's got a real kick, shame. A lot of firepower. I've been angry. I've been sad."

"You've been jealous," she said, laughing.

"I've been jealous, yes. All that terrible stuff. I figured that pretty much covered it on the negative side. You can recognize those guys. You can see them coming. They're parts of life you've know about since forever. And you can survive them the way everyone survives them."

"By blaming other people?" She threw a rock into the water.

"I guess. But you can't do that with shame."

"Slither out from under it," she said.

"Huh?"

"From under the mantle of culpability. That's what one of the bishops calls it. When you blame other people for your problems. Slithering, like a snake."

He asked her if they ever talked about shame in church. She started coughing and almost choked.

She looked at him big-eyed. "Uh, yes, I think the subject has come up a time or two. It's pretty much the foundation of all religions, isn't it?"

"Don't look at me. I dropped out of college."

"I didn't even go."

They both laughed. "Do they teach you how to deal with it?" he asked.

"They teach you how to avoid it."

"What if it's too late to avoid it?"

"You can ask God for forgiveness," she said. She grinned dubiously.

"How do you do that?"

"You just talk to Him."

He asked her if that helped. She said it didn't hurt. Then she shrugged and forced a smile. He got the feeling she thought it was too late for him, that religion for her had been a lifelong journey and this stuff took time and faith and a level of sacrifice.

"But...praying? It can make you feel better?" he asked, trying to sound like he was keeping an open mind.

"I don't know. Yes. I guess. They'd probably also tell you to go out and atone, you know. Do something good. That's kind of the Mormon way. Like helping old ladies, that sort of thing."

But don't smear shit on old ladies, is that her point?

I think so.

He told her atonement and doing good deeds sounded more like common sense than religion. She laughed and told him a lot of what they said just sounded like common sense.

"So then what do you need the Church for?" he asked.

She stood up on her boulder and looked at him like he was an idiot. "Well, for salvation. Obviously." She bent and touched her toes.

There was an awkward pause.

One of us is going to heaven and one of us is not.

Looks that way.

"What did you do, Ted?" she asked. She said it sympathetically, her voice calm.

It's not just morbid curiosity.

She actually cares.

Cammie sat down again. A fuzzy wave of chills coursed through him. His ears started buzzing and he couldn't focus. He closed his eyes, took a deep breath, and it all passed. He opened his eyes, looked at Cammie, and said, "Well, we used to get the newspaper delivered to our house in college."

He finished the long story with the part about walking to his car in the rain. He didn't think the flying turd episode really contributed anything meaningful. "I thought when I first saw you that you were the girl I followed off the bus. I even asked you about it."

"I don't remember."

"Now I can't recall what she even looked like. In my head she just looks like you."

"But that's not the point, is it?

"No. The point is that I felt like a jackass. So I dropped out. I don't feel so bad anymore, but the consequences are still there."

"You can go back to college."

"I don't want to anymore."

"It's a very strange story, Ted."

"I didn't even tell you about Twin."

"Maybe some other time," she said. She stood up and stepped onto his boulder. She sat right next to him, their legs touching. She put her arm around him and nuzzled his neck. She told him all people make mistakes and learning from them is how we grow. He could hear the bishop's voice in her own. She thanked him for sharing with her. He thanked her for listening. He managed to say it without throwing up. But all this gooey emoting somehow seemed okay, even helpful, in her presence. The generic platitudes

275

of a Sunday sermon all sounded like powerful insight coming from Cammie. He *was* glad she'd listened.

The sun by now had set. It was dark out. The stars, as usual, hung low and bright. He couldn't believe they'd been sitting there in the same spot for hours. "Let's go inside," she said. She stood up and offered him her two hands. Taking them, he let her pull him up to his feet. Then she hugged him. Up close she didn't smell like flowers and bubble gum. She smelled human.

"I'm going to sneak you into my room," she said. "It's getting chilly out here. We can talk inside."

They walked to the dorms. He changed again into warmer clothes and met Cammie back out on the lawn. The buildings were segregated male and female, and she treated the business of getting him into her room like some high-risk criminal venture. She became serious and spoke in a whisper.

"You wait here. I'll check the hall and bathroom."

"Got it."

He could tell she didn't break the rules very often, that it made her uncomfortable. But Ted knew she had nothing to worry about. This wasn't the freshman dorms. Cammie motioned to him and he quickly followed her down the hallway and into her room. He shut the door.

Once they were safe inside he told her he didn't think anyone cared about the segregation rule.

"I care," she said, digging through her drawers. "About people seeing you and me together. At night. In a room alone. I don't want them to get the wrong idea."

She had a pile of clothes in her hands.

"What idea would they get?" he asked, setting himself up.

"You know, that you and I are, like, *together*. I'll be right back." She ran out of the room to change. He took a seat on the floor.

I should just leave. Don't push my luck.

You think she's interested?

I'm tempering my outlook.

How very mature of you.

It's just self-preservation. She's lonely. It's not about me.

Not yet.

She needs a friend. I don't want to be her friend.

He looked around the room. Stuffed animals on the bed. A portrait of Christ on the wall. *The Book of Mormon* on the floor still open, like she'd been reading it while stretching.

No.

No.

She came back into the room wearing adorable fleece pajamas.

Yes?

Yes!

He smiled at her, shaking his head. "You're really just some Mormon girl from Boise?"

She nodded.

"That's really the whole story?"

"Yup."

"And you have bunny slippers to go with that outfit?"

"I do." She walked straight over to her closet and produced a pair.

She sat on the floor facing him. She asked if he felt any better about things, now that he'd talked to someone. He said yes, because he didn't know what else to say.

They talked about the pig for a while, and then she went to her bed and climbed under the covers.

"I'm going to sleep," she said. "You can stay over if you want. The bed's real small but I can squish over."

What the hell does that mean?

You know what it means.

He told her he should probably stay over so nobody saw him leaving. He didn't want anyone to get the *wrong idea*. He made finger quotes in the air.

"You silly," she said. "Now no funny business. And no crapping up the bed."

He turned off the light, took off his shoes, and climbed under the sheets, fully clothed. He lay on his back with his eyes open. She told him goodnight, and buried her face in his arm. "You smell like oatmeal," she muttered, and was asleep a couple seconds later.

CHAPTER THIRTY-TWO

"I brought you lots of stuff," Coy said. "You look great, by the way."

Marona stood dumb, blinking her eyes. There was no way she could think of. Not a single possible explanation. She had flown into Guatemala City, taken local buses, ridden in the back of pick-up trucks to this wild jungle camp. She had written no letters, made no phone calls. Only the professor knew anything about her.

The professor! Shit!

"Where's the professor?"

"The who?"

"Jesus, Coy, how are you here? I don't...it doesn't..." Her eyes darted around the room. There was too much going on. The professor was gone. Gone where? She had looked everywhere in the camp. So he was in the jungle then, somewhere, lost, possibly naked.

"This isn't bad," Coy said, amused by the starkness of her quarters. "And there's even power."

"Where's the baby?"

"The *baby*? She's three and a half, Marona. She's fine. She's with my mother."

"And you don't know anything about the professor?"

"Sorry, Marona...and I'm sorry about a lot of things."

"Not now. Not now!" she hollered. "Christ, Coy."

He just smiled though, and started pulling items from a duffle bag. "Shampoo and conditioner, which I'm sure you've been missing." He set the two bottles on the bed. "And animal crackers, hey? You know you love them." He shook the box and the cookies rattled around inside.

She closed her eyes and pressed her palms against her face. "What. Is going on?"

"One of those magazines you love with the pictures of the women wearing the same dress and people vote on who's wearing it best."

"I'm hallucinating. I'm dreaming."

"And like, tons of candy. Airport gummies, the expensive ones you love."

"You have to stop talking. You have to go away!" She was hysterical. "The professor—"

Heinrich Airhorne stepped into the tent. He was a different man than the Heinrich Airhorne she had known. He looked stern, serious, even authoritative. She was glad to see him.

"You," he said, pointing a finger at Coy. "You need to leave. You need to go to your tent."

"Who is this, Marona?"

"Out!" Airhorne shouted.

"I don't even work here," Coy protested.

"What's happening?" Marona asked.

"You can't—"

"Go!" Airhorne shouted. He raised a fist. "Go away. She'll talk to you later!"

Coy stood up, powerless, terrified. He looked at Marona. She looked at Airhorne, marveling at the transformation. Coy walked out of the tent without saying another word.

"That was my ex-husband."

Airhorne looked shocked. "Really? Why is he—it doesn't matter. We gotta talk. We gotta *move*".

"What's going on?" she pleaded. "I'm losing my mind. For real. How did my—"

"It's time, Marona."

"Time for what?"

"Time for the truth. Is that what you're wearing?"

They jogged through the jungle, Airhorne lighting the way with a powerful flashlight. Marona saw no visible path, yet Airhorne seemed to know exactly where he was going. Normally, Marona would have been petrified by the deep jungle at night, but something felt different now. Airhorne felt different. She felt safe. *He* made her feel safe. This buffoon.

The truth, he had said.

She had trouble keeping up. She should have worn different shoes. She should have *brought* different shoes. "You know where he is?" she asked.

"I know exactly where he is."

"Is he okay?"

"Probably, yes. Until we get there."

"Then what happens?"

"That's up to you."

They jogged on. She had to keep a little distance between herself and Airhorne so the bent branches of the underbrush he passed didn't smack her when they swung back.

"How far?"

"Far."

"Where are we going?"

"To the temple."

"Which one?"

"It's a new one...err, an old one. You don't know about it."

"A *secret* temple?" Through her heavy breathing it was hard to fully communicate the sarcasm.

"Yes, Marona, a secret temple."

"Does anyone else know about it? How long have you guys known about it?"

"I've know about it for twenty years."

She stopped.

"Come on," he said running in place. "We have to hurry."

"You said I'd find out the truth."

"You will, you will. Just keep moving. It's going to be amazing."

"*Twenty* years?"

"Yes."

"And the professor?"

"Longer than that."

"What? When was he going to—" Heinrich started jogging again. She sprinted to catch up. "Talk to me," she wheezed.

"He's playing you, Marona."

"Apparently you are as well."

"I'm...I had to."

"Would he say the same thing?"

"Yes."

They continued in silence for another thirty minutes. How far had they gone? Three miles? At least. They were in the deep jungle now. It became clear to her that she would need someone's help to get her back to camp. It made her very uncomfortable to be so dependent on these men, either Heinrich, who she'd *thought* was crazy, or the professor, who she *knew* was crazy. Whatever sense of independence this trip to Honduras may have established was gone now. Without men, she was lost. Literally.

Right back where I started.

She cut herself off. She'd deal with all that later.

Airhorne stopped running. He put his hands to his sides to slow her. He put a finger to his lips and motioned for Marona to carefully follow him. He turned off his flashlight. They stood at the edge of a small clearing in the

282

jungle. It was nearly black dark, but the clear starry sky gave them just enough light to see across the clearing.

He was praying.

She recognized his body position. He appeared to still be naked.

"He's a fraud," Airhorne whispered. "He wants us to find him. He wants us to think his prayers led him here."

"Where is *here*?"

"The Temple of the Smoke Monkey he calls it."

"Where's the temple."

"It's that mound over there." He pointed across the clearing.

"It hasn't been excavated?"

"He just *discovered* it right now, remember?"

"But you said—"

"I said he was a fraud. It's all bullshit, Marona. Your little meetings at night. His whole life. This is his big moment. We're supposed to find him like this, and believe he's communicated with a spirit, that he was led here, inexplicably. We're supposed to be awestruck. But he has known about this place all along. I know that. And he doesn't know I know that. He thinks this will make him the most famous archeologist of all time. He means to legitimize Theological Archeology."

"He lied to me?"

"Yes."

"And he doesn't know we're here?"

"No. He thought it would take days for the search parties to find him."

"So it's all a scam. All bullshit? And he thinks he's the only one around?"

"Yes."

"Then why is he still praying?"

283

CHAPTER THIRTY-THREE

His ass hung off the side of the mattress. Another night in her bed. Cammie Holder, the Queen of the Kitchen. Ted was still fully clothed. Tonight, he even kept his shoes on, to emphasize the absurdity. Earlier, she tongue-kissed him on the hood of his car while a small campfire smoldered and meteors rained down all around them. They had driven down some dirt river-access road. He told her about Travis and the hitchhiking girls. She told him she had five-thousand dollars in her underwear drawer. He told her he wanted to live in her underwear drawer. She got up when he said that and rooted around in the car for a bottle of water.

And then the sheriff pulled up and wanted to know what provisions they had made to extinguish the fire. Did they have a pail of water and a shovel? Ted told him it was under control, that he had been in the Boy Scouts for almost a year, and the sheriff threatened to arrest him for negligence and conspiracy to commit arson. He watched Ted take trips down to the river to fill up the water bottle twelve times and squirt-out the fire, always chatting Cammie up when he was alone with her.

Ted told her more about Jackie's death, how he hadn't moved a muscle to help her. He told her about his hands, the pink gloves, his pride and vanity. She told him what the Mormons thought about pride and vanity.

A fart, long denied, made its way back up through his intestines.

It was the middle of the summer. The half-way point. He had done a pretty poor job of replacing the absurdity of college life with something more grounded. If anything, his life seemed even weirder now. He still felt like he was seeing things through the opacity of oiled paper walls, as if his life was handcrafted by some lazy overseer, who had peopled it with clichés—impossibly beautiful women, quirky sidekicks, and a mall catalogue of vacationing extras. It's why Travis disappeared. He didn't fit in the story. His center of the road Samurai training too good, too much the kind of thing Ted thought he was looking for.

Despite his chaste and achingly unsatisfying romance with Cammie, he continued to feel less and less comfortable. His teeth hurt in the morning from nervous grinding. He schemed in his lost moments at work for ways to get his hands on more bagsful of grits and oatmeal. He pictured himself buying a nice bathtub, one just big enough to fit in the space of his dorm room between the bunk bed and the closet. He imagined filling that tub with warm breakfast. His head would be all that interrupted the smooth wetness of corn-colored textures.

Of course the pig caught on fire.

He tried something a few weeks earlier that he knew would never work. He tried escaping from the escape. He drove to Yellowstone and camped in the backcountry for two nights. Two nights of pissing himself with bear thoughts and abstract fears. Every twig snapping outside his tent was a zombie invasion, and the sub-woofer rumble of rocks readjusting in the river bed was the collective hoof beat of a ghostly cavalry. He just wanted to pass a pretty girl on the trail with her large breasts framed above the chest strap of her pack and to get some thick buttered toast slices and runny fried eggs. Instead he got rained on and a yearling cub stole his peanut butter and he saw a dead wolf on a median strip driving back to Valvert.

And there was a sandstorm and an old guy on the side of the road who said, "You're going to drive through a sandstorm." The kind of guy who when you look back at him in your rear-view mirror he isn't there anymore. He saw no other cars, and the big red thing swallowed him whole. He sat there like Dorothy in a funnel cloud, watching impossible visions spin past his windshield. A giant squid. A houseboat full of spring-breakers. His parent's dog.

Something is broken.

When the woods fail you have to live...not *deliberately*...

But *ironically*?

You don't sit in your car, Ted, and wait for it to pass. You get out and shit on the side of the road, the whole time the storm so bad it feels like someone is funneling fine grain sand into your ears. And then you put the shit in your gas tank, and thirty hours later, when Triple-A arrives, you explain what happened, and then you look at the guy. You watch him.

And that's where it is.

Right there.

About two and a half seconds.

That's all you get.

They say the guy who used to have my job owned a monkey which bit him so he lynched it with a garden hose.

"What are you thinking about?" she asked.

"You've never been to San Diego?"

"No."

"You're sure."

"Come on, Ted, you've asked me that."

"Why does the question bother you?"

"Listen, do you want to come to Boise with me?"

What?

Wow.

"What?"

"Meet my parents, everybody. It'll be fun!"

"Wait," he said, having trouble keeping himself focused. "Why would you want me to come to Boise?"

"I think you'd like it."

"Based on what?"

"I don't know. You just would. My parents are awesome."

"Only if you have a trampoline."

"We do."

"Of course you do."

She rolled over and went back to sleep.

How bad could it be, being Mormon?

You're out of your mind.

It's inevitable, isn't it.

Are you really going to be that guy?

Why not? Are there limits to just how ridiculous my life is allowed to get?

And how exactly does one become Mormon?

I don't know. You take classes. Pledge allegiance.

That doesn't sound right.

No, it doesn't. How could they ever really know if you were a true believer, especially if you professed your faith en route to marrying a girl like Cammie?

So you're getting married now?

Just brainstorming.

They'll know you're just trying to get in her pants.

Maybe they see things differently. What if I just told them Cammie's beauty led me to the One True Faith? How could anyone argue with that? What greater purpose could beauty be meant to serve?

Fair point.

Maybe I'm not taking a large enough view. Leaving college to work as a dishwasher was small time. But full-blown religious conversion...that's *real* change.

At Arnold Schwarzenegger's dinner party Cammie couldn't stop smiling. And the dinner guests couldn't stop smiling at her. She wore a simple green full-length dress and a fresh roadside daisy in her hair. As usual, her attempt to carry herself somewhat modestly became her sexiest feature. Her hair was straight and simple. She wore no makeup, no jewels, not even a pair of earrings. Yet even there, amidst the high rollers and fancy wives, she led all the eyes back and forth to the hors d'oeuvre table, where she bypassed the tuna tartars and stone crab skewers, preferring to snack on the salted pretzels, cheddar cubes, and little Vienna sausages at the kid's station. She drank lemonade from a blue straw.

Tony Reznack didn't leave her side, but Ted wasn't worried. He knew a little bit more about Cammie by then, and there was no chance she would run off with some widower twice her age. Plus, she had invited *Ted* to meet her family, which was good enough for now. His own date, Salton Steve, had cleaned-up nicely. He stood in the corner with Bruce Willis, drinking Scotch, and trying to teach him how to pop his knuckle. Cara, in her little red dress, stood next to them, marveling at the entirety of Salton Steve. She wore that same perplexed and troubled expression she had when she saw the pole in the pig's asshole.

Ted honestly didn't know what to do with himself. Cammie was star struck, and showed little interest in chatting him up. Which was fine. He understood. But he still felt compelled to show her he could handle himself in this setting, that the money and fame were no big deal. And to do that, he'd need to be at least half-drunk. But he didn't want her to see him chugging booze either. So he drank light beer and spent probably too much time talking to

Kevin, the least interesting person in the room. He figured talking to his boss might give Cammie the impression that he was business-minded and mature. It was all ludicrous and all of it went unnoticed.

While he sipped his beer and talked Michelin ratings with Kevin, Cammie had Arnold, her date, and a slew of other fancy-looking people laughing hysterically at her terrible Terminator impressions. She said, "I'll be back," when she excused herself to the bathroom. Her date actually slapped his knee he was laughing so hard.

As the cocktail hour wound down, people kept picking Cammie up and carrying her around. He'd never seen people act so strange.

She's intoxicating.

Literally.

They're going to snatch her up.

Carry her straight to California.

Wouldn't that be ironic?

No, you idiot, that would not be ironic, it would be a coincidence. It would be ironic if they carried her instead to Warsaw and employed her as a seamstress.

Whatever, Gob.

But the truth did hurt. Ted's best-case scenario, lots of baby-making in some semi-rural Mormon utopia, sounded a lot like the life Cammie had just ditched for Valvert.

This party, these people, that's how it happens for girls like Cammie.

One would think.

But she's also just a potato peeler, right?

Not anymore.

What are you suggesting?

She's never going back to that kitchen. They'll keep her here, have new dresses made, put her up in a guest room with a view of the mountains. She's never coming back down to Earth.

Why would she?

Why should she?

By the time they sat down to dinner, Salton Steve was sauced. He did the spoon bending trick for Cara, but he actually bent the spoon. Then he did napkin tricks, with clever folds producing silly rabbit ears and a brazier. He laughed aggressively at his own antics, and Ted wondered how much longer it would take him to go from charming to disturbing. He knew Salton Steve had something up his sleeve and Ted just hoped when it did go down, none of it stuck to him.

But without his date sitting next to him, Ted was bored. Which was depressing. Alone at the table, he felt awkward and jealous, and angry that he couldn't seem to relax and enjoy himself. But he had to wear a happy face, for Cammie's sake. He knew it was pointless to over-analyze everything, but he couldn't help himself. He ate his salad in silence, with a big grin, pretending to zen-out on the ebullient vibe of the beautiful people. Salton Steve came back and sat down. Bruce Willis pulled up a seat and listened intently as Salton Steve explained how to grow pot in an old Salvation Army refrigerator.

The main course arrived. Fresh whole rainbow trout on a plate. No garnish. No starch. No veggies. Baked fisheyes bursting with a hardened fluid. Minimalist and savage, which seemed appropriate to the venue. He couldn't really see Cammie from where he sat, but he could hear her laughter and the commotion surrounding her. He looked down at his fish, at the trout lips, and thought they were moving slightly. *Are you talking to me?* The fish seemed to rock its head slightly, nodding. *You want to tell me—*

"Ouch!"

Fish on my face!

Hot wet fish!

Scales!

On my face! Hot fish!

"What the—"

Ted put his hand to the side of his face and felt a clumpy slime.

Salton Steve shout-laughed so hard the table shook, the fish flopping over in his fist like a melting ice cream cone. Bruce Willis fell straight back in his chair and lay in a fit on the floor, clutching his abdomen and struggling for air.

Ted, in a rage, took up his own fish and feigned a swing. Salton Steve winced defensively. Ted then pulled Salton Steve's collar and dropped the fish under his shirt. With exaggerated panic, Salton Steve stood up, untucked his shirt, and did a squirming jig until the fish fell out and landed on the floor next to Bruce Willis's head. Salton Steve and Ted locked eyes. The room was dead silent. Then Salton Steve bowed. So Ted bowed. And the whole room burst into applause.

Ted cleaned the side of his face and walked over to the bar, the whole room watching and giggling, every exaggerated movement, or simulation of disgust, generating aftershocks of laughter. He got one last encore of applause when the bartender started dumping gin into a tumbler, the way you'd do for a guy who just missing having a piano land on his head.

As the party wore on into the night, the others loosened their hold on Cammie, who wandered to Ted's side as he sat on the arm of a black leather couch listening to Salton Steve explain how the Maya invented potatoes.

"You're quite a popular gal," Salton Steve told her.

"Everyone's so nice here," she said, still in a bemused daze.

"So what's with the rich guy? Friend of your dad's?"

"That's Tony," she said, lightly slapping Salton Steve's arm. "He's sweet."

"Are you guys...what?" Ted asked nervously.

"Me and Tony? It's nothing. You know that. He just wants me to come see his place."

Salton Steve made a cooing noise.

"It's not like that."

"You sure?" Ted asked.

"Look at you Ted, all protective and stuff."

Ted glared at Salton Steve.

"Yeah," Cammie said, "I'm a big girl."

Salton Steve eyed Tony across the room. "With that kind of money you could really do anything."

"He wants me to babysit his daughter."

"I bet he does," Ted said.

Salton Steve echoed Ted's comment in a bratty sing-song: "*I bet he does.*"

Ted got to his feet, suddenly fed-up with Salton Steve. "What is it with you?" he asked. He felt his face muscles quiver. The fish thing had been fun. He got it. It had actually saved him in a way. But he couldn't handle this constant tonal shifting. Were they friends? Enemies? Was the guy just crazy?

How many times are you going to ask yourself that?

I can't pin him down. I can never get him to be the same person for more than ten minutes.

"Why this constant need to fuck with my head?"

"Maybe you should put your drink down, Ted."

"Shut *up*, man!"

"Ted, just relax," Cammie said, moving in close and resting her arm on his shoulder. She smelled like flowers and rum cake.

"This guy's a fucking asshole, Cammie. He is. Aren't you?" Salton Steve shrugged. "He's always working some angle, playing some game. Like this shit with my drink. I've hardly had anything at all tonight and he knows it, but he wants you to think I'm out of control."

"You are kind of shouting," Salton Steve said.

"I'm not shouting, Dicknose!"

"Let's go out on the porch," Cammie said. "The view is wonderful."

Cammie took Ted's hand and led him to the door. Ted glared at Salton Steve, who gave him two thumbs up and a wink.

He's a genius.

I'm just glad he's on my side.

Now Ted was alone with Cammie out on the balcony, with a view of Valvert and the ski mountain in the distance. The big white moon. Romantic and peaceful.

Cammie snuggled up against him, consoling and tender. "Are you coming with me still?" she asked.

"When are you going?"

"Next Monday. Coming back Wednesday. Can you get the time off?"

"Yeah, I'm in," he said, forcing a smile.

"You're still thinking about Salton Steve, aren't you?"

"He's such a dick. But he's also not."

"Who cares? What's he to you?"

"It just bothers me. I don't understand it, that's all."

Before he could react he knew what was happening. The two hands on the sides of his pants. The stiff downward tug. The cool night air on his thighs. He turned to see Salton Steve running tip-toe back into the main room. He reached down and pulled his pants back up.

He looked at Cammie, who had turned away from him. He walked around her until he could get a look at her face. She was shielding her eyes with the back of her hand, but he could see the tears running down along her nose. She stamped her right foot twice, took a deep breath, wiped her eyes and looked at him, and then exploded with laughter and apologies.

"Un-fucking-believable," Ted muttered, turning to look back inside. Salton Steve was doing a blowfish with his mouth pressed against the glass, Cara at his side watching him with a big smile on her face.

"Just relax, Ted," Cammie said. She put her hands on his face and pulled him to her mouth. As they kissed in the glorious expanse of the Idaho wilderness, under the patient and benevolent moon, Ted had one hand behind his back with the middle finger extended. But Salton Steve had moved away and only little Cara was there to see it.

CHAPTER THIRTY-FOUR

Lattistrom started sprinting the second he stepped off the worn stone staircase. She would follow him down, and expect to find him stumbling along the path back to the tent camp, either sulking or still transfixed by yet another one of his visions. When she didn't find him right away, she'd calmly search the camp, and wait until morning to say anything.

To protect you.

It was going to be hard. Hard but necessary. It had to hit everyone equally. Friends, colleagues, locals. It had to look authentic. Twenty-seven years, everything had to be perfect. And as far as he could tell it *was* perfect. Marona had made it so. How lucky that she had come when she had. *She* really was the sign, the call to action.

He found the stash under a fallen log. He put on the robe, drank as much water as he could, took the granola bars out of their packaging and flicked on the headlamp. It might take days for them to find him, hopefully not longer. He wanted it to look like Smoke Monkey was sustaining him, that he didn't need food or water. He could leave no evidence that he had arrived intentionally.

He set off at a jog. The jungle was hot, even on this clear night. There would be a moon later, a full moon.

Which was another perfect omen. Maybe. *Probably.* But it was still a guess. For all his praying, he'd heard only silence. That wasn't unusual though. Gods didn't answer prayers with a voice. He had to have faith. He would always have faith. Faith in Smoke Monkey. Faith in the plan. He had seen purple lightning flash out of the jungle. He had been saved how many times in that one day? Jumping out of moving cars, bullets missing, planes crashing.

I was summoned to a temple. That was all the reassurance he would ever need.

He hadn't been to the temple in twenty years, since he made his last run for gold and scattered the remaining few sheets of fuselage. But he knew the way from Copan. They had the very best maps back at camp. Satellite images of the jungle indicating all known ruins and their excavation status. But nothing near the temple. Nothing to suggest he might have accidentally found it. The nearest structure anyone had actually worked on was three miles south. He suspected Smoke Monkey's temple wasn't even part of the Copan city state. He hoped it was older. He couldn't wait to find out. Though all the years of scholarship had, in a sense, been part of the ruse, he had still developed a genuine love for archeology. Once they found him, they would excavate. He would lead the crew. They would strip off every last bit of grime. Yes, some day in the very near future, he would see the temple clean in the sunlight. He would study the inscriptions and learn. And maybe when he had learned enough, he would know better how to communicate. And maybe one day when he prayed, there would be a voice.

But he was tired from jogging. He walked for a bit. There was no hurry. It would also be great to recover his body, his youth, to toss off this slovenly Lattistrom character and become his old self, Oliver. Fit, healthy. Virile. Oliver Easton.

First thing I'll do is cut this god-awful hair.

She would like that. She was already his, practically. Nobody would be happier for him than Marona. He would give her as much credit as he gave himself.

He started jogging again.

I'm coming.

When he arrived, he noticed a small clearing in front of the temple that he didn't remember. It would have troubled him if he had taken more time to consider why in this of all places there would be a break in the endless density of jungle. He dismissed the observation and focused on the temple itself, or rather the mound which encased the temple. It was such a mundane sight. How much better this moment of rediscovery would have been if he could have seen the real temple, as it was made to be seen, glorious and proud and holy.

He took off his robe and buried it under a log. He took his place naked in front of the mound and dropped to his knees.

Twenty-seven years.

"See me now here in the glorious present, my journey to you complete, attending the next great voyage, as we travel together into the hearts of the new men. I have been your servant through these years, careful for your sake to find the safest roads to revelation. I have brought others who will join us soon. They will come. They will bring their families. They will learn all that has been hidden these years. It is my promise. My promise made and unbroken. Have these promises been made before? Made and been broken by others? I will not abandon you. I will honor you. I will teach them the power of faith. I am your first miracle of the modern age. They will see it all and understand that no science can explain my presence here before you..."

Then suddenly, there was a voice behind him. "Put some clothes on," it said. "It's not such a pretty view."

Airhorne's light found his face as the professor turned his head. "*You*," he hissed.

"Hello Professor. I've brought a friend of yours."

Marona stepped out from behind Heinrich Airhorne and tossed the professor a shirt and a pair of pants. The professor stood up mute and got dressed.

"*How?*" he asked, dazed.

Marona moved forward and shoved him hard with both hands. The professor fell back on the ground and looked up helplessly in disbelief. Then she slapped him across the face, the cold sting echoing through the jungle.

The professor was still looking at Airhorne. He spoke with his eyes. *How?*

I just beat someone up, Marona realized. An old man, granted. But, yeah. Just like that. She looked down at the professor's crumpled body. She tried to spit on him, for emphasis, but the dry white foam mostly just stuck to her lips. Then she opened and closed her fist the way she had seen tough guys do in the movies. There was no pain at all, which made her think she probably did it right. She looked over at Heinrich and smiled.

"Right hook," he said. "Who saw that coming?"

Marona shrugged. The professor rolled over on the ground. She tried to spit on him again.

"Must you?" he protested.

"Must you," Marona repeated, exaggerating his ridiculous academic affectation.

The professor sat up and put a muddy palm to his nose. Then he looked at it. "Bleeding" he said. "It is an older man you abuse this way."

"Oh please," Marona laughed. Then she turned to Airhorne. "What do we do now?"

"We savor our victory," he said, pounding his chest with a fist.

"Can I kick him?"

"Sure you can kick him."

The professor rolled out of range, covering himself in more mud from the jungle floor.

"Look at you," Marona taunted. "Like a big flabby cigar."

"You don't understand," he pleaded. "Either of you."

"I understand that you're a fraud," Marona said. "And I understand that you used me. Am I missing something?"

"I am decidedly *not* a fraud."

She shook her head, remembering the nights in Copan. The prayers. The outfits. The conversations. "Eugene, I confided in you. I told you about my daughter, about my marriage." A thought flashed into her mind. "But that's not even your real name, is it? A Harvard scholar named Eugene?" That never sat right.

Airhorne nodded. "His real name is Oliver Easton."

Now the professor laughed. "Okay, Heinrich. And while you're at it, why don't you tell her *your* real name."

"Both of you? Jesus Christ." Marona put her hand to her forehead and groaned. Fake names? Fake lives. Fake everything, she thought. These fucking men. All of them. All of them liars. "That's perfect," she declared to the jungle. And not the least bit surprising. First Coy, and now these two. Ah, Coy. She had almost forgotten about him, back in the tent camp. Going through my stuff probably.

"Fish!" she had shouted at Coy's father, at their last New Year's Eve party, back in New York. "Coy is a fish!"

She took a deep breath of the tropical air. To say this isn't the life I expected to be living—thousands of miles from home, in the asshole center of a jungle in Honduras with perverts and stalkers and con men. She looked again at Airhorne, her doofus protector. Six-foot-six Heinrich Airhorne.

"Salton Steve," he said.

"Huh?"

"My real name. My real name is Salton Steve."

She just stared up at him. "I'm not calling you that."

"Suit yourself."

"Okay then," she announced. "I'm ready to go home now. Yes, one of you retards needs to take me home."

But no one moved or said anything. The jungle too was still and quiet.

Poised.

She took off one of her pumps and wiggled the heel back and forth. "Ruined," she said. She threw it on the ground and then undid the elastic in her hair and shook out her ponytail.

The professor coughed and spat. "Anyway," he said, "the moon is rising."

"Fantastic. That's fantastic, *Eugene*."

"It's going to come up right over the temple."

Marona ignored him. "Yes, first I'll go back to C.R.," she mused. "Then to Chiquimula, Estanzuela, and Antigua eventually, to a spa. Yes..." Her voice trailed off. And then what, Marona?

The boys were suddenly at it again, arguing. Airhorne was repeating himself. "You can't. You just can't, shithead. Not in this world. Sorry. Manufactured divinity?"

"Your term, not mine." The professor stood up.

"Well that's what it is. And conjuring? Really? In the Ivy League?"

"I was not conjuring. That's nonsense," the professor said, brushing himself off.

"Nonsense indeed!"

She could sense Airhorne tightening up. There was real anger in his voice. Why does the professor make him so mad? Marona wondered. My own rage is certainly justified. But the professor never used Airhorne like he used me. In fact, the two of them seem like they should be friends, or at least professional associates, maybe a journeyman and his apprentice. The professor there to nurture Airhorne's budding insanity, to harness the irrational energy of this seminal brain malfunction. It was hard to tell who was crazier. The professor, for concocting the plan, or Airhorne for waiting twenty years to call him out. Surely some of this must be rubbing off on me, she realized, that these are the people at the core of my existence.

As if to prove her point, Airhorne began lecturing the professor. *Lecturing!* He was telling the professor that this so-called theological approach to archeology was irresponsible. *Irresponsible?* As if Airhorne was some kind of watchdog. This nutcase. This milkman-looking guy. Then he tackled the professor again, and held him down in the mud.

Neither one of them noticed the exact moment when the moon finally did crest right over the temple mound. "Boys," Marona said. She was pointing. The jungle suddenly woke up. Unseen creatures called out. There was movement in the branches above. "Can we please go back now?" she asked. "There's plenty of light." There was a little flutter in her voice that caught her off guard. She realized she was uncomfortable, fundamentally. Something strange was happening, strange even by these current standards. She thought she could feel a very subtle vibration in the ground.

The professor was back on his feet, wiping mud from his face, but smiling now, staring at the moon and the mound. "What are you so happy about?" she asked him. But he didn't say anything. Probably thinking about his temple, she realized. Thinking about the human bones or mummies, the gold and silver, the etchings and scratchings—whatever was there all those years ago when the interred god called to him. To this place he meant to publicly rediscover. Today. Now. With Marona as his witness. But of course that got all fucked up, thanks to Heinrich Airhorne, public avenger.

The ground was now definitely shaking, and a deep unfocused sound vibrated up from somewhere. They all looked around. "It's probably a helicopter," Airhorne said.

"You believe that?" the professor asked.

Marona shushed them both. "Listen, do you feel it? It's an earthquake."

"They don't have—" Airhorne cut himself off as the ground really started shaking. The professor fell to his knees, grabbing Marona's hand and pulling her down next to him. She didn't resist. In fact, she squeezed his hand hard. Her knees sunk into the soft wet ground. She looked at Heinrich, who threw her a jilted glare. She shrugged and smoothed her skirt with her free hand. Right away the professor started in with his praying. She knew he would think this earthquake was a message, a grand sweeping justification. She had asked him weeks earlier about his prayers, how it would be possible for Smoke Monkey to understand English. He told her the same way The Virgin of Guadalupe had understood Mayan. Marona wasn't Catholic or anything, and still the comparison sounded like sacrilege.

But a strange earthquake, she thought, though they're all strange. She had grown up in California and had been through a few. They always left her feeling rough and unsettled. It'll pass soon, she told herself, this shaking, this jungle nonsense, this whole pre-Columbian nightmare. You'll get up, brush yourself off and head back with your one good shoe.

Airhorne wasn't as calm. He ran to the center of the clearing to get out from under the trees. His movements were jerky and defensive, like someone expecting to be struck by lightning. Then she heard a loud crunching noise, as a stunted tree that grew out the side of the mound suddenly lost its purchase and tumbled to the ground. A thin blue stream of light shot from the exposed hole and fixed itself against the trunk of a spiky-barked tree right next to Marona.

The shaking persisted. The professor continued his muttered prayers. Marona plunged forward from her knees

302

and lay flat on the ground like a sailor on deck in a storm. She lay there riding the undulations, with her ear flush against the jungle floor, her arms up over her head for protection. Then she heard something strange, deep within the earth: the unmistakable hissing of pressurized air escaping from industrial hydraulics.

She lifted her head from the ground and looked around. Huge trees flapped their branches as if they were trying to take flight. Airhorne lay on the ground in the middle of the clearing, beckoning to her to get out from under the trees. The professor, covered in mud, was crab-walking towards the mound...and the blue light. She put her head back to the ground and listened. A mechanism of some sort. She could hear it. Like turbines, like a steam engine. Hissing.

There's something down there.

Which was impossible.

Then everything suddenly stopped. There was a brief silent pause.

And then the birds went crazy.

A dissonant crush of sound from all directions. Panic and confusion. None of it really visible at all. Maybe a dark form crossing from one tree to the next. Hard to tell in the half-light. She looked to the mound in time to watch the professor stand over a cowering Heinrich Airhorne, pointing a righteous finger down at his fallen nemesis. She heard his voice come through clear as the bird calls lessened.

"You dared! You dared defy Him!"

Then he turned and ran to the base of the mound. He looked back at Marona and then began to scramble up the side towards the opening and the source of the dim blue light, which continued to reach out across the clearing.

Marona stood up and walked over to Airhorne, everything just pure anger now. She put her spiked heel on his chest. He didn't resist. From what she could tell he was in a state of shock, just lying there with his eyes open. "Who are you?" She pressed down with the heel.

"Salton Steve, for real."

"Are you lying to me?"

"No."

"Who is he?"

"He's Oliver Easton, like I told you."

"Who made the ground shake?"

He took Marona by the ankle and moved her foot. She didn't resist. He sat up. "What do you mean?" he asked. His voice came out weak and defeated.

"The earthquake. How did you do it?"

He smiled. "I don't even know what you're asking me. That was an earthquake, Marona. For real."

"No, it wasn't. I heard...*machines* in the ground."

Salton Steve stood up. He brushed himself off, for all the good it did him. He extended his hand. "I feel like we got off on the wrong foot."

She reached out quickly and grabbed at his nipple. She twisted. He gasped. "Who made the ground shake?" she demanded.

"That was...I don't know Marona."

"Why is my ex-husband in Copan?" She twisted harder.

He slapped her hand away and stepped back. "I don't know anything about that either."

"You told me I'd find out the truth."

Salton Steve shook his head. "I thought I knew the truth." He looked up at the mound. "I guess there's a lot more going on than I thought."

"So the professor...he *is* a professor, right?" Salton Steve nodded. She continued, "The professor is *not* a fraud then?"

Salton Steve threw up his hands. "I don't know anymore. I know what he did was fraudulent, or I thought it was, but...he prayed and the ground shook and there's a light in the temple and...Jesus, who knows?"

CHAPTER THIRTY-FIVE

Earl Bish couldn't believe the untested thing actually worked. Worked *perfectly*. But then why shouldn't it? His were the best engineers on earth. They relished the challenge, and trusted Bish enough to know they would be well compensated if they could turn his abstract ideas into functional realities.

Which is what this whole thing is really about.

In fact, BC Petrol engineers had done things far more complex than this. Like the surface-based tar sand extractors they'd used on lakes in northern Alberta. Or the natural gas receptors they used in the oil wells up and down British Columbia, which harnessed oil deposit gases and reused them to power the pipeline pumps. Or the hydration tubes he'd conceived of for the city of Las Vegas, that would bring salt water from the Pacific and use the natural heat of the desert to desalinate and purify the water while it traveled. Most of it was patented one-of-a-kind machinery designed to deal with a specific environmental factor. Sometimes Earl thought he could make just as much money selling technology as he could selling resources.

He wondered if there was a big market out there for earthquake machines.

The real challenge wasn't in designing the technology; it was in its covert implementation, smuggling everything in piece by piece, finding willing locals with the right connections and then buying their silence. Trusting them to keep their secrets.

Trusting them to do what I could not do. What I promised...what I swore...

Then moving everything to this secret location without locals, government officials, military or paramilitary, or anyone else catching on. And then assembling it. Doing it all without any snooping archeologists seeing the mound and realizing there was a significant unexcavated Maya site just next to Bish's own excavation site.

He really had to give himself credit. There weren't many people on earth who could have pulled it off, working the human angle so well, meeting the essential players in the ports, breaking bread with their families, making promises to educate and employ. And doing it all in a foreign country, with foreign customs, and a foreign language. A beautiful, logical evolution of his abilities. His greatest triumph.

So far.

He sat in the muggy control room with six other men, watching the pressure gauges all fall back out of the red. He watched on the video display as Oliver Easton ducked his head and tentatively entered the upper tomb access, the blue light on his face.

What must he think that is? What is he already calling that in his mind? What fantastic tale to attribute to its origins? None so fantastic, I assure you professor, as the plain old truth. Which you'll have soon enough. To break your heart. But the look on that poor bastard's face—that rich bastard's face. Bug-eyed and determined. Sweat-stained. Enraptured.

"Get my wife on the phone."

He studied Easton's face some more. The image quality was perfect.

I see a man who is actually terrified by the confirmation of his *own* beliefs. That this would be so shocking. Oliver Easton, like some pious supplicant, awed by the reality of his own transmigration. *This bullshit...is real?* That it would be so hard to take the knowledge that prayers have been answered. That we expect failure and are confused by success. Even in faith, where we get make our own rules.

"He's there, honey. It's amazing...yes...everything...on video. In still frame shots. And Salton Steve as well. I know, the little sneaking weasel. Well, we have him...it is, I know...just what he deserves, yes. He looks genuinely broken. The Dilenta woman's giving him hell right now...yes, in her heels...I wish we could see all that a little better. The light's not so good out in the clearing. Once they get in the temple though...*man*, this is the greatest. Call Twin, will you? Tell him it's *on*. Everything is on!"

He mopped his brow with a towel. He exhaled. More high fives with the crew. All calm, professional. Of course it worked, sir.

But *wow!* And what had it cost him? Fifty million all told, give or take. Compared to what they had taken out of the crypt it was nothing. It paid for itself. For the whole operation. For the future of Smoke Monkey. Thank God Easton went back that last time. Otherwise we might never have found the place. Easton will understand, eventually, once he gets the whole of it. If he survives the shock. He'll be angry, sure, and humiliated. Just look at Salton Steve. That's an expression that's almost hard to take.

And what about this Marona Dilenta? She's going to be good. Essential. And it's in her blood. Was it coincidence what they found when they checked on her? Setting her cheating husband up with prostitutes. Small time, sure, but in her heart she understands. And throughout this Copan ordeal she's handled herself perfectly. The right mix of compassion and strength. *Remind you of anyone, Earl?* First the beatdown on Easton, and now she's giving it to Salton Steve. In a tight skirt and high heels. Just awesome. And whose idea had it been to bring in the ex-husband? *Oh, that was mine too.*

Genius.

Earl Bish felt no guilt. Not about the welching or the pillaging. If Easton wanted to persist in his faith, he was free to do that. Smoke Monkey was still Smoke Monkey. The only difference now was that the game was over. There would be no magic revelation to sell the masses. Sorry Oliver. No Theological Archeology chairmanship at Harvard.

But don't worry, I got something a hell of a lot better for you.

Not that Bish could expect Easton to understand. At least not yet. He was twenty-seven years into this thing and his only confidant had lied to him and taken all the money. He was going to be...what? *Angry?* No, no, no. Something far beyond angry. Homicidal? Blood thirsty, vindictive, *and* homicidal? Probably. And we've all seen his ability to stay focused on a plan.

But Bish had considered all of this. Of course he had. It's what he did, professionally. Once Easton got past the pride issue, he might listen. And once he heard what Bish had to say, once he *understood*, he might settle down and join the party.

Yes, Bish thought as he looked at a still frame image of Easton entering the temple. A perfect image of his face. An expression of exhilarated expectancy. Of sheer terror. The others would understand. Once they saw this, they would all come around.

And if they didn't?

Well, fuck'em. They brought this on themselves. They all did.

Even that kid in San Diego.

A member of Bish's team stood behind him, holding a garment bag and a hatbox. "Sir," he said, "you should probably go get dressed."

CHAPTER THIRTY-SIX

Cammie's car was a real piece of shit, a rusted-out red Fiero that swooped and vibrated as they drove it west to Boise, into a brutal wind. The door seals hissed, the antennae whistled, and neither passenger said a word. Ted could feel every imperfection in the road vibrate up through the car's foil-grade chassis.

He looked over at Cammie.

You are way too pretty to be a good driver.

He turned to look at the brushfire again. It burned much bigger now, a horizontal comet-trail of orange and brown smoke floating parallel to the road. He could see the actual flames eating at the ground. Moving upstream into the wind.

"It's too gusty for the Bell 204's," she called to him, her hands firm on the wheel, elbows out, fighting the pull.

You are way too pretty to know so much about helicopters.

It made for a strange mix of emotions. Death, he was certain, would come soon in the form of twisted metal and hot fire. But he was also exhilarated. The two of them on the road, plowing across the elemental thresholds.

Through Fire and Wind!

She sprayed the windshield with cleaning fluid.

Through Water!

When they reach the other side...

Nothing will be as it has been!

"Let's just drive to Vegas and get married," he said.

She laughed.

"I've always wanted to say that."

She patted his thigh, and then readjusted her tight grip on the wheel.

He turned to watch the fire again.

He imagined himself as some ancient criminal archetype. He had stolen Cammie out of a dream, broken the code, angered the gods. Valvert was some fantastic set-up, a playground. She had been put there to delight him and bemuse him. But she wasn't supposed to leave. He had outsmarted her keeper, stolen sacred lightning from a dozing guardian. They were back on Earth now, headed not to some apocalyptic showdown, but instead to the grandparents' house, for an early dinner, and pie.

"I'm worried," she said, looking at the fire. "There's a nuclear thing over there, like a test lab or something. It's top secret."

"Not a good place for a fire."

She shook her head. "Have you made your peace with God?"

"Is that a serious question?"

"Of course."

"Have you?"

"Of course."

"You've been talking to God?"

"I sure have."

"How's he doing?"

She laughed. "He's very busy."

An eastbound semi roared past them, sucking their car briefly towards it. Cammie rolled her eyes and smiled. She refocused on the road. Then she wiped her forehead and shook out imaginary sweat drops with an exaggerated cartoon flourish.

He watched her, amazed.

I *could* become Mormon.

(nodding)

I could do that.

Just then, they passed a guy pulled over on the side of the highway, playing a full-sized drum kit.

What the fuck?

That's Salton Steve.

Playing the drums on the side of the highway.

With the wind and the fire and the nuclear time bomb just in the distance.

"That was Salton Steve!" Ted shouted, twisting his head to get another look at him.

"Seems like something he'd do."

"No, I'm serious. It was him. Playing the drums."

"That's ridiculous."

"Exactly. Go back. I'll bet you."

"You want me to turn around?"

"Please!"

"I don't want to turn around," she said. "We have to push it." She was worried about the fire. "Plus, I don't want to be too late. My twin sister makes some kick-ass ribs. There won't be any left."

He stared at her. She didn't smile, or anything.

He waited. Thirty seconds. Two minutes.

Not possible.

Now she's doing it too.

"*Twin* sister?"

"I'm the smart one and she's the pretty one."

The wind finally died down as they neared the city. Cammie relaxed and pointed out important landmarks. This is where they filmed a Bill Cosby movie. This is where you turn to go to the local ski mountain. This is where you always drive through insect swarms.

Ted hadn't thought much about what they would actually do once they got to Boise, how it might be for him to hang out with her whole family, her six brothers and sisters, her parents, and four grandparents.

All with the spotlight on me.

They're going to be suspicious.

This guy from *California*.

This predatory hormonal atheist.

So Ted was surprised when they pulled up to the grandparents' home in a wooded suburb and he was overlooked and ignored by the stream of family that poured out the front door and surrounded Cammie, lavishing her with love and praise like she'd just clinched the pennant. The fact that Cammie had arrived with a boy seemed not to even register on this group. And that wasn't encouraging.

Either she *always* has boys with her...

Or you're soon to be discarded, like all the other rejects.

It took her verbally introducing Ted to get anyone to even look at him. But once they did acknowledge him, they came around, systematically running him through introductions, from youngest to oldest.

When Cammie's mother Pam shook his hand, he told her it was nice to finally meet Cammie's twin sister, which sent the grandmothers into hysterics.

"She tells everyone that," Pam said. "And I have to say I don't mind."

Well played.

Dad's not amused.

Bruce had kept his distance at first, working with the barbeque over by the house.

He doesn't have a shirt on.

And he's wearing cut-off camo shorts.

He's sizing me up.

Of course he is.

Cammie was still busy with her family, so Ted surveyed the bug count on the front of the car. Then he went around kicking the tires. He tried to look manly in his concern. He nodded to himself.

He's still watching me.

He's coming over.

Ted heard the hard crunching footsteps on the gravel. Bruce introduced himself with a bone-crushing handshake. His fingers were sticky. He asked Ted where he was from and what he did and what his father did and if either of them ever served.

"I mostly wash dishes, to be honest," Ted told him.

"I mean in the military."

"Oh, no sir," he said.

"Your father in Nam?"

"National guard."

He nodded and started to give Ted his own credentials when Pam moved the whole crew inside. They all sat in a circle in the family room, Ted next to Cammie, Bruce across the room. Two of Cammie's younger siblings played with blocks on a big green rug. Cat Stevens played quietly on the radio.

"So Cammie's told us nothing about you, Ted," Pam said to him.

He looked at Cammie. She shrugged.

Then one of the grandmothers broke in. "Where are you from?"

"San Francisco, originally."

Her father did the same cartoon forehead wipe Cammie had done in the car. "Guess we can call off the dogs then," he laughed.

"Dad, not everyone in San Francisco is gay," Cammie said.

"That's true," Ted confirmed.

"And what brings you to Idaho?" the other grandmother asked.

"He dropped out of college," Cammie said. Ted thanked her.

Cammie's two younger sisters sat next to Bruce. "You guys must miss Cammie," Ted said to them.

"Yes, but she'll be home soon," the youngest of the two said.

"Three weeks!" the other cheered.

"Really?" Ted asked, suddenly puzzled. He looked at Cammie.

She told him not to worry about it.

A bowl of Fritos made its way around the circle. Pam told Ted that Cammie's paternal grandfather built the house they were sitting in. Ted said he would love to know how to do something like that.

"Ted can't even change a flat," Cammie said.

He scowled at her.

What's she doing to me?

You're a prop.

For what?

Multi-generational Mormon inter-family dynamics.

So good luck with that?

Pretty much.

"We saw Chuck's mom at the market," Pam said. "They do miss him." Then she rubbed the head of one of the boys and told him she didn't know what she was going to do when *he* went on *his* mission.

Ted's chair was made of hard wood and offered no cushioning. He started to develop a strange feeling in his left buttcheek. He had his wallet in his back *right* pocket so it wasn't that. He casually leaned to the side and felt around the back of his shorts. There was something in the left pocket.

"You alright, Ted?" Cammie asked. He realized it might have looked like he was letting out a fart.

"Yeah, I'm just cramped from sitting all day in the car." He turned to Pam. "Which reminds me, where's your bathroom? I need to make a stop."

She pointed down a hallway and Ted excused himself. He walked slowly down the passageway, studying the photos for pictures of Cammie. He found one of her at a school dance, in a gaudy blue gown, a tall awkward boy standing next to her in his rented tux. Neither one of them was smiling.

Then he found the bathroom. He flicked the light, shut the door, and reached into his back pocket.

A condom.

He stood there mortified.

He didn't own any condoms. He hadn't even seen a condom in two years, much less brought one with him to Cammie's house. His roommate Luc didn't have any either, he was pretty sure.

How did this thing get in my—

Salton Steve.

That motherfucker.

Exactly.

He was in my room yesterday. He brought me a copy of the *USA Today*. I left for a second to get a shampoo bottle from the bathroom. He must have put the condom in my pocket then.

Ted stared at the wrapper.

It's actually kind of ingenious, in terms of a prank.

Don't, Ted.

It is.

You know what would have happened if they found that thing? If *he* found that thing? They'd roll you up in that green carpet, set it ablaze, and throw your ass into the Snake River Canyon. But Salton Steve is kind of a genius, you say.

Well.

Knock it off, Ted. It wasn't a prank. He could have ruined everything for you. What kind of person would travel hundreds of miles to a Mormon girl's house—the house where she grew up, where her family all still lives—and defile her out of wedlock while her little brothers and sisters sleep in the next room?

This condom makes me that person.

Salton Steve makes you that person.

Ted winced. He turned the condom in his hand, unable to fully dismiss its purpose.

Sex with Cammie.

Knock it off!

He couldn't throw it away. He didn't trust Grandpa's do-it-yourself plumbing either. He didn't need the condom floating back into the bowl once he'd left the bathroom. And he couldn't bring himself to put it in his wallet and be *that* guy. It was going to have to stay in his pocket, which had a button, until he could get to his bag in the car and hide it away for good.

When he got back, Grandma Number One told him all the boys were out front at the grill. He found Cammie in the kitchen with her mother.

"You feeling alright?" she asked.

"Yeah, I'm fine. It's not...it's nothing."

They sat on the linoleum floor and shucked corn, while Pam stirred something on the stovetop. "Just like I'm back at work," he joked.

"I thought you were a dishwasher," Pam said.

"He's an awesome dishwasher," Cammie said.

Ted thanked her again. "And Cammie's quite the potato peeler."

"Idaho, born and raised," her mother said.

When they finished, Ted told Cammie he had to go to the car for a second. Her look told him he was acting weird and needed to cut it out. He told her he would just be a second.

He passed the smoking grill on his way to the car, and waved lamely to the three men huddled around it. A black dog ran up to him and buried its head in his crotch. He shooed it away and opened the passenger side door, which concealed the lower half of his body. He fished the condom out of his pocket, unzipped his duffle bag, and dropped it in there. Then he grabbed his favorite hooded sweatshirt to justify his little excursion. He slipped it on and became instantly aware of how hot it was out.

"You cold?" Cammie's shirtless dad called over to him, contempt in his voice.

"I thought I was," Ted said.

"What does that mean?"

"I must have been sitting under a vent," he said. Then he took the sweatshirt off.

"Don't have any vents," Grandpa Number One said. "She's all swamp-cooled."

"Hmm," Ted nodded. They all eyed him suspiciously. He balled the sweatshirt up in his hands.

And he felt something.

Two somethings, in one of the pockets.

Oh my God, I will kill him. I will execute him when I get back.

But it's such an ingenious prank, right?

Fuck off.

There could be *hundreds* of them.

Fuck *off!*

He turned back to the car and put the sweatshirt away, eyeing the ground the whole time in case something fell out. Then he joined the guys at the grill.

"Can't figure this weather out," he said.

"What's to figure out?" Number Two said. "It's hotter'n shit. All summer, every summer."

"Then it rains."

"Right, then it rains."

"I'll try and remember that," Ted said. He stood there nodding while they all stared at him. He looked at the grill. "Charcoal, huh?...I'm with you...if you're going to use gas...you might as well cook inside...but I always burn the chicken it seems...all the sugar in...the...barbeque sauce...did Cammie tell you all about Luau Day?"

She came bounding down the front steps, sunlight in her hair, her breasts flopping around under her T-shirt.

Ted tried not to react.

What do they all see right now? Is it the same thing I see? How does that sort of thing work? How do *daughters* work? Of course they all know she's pretty. But do they know she's *hot*?

They certainly know what you're after.

· They must. They must know it's one of the central—

The central.

Fine. *The* central goal in my life right now to watch this girl undress, to watch her naked body move across the room into my bed. I don't even think that makes me a pervert. They might even know I'd be willing to make monumental sacrifices and alter the entire trajectory of my existence just to make that happen. And yet it's completely normal for us all to hang out and eat dinner together? How can any man ever even look at his daughter's boyfriend?

Then Cammie was next to him. She put her soft hand on the back of his neck and he had to put his own hands in his pockets and turn to the side.

CHAPTER THIRTY-SEVEN

By the time Oliver Easton passed through the low portal and entered the upper chamber of the temple, he was once again focused on his ultimate goal, which was direct spiritual contact with his god. Obviously, things had not worked out the way he had intended. But he wasn't going to look back at those twenty-seven years as time wasted. Rather, it was time spent honing his faith. Without the knowledge he had acquired as an archeologist, without the prayers atop the Hieroglyphic Staircase, he might have been too hasty in his desire for contact.

He was actually happy for the recent trials, the throng of doubters trying to steer him from the path. They just confirmed his faith. And so did the earthquake. Which was...

I don't know what to say about that.

The source of the dim blue light was difficult to identify. It seemed to come from the very stones in the walls. At one time, it had been focused and bright enough to cast a beam across the clearing in the jungle, but now it barely shone strong enough to light the room.

He breathed deeply, taking in the ancient earthy odors. He wished he could close a door behind him. He could hear the other two talking as they climbed the outer side of the mound, fouling the aesthetic. He didn't know what to do next. He could wait, and then surprise them. Overpower them. Push them back down to the jungle floor. Injure them as they injured him.

He looked around the room. He saw a small tunnel in the far corner, leading downward, accessing the lower portion of the temple and the crypt he had discovered all those years earlier. He could go now, but they would just follow him.

The voices grew louder, came closer. He moved back to the main opening and stood just to the side, hidden. They were *right there*, discussing what to do. It sounded like they were working together. Salton Steve would have to bend low just to pass through the portal. It would be an awkward defenseless position. Oliver could go for the knees. A hard sideways kick. Salton Steve would crumble, then tumble.

But can I really hurt Marona?

He hesitated. She entered the room. He didn't move, didn't breathe. She went straight for the tunnel on the other side of the room, like she knew it was there all along.

"Come on," she said without turning around.

Oliver saw the beam of Salton Steve's flashlight moments before he entered the room. Marona must have turned to look just as Easton stepped out of the shadow.

"Look out!" she yelled.

Salton Steve stepped back just in time to avoid Easton's awkward leg kick. Then he lunged forward and had Easton on his back again, pinned to the floor of the room.

Shit!

Oliver closed his eyes. His body went limp. He didn't have the strength anymore. It was just too hard. All of it.

"You were going to send me flying down to the ground," Salton Steve said. "With a kick. That's not very manly of you, to kick. You're not a very manly man, are you?"

Oliver didn't respond. He didn't even open his eyes. He felt the weight of Salton Steve's body lift. He curled into a ball. He closed his eyes tightly, but he couldn't stop the tears. His body convulsed in silent tremors.

"He's crying, Marona."

"Let him cry."

Then they were gone. Down through the tunnel, presumably, to the gold. He could hear their voices fading. Broken, he thought. I am broken and I will lay here unmoving until I die, in the temple of my god, while others defile the sanctity of my heart. Oh, where are you now? Does my weakness offend you? Does my stupidity reveal my unworthiness? I do not blame you for abandoning me so soon after your great revelation. Your great effort wasted. Are you tired as I am tired? Is it all over, then? Do we share this last gasp? Do you too run on the fumes of glorious resurrection, slumped as I am, defeated and sad?

He heard wings flapping. A shifting in the air. He opened his eyes. The light of dusk barely filling the room. The soft blue glow was gone. He sat up. A small black bird stood in the center of the room looking at him. It cocked its head. Then it wiped each side of its beak on the stone floor and picked one leg up and then set it down. It wiped its beak again and lifted the other leg. It made no vocalizations. Oliver just stared at it, his mouth open. The bird cocked its head to the other side. Oliver smiled. The bird leapt into the air and flew back out of the temple.

Then, from somewhere down below, he heard Marona Dilenta scream.

CHAPTER THIRTY-EIGHT

"Earl?"

"Help me out of here, will you?"

Marona lay on the ground next to the great stone block, having fainted from the shock. Candles burning in wall sconces encircled the crypt.

"Earl Bish?"

"Where's Oliver?"

"He's..."

"He's what? Where is he? This is all wrong. Fuck." Bish peered over the edge. "What happened to her?"

"You scared her to death."

"Shit. I thought..."

"Oliver's still back up the tunnel."

"Shit. Help me out of here." He raised his arms and Salton Steve took his hands and heaved him out of the coffin. He was dressed in an elaborate Maya robe with intricate multi-colored patterns. A thick assemblage of gold necklaces looped low across his chest. On his head he wore the skull of a jaguar with polished jade eyes. Bright metal twinkled on his ears.

"What are you wearing?"

"Godkingly garb," he said. He brushed himself off. Then he bent over and touched his toes.

"You look ridiculous," Salton Steve said.

"Yeah, well...is *she* going to be alright?"

"She'll be fine," Salton Steve said, too focused on the absurdity of his old boss Earl Bish, his presence in the coffin, his outfit, everything.

"We should do something about her skirt. You can see all the way to China."

"Did you pierce your ears?"

"No." Bish fumbled with the shining objects and held them in his palm. They're clip-ons. Custom made."

"How did you..."

Bish leaned over the coffin and pointed down. "Oh, there's a tunnel. We built a tunnel. Do you think we can reset this, for when Oliver comes down?"

"I think the cat's out of the bag, Earl."

"I guess it is. Damn. I put a lot of effort into this." He looked around the room. "Well, it definitely worked on her."

"You knew I was bugging you?"

"Not the whole time. Not until you quit and I had you followed. Once we saw what you were up to, following Oliver around, we figured it out. That was clever, I'll give you that."

Marona groaned and sat up, dazed. She looked at Bish and squinted. Then she rubbed her eyes and looked at him again. Then she looked at Salton Steve. "Is that him?"

"Is it...oh, no, this is Earl Bish. We used to work together."

"Okay."

"Are you alright? Can you stand."

"What about the earthquake?" she asked. "I heard..."

"Shhh," Bish whispered. "He's coming. What should we do? Everybody hide. No, there's no...just lie down...like I've smitten you."

"Give it up, Earl," Salton Steve said.

Oliver Easton emerged from the tunnel just as Bish was nervously scrambling for something he could do. Anything to get a rise. But he was caught in this awkward dance looking very ungodkingly. And at any rate, Salton Steve and Marona were just standing impatiently in the center of the room, slightly embarrassed that their host had done such a poor job with the surprise part of the surprise party.

"What's this?" Easton asked. His voice sounded almost chipper.

Bish faced him, gave an embarrassed smile, did a quick jig, and then froze in position. "Ta-da!" The jaguar skull slid off his head and crashed onto the stone floor. The sound echoed throughout the crypt.

Salton Steve and Marona were so uncomfortable they both turned slightly away.

"I don't care," Easton said. "All of you can do as you like, nothing changes...is that you Earl?"

"Hello, Oliver."

"You swore on the *Bible*, Earl," Easton said.

"Yeah, well, looks like I can't be trusted. I guess I'm in good company."

"Your god will punish you for this dishonesty."

"I fully expect you to be angry."

"I'm not angry anymore. At any of you."

"Well now I feel better," Marona said. Easton's presence had brought her wits back. She marched over to him.

"Marona," he said, "I wasn't going to—"

She punched him hard in the stomach. He immediately went down on one knee and shut his eyes.

"Whoa!" Bish called out. He went over to restrain her. She punched *him* in the stomach too. Harder. He fell forward onto both knees, gasping. She straightened her skirt. She glared at Salton Steve, who waved his hands in mock supplication.

"We have to work together," Bish gasped, as he slowly got to his feet.

"Work together?" Marona said, a disgusted laugh in her voice.

"Where's the body, Earl?" Oliver's voice was still strained from the blow. He stood at the coffin, looking down. "Stealing gold is one thing, but to remove the remains—"

"What body?" Bish wheezed.

Easton looked at him impatiently, "The truth, Earl."

"That is the truth. I took the gold, yes, that I did. But it's for all of us. There's so much to explain. This is all getting too confused."

"When I first looked into this coffin I saw the mummified remains of Smoke Monkey. Where is he?"

"Don't look at me," Bish said.

They both turned to Salton Steve. He threw up his hands. "Don't look at me, either. I've never even been in this temple. I followed you here, to the location. But I never—"

"When?" Easton asked.

"The same time I followed you," Bish said. "Right after our last meeting."

"You guys were in on this together?" Easton asked, stupefied.

"No, no, no," Salton Steve said. He explained how he had bugged Bish's office. How he had then quit working for BC Petrol and spent the past twenty years more or less stalking Easton, waiting for him to pull the trigger and lead the way to the gold. "If I'd known you were going to wait this long, I might have chosen a different line of work."

"What about this mummy then?" Marona asked. They all looked from one to the other. No one spoke. "Great," she said. "So there's a mummy on the loose. That's actually not something I ever thought I'd say." There was more silence. "And the earthquake?"

"Oh, that was me," Bish said. They all looked at him in disbelief.

"And my husband," she asked, "or ex-husband, whatever?"

"Me again," Bish said.

Marona looked to Salton Steve for help, then even to Easton. She was incredulous. She approached Bish again, but he ran around the crypt, keeping the stone block between them. She was furious. "Who the fuck are you? You don't even know me. Stop running you little shit." They both stopped. She took in a deep breath and then let it all out, her hair grew bright and red, as if she had summoned some demonic power, her beauty suddenly terrifying as she hollered at Bish, "You will pay, mister!" Bish cowered. She marched over to him. He put up two trembling fists. She faked low and then punched him full across the side of the head. He went down and lay there panting, cradling his cheek. She huddled over him and hiked up her skirt.

"Oh, don't." Salton Steve said.

She aimed the dark stream into Bish's ear canal. He didn't move.

None of this phased Oliver Easton, who watched passively. He took a seat on the stone floor and looked like he might stay there forever.

Marona stood up and pulled her skirt back down. "Now you've seen it, Professor," she said, disgusted by everything. She shook out her hand and took a seat against the wall. "Anytime any one of you wants to take me back to camp."

Salton Steve nodded absently, his brow furrowed and his closed mouth pursed forward. "Well, I'm just going to have a seat as well."

Hours passed. Hardly anyone had moved, except Bish, who now sat up like the others and kept jerking his head to the side to get the urine out of his ear. Each of them had a separate wall to lean against. The stone coffin sat in the center of the room. The candles were almost burned down.

Eventually, Bish spoke. "We have two hundred and thirty million dollars in our general fund."

Several more minutes passed in silence. "What fund?" Salton Steve finally asked.

"Smoke Monkey International."

"Wait, *our* fund?" Marona asked.

"That's right."

"What for?"

"For whatever we want. For special projects. Like this one. This was the first one. Forgive me Oliver, but your plan was going to fail. I told you that from the beginning. But it did inspire me." Bish stood up. From inside his robe he produced three identical photographs of Oliver Easton as he first entered the upper portal of the temple. He handed one to each of them.

"I can't see anything in this light," Salton Steve said.

Earl walked over to the coffin, leaned over it and yelled, "Lights!"

The crypt lit up instantly. The others looked around, noticing small recessed bulbs hidden between stones on the ceiling. Then a voice came over an intercom. "Do you need a medic, Mr. Bish?"

He shook his head. "Just maybe a clean damp towel,"

A disembodied hand appeared in the coffin holding a towel. Bish took it and cleaned his face.

Marona was looking at the picture. She was smiling now. As was Salton Steve. "This is pretty great," he said. "You have to admit."

"I don't even know what to call that expression," Marona said. "Like you're on your way to collect lottery winnings."

"We created that look, all of us," Bish said. "Don't underestimate its importance in the world."

Easton was less excited. "Needless to say, I don't appreciate you manipulating my most sacred beliefs for the—"

"Save it, Oliver," Salton Steve said. "It was all a con. You got conned while you were trying to con everyone else. I got conned trying to con you. This guy Earl conned us all. It was brilliantly played."

"Thank you," Bish said, relieved to finally get some of the praise he felt was his due.

"And I'm just, what, collateral damage?" Marona asked. "That's nice."

Marona had had her pound of flesh already, and Bish was done being defensive. "Not so fast, little lady," he said to her. "Let's talk about New York. You didn't tell your buddy Oliver about *that* did you?"

"What do *you* know about New York?" she asked.

"I know that you paid people to seduce your husband. I know you did it at least four times."

Salton Steve began to laugh hysterically. "That's amazing."

"It's a con is what it is," Bish said. "Look, it's no accident we're all here together."

Marona didn't say anything.

"Two hundred and thirty million dollars." It was Easton who spoke.

"That's right."

"For special projects."

"Yes. Look, this one didn't work out. Sorry, Oliver. But you've shown us the way. You've brought us together. And we're going to try again. And we're going to get better at this." He gestured around the room. "*This* is over. Where do any of you go from here? Back to normal lives? I don't think so. So let's do it again. Only this time we work together. And we don't take twenty-seven years to make it happen."

"Do *what* again? I don't understand," Marona said.

"Manufacture divinity," Bish said.

"Oh, lord," she said, "and how do we do *that*?"

"Oliver tried it his way. It took too long and it didn't work. We need to do it the old fashioned way."

"And what's that?" Marona asked.

"Destruction and resurrection!" Earl said triumphantly. "Or something else. Whatever you guys want. Whatever we decide."

"Why?" Salton Steve asked. "Why bother?"

"Because we can. Because it's fun. Because of the look on the face in that photo. We can make lives mean more."

"By tricking people?"

"You have a problem with that? A problem with power and money, and freedom to bend the rules, with manipulating the lives of deceitful people for your own glory and edification?"

"Vigilantism?"

"To a degree. But we don't punish outright. We have style, class. We fabricate a reality, with all our resources. We are thorough."

"I'm in." It was Easton who spoke without looking up.

"Good, good. Thank you, Oliver. We can get started right away."

Easton continued: "As long as you tell me what you did with the body. Those remains were sacred and I *still* believe."

"That's a mystery, Oliver. All I found in here were the golden potatoes. Many more than you estimated. But no body."

Easton nodded.

Bish turned away from him. He perked up. "Marona? What do you say? A truce? You'll be rich. Think about your daughter."

"Fine," she said. "Why not. I don't even know what I'm agreeing to do."

"Perfect. You'll see. I'll bring all of you up to speed. Salton Steve? Think of the creative potential."

"I guess I'm in too," Salton Steve said.

"Wonderful. Now come here. All of us together. Smoke Monkey International." They circled the empty coffin. Bish forced them all to hold hands. They looked around the room at one another. Salton Steve nodded. Marona nodded too, and even cracked a smile. Oliver Easton did not smile.

"So what do we do now?" Salton Steve asked.

"First we have to go to San Diego. First Class. Smoke Monkey International *always* flies First Class. You ever stayed in the penthouse suite at the Hotel del Coronado, Marona?"

She shook her head. "And what are we doing in San Diego?"

"Stealing newspapers," Earl Bish said.

CHAPTER THIRTY-NINE

After lunch they headed over to Cammie's parents' house. Ted was given the boys' room. They would be sleeping in a tent out on the dead lawn in the back yard. He put his bag down on the bed and looked around the room. The kids apparently had a thing for robots. There were stuffed robots in a basket on the floor, robots on the wallpaper, and a big robot change bank that lit up and moved its arms if you put money in a slot on top of its head, which Ted did. It seemed forced to him, all these robots. Robots were *okay*. But there were cooler things out there. He thought back to his own childhood.

He laughed out loud.

Dinosaurs!

They can't have dinosaurs.

"You okay in there?" Cammie called to him. She was in the bathroom, fixing her hair.

And putting on her swimsuit.

Calm down.

He went outside. He sat at the patio table with a glass of lemonade, waiting for her. The sounds of children laughing and yelling came from all directions, as did a chorus of gritty metal squeakings. Across the yard, past the trampoline and the boys' tent, Ted could see the occasional heads and bodies of the neighbor children on the other side of the back fence, bouncing on their own trampoline. He stood up and walked to the center of the dirt lawn, to get a look at the side fences. To the south, more heads of children crested and disappeared. To the north, still more of the same.

The door opened, and Ted turned around to look at her. She was wrapped in a towel, which covered her suit and made it look like she might be naked underneath. She looked as beautiful and unassuming as ever, smiling and fumbling with her lemonade glass at the sliding door.

Ted sat down and looked back across the yard, to avoid gawking. Cammie came over and stood next to him. She sipped her drink. She set the cold glass on the back of his neck. His muscles seized and he lurched forward.

"Ah!"

"Feels nice, doesn't it."

"Yeah," Ted said, wiping the moisture from his neck and craning his head around to look at her. "You live in a trampoline wonderland."

"I do?"

He pointed. "They have one, and they have one, and they have one, and you have one."

She took a seat next to him. "They also all have cars, you know, and kitchens and bathrooms."

Ted nodded.

Just then, the little dog Taffy came sprinting from the side yard. It dashed across the lawn and jumped onto Cammie's lap. A larger white dog followed, then stopped next to the trampoline.

"Get!" Cammie yelled. "Go on."

She looked over at Ted and frowned.

He stood up and walked toward the white dog. It immediately turned around and ran back across the lawn.

"That's Butchie," Cammie told him. Ted looked at her. "He keeps digging under the fence. He's got a thing for

Taffy." Then she stood up, set the dog down, yanked her towel to the ground and sprinted toward Ted. He watched her body move in a black one-piece, athletic and shiny. She passed him, charging full speed. She put her hands against the horizontal metal frame and did a powerful handspring flip into the air, landing in the middle of the trampoline, her momentum then carrying her high into the air, straight up like a rocket, where she then kicked her legs out spread-eagle and touched her toes before straightening out again and landing with a momentum-absorbing knee bend.

Holy shit.

That's your girlfriend?

This most graceful and erotic.

Prettiest.

Greatest most physically perfect.

Most dazzlingly gorgeous.

Sexually potent girl I've ever seen in my life.

He took a breath. He walked over to the trampoline, dazed. He put his hands on the frame and looked directly into Cammie's eyes. "Cammie," he said. He steadied himself. "Cammie..."

She looked at him. She must have recognized his expression. "Claire!" she yelled, "fire away!"

Ted turned around, still in a fog. Cammie's younger sister was standing on the patio. She took up the hose and sprayed an arc of water over Ted's head, down onto Cammie and the trampoline.

"It's freezing!" Cammie yelled, delighted.

Ted turned again, to see her wipe the water from her face. He watched it drip and run along her body as she bounced slightly up and down, the wet suit tugging at her breasts.

My *God*!

Is this for real?

A cold jet of water then caught Ted in the back and he jumped forward involuntarily. He took off his soaked T-shirt.

"Get up here," Cammie told him.

Taffy sprinted past his feet, chasing the water, yipping at the air. Ted felt a chill and regained himself. He climbed up on the trampoline and stood there facing Cammie while water fell all around them.

Brothers and sisters soon joined the party. Claire brought the hose over and got down on her back, underneath the trampoline. She shot jets of water up at them, anytime a body part touched the black mesh. They called the game *Cold Lava*.

Fortunately, Ted was pretty good on the trampoline. He could flip frontwards and backwards, and do this thing where he would land on his back and fly across the mat and land on his back again and again and again without losing his momentum. They had never seen that one before, and eventually he had everyone trying to figure it out. Then Cammie made the kids all climb down and go inside.

The two of them continued bouncing around alone, Cammie all laughter and smiles. Ted kept catching her looking at him. He had let it go crazy in his head. He would do anything, wait as long as he needed to, believe whatever he needed to. There was never going to be anyone else.

He floated in the air. Cammie made a quick move and had him around the legs as he came down. They fell together in a tangle of limbs while Claire doused them from underneath. It was playful and innocent, and also the most powerfully erotic moment of Ted's life. Her wet suit formed a thin barrier between his bare skin and hers. He could feel her breasts and nipples on the small of his back. And he could smell her sweat mixed with the dead wet lawn and earthy hosewater.

A savage aching pumped though his body. Strewn arms and legs now clutched and held and pulled into each other.

This is her raw physical body, her forehead pressing his shoulder, her hot breath down the back of his arm.

"Dinner in thirty minutes!" Pam yelled out though the open glass door. She held a mixing bowl in one hand and a large wooden spoon in the other. The water jet stopped and Cammie and Ted peeled apart from each other. He tried to catch her eye to see what was there, but she shuffled off the trampoline and jogged to the patio for her towel. He lay there alone for a moment staring up at the big open sky, his pulse beat so strong the trampoline never really came to a full rest.

Shortly after, the fourteen of them sat around a huge dining table and passed bowls of food. Lasagna, garlic bread, salad, dressing, apple sauce, cheese cubes, ambrosia, orange slices, canned corn, something for everyone. Bigger kids helped little kids. Parents helped grandparents. When everyone had a plateful, Cammie's father welcomed Ted from San Francisco to their dinner table and asked him to say grace.

He panicked. "Well, I've never—"

"I'm joking, Ted," he said, playful for the first time since Ted met him. "You should have seen how big your eyes got."

Cammie pelted her father with a dinner roll. Everyone laughed.

He looked over at Cammie, who was smiling at him.

"Holy father," Claire began, "giver of all good, accept our praise and bless our food. Grace, health, and strength to us afford, through Jesus Christ, our blessed Lord. Amen."

"Amen."

Taffy scratched at the door. Pam let her out.

They all dug in. For thirty minutes Ted gorged himself, passively enjoying the scene. He liked watching two of Cammie's younger brothers, who just spaced out, one giving the tablecloth corner an accordion fold, the other trying to get his fork to stand free in a bowl of applesauce. Eventually he had to answer some tough questions about dishwashing and liberalism. Things got loud. They got funny. More rolls were thrown at Bruce.

Cammie stood up and walked over to Ted. She put her hands on his shoulders and kissed the top of his head before going to refill the water pitcher in the kitchen.

Someone, at a grandfather's request, recited her times-nines.

Cammie came back and filled everyone's water. Then she sat down. Ted smiled at her across the table.

Then he heard a faint *tick* on the hardwood floor beneath him. He knew exactly what it was. He had meant to check all his pockets when he changed out of his swimsuit. But he had been all distracted, standing there naked in the boys' room, still raging and lustful from the trampoline.

Fuck.

Shit.

"What's that?" one of younger girls asked him. He looked down at the condom on the floor between their two chairs. The packaging shone black with aggressive neon lettering. He quickly covered it with his foot.

"Nothing," he said, smiling, keeping his cool.

"You dropped it," she said.

"It's nothing." He looked at the girl, shaking his head.

"Is too," she said chuckling. She thought he was playing a game with her. He kept shaking his head.

He looked up. Everyone was focused on him. "This. Was. Delicious," he said.

"What's the problem?" Bruce asked.

"I'm fine. Nothing. Just stuffed."

"He dropped something."

"It's just my napkin."

"That's not your napkin," she said. His napkin, like everyone else's, was a crumpled mess next to his plate.

He froze. The seconds ticked by. Bruce scowled at Ted, sensing something strange was happening.

Suggestions?

Um.

"Oh my God!" Ted suddenly yelled. He pointed at the glass door. "Look at that!"

It worked better than he expected. Thirteen heads moved instantly to see what was happening in the backyard. He used the distraction to casually lean over and palm the condom. He slipped it into his pocket without anyone noticing.

Smooth as silk.

"Oh!" Pam suddenly screamed.

"Taffy!" Bruce shouted. He pounded his fist on the glass door.

Ted looked out the window. Little Taffy was down on her haunches, while Butchie mounted her from behind. Never had Ted seen such an anatomically precise view of intercourse. The big dog's red penis moved visibly in and out, in and out. His wet tongue lolled out the sided of his mouth as he grinned stupidly.

Two of the girls began to cry. "Butchie's hurting her," one of them wailed.

Bruce got to his feet and yanked the door open. He charged outside and literally kicked the dog off Taffy, who then scampered away humiliated. One of the grandmothers started hyperventilating.

This isn't good.

No.

Please don't let me kill another old lady this summer.

Before anyone even had a chance to scold Ted, the eight-year-old girl seated on his *other* side held up her hand and said, "What's this, Daddy?"

Ted stood up and wiped his mouth on the back of his hand. "I'll be leaving now," he announced, without turning to see the condom in the little girl's hand.

"What's a *magnum*?" she asked.

"I appreciate your hospitality, and I apologize for everything."

He didn't even look in Cammie's direction. He turned and walked towards the door without going into the bedroom to get his bag.

He heard nothing from Cammie. Someone called him a pervert. Maybe.

I will kill him dead.

Yes.

Bloody carcass dead.

He opened the front door and stepped out into the stuffy night air.

CHAPTER FORTY

He wandered the streets of Cammie's suburb, feeling physically numb. He hummed and buzzed to block his thoughts. He balled his fists tight and released them. He did it again and again and again. He stopped. He jumped in place and hollered. He moved on. He had a hard time remembering which way he needed to go.

Angry.

Yes.

And I'm no pervert. *He's* the pervert!

So why leave? She's still back there. You can explain. She knows him. She'll back you up.

I can't think about her right now. I mean, *Jesus*, sweet little Mormon girls holding porno-grade condoms, watching dogs fucking?

He plodded along, certain now he'd found the right road, and headed back toward the freeway. There was no plan beyond stopping at a restaurant in the strip mall near the on-ramp and sitting at the bar and getting drunk.

This kind of weird shit just doesn't happen to other people.

Most people don't know Salton Steve. Most people haven't seen Cammie in a wet swimsuit.

I'm not thinking about *that*!

He walked into Chili's and took a seat at the bar. He quickly ordered a beer and some chips and salsa. He watched the Mariners game on TV.

A Washington team is your local Idaho team?

Now *that's* weird.

It's one thing to have to be a Mariners fan if you live in Seattle. That's bad enough. But to have to be a Mariners fan when you don't even live in the same state, or time zone, is just pathetic.

Pathetic?

Yes.

You're comfortable with that word?

Perfectly.

You said you would do anything. And you let it go just like that?

I'm not letting anything go. I'm just going to watch baseball and drink. I love baseball. Baseball baseball baseball.

A group to the right of him paid their bill and stood up. Ted could now see a woman seated at the far side of the bar. She looked vaguely familiar, middle-aged, with long, bright red hair. Very attractive.

Do I know her?

Maybe.

From Valvert? Was she a tourist? I know that hair.

Maybe from TV.

An actress? At a Chili's in suburban Boise?

He ordered another beer. He stole glances at her.

Unusually pretty. Maybe foreign.

Like a sexy Irish Nazi.

He chugged his beer.

There was probably a fight. Her husband's from Boise. They're visiting his parents. She doesn't get their small-town ways. It's all too much for her. Or too little. Too stuffy. They can't handle her. Just needs to get out for a while. Ted can hear the blow-up in the bedroom that was her husband's as a child. He's whispering so his parents can't hear the fight. He doesn't want them to know she's a handful. She, however, is loud as can be. She wants them to hear. She knows how uncomfortable it makes him. Or maybe the problem is that Dad keeps saying inappropriate things. Maybe Dad's even speculated on the color of her pubic hair. If he's a drinker. Well, Dad, the answer is red. I'd bet the farm. If she hasn't shaved it all off.

Not a pervert, Ted?

No.

Just thinking about her vagina?

Yeah, I guess.

The bartender asked him if he wanted to order any food.

Wing sauce red, I bet.

Jesus!

"No thank you, but I will take another beer." He looked up.

A hit for the home team. Man on first and third. Down two. Bottom of the eighth. The bartender was filling the beer at the tap and using it as an excuse to check the woman out. He was trying to see down her shirt, peering through the pickets of proprietary tap-handles. He set the beer in front of Ted. Strike-out to end the inning. An audible groan from someone sitting at a table behind Ted.

"All these fucking base runners," the man said.

The woman ordered herself a shot of tequila.

Maybe I'll have a shot of tequila with her. Drown my sorrows.

Does that even work?

It's worth a try.

Listen, Ted. In some big revelatory chain-reaction, Cammie's going to put all the pieces together. Salton Steve did the condom thing, just like he did the fish in the face thing. The dogs fucking was just an unfortunate coincidence. She'll realize you left the house humiliated and angry when really you should have stayed to explain everything to her family, that this was all one big huge misunderstanding. Is that what the magnums were for? The *big huge* misunderstanding. That's going to be Bruce's joke, to show you everything's cool. You can fix this, Ted. She might walk through that door any second. Do you need her to find you three tequilas in with some older woman, leering and slurring and making an ass of yourself?

Wait. Why *did* I leave like that?

It's what you do.

College?

Yeah, but we can fix that.

Well, it's comforting in a way, isn't it, that I have a pattern of behavior?

That you have a pattern of behavior is comforting? Flies on shit have a pattern of behavior.

The woman threw the shot back and started rummaging through her purse. She was getting ready to leave.

No, no, no don't leave. Just sit there. Please not now. Stay, lady. The game's still on. Bottom of the ninth. They're only down—Jesus, when did St. Louis get three more runs?

She laid some cash on the bar and stood up. She smoothed her hair with both hands and thanked the bartender. She turned to leave and locked eyes with Ted. She walked towards him, strutting, her expression fixed and severe. She stopped just behind his barstool and leaned her mouth close to his ear. He could smell perfume and tequila.

"Do you have a condom?" she asked in a hot whisper.

He could feel his eyes open wider.

What?

He stopped her by holding his arm out, which came to rest on her waist. "Excuse me?"

"It's a simple question." Her mouth was barely an inch from his ear.

344

"What for?"

She stepped back and looked at him. His arm fell limp. She smiled, and then continued on.

He spun in his stool and watched her go. Then he turned to the bartender, who was staring at him. "What was that all about?" Ted asked.

"You tell me."

"She come in here often?"

"Never seen her before. What did she say to you?"

He shook his head and threw a twenty dollar bill on the bar. He jogged out the door and stood scanning the parking lot for some sign of her.

It's like she vanished.

Or was never there to begin with.

I'm hallucinating now?

Well, where is she?

The restaurant door opened behind him and an older couple said good night and walked to their car.

Go back to Cammie's.

I doubt I could find it. I just need headlights to turn on.

She's gone.

She's hiding.

Is that somehow better, that she's hiding from you?

How do I suddenly need this so badly?

He's still messing with you.

Laughing his ass off back in Valvert.

If he's even *in* Valvert.

Yeah, he's probably right around here, driving with that gorgeous red-haired she-devil riding shotgun, the two of them in hysterics. Which is fine, because I'm going to kill him the next time I see him.

Of course you are.

He sat on the curb and stared at a pool of oil drippings in an unoccupied handicap space. After an hour, the manager of the restaurant came out and asked him to move along, implying Ted was a drifter of some sort. He didn't budge.

The next time the manager came outside Ted was already on his feet. He asked the guy for the time. Ten-thirty. The bus station? Downtown. Can I walk it? Take you probably three hours.

He followed a dark frontage road, hoping he would find a hotel each time he came to a freeway off-ramp. Not that he had the money or the desire to stay in a hotel, but the search gave him a clear purpose.

Okay, so say hypothetically Salton Steve was somehow involved in the situation with that woman at the bar.

He was.

Okay, and I know he did the thing with the condoms. So what else? What if this is...

Bigger?

Bigger how?

A longer timeline maybe. Think about the gold figurine. It was like the ones from San Diego, when you worked with Twin. It wasn't identical, but it was close. What are the odds?

This goes back to San Diego?

Well, assume he's crazy. Far crazier than you think. Maybe he's been stalking you, messing with your life for his own entertainment. I mean, look at you right now. You're wandering some frontage road in Idaho. You're a confused wreck, wondering about mysterious golden idols, fantastically beautiful women, and strange conspiracies. There is a certain pathetic richness to your life right now, isn't there? A certain twisted beauty?

It's textbook paranoia, though. Somebody's watching me, stalking me, needling his way into my life, stealing my sanity piece by piece. I can't get on board with that. The reality is that Salton Steve, a guy I work with, put some condoms in my luggage to play a prank on me. He gave me an idol because he's into some new age bullshit just like the people from the office. That's it.

She asked you specifically about condoms. Coincidence?

It's possible.

And then she vanished.

Like the girl on the shuttle bus vanished.

Who looked like Cammie.

As if it's common to look like Cammie.

Exactly.

And didn't he say the idol was Smoke Monkey?

You made the connection when he first gave it to you.

It didn't make sense then.

Well does it now?

I don't know.

Eventually, he arrived at a busy riverfront area just as the bars were letting out. He sat on a park bench and waited for something to happen. Couples stumbled by, arm in arm. A skinny kid leaned over the railing right in front of him and puked into the water. He wiped his mouth on his collar and looked at Ted, and told him in a slurred voice that he was feeling buch metter.

Eventually, it was just Ted and a couple of rats who scavenged on a small lawn area next to his bench.

It's time to go home. *Home* home. I should never have left San Diego. I should have stood my ground.

Like you did at Cammie's?

Damnit.

Look, go home. That's fine. Finish college. Whatever. But if you're not comfortable calling the Smoke Monkey, *Smoke Monkey International* thing a coincidence, then you have to accept that whatever Salton Steve is doing to you predates even Addie Parson.

Addie Parson?

Yes.

Wait. I got something. The firemen. Fire*woman*. The red hair. She wasn't as striking, naturally, but it could have been her.

A vague resemblance, right. Like Cammie and the girl from the shuttle bus.

Okay, if I'm crazy, I'm crazy. But I'm not wrong. Not about any of this. If that wasn't even the real fire department, then how do I know there's even such a person as Addie Parson, or her retarded son Craig?

Yes!

The girl at the house party who threw the turd at me. That was Jeff's old girlfriend. So was he in on it too? All of them, Jeff and Fetcher and all the others. Even Buttsweat. Did he even get to Buttsweat? How? How far back does it go?

To your parents, probably. Maybe all the way back to God.

Where do you draw the line?

Maybe there isn't a line.

What kind of person would do this, take it upon himself to completely manufacture another person's reality, to force that person to endure all kinds of emotional turmoil based on some fantastical construct?

Someone like you.

Fuck! Twin!

He knew all along.

CHAPTER FORTY-ONE

"Did he just leave?" Bruce asked.

Cammie was slumped over in her chair, her face buried in a pile of folded arms. She nodded. Her whole body convulsed. She sniffled long and loud. Then she sat up and looked around, her face bright red and streaked with tears. Then she burst out laughing again.

"He's really gone, dear?" Pam asked.

"I...think so," Cammie said, still convulsing. She blew her nose into her napkin, and then dabbed her eyes.

"What *is* this?" Sara asked, holding the condom in her hand.

"That's a condom," Grandma Bella said. "A man puts it on his penis during intercourse, so there's no baby afterwards."

"Why wouldn't he want the baby?" Freddie asked.

"Well sometimes people aren't ready to have babies."

"Then why have intercourse?"

"Well intercourse feels good. It's a way for two people to feel close. We don't believe anyone should do it until they are married, but not everyone believes the same things we do."

"Was Ted having intercourse?"

Bruce looked at Cammie.

She became instantly serious. "What? No! Of course not."

"And why exactly did he leave again?" Bruce asked, still unable to comprehend what had just happened.

Cammie continue to chuckle. "I think he was just mortified. He probably thought you'd kill him. You're scary, Dad."

"I mighta killed him."

"But the funny thing is," Cammie continued, "is that I bet it wasn't even his condom."

"I saw one on the floor," Jessie said. "He picked it up."

"Right," Cammie said. "There were probably a bunch of them. It was a prank. We work with this guy who's a little nuts. He was just messing around. But...I can't believe Ted just *left*."

"*I appreciate your hospitality*," Pam said, in a dull monotonous drone. They all laughed at her impression. "Where'd you dig him up?"

"He's sweet," Cammie said.

"You going to go get him?" her father asked.

Cammie shook her head. Why should she go after him? He's the one who left. If he comes back, fine. We can all have a laugh about it. But if he's just going to bail on me like that, why should I care? It would've been nice if he'd stuck around and defended himself, fought a little, acted like he cared and wasn't just looking for any excuse to leave. She thought he liked her. He certainly acted like he liked her. And she liked him. In fact, she was starting to like him a lot. But oh well. Better to nip it in the bud.

"Can we give the condom to Butchie?" Sara asked.

Grandma Bella stood up. "Most boy dogs don't need condoms, darling."

"Why not?"

"Well, dear, because we cut their nuts off."

"So they can't have babies?"

"Exactly. Now who's in for brown betty?"

Twelve hands shot up into the air.

Cammie was already looking out the window when the car rolled up. It was two in the morning and everyone was asleep. She crept out of the house and crossed the street. She nodded to the woman in the car and got in on the passenger side.

The interior lights came on.

"You look fantastic," Cammie said. "I love your hair."

"Thank you, Cammie. And you're looking beautiful as ever. We should hit the town together sometime."

"I knew you would come tonight."

"Oh you did, did you?"

"Yup."

"And how did you know I'd want to speak with you?"

"Because of Ted," Cammie said, full of pride.

"And Ted is..."

"Oh stop it, Susanna." She wrapped her playfully on the wrist. "I've figured you guys all out. Not that I understand why you're being so mean to him."

"I'm sorry, I don't understand."

"*Ted.* You know. He's from San Diego. He went to the college where you made me ride the bus. He recognized me. And now he comes to my house and Salton Steve puts all these condoms in his stuff and he leaves and then, *wham*, you show up."

"Salton Steve?"

"Oh, come on," Cammie pleaded.

"The reason I'm here, actually, is to tell you your latest assignment is finished. You don't need to return to Valvert. The one-year waiting period starts today. In fact, we're going to have to insist you do not return to Valvert, okay?"

"Why?"

"It's a yes or no question."

"Okay, yes. Fine. Is there something new though?"

"Oh yes, Cammie. Yes there is. You're being promoted."

"Promoted?"

"Yes. Do you accept the offer?"

"What offer?"

"Just say yes, Cammie."

"Yes."

"Congratulations, then." She held out her hand. "My name is Marona Dilenta. Welcome to Smoke Monkey International."

Cammie shook her hand. "What's Smoke Monkey International?"

"Our organization."

"What do we do?"

"I'll let Earl explain everything."

"Is he the boss?"

"He's one of them."

"Are you a boss?"

"I am."

"Can you answer any of my questions?"

"I can try."

"Who's Ted."

"Ted?" Marona smiled. "Never heard of him."

"Cut it out!"

"Okay Cammie, he's a recruit."

"Does he know that?"

"No."

"And Salton Steve?"

"Earl will explain everything."

"Please!"

"He's the Taskmaster."

"I knew it! What's a Taskmaster?"

"You have to come with me. Today."

"Where are we going?"

"To Central America, to observe. You have a swimsuit?"

"I do, but it's wet. Will Earl be there?"

"Yes. We'll also need to get you an expedited passport."

"Am I a recruit also?"

"No. Not really. Not like Ted."

"So what am I?"

"You're *next*."

CHAPTER FORTY-TWO

The Greyhound station was still open when he got there. An assortment of drifter-types were splayed about the lobby. Insects poured in through an open door and flicked against bright halogen light tubes. A drunk man dressed in rags pounded on a footlocker, trying to get his money out of the coin return slot. Ted bought a ticket for a five o'clock bus to Idaho Falls, which could drop him at a highway junction sixteen miles from his dorm room.

He took a seat on one of the benches and picked up an unclaimed newspaper. He instinctively refolded all the sections to get it back to its original form. Then he scanned through the front page section, reading articles about the local volunteer firefighters, and efforts to fund an arts district in town where the old cattle auctions used to be held.

He checked the completed crossword for accuracy.

He read the comics.

He read an article on Boise's minor league ball club.

And then he saw a small blurb in the national news summary about the confirmed disappearance of an iconic American archeologist who had been working for years in Honduras. He read the short story four times. He threw the paper onto the ground in disgust and moved to a bench on the other side of the room.

That's the same guy I read about back in San Diego, in that weird mystery edition of the Union Tribune. Back when I worked with Twin. Something about a Harvard professor who claimed he could make significant archeological progress by praying to local gods.

And?

It's all connected.

All the way to Honduras?

The building in San Diego was the Smoke Monkey *International* complex.

And so this missing archeologist knows Salton Steve? They're working together? All of this based on a newspaper article you picked up off a seat in a Greyhound station?

Yes. Exactly. Only there is no missing archeologist. The paper's a fake. Just like in San Diego. These guys are thorough. Watch. I'll go find another paper and the story won't be in there.

He stood up and wandered around the room, vaguely aware that some people were watching him. He saw a paper spilling out of one of the trashcans.

You're dumpster-diving in a bus station.

Yes.

He rifled through the pages and found the story. Then he crumpled the paper and threw it in the trash. He wandered back out front. He found a paper box with one copy left. He inserted two quarters and grabbed the paper. Again he found the story. He put two more quarters into the box and put the paper back. Then he kicked the box. He went back inside and took a seat.

An older man with a frazzled ponytail leaned over and asked Ted if something was wrong.

"Yes, something is wrong," he said, without even looking at the man. "There's something wrong with everyone in this room. That's what the bus is for, so people like us can still go places."

"That's an interesting observation."

"I just need to know what the hell is going on," Ted said.

The man seemed to assume Ted meant the comment in an existential sort of way, and just smiled and nodded and told him cryptically that you never got back the hours you wasted waiting for the bus. Ted nodded and thought about the comment.

It doesn't actually mean anything.

"Somebody's screwing with my head," Ted said, knocking on his skull with a knuckle.

The man smiled. "Sure seems that way," he said.

"I'm convinced. It's in everything, like some vast conspiracy."

"That must make you a pretty important guy then."

Ted cocked his head to the side. "I hadn't thought about it like that."

"It is a form of grace to be cursed by God. It means at least he's paying attention to you."

"I never said I was cursed by God," Ted laughed.

"You didn't have to," the man said without smiling.

An ambulance screamed by outside the building, filling the room with spinning red lights.

"Oliver," he said, offering his hand.

"Ted."

"Where you heading?"

"Valvert."

"Fancy schmancy."

"I'm a dishwasher. You?"

"San Diego, via Sacramento."

Ted stared at him, "San Diego, huh. So you're in on it too?"

"On what, the vast conspiracy?"

"Yes. It's actually a serious question. Why are you talking to me?"

"We're all in on it, if that's what you mean, I guess. Everyone together. All for you."

"No, I'm asking you directly."

"I understand what you're asking me. The answer is yes."

Ted stood up. "Not right now," he said.

"Did I say something?" Oliver asked, looking slightly offended.

"None of this Bob Marley zenmaster bullcrap right now, please. We're not all cosmically connected. Lucky for you. Sorry. College was fun. But not today. Thanks, though. I think I just have to sit by myself until my bus gets here."

"Have it your way. Just trying to help."

"Well, I appreciate it, Oliver." Ted walked to the other side of the room, sat down on the floor, and waited.

He took a seat next to the window in the middle of the bus. He was one of the first passengers on board and he watched each new person mount the steps and come down the aisle.

I'm ready, whoever you are. Bring on the vaguely familiar face from my past. One of my college professors, maybe. Or why not try some zany coincidence? Where's the fat bald guy who wants to talk badger hunting and swords? Or the ridiculous scenario. Where's the gorgeous woman who's going to sit next to me but smell like shit? Come on. Just be creative though.

But there was nothing. Until they hit the road.

An hour and a half outside Boise, just as the red sun came blaring over the eastern hills, Ted saw him on the side of the road. Just a quick glimpse. Salton Steve playing electric guitar through an amplifier. Not a parked car in sight. His eyes were closed, his pressed lips twitching through the intensity of an arena-grade solo. In a flash they were past him. Ted looked around the bus to see if anyone else had seen it. But everyone was asleep.

How would he even know what side of the bus I was sitting on? Is there someone on this bus watching me, relaying messages?

Please don't start looking around. This paranoia feels kind of dangerous. You don't want to be *that* guy. This is Greyhound. The major leagues here. Better just simmer down. Just go back to Valvert, pick up your shit, and go home.

He walked the sixteen miles from the bus stop to Valvert, watching the whole time for Salton Steve to barrel past him in his rusted-out Pontiac. But Ted never saw him.

I really am going to assault him.

Good.

I don't care if I've never been in a fight. I don't care if he's been to prison in Texas. He can kick my ass. Fine. It won't matter.

He's never been to prison.

He lied?

It's all a lie.

He got back to his room in the early afternoon. He took a nap. He packed his things and loaded them into his car. Then he casually strolled over to Salton Steve's room at about eleven o'clock.

Ted stood in the hallway.

Use your legs. Lead with your shoulder.

He practiced the motion a couple of times. Fist to palm, elbow out.

Keep your head back and shut your eyes. If it doesn't work the first time, keep trying.

This is who you are. This is what you're doing.

He stepped back from the door, took a deep breath, and charged. The door splintered around the lock but didn't open. Ted staggered back, energized, and caught himself against the wall on the other side of the hallway. He focused on the door and took a breath. He lunged again, hitting the door in the same place. His momentum sent him stumbling into the room. He caught himself against the metal frame of the bunk bed and turned to face Salton Steve.

He blinked.

What the...

"Close the door," Salton Steve said.

What in the...

He did what he was told. The lock was busted, but he managed to get the door to stay shut.

What am I looking at?

The room was lit by candlelight and Salton Steve had his back to Ted, facing a shrine of sorts. He was dressed in a strange robe with a woven checker pattern of white squares, each filled with a colorful image of an animal. And he wore some sort of pelt on his head. He sat cross-legged on a small pile of tiny gold-colored pebbles. Ted had apparently interrupted an elaborate prayer ritual. He stood there dumbly staring at the flickering light of a tea candle on a table draped with a red blanket.

After several minutes of silence, Ted turned and walked out of the room. He made his way up to his own dorm room. It was dark and Luc was sleeping. He climbed up onto the top bunk, drained and exhausted, and fell asleep with all his clothes on.

CHAPTER FORTY-THREE

Pound! pound! pounding! on the door. Ted opened his eyes. He closed them and rubbed out the crust. He opened them again. Late morning light.

Am I supposed to be at work right now?

I thought you were going home.

Oh yeah. Remind me.

Cammie and the dogs and Chili's and the long walk and the roadside guitar solo. Salton Steve in prayer.

My shoulder hurts.

The pounding resumed. Ted slipped down off the bunk. He could sense Luc was gone. Then he opened the door.

Salton Steve stood in the hallway stretching. He wore a tight white tank top, short blue running shorts, thigh-high tube socks with the two blue stripes, and a blue headband. His thick giant glasses perched on his nose.

"Morning, Ted!" he said with a big smile.

Ted shut the door and climbed back into bed.

Seconds later, the door burst open and Salton Steve flew into the room and fell forward onto the ground. He stood up and dusted himself off, still wearing his same stupid grin. He straightened his glasses. "Up and at 'em, Tiger!"

Ted looked at the door. The lock dangled broken. Bits of wood were sprinkled across the floor.

"I brought you something." Ted felt a newspaper land on his leg.

"Fuck off."

"It's a beautiful day skipper, and I'm taking *you* for a hike." Ted pulled the sheets up to his head and rolled over to face the wall. "There's something I want to show you. It's not far from here. It's cool. You'll like it."

Ted flung the sheets back off his body, slipped down off the bunk, and stormed past Salton Steve. In the bathroom, Ted walked to one of the shower stalls and cranked the water to hot. Salton Steve followed him into the bathroom and stood outside the stall.

"Don't shower now," he said. "Do it when we get back. You might get dirty."

Ted got in the water.

"You're going to need a towel, buddy."

"I'm not your buddy," Ted growled.

When he finished showering he saw Salton Steve had brought him a towel. He recognized it as the towel he'd packed away the day before. Packed away in his locked car. And it smelled nice. It smelled laundered.

He broke into my car, took my towel out of my bag, and laundered it.

Maybe he changed your oil too.

He could hear Salton Steve humming to himself just outside the stall. "There's no real hurry," he said.

"I'm not going anywhere with you," Ted said coldly.

"It'll just take a couple of hours."

"I'm leaving."

"I *see*."

"I figured it all out." Ted announced. "You're very clever."

"Okay."

Clean shorts, clean underwear, and a clean T-shirt flew over the wall. Ted caught them. Sniffed them. "I don't need you handling my underpants."

"That's fine," said a voice from one of the toilet stalls. It wasn't Salton Steve's.

Ted got dressed and left the stall. Salton Steve was gone. He found him in the hallway, smiling and stretching. Ted marched past him. Salton Steve followed, then stood there awkwardly watching as Ted straightened things up and put his car keys in his pocket.

I'm not even going to look at him.

I thought you were going to attack him.

I'm just going home. I'm done.

That'll be the third time, Ted. Maybe you ought to handle your business.

He walked back out into the hallway. "Want me to shut this?" Salton Steve asked, pointing at the broken door.

Ted made his way over to the maintenance building with Salton Steve following close behind. Ted flagged down a guy who was driving a forklift and told him that the door to his dorm room was busted. The guy asked how it happened and Ted just shrugged. The guy said they would send someone over to look at it as soon as they could. Salton Steve stood next to Ted nodding ridiculously throughout the conversation. Then Ted recrossed the resort grounds to the employee parking lot. Salton Steve was still walking a couple of feet behind him, humming cheerfully.

Ted opened his car door, but before he could get in, Salton Steve brought his long arm over Ted's shoulder and pushed the door shut.

Ted, having expected something like this, wheeled around and shoved Salton Steve as hard as he could.

Salton Steve stumbled two steps back and fell down.

"You stay the hell away from me!" Ted yelled. His whole face twitched and he sensed that if he said another word his voice might crack and he could even start to cry.

Salton Steve, of course, picked right up on this. "It's a tough world out there, isn't it?" he said, while making fake sniffling noises.

Ted turned his face to compose himself. Then he made a move like he was going to kick Salton Steve, who flinched. Ted wheeled quickly around, opened the door, and climbed into his car. He tried the key and nothing happened. He looked over at Salton Steve, who was still on the ground, but sitting up. He grinned and made pretend steering motions with an invisible wheel.

Ted opened the door. "If you fucked with my car I will have you arrested."

"Can't we just go for a hike?"

"I'll ask again. Did you fuck with my car?"

"I promise this will be the best hike you've ever been on."

"You have thirty seconds to make my car work."

"Please," he said, imploring Ted.

"We're not taking any goddamn stupid hike! Twenty seconds."

"Two hours, max."

"Ten seconds."

"I'll pay you."

"Five seconds."

Salton Steve pulled a roll of bills out of his pocket, licked his finger, and began counting off twenties. "Five hundred dollars?"

Ted got out of the car, shut the door, and walked over to Salton Steve. "You're going to pay me to take a hike with you?"

Salton Steve continued to count off bills. Then he stood up. "A thousand, is that good?" He pushed the money at Ted.

What's driving home really going to solve?

You're such a disappointment, Ted.

It's a thousand dollars.

Spit in his face.

He took the money, counted it, and put it all in his shirt pocket. There was a condom in there and he pulled it out and threw it at Salton Steve. It spun wildly off the mark.

"You suck," Ted told him.

"This way," Salton Steve said, gesturing with his hands.

They left the parking lot, crossed the main road, rock-hopped over the shallow Bigpine River, and started up an unremarkable sage-covered hill.

A thousand dollars. The start-up capital I need to launch a full-scale counter-attack.

I like the idea. But he's out of your league. For all you know he's been doing this kind of thing his whole life. Probably started in a Bigfoot costume back in his early teens.

He does have enormous feet.

Just see if you can get a good shot at one of his kidneys, and then move along.

I did pretty well with Twin, though, didn't I? The light sensors and elevator call button. That was a start.

Twin knew what you were up to the whole time. Remember? As far as you know that's where this all started. You got caught.

They walked along a faint path towards the crest of the hill. Below them, and not far away at all, Ted could see the village of Valvert set perfectly at the confluence of two deep valleys.

I should be appreciating this more, this view. It's one of the main reasons I came to Valvert. The warm sunlight. The foamy white clouds. That alpine blue sky.

And he's ruined it all. Now stay focused. He's wheezing. He's old. You can take him. Lock your hands together and swing them into his back like a club. Really torque your hips.

They came to a giant water tank just shy of the summit. In order for the tank to sit on flat ground a section of the hillside had been cut away. This left a twenty-foot high wall of dirt and rocks in which Ted could see many levels of geological deposits. Salton Steve stood at the base of the wall and ran his hands over the strata. Ted turned away and stood looking down at his very small car parked in the employee lot.

"Do you know who the first white people were in Valvert?" Salton Steve asked, walking over to Ted's side.

Ted took a step away from him. "Nope."

"French fur trappers."

"I see."

"Do you know who came next?"

"No idea."

"Think about it, Ted."

"What did you do to my car?"

"They were gold miners. This was well before it hit in California. For about fifteen years they worked that river below us, the one that branches off into the creek that runs through town."

"Fascinating."

"This thing we're standing on is called a *something* moraine."

Ted looked at him.

"No idea?"

"No."

"*Glacial*, Ted. It's called a glacial moraine."

Ted looked down at his fingernails. "Is this whole lecture part of the deal?"

"Yes. I wanted you to see this."

"The water tank? I can see it out the window of my dorm room. But it's your money."

"Just relax, Ted. I'm going to make this all better for you. You're going to feel pretty great in about twelve hours."

"Enough with the cryptic bullshit!" Ted hollered. He charged and pushed Salton Steve down like he did in the parking lot. Harder though, and with a bit of a running start. Salton Steve crashed backwards.

He doesn't look scared of you.

I don't care.

Ted took the money out of his pocket and threw it in Salton Steve's face. "Now leave me alone. It's my day off."

He started to walk back down the path. Every muscle in his face tightened and he held his breath.

Oh, God.

Do not, Ted, fucking start crying.

He fought it hard, so it came out as a loud involuntary clucking noise. His face began twitching. Then the snot and the tears started.

Why's he so *mean*?

Lord, really?

If he's so smart and clever why not do something good or nice? Is it all some protracted punishment for what I did to Twin? Well, I repent! I repent! Jesus. I just *left* her.

Cammie?

I just let him do that to me. I'm such an asshole. Why did I leave? Why am I crying about all this?

Maybe he dosed your water with estrogen.

He probably did.

Salton Steve called out to him, "I need your help, Ted!" He could hear footsteps coming up from behind. "Okay, okay, okay," Salton Steve said as he approached. "Stop, please."

Ted stopped and turned around to face him.

Salton Steve looked surprised. "Crying?"

"Yes I'm fucking crying. You win. You've made your point. Tell Twin I'm sorry."

"Who's Twin?"

Ted sniffled and shook his head. "Just *stop*, please."

Salton Steve took out the roll of bills again. "How much?"

Ted wiped his nose on his shirt. He looked down at the village below. "All of it. The whole roll." He spit on the ground. "And I want to take a piss on your head."

Salton Steve didn't even hesitate. "Done and done," he said. He emptied his pocket and handed Ted the roll of twenties, as well as all the bills he recollected from the ground. "It's like twenty-five hundred dollars."

"Why are you doing this?"

"Let's get it over with," Salton Steve said. He got down on all fours right in front of Ted.

"I'll fucking do it," Ted said.

"Well hurry up then."

He unzipped his pants, took out his penis and held it there above Salton Steve. He waited. Salton Steve didn't move. He waited some more. A few more seconds...

"You can't even—"

The powerful yellow stream slammed against Salton Steve's cheek and splattered down onto the dry dirt and rocks. Ted resumed crying, the convulsions making it difficult for him to keep his aim. He moved the stream up into Salton Steve's hair where it was absorbed for a few seconds. Then it poured down the back of his neck. Then he moved on to Salton Steve's ear, flooding the canal until it gurgled. Salton Steve did not move. Ted cut the stream off and then shuffled with his pants at his ankles to the other side. He opened up again on Salton Steve's other ear, then moved the weakening stream down along his back and legs.

Before he even zipped up, he reached down and began shoveling handfuls of dry dirt all over Salton Steve's head and body.

That got him to move. Salton Steve jumped to his feet and began spitting violently. Ted pulled his pants up and stepped back.

There.

He wiped his nose on the back of his hand.

Salton Steve was shaking himself out now, visibly disgusted. His entire head was covered in a muddy cake. He jerked to the side to get the urine out of his ear. Then he did the other side.

"Oh, you dick," he said. "If I try to get it out of one ear it just goes down deeper into the other."

"I tried to be thorough."

"Ugh, it's all in my sinuses! *Fuck!*" He shook himself for a few more seconds and then gave up trying to right himself. He set off down the hill with great bounding steps.

I think that was the actual real Salton Steve there for a second.

Nice job. Now if only we could get you to stop crying.

I'm fine. I feel better. Not a hundred percent better, but still.

You did good, Ted.

I'm going to go back to the dorms, call Cammie, straighten out that whole mess. Then I'll deposit my money, go back to work, and move on with my life.

Right here in Valvert.

Yes.

Good.

I've just got to relax.

Exactly.

He reclined on the dusty ground, well away from the pockets of wetness. He looked up at the blue sky and closed his eyes.

Minutes later, he heard a trudging and wheezing Salton Steve making his way back up the hill. When he got to Ted, he stood there above him with his hands on his knees panting. He was soaking wet from his river bath.

Ted sat up on his elbows. Salton Steve reached his long arms to the sky and then bent side to side, stretching. He then took one long breath, exhaled, shook himself out and pointed. "You see these two valleys?" he said.

Ted stood up and looked. "I see them, yes."

"During the last ice age they were gouged out by glaciers which formed on those big peaks you see there in the distance."

"How do you know?"

"Because they moved a lot of dirt when they did it. And that's what you're standing on. See how all the other mountains and hills around us contain solid rock, and bedrock? There's stuff sticking out, the mountains themselves. But look at this." He turned and pointed back to the wall of strata. "See how it's all just rocks and dirt, layer after layer? There's no bedrock, nothing solid. With enough time and manpower you could move this whole hill, stone by stone. You wouldn't need to dynamite it or anything. And see how all the rocks are round? That's because at one time they were in a river of some sort."

"Okay."

"Now, the early gold miners worked the stream down below, and basically cleaned it out. Then they moved on to California, which promised bigger and better things. What they didn't realize is that this whole moraine we're standing on is made up of the same exact geological debris that was in the stream! Therefore..."

"Therefore..."

"Come on, Ted."

"Just tell me."

"If there was gold in the stream then there would be gold in this moraine." He put his hands on Ted's shoulders and looked him in the eye. "You're standing on the mother lode, motherfucker!"

"You have lost your mind," Ted said. He took a step away from Salton Steve and spun his finger around in circles by his ear. "Am I done here?"

"You don't believe me?"

"It's not that I don't believe you. I just don't *care*."

"Where do you think I got all that money I just gave you?"

"Dishwashing."

"Wrong!"

"Robbed a stagecoach?"

"Wrong!"

"Selling drugs."

"Partially wrong! Listen, I've pulled almost eighty-grand out of this hillside."

"How?"

"Well, I'll show you. That's what this is all about. I need a partner."

"You want me to be your partner?"

"Yes!"

"How'd you figure all this out?"

"Through faith and prayer!"

"What?"

"It's true. I can prove it."

"The thing last night? All the candles and the weird outfit?"

"Yes!"

Ted thought back to the scene in his room. Salton Steve had been sitting on a small pile of little golden pebbles. "What was that you were sitting on last night?"

"Gold, my friend. I was sitting on a pile of gold!"

"Just sitting on it. Like a...like a..."

"Yes, like a fucking *dragon*!"

CHAPTER FORTY-FOUR

Cammie didn't feel right about lying to her family, but telling them the truth would have just made them worry. It was better if they all thought she was heading back to Valvert to finish up for the summer.

At breakfast, everyone wanted to talk about Ted. Where did she think he spent the night? Would she see him that afternoon? Would they be working together? Was it going to be awkward?

She answered their questions in vague terms, partly because she didn't want to think about what happened with Ted, and partly because talking about him and Valvert required her to tell more and more lies. And beyond all that, she was just very excited, and she didn't want to let that excitement show. Which wasn't easy.

Mostly, she was excited that her own intuition had been correct. Ted *had* been the purpose of her relocation to Valvert. Salton Steve was working for the same people she was. That it was all connected was thrilling. She still didn't understand the nature or the purpose of Smoke Monkey International, but she knew it was the best thing to ever happen to her. She hadn't realized just how much she dreaded what her life was going to become. She had wanted something different, but she didn't know what it was or where to find it. She knew she had assets, that she was clever and creative, and *okay*, uncommonly attractive as well. It was true. Those things mattered in life. They just did. She had been blessed, and that made her uncomfortable, because maybe her sisters hadn't been blessed in that way, and what had she done to deserve more than they had? But accepting these things about herself had only made the dread worse. Hers was a life that could truly be wasted. And to even have such thoughts made her overly prideful. And that was a sin.

And then Susanna had shown up. Or Marona. Whatever. It had all seemed so absurd at first, the random excursions, the secrecy. But the money had sure been real. And now that she could see the framework better, that she had been promoted, that she was traveling internationally, that she was *next*, her life was as unique and different and exciting as she ever could have hope it would be.

She kissed and hugged everyone, and rolled her eyes when they told her to have fun at work. Then she got into her little car and drove away, watching in the rear-view mirror as two little brothers and Taffy chased her down the street. At the Chili's parking lot, she took out the paper Marona had given her. The directions were complex. Drive west on I-84 to Nampa. Exit the freeway. Turn left. Drive to Kuna. Turn right at the yellow barn and park next to the Winnebago on blocks.

As she drove, she thought more and more about the word.

Next.

They were going to let her do something. Obviously, she had no idea what. But it would be different than before. No more random tasks and following orders. No more keeping her in the dark.

She didn't know enough about the kinds of things Smoke Monkey International did to speculate in any practical way, so she just brainstormed. At some point someone was going to ask her for input, and it would be a good idea to have something to offer.

So she tried to think logically. Marona had originally said they picked her because she was the prettiest girl they had ever seen. Cammie was sure that was an exaggeration, but okay. So her idea should be one that took advantage of her good looks.

The fact that they promoted her meant she had done her job well thus far. She knew at this point that her main purpose had been related to Ted, that they were focused on him and needed her in his life as some kind of supporting element. She would find out why exactly when she met this mysterious Earl. But it was clear, at least, that some sort of game was being played. Like a trick or a prank, but extremely complex, with some deeper purpose. And Ted had no idea it was even happening. Which gave them all a dangerous level of control.

Which must also be a key to the operation.

So it was about beauty, and trust, and control. What Smoke Monkey International had done to Ted seemed cruel, but Marona, clearly, was not a cruel person. Cammie had trusted her instincts about Marona from the first time she met her, on the rainy night several months ago. So the goal of all this was not to just screw around with Ted's life for no good reason.

That's what she came up with. And if she was next, maybe it was her turn to set up some kind of game, a game that incorporated these same elements. So what would that game look like?

And what role would she cast for herself? Salton Steve had made himself a dishwasher. She was sure she could do better than that.

A limousine was waiting behind the yellow barn. Cammie clapped her hands as she pulled to a stop. The limousine door opened and a high-heeled foot and a long trim leg poked out. The rest of Marona Dilenta then emerged. She's so perfectly put together, Cammie thought, admiring Marona's sleek black skirt, her ruby red blouse, and the flowing burning torch of hair, which blew sensuously off her shoulders. The contrast to the surroundings was incredible. Intentional, Cammie thought. All this glamour and precision amidst the rusted fence wires, the dusty potholes, and the dilapidated buildings.

Marona scooped her hair from her face and waved. Cammie jumped out of the car and ran over to her. She gave her a big hug.

"I'm so excited!" Cammie said.

Marona took a step back and laughed. "I can see that."

"I've never been in a limousine."

"Well get your bag and get in there," Marona said.

Cammie ran to her car, grabbed her bag, and ran back to the open door of the limousine. Marona was already inside when Cammie climbed in. Sitting next to her was an older man with a frazzled ponytail.

"You must be Earl," Cammie said, enthusiastically offering her hand.

The man shook her hand. He stared at her for a moment. "I'm Oliver," he said. Then he turned to Marona. "You weren't kidding about her."

"No I was not," Marona said.

"Wow. And that's what she drives around in?" he said, pointing out the window at Cammie's car.

Marona nodded.

"It's my dad's old car," she said.

Oliver nodded. "So, um, welcome Cammie I guess. Welcome to Smoke Monkey International." He leaned forward and tapped on the driver glass. The limousine pulled away. "You ever been to Costa Rica?" he asked. He looked at Marona and smiled.

"Never."

"You ever heard of La Gringa?"

"What's La Gringa?"

Oliver patted Marona on the thigh. "Tell her, Marona. Tell her what's La Gringa."

CHAPTER FORTY-FIVE

They sat in the shade of the water tower. Salton Steve explained the operation to Ted. He'd been working the mine at night, usually from midnight to four. He had one of the pickle buckets from The Spot kitchen which he filled with debris from the moraine using a hand trowel. Then he would carry the bucket down to the river and wash the rocks in a cooking wok, using the same technique the old miners did, swirling the slurry of water and moraine particles in a circle until the heavier items sank to the bottom. The lighter materials would spill over the side leaving little bits of gold.

"It doesn't seem possible," Ted said. "I went to school in California. We learned all about this shit. The only way to get your hands on a real significant amount of gold is to find a seam running through granite. Pick-ax work. Or placer mining. You got a fire hose lying around? Panning in a river was never a way to get rich. It was for suckers and small-timers. You could get lucky and find something big, but it was never consistent."

"You saw what I had, Ted. It's worth tens of thousands of dollars. You're going to put that up against a bunch of stuff you think you remember from grade school?"

"This moraine isn't exactly hidden. And it's been excavated plenty over the years. There are houses on the other side. But you're the only one who's noticed the gold?"

"I couldn't believe it either," Salton Steve said. "But you can't argue with the facts."

"There are no facts. There's just what you told me."

"You saw the gold. Now are you in or out?"

I'm just going to check it out. If he's lying, it'll be obvious pretty quickly. It wouldn't be me looking like the fool.

You wouldn't even know how.

When did you become so sarcastic?

When you stopped thinking rationally.

"Alright," Ted said.

"I'm going to make you rich, buddy. Isn't that exciting? Where's the enthusiasm?"

"Enthusiasm? I don't trust you. There's more to this story. You know it and I know it. I'm just going to keep my guard up so when you do pull the rug out from underneath I'll at least be expecting it."

"You don't trust me?"

Ted looked at him. He laughed. Salton Steve laughed too. He shrugged.

"I mean, admit it," Ted said. He was enjoying himself now. "You're scamming me. Maybe you could get lucky and find a little nugget here and there, but the quantity you seem to have is ridiculous. You're talking about a very small sliver of a huge moraine. If what you say is true, then this site would have to be one of the most valuable in the world. It's not possible."

"What's not possible? That little old you could be someplace significant? That your life might find you connected to important events? That you might be worthy of greatness? Where'd you get such a shitty opinion of yourself?"

"This isn't that, trust me. The employee dorms at Valvert are not situated two-hundred yards from a massive gold deposit. Sorry. You can call it poor self-esteem if you want to. And by the way, coming from you—"

"Coming from me what?"

"I'm not the one who just let someone piss on my head."

"You think that was about poor self-esteem?"

"I'm just saying."

"It's just the opposite, Ted. I let you do that because I'm unflappable. And you know what else? I'm a great man. And at least I have the balls to admit it. You're lucky you know me. How about that? How about today being the greatest day of your life, huh? I think I've heard enough. It's time for you to just shut up and listen." Ted crossed his legs and pursed his lips. "The reason," Salton Steve continued, with an extra dose of smugness, "that I have been so successful is that I've had help. You think just because there's a glacial moraine outside my window that I'd run out and buy a cooking wok and a headlamp and start spending my nights standing in the middle of a river? Of course not. I was directed, you see. Told to come here to Valvert. Told to look for gold in that hillside."

"Told?"

"Yes."

"Told by?"

"Smoke Monkey."

"Smoke Monkey?"

"Yes."

"And does that have anything to do with Smoke Monkey International, a company who rented space in a building where I used to work?"

"I don't know, probably."

"*Probably?* What does that mean? There's a connection. Admit it."

"That's irrelevant."

"It's *not* irrelevant. It's everything. You've been stalking me. Setting me up."

"That's ridiculous."

"Ridiculous? You're the one claiming a Maya god directed you to a gold mine."

"It's true. You'll see. If we go out tonight and there's no gold, feel free to laugh at me and make all the accusations you want. It costs you nothing. You risk nothing. But you do have to pray."

"Like that guy down in Honduras, the archeologist who went missing?"

Salton Steve became very serious. "How do you know about that?"

"I read the paper."

"That's not what I hear."

"What's that supposed to mean?"

"To answer your question, if you're talking about Professor Eugene Lattistrom, well then yes, this does have something to do with that. I knew the guy somewhat. We worked together for a couple of summers in Copan."

"Was this all his idea?"

"Eugene Lattistrom is a remarkable man, yes."

"I saw a story yesterday that said he'd vanished."

"I don't know anything about that."

"You're lying."

"You've got nothing to lose. Trust me with this mine. We'll go down to my room. I'll show you the gold. I'll introduce you to Smoke Monkey. I'll take you out with me at night and you will stand in the middle of the river with your headlamp pointed at the debris swirling around in your wok. You will see gold. And it won't matter what you think of me, whether you think I'm stalking you or whatever. All that will matter is that you will pray to a God, and he will grant your prayers."

"Fine. Whatever. Just tell me one thing, please."

"Okay."

"Why'd you screw it all up for me with Cammie?"

"You screwed that up, Ted."

"You put condoms—"

"You *left*, dumbass. You weren't supposed to leave. You were supposed to laugh."

CHAPTER FORTY-SIX

It disappointed Cammie that even after the ride in the limousine, the first class flight to San Jose, and another long ride in a rented Range Rover, she still didn't have many answers. She had assumed, with her promotion, that she was now an insider in the organization, but the reality was that little had changed.

She had asked plenty of questions and received only vague answers from Marona, who seemed a bit nervous. Cammie's enthusiasm waned. And this made her cross. She knew it was partially that enthusiasm, her gregariousness, that made her such an asset to them, so why quash it right out of the gate? Why the somber tone? Why fly her to another country only to clam up when she asked the most basic questions about what she would be doing?

Observing, she was told.

But *observing what* was such a taboo subject? If there were ground rules for conduct in this organization, well then, spell them out. Don't keep me guessing.

And we had to do this at night? My first time out of the country, driving through a lush tropical landscape, and I can't see a thing. There are monkeys out there, and mossy vines, and toucans. Out there somewhere.

The whole thing reminded her of the church, which made her feel even worse. The way the big answers just brought more questions. Each revelation a maddening false summit. Each discovery a gateway to deeper, more perplexing mysteries.

But this wasn't a religion, this Smoke Monkey International. And it wasn't a business either. So what was it then? A *cult*. The thought made her shudder.

She looked over at Marona, who must have been sleeping. It was too dark in the car to see her face. Oliver rode up front with a local man who was their driver.

"Can we stop," she said. "I have to pee." There was no response. She waited a few seconds and repeated the question. She heard Marona suck in a deep breath. Then she leaned forward and tapped Oliver on the shoulder.

"We need to stop," she told him. Oliver then muttered something to the driver in Spanish. He flicked the lights on in the car and turned around. He smiled at Cammie.

"We'll be there shortly," Oliver said. "Did you get some sleep?"

"Not really," she said. "I'm all jacked up, to be honest. With the traveling and the big mystery and all that. Can't you just tell me what's going on?"

"I know, Cammie," he said, his voice warm and sympathetic. "You will have all the answers you need very soon. But we want to show you something, and it's important that you see it from a different point of view than the one we have. We need to know how it looks from the outside, okay? Does that make sense?"

"Are you guys a cult?"

Oliver laughed. He turned to Marona. "I don't know, are we?"

She rubbed her eyes and arched her back. "A cult? I don't know. Maybe." She cocked her head as she gave the question deeper consideration. "To be honest, I don't think there's a word for what we are. But we're not a cult, no. I feel like cults are bad."

"And you're good? *We're* good?"

Marona and Oliver looked at each other. They both smiled. "I *think* we're good," Oliver said. "But we might not be. I guess it depends. Ultimately, yes, we're good. But we're also kind of messy. And I'll be honest Cammie, we're new at this. You hold a place in the organization that's never been held before, and so does Ted, and you two aren't even in the same place. So a lot of the questions you have are questions we also have. You just need to be patient for a little longer and you'll understand."

"What would be nice," Marona broke in, "would be for you to tell us, once you get some perspective, whether *you* think we're good."

"Or evil," Oliver added.

"Or whether you're a cult or not."

"Sure," Marona said.

"I just want to see some monkeys," Cammie said, exasperated.

Oliver smiled.

A short time later, they pulled off the main road and continued down a long bumpy driveway. Cammie looked out the window eagerly. She could see lights through the forest, growing brighter.

"What's this?" she asked.

"Mission control," Oliver said.

They broke into a clearing and pulled up to a gorgeous colonial mansion. It was a large boxy structure with three floors, shaded verandas, and tall Greek-looking columns. A porter stood by the front door, and when they pulled up, he rushed to the car and opened the doors for everyone. Cammie stepped out, beaming.

Marona took her hand and led her through the front door. They stood on the marble floor in the foyer and took in the Great Room, with its high painted ceilings and period furniture. Abundant plants and teak wainscoting gave the place a cool tropical feel of wealth and leisure. A series of large-fronded ceiling fans circled slowly, creating a subtle draft which brought fresh jungle air to Cammie's damp skin.

"I love this place," Marona said. Her now winsome voice echoing all around them.

"I love it too," Cammie said, unable to elaborate.

"This way," Oliver said, coming up behind them and pointing to the hallway across the room.

"Right," Marona said. "First things first."

The three of them walked down a hallway lit by sweet smelling lamps burning in golden wall sconces. They turned into one of the first rooms and flicked on the light. The room was non-descript, with a couch and a chair. Marona walked over to a closet built into a wall and slid the door open.

"You need to pick out an outfit," she told Cammie. "Anything you like." She took a hanger down as she spoke. She folded a red and white garment over her forearm.

Oliver left the room.

Cammie smiled at Marona. "What's going on?" she asked playfully.

Marona set her garment down and took a seat on the couch. She began to undo the straps on her heels. "I think, Cammie, now that I kind of see how this all might look from your side of things, that yes—" She pulled her blouse up over her head. She wasn't wearing a bra. "This probably is a cult."

She then stood up and wiggled out of her skirt. Cammie stared at her. "You look fantastic," she said.

"Oh, thank you. I've worked very hard for this day." She then took the garment off the couch, shook it out, and draped it over her head.

Cammie clapped. "Oh, wow," she gushed. "That's so great!"

Marona stood modeling her new outfit, a traditional cotton dress, simple and modest, white with red trimming, a high neck-line, and short sleeves.

"And that's it," Marona said, satisfied.

"I want one too," Cammie said, hopping up and down.

"I think there's another in there. There's tons of other stuff too, if you want to look."

"No, I want that. If that's okay."

"It's fine with me," Marona said.

Cammie searched the closet until she found an identical dress. She quickly stripped out of her clothes and put it on. Marona stood looking at her. Cammie smiled sheepishly.

"It's straight to the volcano with you," Marona said.

Cammie curtsied. "What now?"

"This way."

She led Cammie back into the hallway. They passed another dressing room and then turned into a chamber with heavily perfumed air. A shrine of sorts was built into the far wall. Several gold statues stood on a table covered in a red cloth. Candle light reflected off the polished surfaces. Oliver was on his knees, wearing a simple robe of his own. He appeared to be praying.

"*Definitely* a cult," Cammie whispered.

Marona led her forward and they both took their places next to Oliver.

"She's here," he said in a deep voice. "We welcome her."

"We welcome her," Marona repeated.

"From the desert she has journeyed to your shores," he continued, his head bent low, almost touching the floor. "Dreams and visions made whole now, miracles born of faith and trust and perseverance. Obstacles in a world made to deny you, tendrils of doubt and conflict. Fires of burnished malevolence, a crucible of cohorts, of idiosyncratic monotonies."

"Oliver," Marona muttered, her tone almost scolding.

He glared at her.

"I'm not supposed to do this," Cammie said skeptically.

"It's fine," Marona said. She took Cammie's hand.

As Oliver continued the prayer, Cammie silently deflected the words with a prayer of her own, to Christ.

"Tires, once flat, are spinning now, wheels and doors, work their metaphoric magic. Revelations and reservations and prostrate incarnate illuminations." Cammie squeezed Marona's hand. Marona squeezed back. "We dine on lusty legacies and fruit bat back fat. Land crabs and stigmata scabs. Crow horn topographies and blunt benevolence. Master of wits and wills. Sage oil. Falective."

"Oliver!" Marona shout-whispered. "Reel it in."

He looked at her. He nodded. "Remove the tagpole from the fensticide."

Cammie coughed.

When it was over, they changed out of their dresses. Then they walked back to the Great Room and sat on leather couches. Two local men in tuxedos brought plates of food and pitchers of wine.

"Well?" Marona asked, pouring the wine.

"I don't drink," Cammie said. Marona stared at her and filled the glass extra full.

Cammie picked up the glass without looking at anyone and took a long drink. She winced at the taste and set her glass back on the table.

"Well?" Marona repeated.

"Well what?" Cammie asked.

"Questions? Comments?"

"Can I go home now?" She picked up her glass and took another long drink.

Oliver laughed. He smiled at Cammie. He popped an empanada into his mouth. "Seriously?"

Cammie shrugged. "I don't feel safe here." She looked at Oliver. "To be honest, you scare me."

The comment stung, Cammie could see that. But it was the truth. And what did he expect? His little prayer session was clear evidence of insanity. And it was all she had to go on. Were it not for Marona and her knowing hand squeezes throughout the ordeal, Cammie would be in a real panic.

"I'm sorry you feel that way, Cammie. You're of course free to go anytime you want."

"That you even need to point that out is creepy," Cammie said. She brought the glass to her lips and then set it back down without drinking.

"Help me out Marona," Oliver said.

She nodded. "Look, Cammie." She paused and stared at Oliver. "He's not crazy. And he's definitely not dangerous. And he's never going to ask you to do anything you don't want to do."

"This isn't what I expected," Cammie said.

"Isn't that the point?" Oliver asked rhetorically. "Look. You'll understand. I know we keep saying that, but it's true. It's three in the morning. It's showtime, Marona." He stood up and stared down at Cammie. "You really think I'm creepy?"

Cammie smiled uncomfortably and made a pinching gesture with her left hand, leaving a half-inch gap between her thumb and forefinger.

"That much?"

She nodded.

"Fair enough," he said.

They loaded into the car. This time, it was just the three of them, with Oliver driving. A short while later they pulled into a small sleeping town. Oliver turned off the car's lights. They slowly idled along the main street, eventually turning down an alleyway and into a parking lot. They quietly exited the car and entered a cinderblock building through a back door. Once inside, Oliver turned the lights on. They were in a large workroom, surrounded by stacks of flour bags. An industrial grade mixer stood in a corner. Cammie could smell a combination of sweet bread and yeast. Marona set a small duffle bag down on the ground as Oliver got to his knees.

Not again, Cammie thought.

But he wasn't praying. Instead, he took a screwdriver from his pocket and begin to pry up the floor tiles. Cammie turned to Marona to see if she knew what he was up to.

Marona was naked.

Cammie averted her eyes, amazed at the continuing absurdity. She shook her head and laughed to herself.

Oliver had four tiles up, revealing a hole in the ground. He stuck his head down into the dark and called out, "We good?"

"Exit's clear," a voice called back.

"Who's that," Cammie asked.

"That's Earl," Marona said.

"He lives under a bakery in Costa Ri...ca..." The words faded as she looked back at Marona, who was shivering now, and sporting the skimpiest of stars-and-strips bikinis. The top was heavily padded and afford Marona an enormous heaving bust and attendant cleavage. She wore a flowing blond wig and sequined red high heels.

"Wow!" Cammie blurted. "You look fantastic!"

Marona struck a pose and smiled. "Why thank you."

"Who are you?"

"She's La Gringa," Oliver said.

CHAPTER FORTY-SEVEN

Ted arrived at Salton Steve's room around eleven o'clock. A new door hung in the frame. It wasn't the same rectangle of painted particle board they put up in Ted's room. No, Salton Steve had a *real* door. An absurd door, made of deeply stained hardwood and decorated with ornamental inlays. In the center, about head high, a wrought-iron Celtic knot sat in a pane of green stained glass. A sturdy and anger-proof door, comically out of place in that dingy hallway.

When does he have time to buy and install custom doors? He clearly did this all himself. Why waste the time and money? They'll tear it down as soon as they see it, nice as it is.

How'd he do it so quickly?

He must have had it on hand.

A spare door?

He's going to tell me he always travels with a spare door.

Look at it. That's exotic hardwood, custom glass and ironwork.

How'd he even lift it?

And where was he keeping it?

He couldn't have known I would break down the old one. That's not predictable on any metric.

Maybe he has a history of pissing people off.

Spare doors! Panning for gold with cooking woks!

Like a dragon, he said. Like some maniac.

Ted knocked and Salton Steve let him in. There were no remnants of the prayer scene from the night before, just the plain old dorm room Ted knew so well. Where does he keep all the gold and weird-o paraphernalia?

Same place he keeps his spare door collection.

Salton Steve wore the same robe Ted saw the night before, only now he could also see the front of the elaborate headpiece, which was the head of a fox framed in a half-circle of magpie feathers. The rest of the fox's body spilled substanceless down the back of Salton Steve's head and neck like some grotesque mullet.

"Did you kill that fox yourself?"

"I did."

"You butcher it here?"

"I did. Are we not supposed to?"

"There are signs in the bathroom about not cleaning fish."

"You going to turn me in?"

"I don't know what I'm going to do."

"You're going to get rich."

"Just waiting on you, then."

"Did you bring your idol?"

"You didn't tell me to."

"It's okay, I've got it here." He walked over to his small closet and pulled out the idol he had given Ted.

"How did you—?"

"In your car. I put the spark plugs back in, by the way, so you're good to go if you need to."

"You're out of your mind."

"And in good company."

Ted turned the idol in his hands. "Is this real gold or painted lead?"

"It's gold painted real gold." Salton Steve said. Ted nodded. "You need to talk to it, introduce yourself."

Ted hesitated. "I'm not on camera, am I?"

"Well, technically you are. This is a big moment."

"What do you mean?"

"Just say hello. Tell him your name, and we'll get on with this."

"Hello," he said to the small cartoonish face.

"Tell him your name."

"Shouldn't he know it already?"

"He's not *the* God. He's just *a* god. And kind of rusty."

"My name is Ted. It's...nice to meet you."

"Okay great then, we're ready." Salton Steve changed out of his robe and took off the headpiece, which he placed in large plastic bag. He put the robe in a backpack and they left the dorm building and walked in the direction of the river. They moved in silence. They forded along the same series of large rocks they'd used earlier that morning. Then they turned and walked fifteen minutes upriver to Salton Steve's little secret camp a few feet from the riverbank. His gear was hidden amongst a gnarl of dead branches, driftwood, and cottonwood saplings. Ted saw pickle buckets, trowels, woks, remnants of candles, and a pile of dry debris presumably hauled down from the moraine. Salton Steve set his bags down on the bank and took his robe and headdress back out. He also took out two headlamps. He put one on his head and threw the other to Ted. Then he got dressed and stood there smiling in the moonlight.

"You look ridiculous," Ted said.

"Is that all you have, Ted, more of this sarcastic negativity?"

"I wasn't being sarcastic. You really do look ridiculous."

"Despite what you think, this is serious shit. You're here, despite everything, which tells me you're at least willing to give it a try. But we do this a certain way. You have to buy in if you want it to work."

"Well the gold's either in there or it's not, right? What does my attitude have to do with anything? And by the way, if you don't like my attitude feel free to blame yourself."

Salton Steve dug around some more in his backpack and pulled out a second robe. "Now put this on," he said.

He continues to degrade me.

Just put it on.

He stripped down to his underpants and pulled the robe over his head, just to prove his point. The whole thing was vertically striped in simple red and green swatches. It came down to just short of his knees.

"This is the best you could do for me? It's humiliating."

"Exactly."

"Is that necessary?"

"Humiliate, as in *humility*. He's very sensitive."

"Smoke Monkey?"

"Yes. You need to show him you're not overly prideful."

"I look like a gay elf."

"You look great. And put this on too." He pulled a second headpiece out of the plastic bag.

Ted laughed when he saw it. "Is that a possum?"

"It is."

"Tell me you didn't get that on the side of the road."

"As a matter of fact I did," Salton Steve said, cracking a smile. Ted took a step back. "Put it on."

"I'm cool. I don't need fucking rabies."

"You're not going to get rabies. Just put it on. It's the only way this will work."

"Okay, then I'm confused. Is the gold in the moraine there because of some geological reality, or because some long dead Maya godking put it there?"

392

"Geology put the gold in with the rocks. Smoke Monkey's going to put it our pans," he said. "If I show you how this works and I get some gold, will you listen to me and do what I say?"

"Yes. Fine. Don't I always?"

Salton Steve walked over to the debris pile and scooped a couple handfuls of dirt into a wok. Then he waded into the middle of the river and turned on his headlamp. He bent over and let water spill into the wok. He swirled everything around for several minutes.

How do I know he didn't mix the gold in with the debris already? Maybe it's the same stuff he had in his room last night.

Can't be. He'd risk washing a lot of it right back into the river.

Ted took a seat on the bank watching, listening to the sound of the river flowing under ribbons of yellow moonlight. The tall skinny body silhouetted in the stream seemed a right and congruous addition to the overall setting.

Somehow it fits.

Without the headlamp you might take him for some creature of the forest.

Damnit.

What?

I like this. I like him.

He watched as Salton Steve poured a wet concrete-like mixture from the wok into his palm. Then he put the wok between his legs and picked through the material with his fingers. Then he tossed it all into the river, rinsed his hands, and walked back over to the riverbank. He didn't say anything. He scooped more debris and waded back into the stream. He repeated the process six times before he let out a yelp and ran towards Ted, kicking up water.

"Look at this," he said, as he stood there panting. He shined his light down to his hand, which was balled into a loose fist.

"Gold?"

Salton Steve opened his palm. "No! A frog. A little guy. A baby leopard."

Ted looked down at the frog, tiny and covered with mud.

"Here, take him." Salton Steve put the frog in Ted's hand and reloaded his wok. He walked back into the river.

Ted set the frog down on the muddy riverbank and continued to watch Salton Steve work the wok in the middle of the river. "Orange peel chicken!" Ted called out.

Salton Steve shushed him.

Twenty minutes later he called Ted's name and waved him to the middle of the river. The water was colder than Ted expected. He sloshed over and looked at Salton Steve's pale wrinkled palm. He saw several small oblong rocks in a mix of sand and muddy water. Salton Steve took one of the small rocks and put it in Ted's hand.

"That's gold," he said, whispering. Ted turned the rock over in his hand. "Rub it."

Ted started rubbing it under the light of his headlamp. It began to turn a dull yellow color. He rinsed it in the stream.

"Now bite it," Salton Steve said. "If it's just a rock it will crack."

"Or crack my tooth."

"Or crack your tooth, that's right. But if it's gold you'll be able to dent it. It'll move."

Ted put the rock in his mouth and tenderly pressed it between his teeth. He could feel its shape slightly alter under the pressure. He took it out, rinsed it again, and set it in his palm. "That's gold?"

"Wouldn't you say?"

Ted nodded. "How much is it?"

"Say that's a gram. There are about twenty eight grams in an ounce and an ounce is worth about eight hundred dollars. So that's about thirty bucks there. And I think I got a couple more smaller ones here."

"No shit," Ted muttered. He looked up at Salton Steve, who shielded his eyes from the beam of light. "Okay."

"Okay what?"

"You win. I believe you. I'm in. I hate you. You're a fucking asshole. But I believe you, okay. If this is all a scam, it's worked. You can throw yourself a party. Tell all your friends watching at home I'm a gullible dipshit. Just tell me what to do."

"The rumor of your benevolence floats into this valley on a welcome breeze. Drink in the nectar of our devotion. Time spins back upon itself and it is we who are frozen in your gyroscopic modernity. The princely manifestations of your gruesome cartography poison only the minds of the disinclined. Here the Soapspreader is Eighteen Rabbit reborn. Gorge yourself on the brash delicacy of fresh faith, the bloomed flower of remedial articulation comes with a slipshod willingness to evaluate your concentricity. Quartz and elaterite fused forth from the Newsmaker. The Defecator. The Shuttlestopper. This postdated periodontal predecessor."

Ted adjusted his ill-fitting robe and looked at Salton Steve. "Shuttlestopper?"

"You ready?"

"I think my possum is leaking."

They walked over to the stream bed where the materials were kept. Ted took up a trowel and a bucket and walked a hundred yards up the moraine. The night was clear and crisp with flashes of white lightning.

He filled his bucket with dirt and small pebbles from a hole he made directly in the moraine. Then he carried it back down to the bank. Salton Steve had filled his own bucket from a larger debris pile he'd brought down in a full-sized garbage can. Ted put a scoop of his mixture into his wok and waded into the middle of the stream. He asked Salton Steve why they couldn't just rinse the gravel right there on the bank and was told it didn't look *good* that way.

"Iconic imagery helps build a mythos. As does the way the moonlight plays through the ripples and small rapids. It's the same reason we wear the robes."

"We need to discuss my robe."

"Just imagine how this all appears to one observing from a distance. You have to focus on gestures and details. Like an actor. Which is kind of what you are. The scene's been set by the combined forces of time, nature, and divinity. We must attempt to play our roles convincingly, with the appropriate flourish. We must put on a good show, out of respect for our audience, who makes this all possible. You don't want to be some lowly scavenger in a T-shirt huddled on the river bank playing in the mud."

"Which isn't all that different than washing dishes."

"Yes, of course, all the better. And you play that part well, as it should be played. But this is not that. This is prayer, standing out here in this river, dressed in our traditional robes. You have to get that in your head, or this will never work. You must be at all times conscious of his presence in your mind. You must speak to him, ask him for guidance. Did you do that when you shoveled your debris?"

"No."

"Then why would he help you?" He made Ted dump out all the debris he collected.

"Refill your bucket and repeat what I say."

Ted started scooping with the small trowel.

"Oh great and powerful Smoke Monkey."

I don't think I can do this.

Get over yourself.

"Oh great and powerful Smoke Monkey."

"Keep digging."

"Keep digging."

Salton Steve punched him in the arm. "Please continue to help us."

"Please continue to help us."

"Bring us the gold we need to do your work on earth."

"I think I get the idea."

Smoke Monkey, Smoke Monkey.

You should at least try.

I feel like an idiot.

Just try.

Please bless this earth.

Good.

Oh wise and all powerful one.

Just be yourself.

Easy for you to say. Okay. Hi there. My name is Ted. I want to apologize, first off, for my friend Salton Steve. Well, he's not really my friend. He's more like my nemesis. He's kind of a dick, to be honest. But he has presented me with this...ahem...*golden* opportunity...so I'll give it a shot. He says you're from Honduras. That's cool. I'm from California. The Bay Area. So what would be awesome would be if you could put the gold in this dirt here into my cooking wok. Because if you make me rich, I will be able to spread the word about you. Which seems to have worked with Salton Steve. If he didn't have all that money to bribe me with then I would never be here praying to you like this. So there, thanks. Good luck. Bye.

Bravo.

Salton Steve stood next to Ted. He tapped on his shoulder and pointed out a doe with her fawn in a patch of moonlight on the side of the moraine.

Peace.

A beautiful night.

The sound of the water.

The prayer.

I agree.

With his bucket refilled, Ted walked back to the riverbank and loaded a scoop into his wok. He waded with Salton Steve into the middle of the river. They stood side by side under the moon. Salton Steve raised his wok high in the air. Ted imitated him. They stood like that for a minute. Then Salton Steve started methodically washing the rocks in the river water.

Ted watched closely and tried to mimic his actions.

Just a little water. Swirl it around. Be gentle. Let the muddy water spill over the side. Keep the rocks in the bottom.

Slowly, slowly. When all you have is rocks, put them in your hand and inspect them under the light of your headlamp.

He showed Salton Steve what he had. Salton Steve shook his head. Ted threw the rocks into the water and went back for another scoop.

The only time Salton Steve said anything was to make sure Ted continued to pray as he worked. After he'd been at it for over an hour, Ted found his first little nugget. It was amorphous and smooth and he checked it with his teeth.

Good.

That's it? No Eureka?

I guess not. I'm happy. But it's the act more than anything. Just being out here, doing this. It's so relaxing.

Talk to the ankles. They're freaking out.

I can't even feel my ankles.

Salton Steve just patted him on the back without saying anything. He took out a test tube from his pocket and handed it to Ted. He removed the cork stopper and added his nugget to a small collection Salton Steve had already amassed. They both smiled and shook hands.

They closed down the operation at four. Ted had found several nuggets. Not a huge haul, but not bad for a first try. They stashed the buckets, trowels, and woks in the bushes.

Then they changed out of their robes and wandered back to the dorms.

He passed Cammie's window and all the accumulated joy and satisfaction fell out of his body. His knees buckled and Ted collapsed onto the wet lawn. Wordlessly, Salton Steve turned around, scooped Ted up, stabilized him on his feet, and then slapped the shit out of him.

CHAPTER FORTY-EIGHT

4:00 AM on a misty morning somewhere along the border of Panama and Costa Rica. Two men drive a modified four-wheel drive golf cart along one of a thousand muddy lanes of the Produce Americano banana plantation. Clouds swoop down and collide with the ground as the golf cart stops. A man gets down from his seat and walks to the closest tree at an intersection with another access lane perpendicular to the one they are driving on. Both men are smoking. The man still in the cart yells to the man at the tree, who yells something back. The man on foot tears at a leaf and runs his finger along the wound, collecting a sort of sap on his finger. He puts his finger in his mouth, swirls his tongue around and yells something back to the man still in the cart. Then he loads up. The men continue to the next intersection. The cart stops in a large puddle and this time the second man gets out and repeats the actions of the last man. Overhead, a vast network of cables and carts rests dormant in this time of non-harvest.

Water is everywhere. It is thick in the air, dripping from the cables, dribbling across the angular rutted banana leaves. The men themselves are soaked as well. They are used to being wet, and muddy. Everywhere, in their community, are signs explaining how to maintain hygiene, how to prevent bacterial infection, how to prevent cholera. These men know that you must wait until noon before the sky will betray the day's true weather. All mornings are wet. And these men always work mornings.

This is the only place in Central America where there are no birds, no monkeys. Only rats and snakes. The men are used to a peace they will find no place else. This is the good shift. The best shift. They chain smoke. They are hungover. They check the leaves, step in puddles, move to the next tree, and at the end of it all, they will make their report.

Both men are short, with dark skin. They are Maya, with hardly a drop of Spanish blood, though Spanish is the only language they speak. They live with their wives and families in a sort of indentured servitude, where they are paid in company credits. These credits go towards lodging in the company compound, food in the company store, and booze in the company bar. It is a life. There is no consideration of whether or not it is a good life. Happiness and sadness exist irrespective of one's job, one's location, one's prospects.

They smoke more cigarettes and drive on into the mist. The massive tires negotiate the puddles and the mud without incident. Ahead of the two men a large cloud swirls then dissipates. As Norberto looks to the ground to place his foot on dry land before leaving the vehicle, Beto sees a form materialize in the watery sky. A shadow at first no more than an illusion. It grows vivid in a matter of seconds, and before he can call out to Norberto, it has taken a definable shape. The shape of a woman. A tall, thin woman, standing in profile. She has large breasts and flowing hair, now clearly seen as blond hair. In a trance, Beto watches silently as the form takes solid shape. A white woman, in a bikini, unblemished, without a speck of mud on her long tanned legs. Posing there in red high heels. The bikini bottom shimmer with red sequins. The bikini top is

America. She turns her head to look directly at Beto, kisses at him with her full red lips, and is again swallowed by a spiraling mist.

"La Gringa!" he shouts at the top of his lungs. Norberto looks up in shock, but the image is gone. Foot on the gas, Beto takes off in pursuit. But for all his frantic circling, his racing up and down each and every possible banana banked lane, there is no sign of her. Not a footstep, not a heel hole in the mud. Nothing. And he will be the one this time, at the end of the day, in the company bar, to be called out by his good friend Norberto, who will tell all the others what Beto saw: a tall white woman with enormous breasts, high heels, and a stars-and-stripes bikini. He saw her emerge from the fogs and then disappear.

CHAPTER FORTY-NINE

They had Ted in the Spot kitchen that morning. First thing was to finish up the breakfast dishes still left over from the early *early* shift, which was worked by a guy named Petros, who Ted had never met. Petros came in at two-thirty in the morning and spent half his shift prepping breakfast and then the second half working the machine and the pots and pans station. Ted had passed the word on to Petros, through Alfonso, that he didn't need to worry about the grits and oatmeal containers since Ted liked to eat from them occasionally. No doubt Petros was fine with this since those were the two worst items to clean in the whole kitchen.

Ted had been working the two kitchens long enough to earn the right to steal bacon and fries off the line, if he didn't get in the way. But the fresh-squeezed orange juice was still off limits. He didn't ever see anyone drink it. Coffee, of course, was unlimited. And they had good stuff in The Spot. And Ted needed it, having been up late at the mine.

Kevin came down to get his breakfast and wandered over to the dishmachine. They spoke as Ted worked, though the glass racks kept them from being able to see each other.

"I need you to get fitted for a tux," Kevin told him.

"You getting married?"

"It's not a real tux, we just call them that. There's a run on banquets this whole month. We need extra servers. Can you handle the public eye?"

"What about dishwashing?" Ted asked.

"We'll get someone else to take a few of your shifts."

"Is the money better?"

"There's a tip pool you get a piece of, on top of this same hourly wage. Plus people throw you cash from time to time. It depends on the function. But generally, when people are getting a lot of free stuff, especially drinks, they tend to tip well."

"A bowtie?"

"Of course."

"I'm not so sure, Kevin."

"You actually like washing dishes, don't you?"

"I'm good at it."

To prove the point, Ted accelerated his pace. He dumped the silver bucket onto a flat rack and slammed in into the machine. Then he started yanking glass racks down and lining them up along the mouth. Kevin could see him now, as he stacked clean plates from hot wet racks. He pushed them across the counter and Kevin took the stacks instinctively and walked them over to the line, where he added them to the depleted stacks already there. When he turned back around, Ted was squeegeeing the counter.

As Kevin tried to speak, Ted cut him off with the disposal roar.

He shut it off. Kevin opened his mouth again. Ted started the disposal back up. "I can't hear you!" Ted yelled. Kevin was smiling. Ted cut the disposal. "I don't have a choice do I?"

"Not really. Cammie should be there too, if that helps."

"You talked to her?"

"Actually, no. She didn't show up today."

"Really?"

"You know anything about that?"

"I don't."

And I sure as hell don't want to work banquets in a bowtie.

Quit.

I can't. I need the housing.

Do you?

What, camp out in the woods?

Why not?

"When would it start?"

"This evening. It's a late night mixer thing for some film studio from California."

"Till what time?"

Kevin was losing patience. "I don't know Ted, until it's over. What does it matter? You got some hot date? Some better place to be? You finish up here, you head over to Uniforms—they'll have the requisition by then. You get your tux and you're back here at six-thirty."

"And Salton Steve?"

"What about him?"

"Is he—"

"Doing banquets? Are you out of your mind?"

Kevin picked up his lunch from under the heat lamp and walked back towards the elevator.

Lunch was chaotic, as hungry clients from California arrived and checked in. The dishes came in endless waves, and Ted operated his station with a detached grace.

Certainly the weirdest subplot to this whole freakish summer is this discovery that I have some kind of god-given knack for washing dishes. Which is absurd.

So much is absurd.

They say everyone has a talent, that one area of life where they truly excel. Some people get basketball, right? I get this. I get the secret joy of a gleaming dump counter and hot dry plates.

And all the grits and oatmeal you can stuff in a sack.

That's another reason not to quit. I'm actually good at this. I've spent so much time this summer beating myself up, tallying each internal malfunction. It seems like a very bad idea to abandon the one thing that's actually working for me.

CHAPTER FIFTY

"We're clear!" came the voice through the walkie-talkie.

"That's it," Oliver said to Cammie, who sat on a stack of flour sacks, eating Strudel de Manzana and drinking strong dark coffee. Oliver drank whiskey and ate beef jerky from an unseen pouch in his pocket. He set his drink down and stuck his head in the hole on the floor. "Me gusta La Gringa!" he shouted into the darkness.

He stood up. "We did it! We did it, Cammie!"

"That's awesome," she said. "Congratulations. I know you've explained it to me, and it sounds cool, but I still don't really understand. I'm sorry. I don't mean to be a downer."

"It's fine. It's fine. Just...you'll see, once she gets up here with the camera. And you're next, remember."

Cammie was mortified. "I'm not going down there."

"No, no, not there, not this. Something else. Think! Whatever you want. Get creative."

"I don't understand."

"It's fine, we'll discuss later. She coming through. And here she is!"

Marona stuck her head up through the hole in the ground. "Did you guys order a pizza?" she asked, deadpan.

"La Gringa!" Oliver shouted.

Marona threw the blond wig across the floor and set her camera down. Then she reached her arms into the air. Oliver hauled her out. She stood on the floor facing Cammie, her body covered in dry streaks of muddy water. She shook out her hair and exhaled violently. "Wow!" she said. "That was *fucking* great!"

Cammie smiled. "You still look fantastic."

Marona cupped her huge breasts. "I could get used to this," she laughed. Oliver handed her a jacket and some sweat pants. She got dressed. "They were out there," she said. "And the weather was absolutely perfect, all misty and cloudy. They saw me. I know they did. I even heard shouting. They called me La Gringa, if you can believe that. Two of them. They chased me. God I wish I could hear them now. I need a drink!"

Another head popped up out of the hole in the ground. He looked to the left and to the right, scowling. "Wait a minute, there's no *birthday party* for me here," he said. Oliver bent over and hauled Earl Bish out of the hole. They hugged. Earl turned and hugged Marona. Then he looked at Cammie. "And there she is, as advertised," he said. "I'm Earl."

"Cammie." They shook hands.

"Your LDS, right?"

"I am."

"Glass of scotch then?"

"Um, sure."

"What do you think?"

Cammie shook her head, perplexed. "I don't know. I'm still sort of shell shocked. You guys are nuts."

Marona handed the glasses around. "And proud of it," Earl said.

"Cheers!" Oliver yelled. They all reached their glasses together. "To Smoke Monkey International. Shame Salton Steve wasn't here to see it. And welcome, Cammie."

"Yes, welcome Cammie!" they all called out together.

"And to the beautiful and capable Marona Dilenta!" Earl shouted, "Who once pissed in my ear!"

When the celebration died down, they hooked Marona's camera up to a television brought in from the back of the Range Rover. The footage was shaky, and not very easy to follow. But there were several clear shots of men chasing her, particularly at the end, when she was already in the hole, filming through the propped open cover.

"Pause it," Earl said. "Right there." The image was backed up to a clear, still frame shot of Beto in ecstasy, chasing La Gringa, his eyes bugged open, his arms pumping, the swirling mists all around him. "That's it," Earl said. "You're a genius, Marona."

They got back to the mansion around midday. Oliver took them all immediately back to the improvised chapel, for a prayer session. Cammie was happy to see Earl's unguarded reluctance. But clearly, when it came to Smoke Monkey International guidelines, Oliver Easton's fanaticism was to be indulged without question.

Then they ate lunch. After Marona's exploits had been given their sufficient due, attention turned to Cammie. They all wanted to know what she had planned.

"We gotta back up," she told them. "I still don't know what any of this is about. I never have. Nobody's ever explained anything to me. If that's not intentional, me being all crazy and confused, then you need to do a better job of communicating."

"I don't think so," Earl said. "We've been pretty clear. What do you want to do?"

Cammie looked to Marona for help. Marona kept her eyes on her plate.

"I want to go to the beach," Cammie said, finally. "I guess. Is that...okay?"

"It's great," Earl quickly responded. "The beach. Perfect. What beach?"

"I don't know. I'm still confused. Uh, Cancun, I guess?"

"Cancun it is!"

"And what am I supposed...I'm sorry..."

"We'll leave tomorrow. I've never been. You, Marona?"

She nodded with a full mouth, chewing.

"I've heard the water is...very blue," Earl said.

Marona nodded more vigorously.

CHAPTER FIFTY-ONE

The call came in. A waitress stood in the middle of the kitchen trembling. She didn't ask for help or say anything at all. She stood there looking at the ground. Eventually, one of the other waitresses came over and asked if she was okay. She shook her head. Ted looked at Alfonso, who was smiling back at him. The trembling waitress was helped to the drink counter, and hoisted up so she could sit. She was given water. Ted watched what was happening.

Why's Alfonso staring at me?

I don't think you want to know.

"We need to close the lady's room immediately," said the waitress in charge of the situation. "Saul's blocking it right now."

"What is it?" asked Alfonso, without taking his eyes off of Ted.

"It's bad."

"Code brown?"

"We should be so lucky."

The waitress walked over to Alfonso and said something in a low voice.

"Is she okay?" Ted heard Alfonso ask.

The waitress said something else, and Alfonso winced and then nodded. Then he asked a question in a voice loud enough to make sure Ted could hear every word. "How can you even tell the difference between vomit and *bloody* vomit?"

The waitress said something.

"I see. No wonder she can't really speak...like it was dropped in a bag from ten stories up?" Alfonso continued to eye Ted. "The walls too? Like it was intentional? I doubt that." He wiped his hands on his apron and took off his hat. "Oh, Ted," he said. "Can you come over here for a moment?"

Ted turned the disposal on and watched the water get sucked down. He looked up. Alfonso was standing right next to him. He shut the disposal off.

"You need to get yourself some gloves and a mop and...did they ever give you that haz-mat suit? Seems there's a problem in the ladies restroom. Somebody was quite ill. But don't worry, it's just vomit."

He thinks this is funny.

I told you to quit.

Ted put the mop in the empty mop bucket and wheeled it through the kitchen towards the dining room entrance. Alfonso handed him a pair of gloves as he walked by. Everyone stood still, watching him go.

Where is that dirge coming from?

Sorry.

The dining room was empty. He looked at the bathroom entrance.

The gates of hell?

That's a little dramatic.

Saul shook his head as Ted passed him. "Cuidado," he said.

Ted took a deep breath and opened the door. He looked at the wall first and slowly moved his eyes toward the floor, so as not to take the whole scene in all at once. Most of it was pooled in the center of the room, dark red and sludgy on the outer rim, chunkier as it got towards the middle.

Vile.

And you have to do more than just look at it. You have to manipulate it. Push it around. Scoop it up.

It's on all the surfaces too.

You're also going to need to take a breath soon. Mouth only.

Like I'm *eating* little bits of it. I can't do this. I won't.

If not you, then who?

That's not my problem. They can't force me.

They can fire you.

I'm not doing this.

He walked back out of the bathroom and took a deep breath. Saul was sitting at one of the tables nearby. His expression seemed to indicate that if Ted refused to do his duty, the honor would fall to him. "Sorry, buddy," Ted said. "There's just no way."

He walked back into the kitchen and without making eye-contact with anyone, he took his place behind the dump counter and began sorting clean silver.

"Ted...Ted...it's your job."

"Actually, Alfonso, it's *your* job, right. You've got me, and Saul, and maybe Salton Steve upstairs, but I think we both know what he'll say. And I'm out. There's no fucking way I'm dealing with that."

He looked up at Alfonso whose indignation barely hid the terror.

This is awesome.

He's doing the math right now.

"And Saul didn't exactly offer to help me. Maybe you've got a shot with him. But maybe not."

Alfonso leaned in close. He was gritting his teeth. "Please, Ted. Please do your job."

It *is* my job.

Not if you quit.

You're the one who's always telling me to handle my business.

This is where you make a stand?

I guess.

Not with the girl? Not with college?

I have to start somewhere.

"I'll do it, but I have conditions."

"There are no conditions, Ted. That's not how it works. You do your job or you don't. There may be something in it for you, but that's not for you to decide."

"Fine. But I'm hosing it down. I'm not mopping it up. I won't."

"What about the chunks? Aren't there chunks?"

"There are lots of chunks. We just push them down through the drain."

"You know where the drain is?"

"I can find it."

"Thank you, Ted."

It took two hoses, joined by a coupler. He stood just outside the door. He yanked twice on the hose. Ten seconds until they'd turn the water on. He took a deep breath, opened the door, and went inside. He couldn't find the drain."

It's under the pool.

Not draining.

It's clogged already!

The water shot out the end of the hose, which Ted directed to a corner of the floor. But it quickly found its way along the slightly sloping tiles and mingled with the pool of vomit, expanding it.

Fuck!

He kinked the hose and yanked three times on it, which was the shut off signal. He could feel the pressure in the hose continuing to build. With so much hose length in play it wouldn't be easy to redirect the pressure back into the ground pipes.

This hose is going to pop.

That coupler in the middle of the kitchen can't be happy either.

He ran out of the bathroom carrying the hose, ultra-fine jets shooting from the end.

He charged back through the dining room, into the kitchen, past a small group of employees. Alfonso had the leaking coupler in his hands to keep it from spraying. "Coming through!" Ted shouted, and ran out the back door. He let the kink out and shot a jetting stream into the base of a spruce tree. Saul was standing next to the spigot, watching with amazement.

"Que paso?"

"The fucking drain's clogged."

So how much water got in there?

I couldn't tell. A lot, I think.

I think it looked grosser the second time, don't you.

Some congealing, is that what you mean?

Yeah.

I still haven't had to smell it yet, at least.

Alfonso came out the back door and looked at Ted. "That was fast."

"That drain's clogged in there, Alfonso. This is officially a plumbing problem, right, not a restaurant problem. That's a whole different department, right? We're off the hook. Plus I was thinking, with the blood and all, doesn't that make this a biohazard? I mean, I don't think I even have the proper training or authority to deal with something like this."

"The sooner you start, the sooner it will all be over."

He walked into the bathroom. The puddle was twice as big as before. And the force of the water had pushed it into new areas. He took a mouth breath.

I can't get at what's under that drain, so some plumber is going to have to snake the pipe through the puke.

This is still worse.

415

Obviously. But it's not just me, that's my point. And if something in there moves I swear to God I'll soil myself.

And you'll have to clean that up too.

He dropped the mop head into the center of the puddle and twisted it around.

If I watch through the mirror it's not as bad.

Then he put the mop head in the squeeze mechanism on top of the bucket and pulled the handle. A small amount of liquid pooled in the bottom of the bucket. He redipped the mop head into the puddle. He squeezed it out again.

I wonder what this woman looks like?

Does it matter?

Kind of.

Like if this was Cammie's puke it wouldn't be so bad?

Right. She took a shit when I was at her house and I caught a whiff of it coming out of the bathroom and I didn't mind.

That's repulsive.

I didn't say I *liked* it. I just didn't mind it.

He repeated the process until the bucket was half full. He walked into the only stall that still had a clean floor and lifted the toilet seat.

Why do the toilets seats in women's restrooms even have the option of up or down?

For moments like this I guess.

He walked back to the bucket and lifted it off the floor. The liquid sloshed around.

Carefully, if you get the right slosh movement it'll jump right out of there.

Don't, please.

He poured the contents of the bucket into the toilet and then took the bucket back by the door and set it down again.

An hour later he was just down to stains and chunks. The mop wouldn't pick them up. He walked back into the kitchen, making eye contact with nobody. He picked up the

416

broom and dust pan from dry storage and took it back to the bathroom. A woman was leaving the restroom with a horrified look on her face.

"The restroom's closed, ma'am."

"You could have put a sign out front or something."

"The restaurant's closed too, until 5:30."

"You deserve a medal, young man."

He swept the chunks up into the dustpan and flushed those too. All that remained was to scrub out the stains and disinfect. He wheeled the mop bucket back through the kitchen and out the back door. He washed it out with the hose. He filled the bucket with water and rinsed the mop until it was free of any pinkish liquid. He dumped the water at the base of the spruce tree.

Inside, he loaded the bucket with disinfectant, mixed in some water, and wheeled it back to the restroom. Twenty minutes later, he was done. He tried his first nose breath in there and was satisfied that he could smell no puke. The last thing he did was pour straight bleach into the drain which was clogged about an inch below the grate.

Back in the kitchen everyone was gone. Someone had finished up the dishes for him. He took a garbage bag from dry storage and walked back to see if the grits and oatmeal had been dealt with.

Of course they haven't.

Lucky for you.

Come to papa!

He spooned out about a quarter bagful, half of each. Then he slung the bag over his shoulder, and went to punch out. An envelope was stapled to his time card.

What's this all about.

Money from the puker.

You think.

I know.

He opened the envelope. There was a note and five twenty-dollar bills. He read it: "My wife wanted you to have this. She is in the hospital and feeling much better. Thank you."

Unsigned.

That's not surprising.

He walked back to his dorm. Luc was there, napping. He woke up immediately.

"What is the smell?"

No *pee-you*? What the hell?

"You can smell it on me?"

"Where are your close? I sought you are leefing."

"They're in my car. It's a long story."

"What's in zee bag?"

"Shampoo."

He took the bag with him out to the car and got a duffle with his clothes in it. He carried both bags back to his room and set them down on his bed. Luc was back asleep. Ted took out some shorts and a T-shirt and carried them along with the garbage bag back into the bathroom. He cranked the hot water, and got in, bag and all.

CHAPTER FIFTY-TWO

Xochitl Mera was born in Merida, Mexico. She made the first trip to Cancun when she was seven years old. From there, they caught the ferry to Isla Mujeres. At first she just followed her mother, as she walked the scorching beaches with her hand-made wares. On her fingers, her mother carried woven bracelets, beaded bracelets, and silver bracelets, rings and decorative necklaces with pendants made from stones or shells or glass. On her arms were hooked various garments, airy beachwear in all colors and sizes, tube tops and linen shirts. Over one shoulder were looped hammocks with NFL color combinations, wrapped in tight knotted bundles. On the other shoulder, a small papoose with Xochitl's youngest sister dangling in silent obedience. The other arm was loaded with leather belts and hand bags and small coin purses, some made with simple beaded polyester, others built of braided palm frond and a sort of loomed wicker. On her head, despite the heat, she wore a pile of hats of all styles: straw fedoras, woolen caps, and sequined sombreros.

At least 250 different items she carried on any given day.

At first, Xochitl would just follow her, carrying simple bundles of lychee nuts, which she offered for ten pesos.

Mother brought little food and no water.

They moved relentlessly from one lounging tourist to the next, calling out their wares in a Mayan tongue nobody could understand. From sunburnt Danes, to large congregations of vacationing Mexicanos. Americans caking on sunscreen, Aussies drinking beer, Germans fussing with their masks and snorkels. Dutch girls reading. The response was almost always the same: "No, gracias." Many didn't even bother to look up until they'd passed. Then Xochitl could feel their eyes on her and her mother, more interested in who they were than what they were selling.

Sometimes the strangers did stop them. They always asked the same question: "Quantos." How much for this, how much for that? They scoffed at the prices, as if they'd expected it all to be free. They bargained them down to nothing, and then most said no anyway. Or said, "Mas tarde." Later. Can you come back later. My husband has all my money.

Though sometimes they bought things. Mostly, they bought Xochitl's nuts. They'd never seen nuts like that. She watched them eat skeptically. Most pulled them out of their mouths instantly to look at them, and then threw them into the sand and then looked at the bundle they now owned.

But sometimes Mother made a real sale. Once, twice a day in the high season. Once, twice a month in the low season. They gave her large bills, assuming she carried change. Sometimes she spent hours begging the beach club bar owners to help her change the large bills. They usually helped.

All this in the heat, in the sand, in the mosquitoes, and the passing thundershowers, under the perpetual menace of the falling coconuts. Mother never complained, never gave up. She'd reach the end of the beach and turn around and head back. She never unburdened herself, not until they were on the ferry dock. Some days they didn't even make enough to cover their traveling costs. But there were good days. Days they sold the belts and hammocks to drunk men, who sometimes mixed up their bills. Mother's expression never changed. A sale never seemed to make her happy. A wasted day never made her cry.

By the time Xochitl was seventeen, she traded days with her mother, traveling on the collectivo to Cancun and then riding the ferry to Isla. Her luck was no better than her mother's, though Xochitl was pretty, with dramatic features, dark skin, and intense eyes. They didn't ignore her like they did her mother. Instead they tended to stare, to imagine her life, or perhaps conceive of some better alternative. Men sometimes talked to her, but she couldn't understand their words. She only spoke Spanish numbers, and a few simple phrases in English: "Very cheap, almost free. Happy hour today. Second one half-price."

Back and forth on the beach. About ten such peddlers on any given day. The Mexican who sold coconuts he scavenged from the ground did good business. But he knew English and made people laugh. Other local island boys sold fruit and empanadas. Food seemed to sell better than anything else. Often she was asked for cerveza. "Poque no cerveza?" they asked. She understood the question. They were trying to say she would sell a lot more beer than woolen caps. But she didn't sell cerveza. It wasn't a question of why or why not. It's just not what she sold.

On her best day ever, she sold one hammock, three rings, six bracelets, and a necklace. She took the ferry home with 600 pesos. A small fortune.

Then something strange happens. It is a day in late August, especially hot and humid. She walks from the pier to the southeast end of the beach and begins her journey. Almost immediately, a white man with a very bad sunburn tells her he needs two hammocks. "Now, now, ahora, ahora." He is tapping his watch. He points to a green and yellow Packers hammock, and a blue and silver one as well. She begins unloading her hands and arms just to get her hammocks free. He keeps demanding, "Quantos, quantos?" She tells him five-hundred each. It is a bold price to offer, but the day is just beginning and the man seems desperate. Maybe he needs to catch the ferry. Maybe he is heading home and needs gifts to bring back. It doesn't matter. He peels off two bills from a stack and hands them to her. He takes the hammocks and bows and thanks her and runs off.

Already, it is the most successful day of her life, and she has only just begun. She walks the full length of the beach without making another sale. But coming back, a Mexican couple sitting on the ground under a coconut palm asks to see her rings. The man buys the woman a simple silver ring for fifty pesos. She thanks them. Then the woman looks into her eyes and says, "Muy bonita." Xochitl blushes. The women asks about handbags. She buys one for two-hundred pesos.

A miracle, Xochitl thinks. She crosses herself.

She continues on. A fat man calls her over. He isn't dressed for the beach. Instead he is laying under one of the palapas on a beach recliner from an expensive resort, wearing jeans and a sweat-stained green shirt. He holds out a finger to Xochitl and she then watches him pull his belt out from around his waist. He shows it to her. "I'm too fat," he says. She doesn't understand. He stands up and holds his hands out to his side. He points at her belts. They don't fasten through loops, but rather with a clamp. They work at any size. She tells him one-hundred pesos and he buys it. He offers to give her his old belt, which is such a strange gesture.

Then, she thinks her luck has run out. Three more times up and down the beach, like any other day. Eyes follow her and politely decline.

At the far end of the beach, where fewer people stay, she is called over by an odd young couple. The woman is not wearing a top and her small breasts are covered with wet sand. The man with her is acting strange, pouring handfuls of dry sand onto his head and giggling like a small child. His eyes are wild looking. The woman's bare chest makes Xochitl uneasy. The woman wants to see all the bracelets. The man is now making strange chirping noises. The woman asks questions in a language Xochitl doesn't understand. She takes three bracelets, one woven, one silver, and one made of small white shells. She smacks the man on the back and says something to him. The man puts his hands in the air. She points to his pockets. He pulls out a wad of bills and sprinkles them on the sand, looking at them as if he doesn't understand their purpose. The woman points at the money, indicating Xochitl should take what the bracelets are worth. She takes a hundred peso bill and sets off again.

She can actually feel the load lighten. This has never happened before. She's never sold enough for there to really be a difference. At this point she becomes convinced that the Virgin is watching over her. She crosses herself now every twenty steps.

A white man with a frazzled ponytail walks past her and gives her a small bottle of water. He insists she take it. Nobody has ever done this for her.

Back now on the main section of beach she passes another woman she knows from Merida, who carries similar products. Xochitl doesn't say anything about her good fortune, and she hopes the woman won't notice her depleted stores.

Onward. She sells two more hammocks, to two men with many strange tattoos on their legs and arms. They are surrounded by a small fence of green beer bottles. As she is leaving two women sit down next to the men and seem upset about their purchases. Xochitl fears they will force the men to try to give the hammocks back, but instead they seem only upset that the men have spent money on themselves and not on their girlfriends. They ask to see the summer dresses. Xochitl presents the hangers. The women hold different dresses against their bodies and pose for one another and giggle. They each buy one. Feeling bold, Xochitl offers bracelets as well, and the women speak to the men, who are busy stringing their hammocks between palm trees. They dig through the men's possessions, producing wallets. They pay Xochitl for the dresses and bracelets. Out of kindness, Xochitl tries to explain that the men should not put their hammocks on those palm trees because the nuts will fall and hurt them. The women nod but do not say anything to the men.

Midday. Almost nobody says no to her. At one point there's even a line, people waiting to see what she has, picking up on her popularity and taking it as a sign that she has something special going on. She begins to consider the possibility that she might sell everything. It is not something anyone in her position would ever even bother thinking about. Women like her do not carry twenty dresses hoping to sell them all. They do it to make sure the one woman who might buy a dress has plenty of options to choose from. She also starts worrying about the amount of money she has in her pocket. She dares not take it out and count it. She doesn't even think about how much might be there. She's already made up her mind to give half to the church, to thank the Virgin for her blessing.

She sits down in the shade of an abandoned restaurant's awning and eats her modest lunch. Chicken and tortillas and fried plantains.

Just as she is gathering her things to start up the beach again, it starts to sprinkle. She looks at the dark clouds above. The rain quickly intensifies. She watches it pelt the dry white sand. This happens every day. At least she has shelter. Then she sees a flash of lightning, bright and green, right out over the ocean. The rain falls harder still. This is a big storm. An unusual storm. The thunder shakes the earth. She hears a few children screaming. Never so loud, she thinks, this thunder. She can see people running from the beach.

Another bright flash. A terrible clap of thunder. She shudders. Never before like this. It is hard to think. Another flash. And this time the loudest boom of thunder she's ever heard. Impossibly loud. The air seems to shake and wobble. It is horrifying. The wind blows thick drops in under her shelter. She cowers alone, shivering. She mutters a prayer to the Virgin. Everything forgotten. Who am I? Where am I? What are these things I carry? Another flash. An instant boom!

She is crying now. Never like this. Stop. Please stop.

Please stop.

Stop.

Like a faucet turning off, the rain stops. She sees the dark clouds move off over the ocean, a veil of water touching the surface. Lightning in the distance.

She is soaked. Her wares are soaked. The beach is deserted. She staggers out from under the shelter, her reduced load now heavier than normal. She shuffles down the beach, sniffling. She arrives at the pier and sits on the bench to wait for the ferry. The sun is back out, the air thick and humid. She tries to think. I must buy my ticket. I must go home. She stands and walks to the ticket window. She knows the woman behind the glass, who indicates that she too has been horrified by the thunder.

Xochitl reaches into her pocket to pay for the ticket and feels the bills, the fifties and hundreds and two hundreds and five hundreds, so many of them. She blushes. She thanks the Virgin. She takes out a fifty and slides it under the glass.

The woman asks her why she is crying.

She sits to wait.

On a bench across the walkway, four tourists eat ice cream. The girl on the end is beautiful, glowing. The others keep putting their hands on her shoulders, shaking her, as if to congratulate. She is blushing. Something wonderful has happened to her. It is for her, a glorious day.

It is for both of us.

CHAPTER FIFTY-THREE

"Close the lights," Luc said.

"Ten seconds, then I'll be out of your hair." The bowtie was already on the floor. Ted began stripping off his new uniform, the pressed white shirt, the black pants, the black socks.

"You have been working?"

"Yeah, banquets. It's two in the fucking morning."

"So late. You are going out?"

"I'm all jacked up, you know. Can't sleep now."

"And you are still with the dishes?"

"Everything, Luc. I'm doing everything, all the time. Back in the Spot in eight hours, Then the IR tomorrow night. *Tonight.* Shit."

"You are a rich man, I'm thinking."

"I need more hours in the day." Ted threw on a pair of shorts and a T-shirt. "Sorry to wake you."

He sprinted down the hall, down the stairs, to Salton Steve's room. The new door was still there. Ted knocked and Salton Steve appeared immediately, backpack in hand.

"It's late," he said.

"Open bar. These people would not leave." They walked briskly out of the building.

"How's banquets?"

"Better than the kitchen in a lot of ways. But I don't really like having to meet a whole new crew of people."

"Being the new guy."

"Right. The new guy who doesn't know what the hell he's doing. I made tons of tips though, which is weird because I don't even give a shit about the money." They crossed the lawn, then the road, then the river.

They arrived at the little camp, and Salton Steve began to dig out their outfits and supplies.

"My face is still sore," Ted said.

"You needed that."

"Well, don't do it again."

"That's up to you."

"I was tired and I miss her. What's wrong with that?"

"I need you focused."

"This is as focused as I'm going to get. You guys overdid it with her."

Salton Steve laughed. "The conspiracy?"

"I don't know. I'm tired. I'm always tired. And I'm overwhelmed. I think I need to just quit Valvert, especially if this mine produces."

Salton Steve shined the headlamp beam directly into Ted's eyes. "Do *not* quit your job. Do you hear me? Do not." His tone was harsh and direct.

"Why not?"

"Why do you think?"

"Housing, I guess, but we could just camp out."

"No, we can't. This is private property."

"The national forest starts half a mile up the road."

"Don't be an idiot, Eighteen Rabbit, we need a reason to be here, in the area. We need jobs. Otherwise we're just vagrants."

"What did you call me?"

Salton Steve tossed him his robe. "Eighteen Rabbit. Out here, that's who you are, from now on. An ancestral godking. A defeated rival. It's a way of showing humility."

"And you are?"

"Call me Head on Earth."

"Sounds presumptuous."

"It is, a little. But my intention is clear. I mean to honor the founding godking, not assume his power. Smoke Monkey understands."

"Of course he does."

Salton Steve gave a disapproving glare. "Have you said your prayers?"

Ted shushed him as he slipped into his robe.

I'm back. Another thanks for last night and all the gold I found. You really are amazing and powerful. I've been thinking about you all day. It is really such an honor to come out here and be with you in this beautiful land. I couldn't sleep last night when I left the mine. I was awed by your power. It's unlike anything I've ever experienced before. I can only imagine your greatness, all those years ago, when an entire city-state bowed before you. But don't worry. This is just the beginning. We will bring you many many followers with this gold. We will build your temples back. We will bring you the glory you clearly deserve.

Ted stood in the middle of the river now, next to Salton Steve. He had a wok-full of debris from his own hole, the one slightly up the moraine, away from the debris pile Salton Steve used. The moon was already setting behind the trees along the western bank. A thin layer of still mist hung just above the water. Ted dipped his wok to let in some water. He swirled it around, studying the slurry under the beam of white light.

Him.

Yes.

He's on my mind. Not the god, but the historical figure. I think about his life, or what I imagine his life must have been like.

What do you know of the Maya?

Nothing. That's kind of the point. I don't have any context. I imagine him sitting on some great stone throne on top of some massive structure, looking down at his minions. People coming up to him and bowing, and making offerings.

And that's interesting to you?

It is. Just that it happened, historically. I should go down there. Maybe that's the first thing I'll do with the money. Like a field trip. I'll go check out Smoke Monkey's home town. Take some guided tours. Learn a bit about his life. I mean, *King*. Think about that.

You are.

You know what I mean. Commissioning great works to be built in your honor. The pageantry and ritual and ceremony.

The women.

The women, yes of course. Beautiful queens from other tribes, offered as a peace pact, as a treaty.

The hunt.

Yeah. Probably a jaguar hunt or something. Surrounded by great warriors all done up in crazy outfits. Pretty awesome. Stalking through the jungle with bows and arrows and clubs. None of this modern day crap, these needlessly complicated lives.

Yeah, but nobody's trying to kill you, or usurp your throne, right? You may clean others people's puke from bathroom floors, but at least nobody's looking to toss King Ted into the volcano. You think Smoke Monkey had a minute's peace?

Ted threw out the last of the debris and walked back to shore. He reloaded the wok and started back at it. A flutter in the air above him and a loud whoosh. Salton Steve jerked his head down.

Then he shined his light downriver. "Owl," he said. "You see it?"

Ted could see a large object moving just above the water. "Almost hit you."

"I'm too damn tall," he said. Then he laughed. A deep satisfied laugh.

There he is again.

The real Salton Steve.

Last time I saw him he was covered in piss.

Kind of weird that *this* is where he's himself. Three in the morning in the middle of a river, panning for gold in Maya robes, praying. What were the odds he'd find his happiness?

Got one!

"Got one!"

Salton Steve walked over and put the beam on Ted's palm. He nodded. Then he took out a test tube and unstoppered it. Ted dropped the small nugget in. Salton Steve patted his shoulder and set to his work again.

King Ted. I almost had a queen. That's as close as I'll get to royalty. I can just see him there. Probably a short guy. Anything he wants to eat. He just asks and they bring it to him. And think of the way you could just change lives. Just on a whim. You cruise around in your little box-thing.

Your litter?

Right, and you see some person down by the river, maybe they're washing their clothes or bathing or watering their animals, and you just decide you like that person, you feel good about them, and you can just bestow happiness on them. Land. Food. Power. Influence. A home. Servants. Whatever. You can just go around blessing people's lives.

Ted the Benevolent.

Okay, or you can also fuck endlessly with people's lives.

Ted the Asshole.

Round up your enemies. Can you imagine. Just say, *round up my enemies*, and like three hours later you have every dick in town groveling at your feet.

A Maya king though? You sure. In the jungle? What about a medieval king?

Salton Steve was tapping on Ted's shoulder. Ted looked at his palm.

"That's huge," he said, staring at the rock. Salton Steve nodded and then fixed his fox pelt crown. He dropped the gold into the test tube.

A King Arthur type?

I think that's more your speed.

I think the food would be better, for sure. Roast mutton and gravy and that sort of thing. And I would probably rather live in a castle than in some Maya pyramid. Maybe I'll pull enough gold out of this river to buy my own kingdom.

A fiefdom.

Salton Steve found another nugget. He held it up for Ted to shine his light on. Then Ted watched him offer up some sort of prayer.

He really believes, I think.

Don't you?

No.

After all this?

What, the gold mine?

No, *all* this.

I don't know. I need proof.

There isn't proof everywhere you look?

I need real proof.

Like what, a visitation?

Yes, or communication.

Okay. Hello Ted.

Very funny.

It's me.

No, you're *me*.

No, you're *you*, Ted. So who am *I*?

They quit just as the sky was lightening. Ted stripped out of his robe and sat on the river bank rubbing his feet. "Can't we get some fishing waders or something?"

"I'll pick us up some today."

He got back to the dorm room just as Luc was leaving for his pastry shift at the bakery. They nodded to each other. Ted climbed into bed and put his head on the pillow.

He called Cammie when he woke up. Her mother answered. She was very friendly, immediately telling him how sorry they all were that he had left. But that Cammie was back in Valvert. Hadn't he seen her at work?

No, he hadn't.

Pam told him they ought to try and work things out.

He thanked her and hung up.

She's not here.

No.

She hasn't been to work. I haven't seen her. Salton Steve hasn't seen her.

He worked dishes, and banquets, and the mine. They kept the gold in Salton Steve's room, in a secret compartment under the floorboards. Every few nights, before they went out to the mine, they'd sit in Salton Steve's dorm and just look at it, run their hands through it, estimate its weight and value. Salton Steve pooled what he already had, which was generous, but also cemented each of their places in the hierarchy of the partnership. They guessed they had around a hundred grand worth, which was ridiculous. Impossible. Yet there it was. Ted's robe was upgraded as well. Something less humiliating, though the possum crown remained, mostly because Ted wasn't comfortable killing anything else.

He stopped questioning Salton Steve. If there was some grand conspiracy, all it had done was lead him to this place of relative contentment. He missed Cammie, missed

433

looking at her. But he realized what a danger she was too. With her in his life, nothing else would be possible. And there were no more thoughts of returning to college, or quitting Valvert. This was a long-term situation. They planned a trip to Honduras for the fall, to visit some of the ruins.

"You're happy, then," Salton Steve asked him one night as they shared a beer on the floor of his dorm room.

"I guess I am."

Which is the truth. I did it. Somehow I managed to pull it off. And I'm rich, or getting there. I'm young, and once we cash some of this gold in, I'll have every opportunity imaginable.

Like a king.

A king without a kingdom.

"We need to cash this gold in," Salton Steve said.

"I was just thinking that."

"Probably somewhere in Boise. We both have tomorrow morning off. There's got to be a place to do it. We're not the only gold miners in Idaho. But I'm worried we've got too much. I don't want anyone figuring out what we've got going on. Follow us back here. Any suggestions?"

Ted had thought about this before. "Are there larger operations that do their own, what, bulk-smelting?"

"There are. Mostly in Canada though."

"Can we get them to take it? Someone who'll think our haul is puny? Have them buy it?"

"They'll want a cut. So which is better, take the risk in Boise, or lose a percentage with the big boys?"

"Why don't we just take a little to Boise and scope it out?"

They took Ted's car and one test tube of nuggets. First they stopped in the Oresite library and looked through a Boise telephone book. They found three places listed. Ted suggested they start with the one that claimed to have been in business since 1911.

"Maybe the guy who runs it is an old-timer who's seen some miraculous hauls. Might be harder to surprise him," Ted reasoned.

They drove on.

"I'm upset with myself," Salton Steve admitted. "I didn't think this through. I'm worried. We need our own smelter, to make our own bricks. Then we can claim they were investments and sell them at auction."

"So we buy a smelter. That's a better plan. What do you need? Just a brick stove..."

"A crucible. Bellows."

"Brick molds. We could put his name on our bricks."

Salton Steve smiled. "I'd like that. But where do we do it?"

"We buy a little shack somewhere. I'm just trying to picture this. We'd need some leather aprons and funky smelter's goggles."

"Okay, Ted. That's a plan. A good plan. We'll see what happens today, and then start looking for a place."

They pulled up in front of the dusty old shop. It was on a side street off the main drag. Ted could see a large metal chimney coming out of the roof. He looked at Salton Steve. "Why not just buy this place? It looks like it might have a little smelter. Maybe the guy would be willing to sell."

Salton Steve nodded and smiled. "Let's go in and have a look." He took the test tube out of the glove box. Ted noticed his hands were shaking.

What's wrong with him?

Never seen him act this way.

Should I be worried?

Go ahead, why not?

Worried about what though?

Just be careful.

435

"You okay?" Ted asked.

"I'm fine. I'm just giddy. Excited you know. This is where it gets real, when we walk out of here with cash in hand."

They got out of the car and walked to the front of the shop. An "open" sign hung in the window. It was too bright outside for Ted to see anything inside. He pushed open the door and heard a little bell jingle overhead. They walked in and the door shut behind them. A middle-aged man with a ratty ponytail stood behind the counter with glasses on, holding some rock up close to his face. He looked up at them. Ted's eyes adjusted. There were pictures on the walls. Lots and lots of framed pictures. And a large poster behind the counter, partially blocked by the shopkeeper. Ted looked at the poster, trying to make sense of it.

It was a very odd image.

A greenish photograph, slightly blurry, like a still frame shot taken from a surveillance video. In the photograph a young man was standing on the floor in a strange crouching position. He didn't appear to have any pants on...and there was a newspaper on the ground underneath him...and something oddly shaped protruding from...

Oh God.

That's you.

That's me. Shitting.

Is that what it looks like?

Shitting on the newspaper.

His eyes darted around the room. More photographs. Some this same surveillance grade, some black and white, some crystal clear color shots. Ted everywhere.

Everywhere!

Ted on the shuttle. Ted in class. Ted at work. In his car. In his dorm room. In the middle of the river. Ted with Cammie.

In her house! On the trampoline. In the Greyhound station.

Talking to Jackie.

Talking to Twin. Videotaping Twin.

He wandered around the room looking at the pictures. Salton Steve and the shopkeeper didn't move or speak.

There he was on the banks of the Bigpine. In Cammie's bed. Talking to Fetcher. Arm-wrestling Buttsweat. So many shots of him in his gay elf robe.

A whole series in the shower with the grits and oatmeal. His face enraptured. Caked in breakfast. In the cafeteria. Reading on the lawn.

Luau Day!

The pig on fire.

At Schwarzenegger's party. Covered in fish scales. Making out with Cammie.

A hundred photos of Ted. He sat down.

"Welcome, Ted," said the man behind the counter. Ted now recognized him from the bus station, but didn't bother to say anything. He put his hands to his face, covering his nose.

This.

This!

What is this?

He stood up and walked over to the nearest wall and looked at a framed picture of himself sitting on a curb in the rain in San Diego. He took it off the wall and flung it Frisbee style at Salton Steve, who danced to avoid it, though it missed way wide.

He took down the next framed photo, of him peeing in a yard at a house party. He flung it much harder this time, and it whistled through the air and exploded against the poster behind Oliver Easton. He took down as many as he could. Some he threw. Some he sent crashing to the ground. He took up a shard of glass and clutched it and turned to Salton Steve. Blood dripped down from his fist.

"Ted."

"Ted, we can explain."

"Ted, you have to listen."

He threw the glass. He took down more pictures and flung them at the shop windows. He went to the corner of the room and took an American flag on a pole out of a floor stand and threw it at Salton Steve. Then he picked up the heavy floor stand and threw it into the front window, which shattered. A woman on the street yelled.

"Shit, Oliver," Salton Steve said.

Ted picked up the flag and pole and faced Salton Steve. A ferocious rage now boiling in him. He tore off the flag and swung the pole in great threatening arcs. He didn't say a word. He moved his hands to the middle of the pole and faked a front angle swing and then caught Salton Steve across the head with a back motion. Then he moved his hands to the bottom of the pole and swung again hard, this time at Salton Steve's legs. Salton Steve groaned and fell over.

A woman peering in the window yelled at Ted, "Stop! Stop! I've called the police." Ted looked at her.

What is that?

A woman, I think, a person.

Can I hurt her?

No, don't hurt her. Hurt the guy behind the counter.

Salton Steve was rolling on the ground, clutching his knee. Ted swung the pole down on him again, connecting with his ribs.

"Oof!" Salton Steve gasped. "Why'd you leave a fucking pole around, Oliver!"

Ted charged through the broken glass on the floor. Easton hid behind the counter, and all Ted could do was jab the pole down at him, poking.

"Please, Ted, I can explain."

Get on the counter.

Yeah.

He hopped up on the counter and could now swing the pole down on Easton. He broke it in half across his head and the man slumped and stopped moving.

Then he leaned against the back wall and tore the poster away. He stood there on the counter tearing little bits of the poster and sprinkling them down on Easton's body. Then he bent over and tried to pick up the cash register.

"Don't," Salton Steve said.

"Don't what?" Ted grumbled.

But the register was bolted to the counter.

He looked around. There was a surveillance camera in the corner of the room. He picked up one half of the pole and started walking along the counter.

"Freeze!"

"Drop the weapon!"

He turned around. Two police officers were silhouetted in the doorway, guns drawn, backlit by the bright sun outside. Ted dropped the pole. Easton groaned on the floor underneath him. Salton Steve sat up, clutching his knee.

"We'll post your bail," Salton Steve whispered.

Ted put his hands in the air, hopped off the counter, and walked slowly to the front of the shop.

Anger is

The best emotion.

CHAPTER FIFTY-FOUR

"I'm going out there," Cammie said. She stood inches from the monitor, her hands pressed against her cheeks.

"Don't," Marona said. "It's just going to make things worse."

"He'd have killed Oliver with that cash register."

Marona stood up. They could hear the commotion on the other side of the door. "Just let the police handle it."

"I thought you guys knew what you were doing!" Cammie yelled, turning to Marona with a flushed faced. "He's going to jail now. There's blood, Marona!"

"It'll be fine. We'll bail him out. We'll sit him down and explain."

"Explain what? That this is all *your* fault? How's that going to help anything?"

The door opened and two officers walked into the room. Cammie looked at the monitor and saw Ted being led from the building in handcuffs.

"Does that record," one of the officers asked, pointing at the monitor.

"Yes," Marona said.

"Did you see the whole thing?"

"Yes."

"He seemed to know those two men."

"Are they alright?"

"They should be. Did he know them?"

Marona looked at Cammie. "Not that I know of," Cammie said.

The officer turned to Cammie. He smiled. He took off his hat and fixed his hair. "Can you tell me what happened?"

"He rejected our bail," Salton Steve said, limping toward the booth where the other four were seated. He had medical tape above his left eye.

"Can you even do that?" Marona asked.

"He'll come around," Earl said. "It's fine. At some point this was going to get real. We all knew that."

Cammie glared at him. It had taken all their effort just to keep her from going home. She still hadn't said a word to anyone. The waitress brought over two bowls of chips and took a drink order.

"It's my fault," Salton Steve said. Nobody disagreed. "I didn't think things through. I thought he'd just be amazed, you know, *impressed*."

"We have to do better," Earl said. "You hear me Cammie? If you don't like how things turned out. It's up to you now. If you think we went too far."

"It's not that," she said, finally. "It's not that you went too far that's the problem; it's that you didn't go far enough."

Marona smiled. "Oh?" she said, picking up on something in Cammie's tone.

They all perked up.

"You need to think big," Cammie said. "*Big*, big." She made a sweeping arc with her arms above her head.

"Just tell us what to do," Earl said, bouncing in his seat.

CHAPTER FIFTY-FIVE

It was early in the morning, with the orb of the sun directly visible through the glass doors. Each of the polished floor tiles refracting a tiny explosion. He had to use both hands to shield his eyes. He moved forward tentatively, two guards in lock step behind him.

It's going to be cold out there, despite the sun. Like mornings in Valvert.

You're not in Valvert.

I just hope they bring Cammie this time. I want to look at her.

You're sure she's involved?

Of course she's involved. We've been through this. They'll bring her if they're smart. They have to realize at least I'm not going to beat her up or light her car on fire.

Are you going to listen this time?

Probably.

The glass doors slid apart. This was the third time he'd had this experience, though usually it happened in the afternoon. The first time was after his initial thirty days, for assault, though the charges were eventually dropped. He'd technically not even left the county property that time, punching Salton Steve repeatedly in the lower back.

The kidneys!

Salton Steve hadn't seen it coming as he stood outside the limousine they'd sent to pick Ted up. When he turned to open the door for Ted—

Wham-o!

With your hands interlocked like a big club.

Salton Steve was dressed in a tuxedo and looked like an entirely different man than the one Ted knew in Valvert. He pooled in the gutter, wheezing for breath.

The second time they just sent a driver, someone Ted had never seen. He was taken to a large house on the outskirts of town. He made sure to pocket the matches from the ashtray. The driver let him out of the limousine and gestured to the front door, indicating where he should enter. The driver then pulled away. Ted noticed three cars parked on the gravel at the side of the house. One was an old Jeep, another was a brand new red Mercedes, and the third was a polished black Towncar with a vanity plate that read "SMONKEY." Rather than walk to the front door, Ted sprinted to the Jeep, leapt onto the hood, climbed onto the roof, and quickly undid the cordage fastening two red gas cans. He threw them both to the ground and then jumped down. He took up the first can and opened it. Then, he began dousing the entire Jeep, the interior, the tires, and the surrounding gravel. Then he trailed the liquid to the Mercedes and covered all four tires and the roof. With just a little left in the can, he forced it under the low profile of the car. He took up the second can just as he heard the front door open. Two men shouted at him, but Ted kept working furiously. He trailed gas from the Mercedes to the Towncar and covered it with all but the last quarter of the can.

The men sprinted in his direction. Ted trailed a liquid fuse as he ran away from them.

He crouched fifty feet from the cars. He struck a match and dropped it on the ground. The trail of fire was invisible in mid-day sun.

"Watch yourselves!" he called to the men, who were just passing the cars. Realizing what was happening they circled wide around the cars, but kept coming.

He saw the cars go up. One. Two. Three. And then they were on him, tackling him, and holding his face in the gravel. He could feel the heat of the flames. Then one of them whispered through heavy breaths, "It's called auto insurance, dumbfuck."

The arson charges were also dropped.

He took his hands from his eyes as he passed through the doorway and saw Cammie standing there all alone in front of a brand new Towncar. She wore a black dress which hung modestly past her knees. Her brown hair was shorter than it had been, just barely to her shoulders.

God, look at her. I love to look at her.

Yes.

The sun sees it and the birds see it and the drops of dew on the shaded parts of the lawn see it.

The guards see it.

They aren't releasing a prisoner. They're just transferring custody.

He approached Cammie and stood in front of her, and then turned to see if the guards were still there. They were, both of them eyeing Cammie. Ted turned his palms upwards. "Is there something else?"

As if coming out of a daze, they looked at each other and turned and walked back towards the building.

"Hi Ted," she said.

"I'm glad they sent you this time."

"You're not going to hurt me, are you?"

"No, I'm not going to hurt you. It's so good to see you." He held out his arms. "Can I?"

She hugged him. He felt his whole body go weak.

Was I ever this bad for her?

"I've missed you, Ted," she said in his ear. "I really have."

"You're beautiful."

"Stop it. I can't believe I'm picking you up from jail. I did not see that one coming when we were living in Valvert. You don't seem like the jail type, beating people up and lighting cars on fire. They really got to you."

"So you know what they did?"

"I do."

"And you were in on it?"

"Let's get in the car. We can talk and drive."

The unseen driver behind the tinted screen pulled the car away from the building and drove in a familiar direction. Ted knew immediately that they were taking him to the large house where he had burned the cars.

Cammie explained to Ted that she was and was not involved. "They paid me a bunch of money to go to San Diego and ride around on a shuttle bus. I had no idea what for. They gave me this walkie-talkie and kept telling to run over here and run over there. I had no idea what for, honestly."

"You couldn't tell me that?"

"They'd withhold half of my money if I said anything within one year's time."

"It hasn't been a year."

"Well everything's changed now. They didn't really know what they were doing back then. They're a lot more focused now."

"And Valvert?"

"Same thing. They just told me to go there and work for the summer. I think they pulled some strings to get me into Kitchens, but I had no idea what their plan was. I had no idea it had anything to do with you. They offered me even more money for that." She stopped her story and looked imploringly at Ted. "They never told me to pursue you. That was never part of the deal."

"Is this what they expected to happen?"

She moved closer to him. He watched her thighs slide across the black leather of the seat.

"Of course not. It's not like that."

"Okay. But the minute you leave me alone with them I will start to destroy things," he told her. "I have to. I don't know what else to do. Aggression is the only appropriate response."

"You need to listen to what they have to say."

"Why?"

"You need to understand what has happened to you, and why. They explained it to me. There's more to the story, Ted. I'm sorry for my role, whatever it was, for any pain I caused you. But trust me, please. They're really not bad people. They're just weird. And they're interesting, and they can offer you things."

"What kind of things?"

"All kinds of things."

"What did they offer you?"

"A turn."

"A turn? Like in a game?"

"Yes, exactly. This is all a game, Ted. A wonderful game."

"What will they offer me?"

"Your own turn."

"Who's turn is it now?"

"Salton Steve's turn just ended."

"And who's next?"

"We are, Ted."

The car moved onto the long gravel driveway, past the spot where Ted had lit everyone's car on fire.

"The red Mercedes wasn't yours was it?"

I think you know whose it was.

"No," she said. "It belonged to someone else." Her voice was suddenly detached, as if she had something else on her mind. "Look," she said. She seemed to be weighing her words. "You *have* to listen to what they say. Please." She took his hand as the car came to a stop.

It's the only way for her to stop feeling guilty.

She *needs* this from you.

I can hardly stand it when she looks me in the eye.

She slid right next to Ted, seductively pressing her chest against his. She moved her mouth to his ear and spoke in an uncharacteristic sultry whisper, "Ted," she said, her hot breath spilling down across his neck. He shut his eyes. "Anything."

In one quick motion she turned her body on top of him. Her dress slid almost all the way to her hips. She put her hands on the side of his head and pulled his mouth to hers. Their lips pressed together, and his hands went to her sides, pulling her body even closer to his. She jerked her head back and he opened his eyes. "*This,*" she whispered, her eyes locked on his. "This is *nothing.*" In another quick motion she was off of him, her hand moving to the door latch, her eyes pressing him. "You can have *anything,*" she said. "What do you want?"

"*Anything*?" he said, exhaling, trying to steady his pulse. He smiled at Cammie.

"Yes," she urged.

"Well, then, I want to be King."

Made in the USA
San Bernardino, CA
15 November 2013